THE
HOUSE OF
ROMANCE

FROM THE HOUSE OF ROMANCE COLLECTION
OF GREAT LOVE STORIES

THREE FULL LENGTH NOVELS IN EACH VOLUME

TRIO 1
CUPIDS AND CORONETS	by Charles Stuart
LOVES TREASURE TROVE	by Julia Davis
THE HEART'S OWN SWEET MUSIC	by Georgina Ferrand

TRIO 2
TOPAZ	by Francis Hart
THE TROUBLED SUMMER	by Janet Roscoe
A GIRL CALLED DEBBIE	by Elizabeth Brennan

TRIO 3
TWO AGAINST THE WORLD	by Harriet Smith
LOVE DANGEROUSLY	by Peggy L. Jones
NO EDEN FOR A NURSE	by Marjorie Harte

TRIO 4
NURSE IN DANGER	by Edna Murray
MAN FROM THE VINEYARDS	by Marjorie Stockholm
STRANGER IN THE SHADOWS	by Angela Gordon

TRIO 5
LOVE HAS A HARD HEART	by Kathleen Bartlett
SPRINGTIME OF JOY	by Georgina Ferrand
RUN AWAY FROM LOVE	by Grace Richmond

TRIO 6
THE CRYSTAL CAGE	by Juliet Gray
TOMORROW'S PROMISE	by Iris Weigh
THE INCONVENIENT MARRIAGE	by Winnifred Mantle

TRIO 7
TESSA JANE	by Joan Warde
VICTIM OF LOVE	by Joan Marsh
LOVE IS A NEW WORLD	by Helen Sharp

TRIO 8
WHISPERS OF FEAR	by Brenda Castle
LOVE HAS A DOUBLE	by Beth Gorman
ANGEL IN ABBEY ROAD	by June Mortimer

TRIO 9
GOLDEN CARE	by Renee Farrington
THE HAPPY HOSTAGE	by Charles Stuart
FLAME OF THE FOREST	by Doris Rae

TRIO 10
ENCOUNTER IN ATHENS	by Georgina Ferrand
RIDE TO ROMANCE	by Joan Murray
BROKEN VOWS	by Christine Wilson

3 Great RomanceS

THE HOUSE OF ROMANCE

THE HOUSE OF ROMANCE — TRIO 10
ISBN 0-88767-011-3
Published April 1977

The stories in this volume were originally published as follows:

ENCOUNTER IN ATHENS
Copyright © Georgina Ferrand 1976
First Published in U.K. by Robert Hale & Co. in 1976

RIDE TO ROMANCE
Copyright © Joan Murray 1969
First Published in U.K. by John Gresham & Co. in 1969

BROKEN VOWS
Copyright © Christine Wilson 1966
First Published in U.K. by Robert Hale Limited in 1966

HOUSE OF ROMANCE is published by 'Round the World Books Inc., Toronto, Canada

The words "The House of Romance" and line drawing of a house within a circle, is the trade mark of 'Round the World Books Inc.'

Exclusive Distributor — U.S.A. — Promarketing Inc., New York, N.Y.

Encounter in Athens

❧

Ride to Romance

❧

Broken Vows

Encounter in Athens

Georgina Ferrand

It was as if everything she had ever said and done and wanted was leading only up to this moment of truth.

"It has nothing to do with the legend," she murmured as he enfolded her in his arms.

"Must you argue even at a moment like this?" He asked, but there was no irritation in his voice, just tenderness.

Chapter One

There was someone outside, across the street. Nicole hadn't been sure at first but now she was certain, and she had the strangest feeling he was there to watch this window. With a jerk of her hand she drew the curtains together and turned her back on the window. Paul was on his knees on the floor changing the record that had flooded the room with soft music. Nicole just stood with her back resting on the window ledge and watched him for a moment or two and then, when the room filled with music once more, he looked up at her and smiled.

Her heart leaped violently in her breast at the sight of that smile. She had never known anyone so perfectly handsome; he possessed a profile more normally seen on ancient Greek coins. And by some incredible chance he loved her—Nicole Carrington.

'Well,' he said softly, 'do you intend to give me an answer?'

To his surprise she began to laugh and his mood

5

quickly changed to one of irritation. 'Amusement? Is that all my proposal means to you?'

Her laughter died quickly and she went across to him. 'Oh no, darling. It's just the sight of you, on your knees, talking about marriage. You look so roundly old-fashioned. If only you had bushy side-whiskers and a top hat!'

He got to his feet quickly then and brushed off his trews with one flick of his hand. 'I would go down on my knees if I thought it would make any difference. You seem to think I'm not being serious about this.'

She moved away from him and went to sit down on the sofa. 'Yes, I believe you're serious, right at this moment, but for me, Paul, it's the wrong time.'

He came to sit by her side. 'Don't you realize, Nicky, I want to marry you? How can there be a wrong time for that?'

'You have a career and if you lost your job there would be no problem for you; your brother would support you well. I haven't had that kind of security since my parents died, but it's different now. It's only a year since we opened the boutique and yet business is improving all the time. Not only that—I'm designing for more and more people now. They're coming to seek me out and it's what I've hoped for all these years.' He said nothing; he just kept on looking at her. 'Paul, it wouldn't be fair to Sally.'

'Why not?'

'If I married you now she would have more than

her fair share of running the boutique thrust on her. Face facts, Paul, you haven't much time for career women, but I would really like to have a try at making mine successful before I settle down to a home and children.'

'Who said anything about children?' He smiled slightly. 'Anyway, in my country to be a wife is a career, and one every woman delights in.'

'When I do marry it will be my only consideration; but you've just made another point; I think you should go back to Greece before we come to any definite agreement about the future.

He stood up, strode across to the record player and lifted the arm from the record. The silence was suddenly quite dramatic and Nicole watched him curiously for his complexion seemed to have paled.

'You seem very anxious to put every obstacle in the way, and now you want to be rid of me.'

'Paul,' she said gently, 'you are living in a foreign country, away from your family and friends and all that is familiar to you. All I say is, perhaps that is why you want to marry me. If you go back at least you will know.'

'I know already; I love you. Is there anything else I need to know?'

'I still think you should at least visit your brother and tell him of your plans. You were very close to him.'

'I still am.' He began to put the record back in its

sleeve and Nicole wandered back to the window and drew aside the curtain slightly. The shadowy figure was still there and the sight of him gave her something of a shock although he had been at the back of her mind, nagging at it since she first caught sight of him.

'Paul, I think someone is watching your flat.'

To her surprise he dashed across the room, almost flinging her aside in his anxiety to reach the window. 'There's no need for that!' she protested, steadying herself against the wall.

'Where did you see him?'

He stared out anxiously, scanning the street. 'Over there in the shadows.'

'I can't see anyone.'

Nicole drew her eyes away from him to look out again. 'Neither can I now.'

He let the curtain drop and she added, 'Of course I might have been mistaken.'

He drew a handkerchief out of his pocket and dabbed at his perspiring brow. 'You must have been. The cinemas will be closing now and all the pubs; a lot of people must be going home.'

She continued to watch him worriedly. 'There are lots of odd people around, usually harmless. There's no need to get so alarmed.'

He moved away from her and laughed harshly. 'It's just that you've got me so rattled, Nicole. I hope you don't imagine you've changed the subject.' He turned to look at her again. 'I want to make my home here with you. I don't want to go back.'

She went across to him and put her hand on his arm. 'Why not? That awful regime is ended and you have nothing to fear any more. We can go there together if you like, later in the year.'

He twisted round almost sending her off balance. 'No! And I don't want to hear you suggest it again! That life is finished for me and this is where I belong now.'

Nicole steadied herself again, almost recoiling from such rarely expressed anger. 'Paul,' she whispered, 'what *have* I said?'

He took hold of her and pulled her towards him despite the fact that she resisted slightly. 'I'm sorry, Nicky. I didn't mean to lose my temper with you.' He smiled again, once more the good-tempered man she loved. 'The fact is, you're driving me to madness. Just when I begin to think you're mine you elude me again. I feel as if I shall never possess you. It's a very rare quality in a woman.'

He kissed her and she responded gladly and then with her cheek against his she said, 'You've never talked to me about what happened, why you left. It must have been bad to make you feel so strongly about going back now.'

He had stiffened against her. 'I don't want to talk about it.'

'We must, Paul.'

9

He thrust her away from him. 'And I said I don't want to. The only issue as I can see is whether you love me or not. If you did you'd say you wanted to marry me without making all these ridiculous excuses.'

With some difficulty she extricated herself from his furious grasp. She rushed across the room and grabbing her jacket and handbag she said, 'Perhaps you are right, Paul. Perhaps I don't love you enough, but it's quite obvious you don't trust *me*.'

She ran out of the flat and he made no effort to follow her. By the time she reached the street and her car, tears were streaming down her face. For some minutes it was impossible for her to attempt to drive away and then, making a concerted effort, she dried her tears and switched on the engine. As she glanced in the driving mirror it gave her a start to see the shadow of a man standing motionless on the other side of the road. He was looking across to Paul's flat, his face turned up to the lighted window and then, as if aware of her interest, he looked directly across at her. She couldn't see him well enough even to describe, but something about him made her shiver. As he moved slowly forward, as if he were about to approach her, Nicole started up the car and drove away as fast as she could.

Nothing but silence answered her knock. Nicole glanced at her watch; it wasn't too late for him still to be at home and yet not too early for him to be up. She knocked on the door more impatiently now, becoming alarmed at the unusual silence which greeted her.

She had spent an almost sleepless night, and as dawn finally came she realized that it was not regret at refusing Paul's proposal which was causing her so much anguish, rather his own unease before she had left him. She knew she would not be easy in her mind until she had seen him again.

It was the door across the hall which finally opened. Nicole swivelled round on her heel to see Paul's neighbour peering out at her, and for once she swallowed the irritation this woman usually created in her.

'Good morning, Mrs Dawson. I don't seem to be able to make Mr Stalis hear me. Have you, by any chance, seen him at all today?'

The door opened wider and as she came out into the hall Nicole could see that she still wore a shabby dressing gown and her hair was still in rollers.

'Well, I did see him first thing this morning,' the woman told her, her voice low. 'Very early it was. He left carrying two suitcases when the taxi came to collect him. Not a word to me though. You'd think he would say something, wouldn't you?'

Nicole's eyes opened wide. 'Paul has left?'

'Didn't he tell you he was going?'

She shook her head and the woman said, her eyes

kindling with interest now, 'Fancy that. Perhaps he's
left a note inside the flat.'

Nicole suddenly remembered that Paul had the
habit of leaving his key underneath the mat and,
still watched by Mrs Dawson who was an undeniably
curious woman, she stooped down to look for it. On
this occasion it was not there and, disappointed,
Nicole straightened up again and shook her head.

'It's not there.'

'I'm not surprised because he left in that much of
a hurry.'

'What time was that?'

'Early. I don't sleep so well these days. Must have
been two hours ago.'

Nicole's mind was in a whirl. Where could he have
gone? she asked herself. And why? She could have
taken an oath that last night he had no plans for
going away.

Almost absently she tried the door and to her
amazement it opened. Mrs Dawson laughed and
Nicole had the feeling she would have followed her
inside if she hadn't closed the door firmly behind her.

The flat was, as far she could recall, the same as
it had been the night before. Their empty coffee
cups were still on the table, the record lying in its
sleeve on the floor. She glanced around her quickly,
seeking some note, some explanation of this sudden
flight, but there was none.

The bed was not made, although this in itself did

not surprise her. Paul never troubled himself with household matters; she knew he had been brought up in a wealthy household where everything was done for him, and today was not the day his domestic help came in.

She opened the wardrobe and peered inside. Paul dressed well and his wardrobe was normally full. Now hangers swung emptily, mocking her as she gazed at them. Some of his clothes were still there, but, she noticed, they were all heavy winter clothes. That meant little, for the weather was much warmer now and wherever he had gone he would not need those clothes he had left behind.

Automatically she reached for the telephone and dialled Paul's office. 'Is Mr Stalis there, please?' she asked in a small voice.

'He's not expected in today,' came the answer. 'May I take a message?'

'No, I must reach him immediately; it's very urgent. Do you know where I can contact him today?'

There was a pause. 'You could try his home. You might catch him there.'

Nicole replaced the receiver with a whispered, 'Thank you.'

As she walked back slowly into the living room she wondered when she might hear from him and if it was her behaviour that had caused him to leave, if he were trying to punish her for refusing to marry him immediately. Somehow it would not surprise

13

her. In many ways Paul could be very childish.

After glancing round once more, reluctantly she realized she would have to go; nothing useful would be served by remaining and Sally would be wondering what had happened to her. There were stock inventories to be made, ordering done. Nicole knew she had no choice but to carry on as normal and hope that Paul would contact her soon.

As she opened the door again something scuffed against her shoe. Looking down to the floor she saw that a screwed up piece of paper lay at her feet. She quickly scooped it up and smoothed it out. It was a plain white piece of paper and written on it were just two words; but they were in Greek, and although Paul had taught her several words and phrases she could not attempt to read what was printed here.

Nicole stared at the paper for some few moments. There was something ominous about those strong black letters. Her mind returned to last night; the man in the shadows. Of course there need not be a connection between him, the note and Paul's disappearance, but Nicole was sure there must be, and she was suddenly afraid.

The door opened and she started. 'Found anything,' Mrs Dawson asked. 'A message, I mean.'

She had dressed and removed the rollers. Her hair was now brushed out into a fluffy style that was too young for her.

Nicole clutched the note to her chest. 'Yes,' she

answered breathlessly. 'He's had to go away for a few days—for the newspaper. He'll be back shortly. It's nothing to be alarmed about.'

And before the woman could question her further Nicole edged her out of the flat, slammed the door and rushed down the corridor.

Sally's monkey face wrinkled into a grin when she saw Nicole. 'Well, where have *you* been? I heard you leave the flat this morning and thought for sure you'd have opened up by the time I arrived.'

'Oh, I am sorry, Sal. I went out early because I had to see Paul before I came to work.'

'It must be serious!'

The bell tinkled as a customer came in. While Sally hurried to attend to her Nicole went to hang her jacket in the back room where the other girl joined her moments later.

'She just wants to browse. Mrs Filmington-Conner rang first thing. She wants you to design some holiday clothes for her. Madeira this time. Honestly, with customers like the fair Josephine who needs a boutique?' Nicole laughed and Sally went on, 'I told her you would ring back as soon as you came in.'

Nicole nodded and went to switch on the kettle.

'Far from everything between you and Paul being rosy, I think there's something wrong,' Sally went on, watching her friend closely.

Nicole put one hand to her head. 'We had a quarrel

15

last night. It was all very silly but we both got a bit heated and I walked out on him.'

'And you went back this morning hoping to make it up.'

Nicole nodded. 'I hate unpleasantness, and Paul is usually so even-tempered.'

The water was boiling and the customer wanted to try on some skirts. Sally went to attend to her and Nicole made herself some coffee. By the time Sally had returned Nicole had finished it and had made some for her friend.

'She bought two. Not bad for a Monday morning. We'll be holidaying in Madeira ourselves before long,' she added, laughing.

She settled herself into one of the two chairs in the tiny room and looked at Nicole. 'From the look on your face I gather your quarrel wasn't made up, or perhaps I shouldn't be asking.'

'He wasn't there.'

She laughed again. 'Even Paul has to do something some time. He has probably gone to work.'

'He never leaves before ten. Besides he left in a taxi, in a hurry, with two suitcases, according to his neighbour who misses very little that goes on in the entire block of flats.'

'Perhaps he had a telegram from home. Someone might be ill or had an accident. It sounds like something of the sort, doesn't it?'

'I suppose so, only why haven't I heard from him?

16

You'd think he'd have taken a few minutes to let me know.'

'Not if he'd had a telegram. Shock would send all other thoughts right out of his mind. You might hear from him when he arrives in Athens.'

Nicole looked up sharply. 'He wouldn't go there. He says he'll never go back there again.'

'If his brother were ill. . . .'

'I'd have found the telegram; he'd have let me know!'

'Have you tried the newspaper?'

'He didn't turn up, but he is more or less freelance, so that isn't unusual.'

'He just might have had the scent of a scoop! You know what journalists are like.'

Nicole laughed brokenly. 'Not Paul. He couldn't care less. He's only in journalism because his brother owns a newspaper.'

Sally sipped at her coffee. 'Well, I think you're getting agitated about nothing, Nicole. There is probably a very simple explanation for all this.'

'I wish I knew what it was.'

Another customer came in and it was Nicole who went to attend to her, returning a few moments later. 'We haven't got what she wanted, Amazing, isn't it? Every colour except the one she wanted. Customers!'

Sally eyed her friend curiously. 'Just what was your quarrel about?'

Nicole stared uncomprehendingly for a moment or

two at the other girl. She had almost forgotten about it in her new anxiety.

'He asked me to marry him and I wanted to wait a while.'

Sally let out a long, low whistle. 'You *are* mad. If Paul Stalis had asked me to marry him I would have dragged him to the altar before he had a chance to change his mind.'

Nicole smiled faintly. 'It wasn't the first time he'd asked me. I need to be very sure first, Sally, before I'd marry anyone.'

'You should be. Paul Stalis is a dish, and rich too, isn't he?'

'I believe his brother is quite well-to-do.'

'Same thing!'

Nicole sighed. 'I'm not sure we're ready for marriage yet. In many ways he's very immature. I gather his brother has always treated him as a child—his child—and I don't think Paul has ever been given much responsibility.'

'He seems anxious to take on the responsibility of marriage.

'Marriage isn't a game, but sometimes I think Paul believes it is.' She sighed again. 'To be quite honest, Sally, I'm not at all sure I didn't make the wrong decision last night. My arguments sound weak in my own ears. All I want to do is find him and start again, only I don't know where to begin looking for him.'

'It shouldn't be too difficult. There can't be many

people he knows in this country. Try all his friends.'

Nicole shook her head. 'I'm sure there isn't one he would want to stay with. He'd discuss it with me first anyway. I can't imagine *where* he might have gone.'

'Athens.'

'No.' Nicole brought the paper from her handbag. 'Last night when I left I'm sure someone was watching the flat, and this morning I found this note on the living room floor.'

Sally stared at it. 'What does it say?'

Nicole laughed unevenly. 'That's just the problem—I can't read Greek, but I have the feeling it's all to do with Paul's disappearance.'

'I still think you're making too much of this, Nicole. It's probably just a message he jotted down and forgot about.'

Nicole spread it on the bench. 'No. Paul always wrote in English. Besides, look at it, Sally; it's printed so carefully, just like a threatening or anonymous letter.'

'Why should anyone threaten Paul?'

Nicole covered her face with her hands. 'I don't know!'

'Nicole, if you feel so strongly about it I think you should find out what is written on that note.'

'How?'

Nicole looked at her hopefully and the girl came up to her and put one hand on her shoulder. 'Obviously someone who knows Greek. What about that

19

Greek restaurant Paul often took you to? You became quite friendly with the proprietors. Are they really Greek, or the English kind?'

'Ann and Spiro! Of course! They were born in Greece and I'm sure they would be able to tell me.' She reached for her jacket. 'Even allowing for the traffic I can be there and back in an hour.' She rushed into the shop. 'Bless you, Sally. I would never have thought of it myself. I'll be back as soon as I can.'

When she returned there were three customers in the boutique, which made it appear full as the shop was a small one. Sally eyed her curiously but there was no opportunity to talk until all the customers had been attended to. When the last one had gone with her purchase Sally lost no time in following her friend into the back room.

'Could they help you?' Nicole nodded. 'Well, don't keep me in suspense. What did the note say?'

There was a look of total bewilderment in Nicole's hazel eyes and she raised them to her friend's face. 'Just two words and they don't make sense; Remember Maria. That doesn't help me at all.'

For a moment there was silence between them and then Sally, in her customary commonsense manner, suggested, 'It could simply be a reminder to send a birthday card.'

'He doesn't know anyone called Maria. If he did I would know it too. Besides, Paul wasn't the type to send birthday cards or presents to anyone but those closest to him. It isn't Paul's writing on that paper. Someone else wrote it and pushed it through the letter box. And there's something else that's been troubling me. One day a month or two ago Paul received a letter from his brother. It upset him terribly but he wouldn't tell me why. I remember thinking it odd because the military government had just fallen and Paul was so happy about Greece's return to democracy.'

'There's something terribly wrong, Sally. I know it but I can't think what it could be or what to do about it.. I feel so helpless.'

'Why do you think he had this reluctance to return to Greece?'

'That's another puzzle. He loves his country; that much I do know, but he was arrested during some student trouble a year or two ago, and from what I can gather it wasn't a very pleasant experience. He hasn't told me about it but you've read the newspaper reports about political prisoners in Greece. When he was released his brother got him a job with a newspaper over here because it wasn't safe for him to stay there any longer.'

Sally frowned. 'The junta is finished, so why doesn't he want to go back? You'd have thought he would want to catch the first available plane.'

'That's what I wondered. So many of his compatriots did, even some he knew here in London. At the time I wasn't too sorry he decided to stay, because I wanted him here with me.'

'From what I know of him I appreciate he's not particularly fond of work, so returning to a job with his brother would be ideal now there's a new regime in Greece.'

Nicole nodded her agreement. 'I expected Paul to announce his intention of going back every time I saw him. I just can't understand why he didn't.'

A customer came in and, reluctantly, Nicole went to attend to her. The woman couldn't make up her mind between some jeans in powder blue or the pair in burgundy. Normally endowed with endless patience Nicole couldn't even concentrate on what the woman was saying.

She couldn't understand why she had been so reluctant to agree to marry Paul last night. If he appeared now she would be willing to do anything he asked of her. If only he would appear. . . .

The customer finally decided on the burgundy pair which she reckoned would be more useful. Nicole heartily agreed and when she returned to the back room at last Sally was just finishing a telephone conversation.

'Was that Mrs Filmington-Connor again?' Nicole asked. 'She must think I don't want the work.'

'She rang again while you were out. I explained you had a personal problem that needed urgent attention and she was very sympathetic.' She paused, saying after a moment, 'This was my own call.'

Nicole was about to reach for her sketching pad when Sally said, 'I was speaking to the airport.' Her friend looked at her. 'Paul Stalis was listed amongst the first class passengers on the ten o'clock flight to Athens this morning.'

Nicole stared at her. 'I don't believe it,' she said in a voice hardly above a whisper.

She sank into a chair and Sally said, 'The girl I spoke to remembered him easily because it was a last-minute booking, a cancellation. It would be too much of a coincidence for it to be any other Paul Stalis, don't you think?'

Nicole nodded, staring ahead of her sightlessly. 'Something terrible must have happened to make him go back there, Sally.'

'What are you going to do now?'

Nicole raised her eyes and looked into her friend's worried face. 'Nothing. I shall just have to wait until he writes to me from Athens.'

Chapter Two

Waiting was something very difficult for Nicole to endure patiently during the next few days. By the time a week had passed and no word had come she could scarcely eat or sleep or do her work for the worry and speculation that plagued her without mercy.

'You will have to do something,' Sally told her, 'or you'll be ill. Personally, if I see Paul Stalis again I shall black one of those gorgeous eyes of his.'

Nicole smiled faintly. 'What can I do except wait and hope?'

'There is only one thing left to do now; you must go to Athens yourself.'

Nicole laughed. 'You must be crazy. How could I begin to look for him there?'

'You wouldn't have to look far; his brother is an influential man. I'm sure you'd be able to locate him very easily. Paul wouldn't go back to Athens without going to his brother.'

Nicole sighed. 'Oh, I couldn't do it. For one thing

I couldn't leave you to cope alone. You've done more than your share this week. It wouldn't be fair to go now and leave you.'

'It would be fairer than my having to look at you at the moment. I don't have to be on my own either; my sister-in-law would come in to help; she's growing tired of being just a housewife and she would welcome the change for a while. Truly, Nicole.'

She looked at Sally uncertainly. 'Do you really think I should? It's an awfully long way to go just on the offchance that Paul might be there.'

'It's a good chance, and you'd best go if you don't want to drain away completely. I'm not being entirely selfish, Nicole; Bob and I want to go camping later this summer and if you take some time off now I'll feel happier about it when the time comes.'

Nicole smiled. 'Well, I'm not going to stop worrying until I find out where he is and why he went, so I have nothing to lose except the fare money. Pass me the telephone directory and I'll see about booking a seat.'

It was three days later that she arrived in Athens, three days in which she had felt both impatience and reluctance. Once she had decided to go the time could not come quickly enough, but on the other hand she wondered if she were being too anxious. The thought that she might be making a fool of herself in Athens whilst Paul was pursuing some great

25

journalistic scoop in England, haunted her constantly. Anything was possible.

As the aeroplane came in low in its approach to the airport she peered out of the window eagerly at the city laid out below. The sun shimmered on white buildings and on the sea to one side of the plane.

Once on her way she had fretted at the length of the journey, only wanting to be there and on with her search for Paul. Some little warning voice told her finding him might not be so easy. On the face of it the task was a daunting one. She was unfamiliar with the country, knew nothing of the language except for a few basic phrases, and her only lead to Paul was Alexander Stalis, and if he wasn't in Athens or didn't know where his brother happened to be. . . .

The first thing that struck Nicole as she stepped on to the tarmac was the sweetness of the air. It was so bland and fragrant. The summer was too young to have brought the blistering heat which would hit Greece in a few weeks, but the sun was far more warming than it had been in London when she had left. That in itself seemed a good omen, that and the fact she was on solid ground.

Nicole didn't ever enjoy air travel and always regarded it as a miracle when she arrived safely, but this time it was more than relief that she felt; it was an overwhelming gladness that at last she would be doing something to find Paul.

Twenty minutes after arriving Nicole stepped out of the airport building. As she approached one of the waiting taxis the driver opened the door for her, but before getting in she handed him a slip of paper on which was written the name of the hotel given her by the proprietors of the restaurant she and Paul frequented. They had even been kind enough to send a telegram to the hotel to reserve a room for her.

The driver looked at the paper and then to her surprise said, 'Are you English?' She nodded and he grinned. 'I speak English very well.'

'You certainly do. Will you take me to the Argos?'

He nodded vigorously. 'No need to worry; I take you where you want to go.'

She got into the taxi and it set off at breakneck speed.

'Where did you learn such good English?' she asked.

'In the war I fight with the English. Do you stay in Athens all the time you're in Greece?'

'Yes, at least I think so.'

'You find most people speak English.'

Nicole laughed. 'I'm glad because I don't speak Greek.'

The road into Athens ran by the sea and Nicole sank into the seat and watched the yachts and boats bobbing on the gently rippling water. Oh, if only I knew that Paul was all right, she thought. In her

mind a fear for him had become fixed and no amount
of reasoning could dispel it.

'The Argos is a good hotel,' the driver told her as
the coast road was left behind. 'You will find it comfortable.'

'It was recommended.'

'Good for sightseeing. You come on holiday?'

'I've come to see my boyfriend,' she answered, more
hopefully than she really felt. 'But if I can get in some
sightseeing while I am here then all the better.'

'You can't come to Athens without seeing the
Acropolis and then Epidaurus and Delphi.'

Nicole said nothing. The traffic was becoming
thicker and she felt impatient every time they had
to slow down. When the ruins of Hadrian's Arch
came into view she knew they had arrived and she
was possessed of a sudden fever of excitement. In
other circumstances she would have been delighted
to be in Athens, to sample its east/west flavour, to
see its famous sights. But all that must be disregarded
until she found Paul.

The taxi pulled up outside an imposing-looking
building situated in what appeared to be the hub
of the city. 'Here is the Argos,' the man told her. As
he helped her out he said, waving his arm, 'Up there
is Constitution Square. See, where that building is,'
and, as she nodded, he flapped his hand in the other
direction. 'And there is the Acropolis.'

Nicole caught her breath at the sight of the

28

Pantheon, rising majestically above the city. Having seen it in countless films and photographs, she still wasn't prepared for the magnificence of white marble outlined against a clear blue sky. High up on the Acropolis hill it still dominated the city even in its ruined state.

'Good?' the driver asked, obviously pleased at her reaction.

'Oh, very good!' she agreed. 'I only hope to have a chance to see it at closer quarters.'

She paid him what he asked, fumbling with the unfamiliar money, and added a generous tip for his kindness.

'Have a pleasant stay, young lady.'

She started towards the hotel and then turned to him again. 'Oh, wait a minute.' He paused. 'Do you happen to know of a man called Alexander Stalis?' He owns a newspaper in Athens.'

The man grinned. 'Sure, I do. Is he your boy-friend?'

'No, but his brother is. Where can I find him?'

He frowned for a moment or two and then his face cleared. He took her arm and led her in front of his taxi.

'If you walk along this street towards the Square, there is a white building just before you get to it. There, you see it juts out a little more than the others. That is where you will find him.'

'I'm very grateful to you,' she told him.

29

'It is a pleasure to be of service to such a charming young lady. *Herete*, and I hope you enjoy Athens.'

'Goodbye,' she echoed and watched his grey taxi until it was swallowed in the mass of vehicles choking the street.

Nicole found that matters were moving smoothly. The hotel had received the telegram and there was a room reserved for her, but no message had arrived. (Sally was to pass on any word if it came after she had left for Athens). After more than a week she really did not expect any.

Her room had a view of the Acropolis which would have, in normal circumstances, delighted her, but Nicole only glanced at it perfunctorily now. There would be no time for sightseeing until Paul was located. Like so many other people she was here on business.

Alexander Stalis's whereabouts had been discovered much more easily than she had dared to hope, and now she intended to see him as quickly as possible. But first she unpacked her case, knowing she would have to have a bath and change her travelling clothes before she could face Paul's brother.

She stayed in the bath far longer than normal, mainly because now she had arrived she was suddenly shy of facing the man who had had so much influence over Paul; the man who had been as a father to him. But the bath did more than wash away grime of travel, it eased some of the tension which had built up over the past ten days.

For some reason she took great pains with her appearance. Her clothes were of her own design and well made by a dressmaker who was particularly gifted, and when she had finished brushing her shoulder length brown hair and put on a little light makeup she felt equal to facing Alexander Stalis, a man known even to Athens taxi-drivers.

'Is everything to your satifaction, Miss Carrington?' the receptionist asked as she handed in her key.

She realized then that she must have been looking very tense and she smiled reassuringly at the girl. 'The room is very comfortable.'

Outside the Argos traffic continued to whizz past towards Constitution Square, the majority of the vehicles being uniformly grey taxis and the others buses and trolleys.

It took her only a few moments to walk to the building that the taxi driver had indicated. There was a plaque on the wall outside which indicated the name of the company, only Nicole could not read it. It was later than she would have normally considered calling on someone's place of business, but she was aware this was not England and after a siesta in the afternoon business establishments, like the shops, remained open until late.

She stood outside the building for a moment or two and then walked slowly on, to Constitution Square only a few yards away, where the former royal palace looked out to the Acropolis, across the more mundane pavement cafés and airline offices.

Nicole went to the nearest outdoor café, sat down and ordered a coffee. The Square, the heart of Athens, was a hub of activity on such a fine day. Tourists and Athenians milled together, shopping and enjoying a restful moment at an outside table. But Nicole found she was not as relaxed as all those around her; she was trembling. What if something awful had happened to Paul? Or his brother? The coffee arrived; it was far too strong but she drank it down quickly and felt better for it. She paid the waiter and went back the way she had come.

This time she did not turn away; she walked straight inside without a moment's hesitation. A receptionist sat in the marble foyer of the building and Nicole went directly up to her.

'Do you speak English?'

The girl smiled. 'Can I help you?'

'I'm looking for Mr Stalis. Alexander Stalis. I believe that his office is in this building.'

The girl's eyes narrowed with curiosity. 'Take the lift to the top floor. You will find Mr Stalis's secretary in the first room to the right of the lift as you get out.'

Nicole thanked her profusely, realizing she had expected to hear that Alexander Stalis was ill or even dead. Paul had not rushed back to Athens for that reason; this much she had learned already. Nicole didn't know whether she was relieved or not, but, as she pressed for the lift, she did vow to stop asking people if they spoke English.

Up until now she had not given Paul's brother much thought, although she did know quite a lot about him. Naturally, Paul spoke about him constantly, with an admiration that was akin to hero-worship, which tended to annoy her at times. No one could be that perfect.

Alexander Stalis was Paul's only living relative. He was much older than Paul and after their parents had died when Paul was only a baby, Alexander had taken charge of his up-bringing at the same time carving out for himself a sizeable fortune in the world of business. Nicole usually took little notice of Paul's boasting about Alexander and it was not until the lift was approaching the top floor of the building that she realized he had not exaggerated about his brother at all.

Alexander Stalis's secretary was busily typing when Nicole went into her office. She stopped her work and smiled at Nicole who said, 'I would like to speak to Mr Stalis, if he can spare me a few minutes of his time.'

'Oh, I am sorry. You must excuse my English; it is not very good. Mr Stalis is not here. Perhaps you will come back tomorrow.'

It looked as if she might continue with her work when Nicole said, 'No! I must speak to him straight away. I've just arrived from London. I came especially to see him!' The girl looked at her blankly and, wondering how much of that she had really understood, Nicole took a deep breath. 'I am a friend of Paul Stalis—his brother—who has disappeared. I know something has happened to him!'

Whether she understood, the tone of Nicole's voice left no doubt that something was wrong and the girl looked startled, almost as if she were unsure of Nicole's mental state.

'Please, let me know where I can contact him. It's very important. Do you understand? It concerns his brother.'

It seemed that Nicole had said the right thing, for the girl murmured. 'If you will wait a moment I can see what to do,' and she lifted the telephone receiver.

Nicole hoped she was not calling the security men to have her evicted from the premises, but had no choice except to wait and see.

The girl kept one wary eye on her as she dialled and, unable to understand the ensuing conversation, Nicole drummed her fingers on the desk as she waited, trying to stifle her growing panic and frustration. At last the girl replaced the receiver and Nicole looked at her hopefully.

'Mr Stalis has an engagement this evening but he will not be leaving for a while. If this matter is so very urgent he is willing to spare you some time, but you will have to go to his home.'

34

'Yes, yes, of course I will,' Nicole answered eagerly. 'You must tell me where it is, because I have no idea. I have never been to Athens before.'

'That is no problem. I will write down the address and a taxi will take you there in only a few minutes.'

Clutching the slip of paper Nicole hailed a taxi outside the building and sank back breathlessly into the seat as it set off again. The taxi turned into Constitution Square, becoming caught up in the choking traffic. She leaned forward anxiously as the taxi crept forward at a snail's pace, and then at last it swept into a wide avenue which ran behind the Royal Palace. She relaxed again and gazed out of the window with interest. This area was obviously a good one. Large villas and blocks of luxury apartments fronted on to the avenue and when, a very few minutes later the taxi turned into a steep street, she realized this was the lower part of Lykabettus Hill. Here, all the buildings were sparkling white apartment blocks of the better kind, rather opulent in appearance. The taxi drew up outside one of them and Nicole hurriedly scrambled out and paid the driver.

Alexander Stalis lived in the topmost apartment. The lift whisked her silently upwards and the door of the apartment opened almost at the same time as she rang the bell.

'I have an appointment with Mr Stalis,' she said breathlessly as she stepped inside.

The elderly woman, dressed in black, nodded, although Nicole was certain she did not understand what she had said. She followed the woman into a thickly carpeted living room. For a moment Nicole forgot why she had come, for she was lost in admiration of her surroundings. The room was a large one by any standards and its spaciousness was enhanced by the minimum of furniture and a pure white carpet which covered the floor, stretching from wall to wall. The walls themselves and the ceiling were painted white too, and black sofas and rugs were a calculated contrast. No other colour was allowed to intrude.

Here and there abstract paintings shattered the stark bareness of the walls, and on pedestals stood weird shapes of modern sculptures. It was all aesthetically pleasing, but it was certainly not conducive to easy living. The woman indicated that Nicole should sit down and wait, and then left her alone.

Nicole remained standing, for she felt this was not a place in which to live, only to see and admire. She could not violate those sofas by sitting on them, nor could she imagine throwing off her shoes and putting her feet up on one of them, as was her habit at home. It was impossible to visualize, too, any jammy-fingered child spoiling the walls or carpet, and she supposed any person likely to commit such a crime would never be invited here.

Although the decor of the room had attracted the artist in her it was the windows which drew her immediately, for they spread across the entire length of one wall. Her footsteps were silenced by the thickness of the carpet as she crossed the room. There below the window spread modern Athens, streets choked with traffic, and on soil walked by the people of antiquity rose modern apartment buildings like this one. And beyond it all, the Acropolis and its cluster of ruined buildings, of which from this window there was a perfect view.

'Marvellous,' she breathed.

'I think so too.'

Nicole turned around on her heel but the dying sun had dazzled her and she could see only a shadow of the man who had come into the room unheard. She moved away from the window and he came further into the room. She was able to see him better then and she experienced something of a shock. Alexander Stalis was not the middle-aged man she had imagined him to be. He was young and although he did not possess such perfect features as his brother, he was not ill-favoured at all. Moreover, in those first few seconds Nicole realized that, whereas Paul had over abundant charm, his brother had less of it, but a great strength of character. She was certain he would be a dangerous enemy to those who crossed him.

She wondered, a little uncomfortably, how long he had been there, observing her unseen. Nicole suspected it had been quite some time.

'I can spare you only a few minutes of my time, Miss Carrington,' he said in clipped tones which made it quite clear she was far from welcome, 'as my secretary probably told you.' Like Paul, his voice bore only the trace of an accent. His English was faultless, somehow putting her at an immediate disadvantage she did not like.

Responding in much the same manner, Nicole drew herself up as straight as she could. 'I shall endeavour to keep you no longer than that, Mr Stalis. I've come here to Athens to find Paul.'

His eyes opened wider, but his gaze was still fixed on her, disconcertingly. 'Why should you think I can tell you where he is?'

Some of her precious self-control was beginning to crack. 'Please don't play games with me. I've been quite out of my mind with worry since he disappeared last week. I know he's in Greece and I'm certain he wouldn't come back here without your being aware of it.'

'How can you be so sure he's in Greece?'

'A friend of mine rang the airport and discovered that his name was on the passenger list.'

'That was a very enterprising thing to do. '

'I came here only to find Paul, and to know if he's safe.'

'Why shouldn't he be . . . safe?'

'I don't know! But people don't just disappear for no reason without telling someone where they are

38

going and why!'

He came towards her, moving with an effortless elegance she couldn't help but admire. There was less hostility in his manner now she noticed with with some relief.

'Please, Miss Carrington, do not distress yourself. I assure you there is no need. Come and sit down and we will discuss the matter further.'

She allowed herself to be led to a sofa and when they were both seated she said, 'Did he never mention me in his letters? Nicole Carrington. We saw a great deal of each other in London.'

He shook his head slowly. He was dressed for the evening, so it was probably true he had an engagement. It was not an excuse to be rid of her.

'Not to my knowledge. Your name is not at all familiar to me.' He smiled apologetically then. 'Paul has always been so bad at writing letters, and when he does they are very brief.'

'Obviously,' she said, swallowing noisily, 'you don't believe I knew Paul well at all. You wouldn't know that the night before he disappeared he asked me to marry him, and it wasn't the first time, so there is more than just friendship between us.'

There was nothing easy about his manner now. His eyes sparkled with anger, but a moment later he got to his feet and went across to a liquor cabinet. It gave Nicole some satisfaction to know she had surprised him and he was at that moment giving himself pause for thought.

'May I offer you some refreshment, Miss Carrington? I have most of the usual drinks.'

'Do you have a gin and orange?'

'I believe so. Ah, yes, here it is. More orange than gin for you, I think.'

Within a minute or two he was back with their drinks and as she sipped self-consciously at hers he continued to watch her in that disconcerting manner of his.

'Well,' he said at last, 'if what you say is true . . .'

'Of course it is!'

'. . . I must congratulate my brother on his excellent taste.'

'All I want to know is if he's safe.'

'I can assure you of that.'

'Then he is here!' she cried.

'No, but he's quite safe and happy, I promise you.'

'Safe? Then he must be in some danger,' she said uncertainly.

'An unfortunate figure of speech. The matter is quite simple—he needs a rest.'

He finished his drink and she said, 'Who is Maria?'

Slowly his eyes met hers. He gazed at her steadily without the trace of a flicker in those dark, fathomless eyes and said, 'I have no idea. Should I know her?' But Nicole knew without the shadow of a doubt that he was lying.

'Are you going to tell me where Paul is, or do I

40

have to try and find him myself?'

He sighed and sank back into the cushions of the sofa. 'Miss Carrington, it would be so much more simple if you were to return to your home.'

'I have no intention of doing that until I have spoken to Paul.'

There was a momentary silence between them as Nicole stared at him fiercely. He rolled the glass between his palms and seemed deep in thought. At last he said heavily, 'You don't make matters easy for me. You don't seem to realize that Paul is very young—not so much in age, but in his ways. I take no pride in that because it is mostly my fault for sheltering his existence so much, but however painful it is to us both I must ask you to consider that, having asked you to marry him, it is possible that regretting it, he decided to run. It has been done before.'

Nicole toyed with her glass. He was feeling no pain at what he was saying to her and he wasn't even pretending that he did. She would have loved to have thrown her drink in his self-satisfied face, but at last, subduing her anger, she said in a soft voice, 'I doubt if that was his reason, Mr Stalis. I didn't come halfway across the world just to force him to marry me. Remember, I did refuse *him*. Besides, there was a man watching his flat and I found a note which said 'Remember Maria'. I think that is the reason he fled, not because of me.'

She watched him carefully but he was too clever

to show any surprise. Alexander Stalis would be an expert at hiding any emotion he might be experiencing. He got to his feet again and went to the window where a purple dusk was rapidly falling on the city.

'I'm sorry,' he said abruptly. 'Paul cannot see anyone but I will ask him to contact you when he returns to Athens. I take it you will be going back to London very soon.'

'No, I've already told you I won't. What are you afraid of? Is it to do with the trouble he was in a few years ago, before he came to London?'

'Trouble,' he scoffed. 'What a lame word. Paul was no hero and I hope you realize that.'

'I'm very proud of him, Mr Stalis and I think you should be too.'

'There was no glory in what he did. It was only because he was my brother that he got off so lightly. He would have been in dreadful trouble otherwise. More than you or he could know. Paul is not equipped for martyrdom.'

'And who's fault is that?'

'Mine, Miss Carrington. Mine,' he said in a weary voice.

'You can't forgive him even now for going against you just this once in his life, to have principles of his own, not an echo of your own. I am very proud of him.'

She stood up and he jerked the curtain cord, shutting out the night and the view of a million lights below.

'You know nothing about it,' he said, turning on her again. 'Those paragraphs in the newspaper, so many killed, so many arrested. You have no idea how painful it is to have had principles in Greece during the past few years.'

Nicole had to look away from him. He was no coward. She knew that instinctively and although he had not opposed the government he was a man of principle too. She wondered how it was possible to reconcile the two aspects of his nature.

A moment later he was pouring another drink for himself and she said, 'Paul and I became very close in London, close enough to consider marriage. I believe he was sincere the two times he asked me to be his wife, but if he no longer wishes to marry me I would like him to tell me to my face. Then I shall be satisfied and go back home.'

She started towards the door and as she did so a woman came out of one of the other rooms. She was so stunning that Nicole stopped to stare at her, and as if she were well aware of her effect on others and used to it the woman smiled. Dressed in a simple white silk evening gown and with dark red hair piled high on her head, Nicole thought she was one of the most beautiful women she had ever seen.

Alexander Stalis said something to her in their native language and she passed by, going into the room. Then, to Nicole's surprise, he came to the door with her. His manner was still remote but his anger had gone.

'Where are you staying?' he asked as he opened the door for her.

'At the Hotel Argos.'

'I shall contact you there in the morning. Good night to you, Miss Carrington.'

'*Kalispera,*' she responded, but by then he was gone.

She sighed and went towards the lift. What a strange man, she thought. Dangerous almost, if anyone dared to cross him. To be fair he had looked after Paul wonderfully well, only Paul had surrendered his own will to that of his brother in payment. Having met Alexander, Nicole could see that all too well now. If she were to marry Paul after all she would make sure there was an end to that. If. . . . She couldn't see Alexander Stalis approving a match between her, a nobody, and Paul.

She reached the street which was now dark and deserted, and she began to walk down the hill in the direction of the avenue where she would be able to find a taxi to take her back to the hotel. Before she had gone many yards she heard the sound of female laughter and automatically turned round to see where it had come from.

Alexander Stalis and his beautiful companion were coming out of the apartment block and Nicole paused to watch them as they got into a car which was

44

parked outside. As they started to drive slowly away, quite unaware of her scrutiny, the lights of another car, which had been parked some way further up the street, came on and it too began to move forward. As it passed Nicole the man at the wheel turned his head to glance at her, and then he was gone.

Nicole had the oddest feeling that he was following Alexander Stalis, but then she decided she was being fanciful. It was merely a coincidence that he set off at the same time. It was, surely, the strange circumstance of Paul's departure from England which was causing her imagination to work too hard. If someone had been watching Paul in London, it would be too much of a coincidence for another person to be following his brother in Athens.

She dismissed the matter from her mind. All she must do is wait until she heard from Paul's brother who would by now be enjoying himself at some sophisticated nightspot, having forgotten for the moment her very existence.

As she started on her way again Nicole thought that she had never felt so alone.

Chapter Three

It was the insistent ringing of the telephone that awoke her the next morning. All her unaccustomed activity had worn her out and, far from staying wakeful in strange surroundings, Nicole had slept deeply.

Automatically she reached out for the telephone which, unmercifully, tugged her back to consciousness.

'Miss Carrington?'

'Mmmm.'

'Alexander Stalis.'

'Oh. Oh!' She was suddenly wide awake, struggling to push back the stifling covers.

'Are you all right, Miss Carrington?'

'Yes, but can you wait for just a moment please?' She put the receiver down and struggled into a sitting position before picking it up again. 'I'm sorry about that. I was asleep.'

'Do you want to see Paul?'

'Yes!' Every vestige of sleep had gone.

'You must go along with some elementary precautions. I hope you will be agreeable.'

'Of course. I'll do anything you say. I just want to see Paul.'

'Very well.' His voice was very businesslike and Nicole was intrigued. He was not, she was certain, a man to indulge in needless complications. 'You are to check out of you hotel this morning and take a taxi to the airport, just as if you were catching the morning flight to London. When you arrive at the airport lose yourself in the crowds around the check in desks, but make for the powder room and stay there until the flight has gone. Do you understand?'

'Yes, but *why?*'

'Please don't ask questions. There isn't time to answer them. Just do as I ask. I'm relying on you to obey my instructions to the letter. That is very important.'

'Paul *is* in trouble, isn't he?'

'Let's just say some hothead thinks he has a grievance against my brother.'

Nicole wondered who would dare to threaten Alexander Stalis's brother. It was hard enough work being in love with him at the moment!

'It must be a very strong grievance.'

'I have no time to elaborate just now. Are the instructions clear to you, Miss Carrington?'

'Yes. What do I do then? Wait in the powder room until Paul arrives, dressed as a woman, of course.'

47

'This is no time for jokes. It is a very serious matter and unless you are going to treat it as such there seems no point in continuing.'

Immediately contrite, Nicole said quickly, 'I'm sorry. Please go on, only it's all so difficult to take seriously when I don't know what is happening.'

'You know enough. When ten minutes have passed leave the airport by taxi and tell the driver to take you to Vouliagmeni.'

Nicole repeated the name and he went on, 'There is a marina there. A boat named *Melisande* will be moored there and it will take you where you want to go. Are you confused at all?'

Nicole half smiled to herself. 'Not about the instructions. They seem clear enough.'

'Then you'd better repeat all those directions to me just to be sure.'

She did so and he expressed satisfaction. 'As long as you do everything I have asked all will be well.'

'Am I in any danger, Mr Stalis?' she asked as he was about to ring off.

There was a momentary silence before he answered, 'None at all, Miss Carrington. It is only a precaution in case you are being followed.'

'I'm beginning to be alarmed. If Paul is in danger why not tell the police?'

'It is not a police matter, and now I must say goodbye to you, Miss Carrington. *Kalimera.*'

The line went dead but Nicole kept the receiver

in her hand for a few moments and then, sighing, she put it back and began to prepare to leave.

Nicole was determined to obey all those intriguing instructions even though she did feel rather foolish in doing so. Beneath her apparent composure she was very frightened; Paul's brother would not insist on such stringent precautions if they were not necessary, so something must be very wrong.

It seemed an age before she was thankfully able to climb into a taxi outside the airport and direct him to take her to the marina at Vouliagmeni. Even as they drove away she couldn't help glancing behind, but no one appeared to be following her.

The journey to Vouliagmeni was quite a short one and very pleasant as the road passed through holiday resorts and the sea was always in sight. Even though she was in a fever to be at her destination Nicole found herself admiring the small villas in palm-shaded gardens which faced the sea, and she envied all those able to sunbathe in such a carefree way. She wished she could join them and forget the fears and the problems which plagued her. There were moments when she wished she had stayed in London.

The taxi sped along the coast road, the sea sparkling in the sun on one side and purple hills in the distance on the other. Vouliagmeni was a small resort, quiet at that time of the year as the main holiday season had not yet begun. However, there were quite a number of people about but no one who seemed particularly interested in her.

The marina itself was picturesque, crowded with boats and yachts of many sizes. Nicole quickly paid the taxi driver and, clutching her suitcase, she walked towards the quay. She peered anxiously at the hulls of each boat she passed. Many of the names were printed Greek and for a few moments she knew panic until she spotted the *Melisande*, which fortunately had its name written in English.

The boat was a medium sized cabin cruiser with paint that looked new and woodwork which sparkled in the sunlight. Nicole still felt tense but all these boats had a festive air about them which made her feel brighter.

The boat looked deserted but as she approached it a swarthy-looking man, whose muscles were bulging through his tee shirt, came out of the cabin and on to the deck.

'Mr Stalis sent me.' she shouted up to him.

He waved her up the gangplank and when she came aboard he took her suitcase. She followed him into the cabin where he showed her a small basket on the table. Nicole lifted the lid and peered inside and when she realized what it was she couldn't restrain a smile. Inside there was a selection of cold meats, chicken, rolls, sweetcake, fruit and a bottle of wine. No one could say that Alexander Stalis did not think of everything, but Nicole, despite missing lunch, could not face any food however tempting. Her stomach was too tight with tension. For whose benefit had she staged that masquerade?

As the boatman went out of the cabin Nicole said, 'Where are we going?'

'You make yourself comfortable,' he said in a thickly accented voice. 'We get there in about one hour and a half.'

'But where?'

'You see.'

With that she had to be content, for it was obvious he intended to say no more on the subject. Moments later the engines began to throb and then the boat gently vibrated as they started to move. Earlier she had dressed as if for a plane journey and during the taxi ride she had felt overdressed and hot. She peered into the adjoining galley and seeing that the door had a lock on it she took her case inside and changed her suit for a pair of jeans and a tee shirt.

By the time she came out onto the deck they were well away from the shore and a brisk breeze was blowing. It was much cooler than it had been on land but Nicole did not care. Her hair streamed back from her face and she felt gloriously alive. Soon all that could be seen were purple hills of the mainland. Before the coast was out of sight she felt hungry and went back into the cabin to get the picnic basket. She offered some food to the boatman who shook his head, but he did accept some of the wine. Nicole sat by his side on the co-pilot's seat and ate cold chicken, rolls and some fruit, enjoying them far more than she would have imagined when she started out.

By the time the boatman, whose name she discovered was Demetrius, waved towards land she was beginning to wish they need never stop. She was enjoying the journey and beyond it were problems and puzzles she would rather not face. Alexander Stalis had told her Paul was safe and well; that should have been sufficient.

The *Melisande* puttered along the rocky coast of what appeared to be a small island. As it rounded a headland Nicole stood up to view a little village situated in a natural harbour. A few fishing vessels were moored against the quay, and nets were stretched across the cobbles. Fishermen's cottages, dazzling white in the sun, were banked against the rising hillside and looked like lumps of sugar. Beyond the village, in the centre of the island, where it rose to some height, stood what appeared to be a ruined temple. Nicole let out a long sigh of sheer delight; she hadn't expected to venture further than Athens, and certainly not to any of the the famed isles. Now it appeared she was about to visit one of the unspoiled ones

When Demetrius made no attempt to steer the boat into the harbour Nicole said, 'Isn't this our destination?'

'We don't go to to the harbour. There is private mooring near the villa. You see.'

'Whose villa is it? Mr Stalis's?'

For the first time he loked at her with interest. 'The villa belongs to Kyria Adrianou.'

Nicole decided to ask no more questions, for any answers Demetrius might give were of no help. The boat hugged the rugged coast of the island for a while and when they rounded another headland Demetrius killed the engine. A small landing stage jutted out from the rocks. Nicole waited until he had tied up and then he helped her on to the landing stage. She looked around her, for there was no sign of any villa. The cliff behind them looked sheer, but Demetrius, understanding her perplexity, indicated some steps hewn into the rock and it was only a short climb to a garden that was alive with oleanders, bougainvillea and the glorious flame-coloured hibiscus which rioted everywhere, dazzling the eye.

Nicole followed the path through the garden until it opened up on a swimming pool terrace. She stopped in her tracks when she saw Paul so unexepectedly before her. He was wearing swimming trunks and was stretched out on a lounging chair at the side of pool. He was far more relaxed than when she had last seen him ten days before and quite sunburned. The sight of him lying there, reading a newspaper as if he had not a care in the world, when she had been sick with worry and had come thousands of miles to find him, filled her with an unreasoning anger.

He remained unaware of her for a few moments until Demetrius came noisily up the path behind her and attracted his attention. Paul looked up and dropped his newspaper, jumping to his feet.

'Nicky! Oh, how marvellous to see you!' He came bounding up to her. 'I just can't believe you are actually here.' He paused to direct a volley of Greek at the boatman who grinned and went on towards the villa. Paul held her away from him. 'Well, why are you loking so solemn? Aren't you glad to see me?'

'Oh, Paul,' she said, her anger melting, 'I was so worried about you.'

He drew her close and kissed her longingly and Nicole could not resist him. It seemed such a long time since she had been in his arms. He held her close for a long time and then he drew her towards the chairs dotted around the pool.

'I'm sorry, Nicky. I never intended you to be worried about me, although if I'd known my going away would have this effect on you I might have tried it before.'

'You are a brute. I'm beginning to think you did do this to test me. Why on earth didn't you let me know where you'd gone?'

'Bcause *I* wouldn't let him.'

Nicole pulled away from Paul and they both whirled round. Alexander was on the verandah of the villa watching them. He was leaning negligently against one of the pillars. He was wearing a light sweater and fawn trousers and his hair was wet, slicked closely to his head, as if he had recently been swimming in the pool. He looked cool and elegant, and had probably been watching them for some time, which angered Nicole, especially when she remembered Paul's kiss and her eager response to it.

For some reason he was the last person she would have expected to see here, and the sight of him had shocked her deeply. Only last night he had been enjoying the sophisticated delights of Athens, but then, she realized, so had she.

He came down the steps and walked towards them. 'I do hope your journey was a comfortable one,' he said, smiling at her in what she now realized was a deprecating way.

Nicole felt almost defensive. 'It was very comfortable. Last night you said you'd never heard of me before, so why did you forbid Paul to contact me?'

'I hadn't heard of you, but I instructed Paul not to contact anyone at all. We weren't to know he had a friend who was so tenacious and would follow him here.'

She flashed him a furious look and then turned to his brother. 'And I suppose you *had* to take notice of him?'

Paul shrugged and his brother answered, 'Paul, as you've already realized is in rather a . . . difficult

55

position at the moment. If I am to help at all he must co-operate with me.'

He looked so self-satisfied that Nicole was, for the second time, assailed with the desire to hit him, but being well aware of his influence over Paul and that she was here only by virtue of his goodwill, she restrained herself. But she was boiling with indignation and she had the oddest feeling he was aware of her longing to hit out at him, for there seemed to be the hint of a smile behind that inscrutible face.

He glanced at his watch. 'It's time I was going to the village.' He looked at Nicole. 'When I'm here I always have a glass of ouzo at the village café. I don't suppose there is any point in asking you two to come along with me today?'

Paul laughed and put his arm around Nicole's shoulder again. 'Nicole and I have ten days to catch up on, Alex, and you know what that means.'

Paul's brother shrugged and as he walked away he raised his hand in a mocking salute. When he had gone Nicole's tension drained out of her as quickly as it had come.

She looked up at Paul. 'So much for Alexander. He doesn't like me.'

'You obviously don't like him.'

'He's too domineering.'

His eyebrows went up a fraction. 'It's generally believed that women like a man who is domineering.'

'I don't.'

Softly Paul said, 'He's been more than a brother to me, Nicole. I want you to like him. It's important.'

She sighed and gave him a tremulous smile. 'I know, and I will try to get on with him for your sake. After all, he did arrange for me to come out here to join you and I'm grateful to him for that.'

At that Paul threw back his head and laughed. 'You should be grateful to *me*. I got you here only after a furious struggle.'

Nicole watched him curiously. The afternoon sun beating down on her back felt glorious but she was only half aware of it at that moment. 'What do you mean?'

'Alex turned up here last night very late. In fact I was already in bed. He was furious about you.' His eyes gazed into hers. 'But I soon enlightened him about our relationship and made it very clear if he didn't have you brought out here to me I would go to Athens myself to see you. That did it, of course.'

Nicole walked slowly across to one of the chairs and sat down on the edge of it, staring into the blue depths of the pool.

'I wonder why he is so against me.'

Paul reached out for his white bathrobe which contrasted against his newly-acquired tan. As he wrapped it around himself he answered, 'It isn't anything personal against you. It's just that Alex is used to having his own way with me, and in the back of his mind there's a wish to see me married to a Greek girl—

57

from a very good family, of course. Also marriage is a big step to take and naturally he'll be worried in case I've made the wrong choice. He doesn't know you as I do.'

Nicole continued to stare into the pool. Her worry for Paul's safety had faded from her mind and now she wondered why she had bothered to come. There was another problem to be faced here and she didn't think she could cope with it.

'I understand now, because his feelings are very natural and as you say he doesn't know how we feel about each other.' She looked up at him then. 'And how do you feel about the matter now you're back in Greece?'

He came to sit beside her and put his arm round her shoulder, drawing her reassuringly close. 'You know how I feel, Nicky. I love you—nothing and no one can change that. And while you are here Alex can get to know you better and then he will be in no doubt too.'

'So,' she said, attempting to inject some lightness into her voice, 'I'm to be on trial here.'

He laughed, 'Of course not. If I'm firm enough he'll come round. Anyway, how can he help but like you?'

He was about to kiss her when she said, 'Oh, he can help it all right. I have the feeling he has already made up his mind about me very firmly.'

He looked surprised. 'Why do you care so much?'

Startled Nicole answered, 'I don't, but we can't

disregard him. He is your only living relative.'

'Until you are my wife.'

His eyes held hers until quite unexepectedly there came the sound of raised voices just inside the villa. Paul drew away from her, frowning, and got to his feet.

'I wonder what that can be?'

No sooner had the question left his lips than a girl came running on to the verandah. She stopped when she saw Paul and then another woman appeared behind her, apparently trying to pull her back inside. She was middle-aged, her dark hair turned grey, but the younger one was possibly still in her teens and very attractive.

She managed to pull herself free from the restraining grip of the older woman and came running down the steps her arms outstretched to Paul. She threw herself into his arms when she reached him, holding on to him possessively and flashing a furious look at Nicole as Paul struggled to free himself of her grip. He began to shout at her too until the older woman came hurrying along the path and between them they managed to free Paul.

They were all shouting together and at last, when Paul spoke sharply to her, saying, *'Fiyete'*—which Nicole knew meant 'Go away'—the girl burst into tears and allowed herself to be led away by the older woman who continued to scold her as well as, apparently, shouting apologies to Paul over her shoulder.

59

Paul watched them until they had returned to the villa and then drew a sigh of relief, turning back to Nicole.

'What was all that about?' she asked.

He sat down again, glancing worriedly at the villa as if expecting the girl to appear again at any moment. 'The old woman is Chloris, our cook/housekeeper. Sofia is her daughter. They were having a quarrel.'

'Over you, I believe,' she said tersely.

He looked alarmed. 'Oh no. What makes you think that?'

Nicole laughed harshly. 'It was obvious. I'm not a fool, Paul. Besides, you did teach me some Greek words and phrases. Things like "darling" and "I love you". Remember?'

He stared at the ground. 'Sofia is a little fool. She's jealous of you, if you must know.'

'Why?'

'Because she has what is known as a schoolgirl crush on me. She always has, ever since she was very small. It's very embarrassing.'

'Have you given her any encouragement?'

'Of course not! She's only a child.'

Nicole laughed again. 'Hardly, Paul. She's very attractive. You'd be the first to notice that.'

He glared at her. 'I've never given her cause to think she means anything to me.'

Nicole put one hand over his. 'You only have to

say "Hello" to a girl and she believes she must mean everything to you.'

'I love only you,' he said softly.

She believed him; she also believed he had been engaging in a mild flirtation with that girl in her absence. In that respect she knew Paul rather well.

'Don't *you* be jealous, Nicky.'

She smiled. 'I'm not,' she said, and meant it.

He would have kissed her again but she disentangled herself from his embrace. 'First of all, Paul, there are some questions I want answered.'

The laughter died out of his eyes again. 'Can't they wait?'

'No. First of all, where are we?'

She fancied he relaxed a little. 'Kyros.'

'And where is that?'

'An island, just off the southern tip of Greece. It's not a tourist spot except for a few private yachts which call during the summer. It's very private.'

He tried to take her in his arms again but she asked, 'Privacy is obviously of prime importance to you, so who are you hiding from?'

There was a short silence. Nicole knew he would rather not answer, just as Alexander hadn't wanted to, but she continued to stare at him until he said, irritably, 'It's really a lot of nonsense.'

'I would hardly call it that considering the elaborate charade your brother put me up to before I was able to come here.'

He sighed. 'You should realize that Alex during the past twenty years has made a great many enemies . . .'

'You are the one who is in hiding, Paul.'

His eyes met hers. 'I'm trying to explain as best I can. I'm his brother although most people believe I have been more like a son, so anyone wishing to strike back at Alex because of some petty grievance couldn't do better than threaten me. It's as simple as that.'

Somehow she didn't think it was so simple and as if he could read her thoughts he went on, 'It might seem impossible to you, being British, Nicky, but you must remember we are not. Some Greeks, like the Spaniards and the Italians, can be very hot-headed. Grievances you, or even I, might forget live long in some people's minds.'

'Who is Maria?'

He stared at her. 'Maria?' he stuttered. 'I don't understand. . . .'

'It's quite simple, Paul.' She was playing with the strap of her shoulder bag. Somehow she could not look at him any longer. The garden was filled with fragrance, shaded by lemon and orange trees which were heavy with ripening fruit. It was a place in which love could ripen too, but Nicole was aware only of his unease, his evasiveness. 'Do you know a girl called Maria?'

He laughed, but it was an uneasy sound. 'How far back do you want me to go? School, university? I've known dozens of Marias. It's not an uncommon name in Greece.'

'I think this was more recent. In your flat after you'd left I found a note. It said "Remember Maria".'

'I can't remember everything I scribble down.'

Her eyes met his. 'I'm getting rather tired of asking that question and getting an evasive answer. Do you, or do you not, know a girl called Maria?'

He laughed again. 'Good heavens, Nicky. You really are the jealous kind after all.'

'Stop being flippant,' she snapped and he looked alarmed. 'Are you going to answer me?'

His laughter died. 'Of course I do.' He paused. 'The note probaly referred to a girl called Maria Stephenson—she's a typist in the office and she's being married next month. The boss asked me to organize a collection for a present amongst the staff.'

Nicole kept on looking at him. His eyes gazed into hers, frankly, but just as she hadn't believed his brother's answer to that question the night before, now she didn't believe Paul's.

Chapter Four

They seemed to have been walking for ages, but that was only because the going was all uphill. The island was a very small one—only three miles across —but it was rocky with almost no flat land at all, except for a strip around part of the coastline.

'How far is it now, Paul?' she shouted.

He was striding on ahead of her, but then he was used to the island and the heat, which sapped her energy and seemed to be growing more fierce with every step she took. It hadn't seemed nearly so hot when they started out from the villa such a short time before.

He stopped and waited for her to catch up with him, holding out his hand to help her. He shook his head and laughed. 'And I'm the one carrying the picnic basket!' As he pulled on her hand he said, 'It's much easier going down; remember that.'

'I doubt if I shall even get up.'

'We're almost there.'

She stumbled over some stones and Paul steadied her, then she flopped down against a marble pillar at the top of the hill.

'At last,' she breathed. 'I thought we'd never get here.'

Paul put the picnic basket down on the ground, in the shade of an olive tree and walked a little way away from Nicole, who was rubbing her perspiring brow with a handkerchief soaked in eau de cologne.

'As soon as you get your breath back you must come and see the view. It's magnificent.'

'There has to be some reward for the climb. The trouble is, I'm out of condition.'

'You shouldn't be after all the walking we've done this week.'

After a minute or two she scrambled to her feet and went to join him. She walked carefully as stones jutted out of the ground at every step, like teeth waiting to snap at the unwary. He was standing at the edge of what seemed to be a precipice from which they could view the island and the sea which lay all around them, shimmering in the mid-day sun. Up there a cooling breeze fanned them and Nicole felt immediately better now she had rested.

When she came up to him he put his arm around her waist, drawing her close. 'Look down there. It's the roof of the villa.'

'It looks as if it's miles away.'

'It isn't really. Come over here and see the view

65

from the other side. It's even better.'

They picked their way gingerly across the mass of jutting stones until they reached a vantage point from which they could see the village and the harbour. The houses looked like doll's houses and the boats like toys. The village looked as though she could grasp it in one hand.

'Oh, I'm so glad you brought me here, Paul!'

'It's worth the climb, isn't it? Over there you can just see the mainland on a clear day.'

Nicole shaded her eyes with one hand. 'It looks so mysterious. Like a lost land shrouded in the mists of time.'

'Greece is a land full of mysteries, myth and fable.' He held her tighter against his body. 'You *are* glad you came, aren't you, Nicky?'

She leaned her head on his shoulder and sighed. 'You know I am.'

It was true. Almost a week had passed since her arrival on the island and she had enjoyed every minute of it. There was a mystery concerning him but she had managed to put it to the back of her mind, for no one else seemed concerned. The days had gone past with amazing speed. They had swum together in the pool and sunbathed afterwards on the terrace, sipping drinks brought to them by Chloris. There were afternoons when they walked to various coves on the island and passed pleasant hours in the evening wandering to the village to watch the fishing boats return with their catch. Nicole was relaxed again, she slept dreamlessly and had acquired a painless suntan which did nothing but enhance her appearance.

Even the continuing presence of Paul's brother cast no shadows on their enjoyment of each other's company. Alexander, to her surprise, remained at the villa with them but his presence did not obtrude. He joined them at mealtimes, but when he was not in his study running the newspaper by remote control, he was out in the *Melisande* with Demetrius, fishing, or swimming, or in the late afternoon, in the village.

Nicole found her initial dislike of him lessening because of this unexpected tactfulness, but whenever he was around she often caught him looking at her and sometimes frowning, and she was never able to forget that he disapproved of her and would have her part from Paul.

She drew away from Paul at last and looked around at her immediate surroundings. 'What is this place?'

'It was a temple in antiquity, built, it is believed, to the goddess Aphrodite.'

Nicole gazed around. All that was left were the stones, rounded by age and exposure to the elements, and one marble pillar against which she had rested. In the centre of what was once the temple stood one olive tree, old and knarled, and amongst the stones

67

wild flowers had pushed their way, making a pretty carpet for their feet.

'Aphrodite was the goddess of love, wasn't she?'

'That's right. The islanders of Kyros worshipped her deity. It is still believed that if a couple come here when the moon is shining they will fall in love and be bound to each other for ever. We must come here by moonlight before you leave, Nicky.'

She laughed and walked away from him. 'Who would have thought you were such a romantic, Paul. Besides, that would be too elementary for us now.'

He came up to her and lifted her chin so that she was forced to look into his eyes. 'Is it, Nicky?'

After a moment or two she disengaged herself, smiling uncomfortably. 'We are mortals, Paul, not gods and goddesses. I'm hungry.'

He laughed too. 'It's a long time since either of us has enjoyed so much fresh air and exercise. I'd almost forgotten what it was like to be here. In fact I've just realized that in all the time we've known each other we've never spent so much time in each other's company. We're still happy together, so that must be a good sign.'

'It's a very good sign,' she sighed as she kneeled down and began to set out the food, envying Paul his ability to think only of today.

She flicked an insect away from her nose and rested her head on the trunk of the olive tree. It wasn't

the most comfortable pillow but after the picnic and
all the wine she had consumed it didn't matter at
all. Paul lay with his head cushioned on her lap
and he waved away the insects with a blade of grass.

'I feel as if we're completely alone in the world,'
she sighed. 'That no one else exists.'

'It's true in a way. We are all that matters in the
world, the two of us.'

'Oh no, that isn't right. We are all beholden to
others whether we like it or not.' She was thoughtful for a moment or two and then asked, 'Who is
Kyria Adrianou, Paul?'

He lifted his head to look at her. 'Why do you ask?'

'The villa belongs to her, doesn't it?'

'It's in her name,' he answered after hesitating a
moment, 'but I believe Alex has actually paid for it.'

'Who is she?'

'The beautiful Xenia,' he said with a sigh, and
Nicole frowned. 'She's officially been a "friend" of
my brother's for years. Naturally there is more to it
than that, and I for one don't blame him—or for
that matter Xenia either. She was married to a man
years older than herself, hence the need for a convenient hideaway not too far from Athens. He died
last year and I expect once a decent interval has
passed they'll get married. It's only a matter of time
now.'

Nicole digested this information which indicated
that Alexander Stalis was human after all. She re-

called the woman she had seen in his flat and guessed that this must be Xenia Adrianou. He obviously had exemplary taste in his women as well as everything else. Nothing jarred.

'I think I've seen her. She's very beautiful, has dark red hair and a wonderful figure. She's the sort of woman who gives everyone else an inferiority complex.'

'That sounds like Xenia, but where did *you* see her?'

'In your brother's flat the night I went to see him.'

He nodded. 'She has her own place not far away, but I don't suppose she stays there very often. I know for a fact she chose all the furnishings for Alex's place. All those weird sculptures are her own work.'

'So she's talented too.'

'Call that talent?' he said scornfully. 'She's just a wealthy widow with nothing else to occupy her.'

'Take my word for it, Paul, she is talented. If she wanted to take it up commercially—in London at least—she would have no difficulty in getting commissions.'

She laughed harshly. 'Knowing Xenia Adrianou, I'm surprised you even looked at me. No wonder your brother disapproved of your choice after setting you such a good example.'

He sat up straight. 'Xenia might be a living doll—yes, she's just that to look at—but I happen to like a real woman, Nicky. Poor Xenia, I suspect, despite all the elaborate window-dressing, isn't that.'

'I don't believe it. She's all woman. It couldn't just be *window-dressing*.'

He waved his hand in the air. 'Believe what you like. I know Alex and he is too concerned with his day to day business to involve himself with a woman who might demand too much of him. When they are married Xenia will have a status once more in Athens society, and Alex will have an influential wife to host his parties, who will demand no more emotionally than he is prepared to give.'

Nicole drew back so she could see him better. 'You sound almost as if you didn't like him.'

Paul laughed. 'That must be wishful thinking on your part, Nicky. I only wish I could be more like him. I get too involved, that is my trouble.'

Hurt, she answered, 'I can soon remedy that—by leaving.'

He caught her hand. 'No!'

'Well, I can't stay here for ever.'

'Why not?'

She laughed. 'Because I run a business, Paul, and I must go back soon to attend to it.'

'I want you to stay here and marry me.'

'If I do marry you it won't be here or now. You have a job too remember and it's high time you gave a thought to your employers. I don't suppose you've informed them where you are or what you're doing; they'll be as puzzled as I was.'

'No, they're not puzzled any more. I've resigned.'

She recoiled from him. 'Paul! Why?'

'Isn't it obvious. I've decided to stay here in Greece where I belong.'

'But this man. . . .'

'Oh, that. You don't imagine Alex will stand for that nonsense for long. It will be over soon and then we can all settle down again.'

'But when I talked about your coming back you were angry with me. You wouldn't hear of it less than a fortnight ago.'

'Things have changed. The new Greece is marvellous. I had such bad memories I'd almost forgotten how wonderful this land is. You've realized it too in only a week. The sky is so blue and the sun so bright. Why, Nicky, within fifteen minutes of leaving home in Athens we could be on a beach soaking up the sun and enjoying a great life.'

'There are other considerations apart from basking in sun, Paul. You had a job.'

He hugged his knees and stared moodily ahead of him 'As a reporter on a piffling little weekly. That was just a temporary measure. It was never intended as anything else.

'Alex owns one of the most influential and successful papers in Greece and it will all belong to me one day. I'd be a fool to give that up for nothing but a meagre wage every week. Don't you want to share that with me?'

'I'd prefer to have a man who can stand on his own two feet. You're a man of principle; you proved that in rather a painful way. Don't be his lapdog now, Paul.'

'Don't talk so much rubbish. You're talking about Alex as if he's a sinister influence on me. He saved my life. When our parents were killed he hid me in a goatshed, otherwise we both would have been killed too. He's my brother and he's my only relative. I owe everything to him.'

She moved to sit front of him so he was forced to look at her. 'I'm not trying to come between you two, Paul, but don't you realize that if he does marry Xenia Adrianou she is young enough to give him several children of his own and then where would that leave your expectations?'

He smiled then, quite unexpectedly. 'She has one already. Helen Adrianou is eight years old and a delightful little girl. She also happens to look very much like Alex.'

Nicole wasn't sure what expression was on her face but it made him laugh. 'Don't be such a puritan. I told you her husband was much older. Of course, she might give him half a dozen sons and in all probability she will, but that won't make any difference. I'm his heir and that's what I will remain. Don't let your personal dislike of him cloud the issue. We still have a strong sense of family here in Greece.'

They sat in silence for a few moments whilst she

73

pulled up a few wild flowers, mauve ones which looked like minature orchids. After a while she said thoughtfully, 'Doesn't it mean anything to you that when you had to pay very painfully for what you believed in, he sat on the fence and did nothing to support the cause you felt strongly about?'

Paul's face clouded and he jumped to his feet. 'You don't know what you are talking about. I was a fool. He warned me about it and I took no notice of him.'

'Hasn't it ever occurred to you that sometimes, just sometimes, you might be right and he could possibly be wrong? It is possible, you know.'

His face twisted into a mask of bitterness and despair. 'It never has been up until now. I should never have got mixed up in matters I didn't understand!'

He walked away from her and she too got to her feet. 'So what if you were wrong. There is no shame in that, only be sure you do think you're wrong and not just repeating his words, because I believe that's all you're doing and you've got to stop it! Think for yourself, Paul, or there can be no future for us.'

She went towards him and put her hand on his arm. 'Paul, can't you see that you're always thinking with his mind?'

He jerked his arm away from her and dashed forward as if he wanted to escape her. Nicole could only stand and watch him, but he had gone only a few yards when he stumbled and crashed to the ground, crying out in agony. She rushed to him then, stooping down at his side as he tried to raise himself.

'Are you hurt?'

'Only my ankle, I think. It twisted under me as I fell.'

Nicole sighed with relief. 'Just stay where you are; it might get easier in a minute or two. This really is the wrong place to run.'

'I know,' he gasped. 'I was just so angry when I realized you were speaking the truth, but it doesn't make any difference. I can't turn my back on Alex or his world and make my own. If you want me you'll have to accept that too.'

Her heart sank. 'Let's not discuss it now, Paul. How is the ankle? Does it feel any better now?'

He tried to move it, which resulted in him gasping with pain. 'It *hurts*,' he said in the tones of a child who could barely believe the fact that his mother might slap him.

Nicole might have been tempted to laugh if his distress hadn't been so real.

'It might be broken,' she said doubtfully.

'I don't think so, but it is throbbing like mad.'

She straightened. 'All I can do is go back to the villa and bring help. I think that's the best course, don't you?'

'No!' She stared at him. 'It will be dark by the time you get back and I don't want to be left here alone.'

'I really won't be long.'

'No, I don't want to stay here on my own.' He shivered convulsively. 'I can't bear to be in the dark alone.

'Wait for a few more minutes and then you can help me.'

She gathered all their things together and then helped him to his feet. The ankle looked to her as if it was badly sprained and it was already swelling Even leaning against her he was in constant pain and they progressed at a snail's pace. Nicole supported him as best she could, but he was so much bigger and heavier than she and even though they were going downhill it did not make the task any easier. Every few yards they had to stop so Paul could rest and Nicole was afraid untold damage might be done to the ankle.

By the time they reached the villa it was totally dark. They went in by way of the verandah which led to the living room. Alex was mixing himself a pre-dinner drink when they came in and at the sight of his brother, looking far more grievously injured than he really was, his face grew pale.

'What has happened?'

'Nothing to be alarmed about,' Paul told him quickly. 'I was acting about like a fool and fell.'

Alex looked immediately less tense and he rushed over to take support of his brother, for which Nicole was grateful. The pressure Paul had put on her had at times been nearly unbearable.

As Alex helped his brother to the settee Nicole explained, 'We were up at the ruined temple and Paul twisted his ankle on a stone.'

Alex kneeled on the floor at his side. 'Get him a drink, Nicole, will you?'

She did as she was told whilst Alex stripped off Paul's sandal. 'It looks like a bad sprain,' he murmured as he examined it carefully.

Paul gasped in pain. 'For heaven's sake, Alex, go carefully. It's pretty bad.'

As Nicole mixed him a whisky and soda she found her hands were shaking. When she gave it to him he drank it greedily.

'He hasn't broken any bones, has he?'

'I don't think so.'

'How can you tell?' Paul demanded. 'It hurts like hell and you're not a doctor.'

'I know a sprained ankle when I see one, but if you prefer I can have a doctor sent out from Athens to look at it.'

Paul let his head drop back. 'No, don't bother. I'm sure you're right, only this is the last thing I wanted while Nicole is here.'

Alex smiled as he got to his feet and dusted off the knees of his immaculately cut slacks. 'No, it isn't the best encouragement for a romance, is it?'

'What would you know about romance?' she retorted before she could stop herself.

To her surprise he did not react with anger as she

expected him to do. He merely smiled at her, even though there was a mocking quality about it.

'I have had my moments, Nicole.'

She felt her face growing red and was glad when Paul put one hand to his head and said, 'This is no time for you two to start hating each other again.'

'I'll go and get a bandage to strap up that ankle,' Alex told him. 'Then I think, you'd best go to bed.' He glanced at Nicole again. She didn't know what showed on her face but he said in quite a gentle way, 'Why don't you get yourself a good strong drink?'

When he had gone she did as he suggested and then took her glass and went to sit at Paul's side.

'How does it feel now?' she asked.

'A little easier, but it still hurts pretty badly. Who would have thought a mere sprain would?'

'It once happened to me and I thought I must have broken a bone. You'll have to rest for the next few days and then you'll be as good as new.'

He pulled a wry face. 'I hate the thought—not being able to go off alone with you.'

'We'll probably survive.'

She rubbed absently at her aching shoulder and he brushed a lock of hair away from her face. 'I'm surprised I didn't break your arm. Here, let me massage it for you.'

She relaxed against him as he gently massaged her aching shoulders. 'Ah, that feels so good, Paul.'

'You didn't complain once.'

'I was too worried about you, even to notice it at the time.'

'You seem to spend a great deal of you life worrying about me.'

She laughed. 'I don't know why. Whatever happens, you always seem to survive.'

His hands dropped from her shoulders and a bleak look came into his eyes. It was so sudden and so unexpected that it shocked her. 'What is it?' she asked.

He looked at her again and smiled. 'Nothing. I was just thinking how bored you'll be if I'm laid up for the next few days.'

Nicole was just about to tell him she would probably be preparing to go home when a voice answered for her. 'Don't you worry about Nicole.' She stood up and walked away from the settee as Alex came back into the room. 'If she can just be near you she will not be bored. Not for an instant. Isn't that so, Nicole?'

She turned to smile at him even though there was no warmth in it and he knew it. 'Certainly. Even in London, if we just spent the evening in Paul's flat or mine we enjoyed ourselves, and such surroundings aren't in the least exotic.'

As Alex stooped down to strap up his brother's ankle Paul said with evident satisfaction, 'You see, Alex, how much she loves me.'

79

Nicole finished her drink and put the glass down on the table. She felt much steadier now. Alex had his back to her so she didn't know if he were being sarcastic or not when he said, 'You are a very lucky man, Paul.'

Paul himself seemed unaware of any sarcasm, for he smiled reassuringly at Nicole over his brother's head.

'There,' Alex said a few moments later, straightening up again, 'that's as good a job as any doctor could do.'

Nicole came forward again. 'I imagine you can do most things well.'

He looked at her and she had the feeling he was mocking her again. 'There have been times when I've had little choice.'

'And you never fail to remind people of the fact.'

His eyes grew hard and Nicole knew a momentary thrill which died as a second later he turned to put one hand on Paul's shoulder. 'Does it feel easier now?'

'Much.'

Alex looked at Nicole again but she could not meet his eyes. 'It will be all right in a day or two, but until then you will have to be confined to the grounds of the villa.'

He was talking to Paul but his eyes remained on her and she was certain he was deriving more than a small amount of satisfaction from the situation fate had thrust on them.

Chapter Five

Nicole was not bored by being confined to the villa.
How could she be? The place possessed every luxury.
There was a maid to wait on her every whim, the
garden and the pool were as lovely a place to be as
anywhere she had ever seen, and she still had Paul's
company. Boredom was never the danger, but because Paul had to be helped everytime he moved,
Alex was there most of the time. Nicole felt he was
exploiting the situation, glad to prevent any private
conversation between them and having Paul well
within his domination again.

One part of her was urging her to stay and fight
for Paul's independence, the other to cut and run
while she could. Lying there in the sun she wondered
if life in London could ever be the same again and
she was still undecided whether she loved Paul
enough to marry him. Her head told her she did, but
her heart warned her she could not share him with
Alex, and she was unable to make up her mind about

so important a matter when so many questions still plagued her.

'Why don't you go for a walk, Nicole?' Paul suggested.

She opened her eyes as he jerked her out of her thoughts. 'I'm not leaving you here alone.'

'I won't be alone,' he protested with a laugh. 'Alex is somewhere around and so is Chloris, if I need anything.'

'I'm all right, really I am. I've been into the pool several time. . . .'

Her voice tailed away as she caught sight of Alex coming out of the villa. As always she felt acutely uncomfortable when he was around, and this time she sat up and put a robe on over her bathing costume.

'I'm trying to persuade this stubborn girl to take a break from me for a while,' Paul told him, 'but she won't listen.'

'You should take notice of what Paul is saying,' Alex told her as he came up to them. 'It will do you good. You haven't been out of the villa grounds since Paul's accident.'

'I'm perfectly comfortable here.'

'I am going to the village; perhaps you would like to walk with me. It will be company for me and a change for us both.'

Nicole was too shocked and surprised to answer but Paul said, 'That's an excellent idea, Alex! Go on,

Nicole. It's time you two got to know each other better.'

Nicole knew that to protest further would only make an awkward situation worse, so, philosophically, she shrugged and went indoors to put on a skirt and blouse.

Alex was sitting on the edge of a lounging chair, talking to his brother when she returned. He got up immediately, his eyes taking in every aspect of her appearance. 'Ah, you look very nice. You dress sensibly. The islanders are still very primitive in their ideas about women. Bare flesh offends them.'

Nicole chose to ignore him and went to take Paul's hand. 'Try to rest while I'm out. I won't be gone very long.'

'Be as long as you wish. I don't mind if it's Alex you're with. It's other men I wouldn't trust with you!'

She felt self-conscious being alone in his company for the first time since they met in Athens, and for a few minutes they walked along the dusty donkey track in silence. The track was shaded by ilex trees and the occasional olive tree, which made it more pleasant than usual walking at this time of the day.

'Where did you first meet my brother?' he asked at last.

'In London about six months ago. We were both guests at a party given by a mutual friend.'

'Then you are not connected with the world of journalism.'

83

'Far from it. I'm half owner of a fashion boutique and most of the clothes we sell are our own design. I do some private commissions too. One day, if we're successful enough we might be able to move into a West End shop.' She laughed self-consciously. 'I'll be the poor woman's Mary Quant.'

He glanced at her. 'I'm sorry, I don't know this person.'

She laughed again. 'That doesn't surprise me. She designs very modern clothes and she's very successful at it.'

He glanced at her again and then away into the distance once more. 'That's interesting. I have a friend who might like you to design clothes for her.'

'If it's the friend I saw in your flat, you can forget it; I'm not in her class.'

He looked startled. 'Judging from your own appearance I would not agree.'

Nicole was surprised he had even noticed. 'All clothes are the same to most men. As I said, if you refer to Kyria Adrianou, I don't think she would like my work.'

He did not press the point; instead he asked, 'You must have studied designing at some art school. That is the usual procedure, I understand.'

'It is and it was my intention, but just after I left school my parents were killed—a drunken driver crashed into them as they were crossing the road one night—and instead of art school I had to take a job immediately. It didn't work out too badly because I learned a great deal about retail selling and I met Sally—my partner—at the place where I worked, and we decided to open up on our own as soon as we had enough money. So I'm doing what I've always wanted anyway.'

'Your determination is quite admirable.'

She smiled. They were coming into the village. 'You would know all about that. Paul has told me a great deal about you and how you cared for him.'

'There was no one else.'

'Paul was very young when your parents died.'

'He was only a baby.'

They were walking through the cobbled streets of the village towards the harbour.

'Before I met you I somehow believed you were much older than you really are.'

'There are fourteen years between us. It is quite a space between brothers.'

'You were only fourteen and yet you looked after a baby. I find that quite incredible.'

He laughed. 'I did not look after him myself at first. We had other relatives alive then and they actually looked after Paul for me, but they were very poor and another mouth to feed was a serious business, so I had to work to provide the money for his upkeep. It was a good arrangement.'

They stood on the quay watching some of the fishing boats returning with their catch. 'You provided for him very handsomely,' she admitted.

'Hunger is a severe taskmaster.'

It was hard to believe this suave and well-dressed man had ever been hungry, and yet she did believe it, and she felt sorry for many of the uncharitable thoughts she'd had about him. He was stubborn and maddening, but she guessed he had suffered considerably in his struggle to provide so well for the child left in his keeping.

'This is a most beautiful island,' she said after a moment or two.

'Greece has many beautiful islands, but this one has the distinction of being totally unspoiled—one of the very few left nowadays.' He took her arm and began to lead her away. 'Come, I have a call to make here in the village before we return.'

His call was at one of those cube-like houses which were so common to many of the Greek islands. Nicole wondered what business Alexander Stalis could have with these simple people, but she did not have to wait long to find out. The door swung open to his knock and a brown wrinkled face peered out at them. When the old woman saw who it was, her face broke into a toothless smile and she waved them inside, chattering excitedly to Alex all the time. The walls of the room into which they were ushered were as sparklingly white as the outside and everything was scrupulously clean.

The woman left them and moments later an old

man came in. His hair was stark white and his face brown, lined with a thousand wrinkles. He too greeted Alex joyously and they talked for a few moments before Alex turned to her, explaining her presence, no doubt, to the old man.

He poured some wine for them and although Nicole hated the taste of it she knew she must drink it or else the old man would be insulted. After a few minutes the old man produced a stick which he gave to Alex. The two discussed it between themselves before Alex took Nicole's arm and led her towards the door.

Outside the sun dazzled her as, having said goodbye to the old man, they began to walk back through to village. Alex showed her the stick, which was a stout one, intricately carved.

'Stavros is an old man and he can no longer go out in a fishing boat, but he is good at carving. This stick is made from olive wood and I think it will help Paul get about better.'

Nicole was too taken aback to answer for a moment and then she said, 'That's a marvellous idea, Alex. Paul will feel much better if he can get about more and without troubling you all the time.'

They were passing the village café where the elderly men of the village sat, eyeing them in silence as they walked past.

Alex said, 'Don't think I am being rude in not asking you to stop for a drink. I'm sure you'd like one and so would I, but women are rarely seen in provincial cafés, and certainly not in the afternoon.'

'I've noticed that I've received some odd glances when we've been here on an evening. Of course, Paul always goes in and brings the drinks outside so I'm sure it gives no offence. Why is it still like that?'

'Times change slowly where the tourists do not come. It's still like this in many places in Greece. Of course, in Athens it's quite different.'

'Attitudes will change here too before long. It has to. Women eventually realize that they are more than merely the chattel of some man.'

He laughed. 'That is something you will never be, Nicole.'

'That's certainly my intention.'

'Yet, here in Greece, many women regard it as quite natural. They would not have it any other way.'

'I think you are giving me some kind of a warning, Alex.'

He laughed again. 'Why should I do that?'

'I thought perhaps you might be suggesting my life with Paul would be like that.'

He threw back his head and laughed. 'With Paul! Oh, Nicole, I think you would have my poor brother wrapped around your little finger!'

She drew back. 'That's not true! Naturally, I shall keep my independence, but I'm no Amazon. Paul will always be the head of the family.'

He was using the walking stick, leaning on it heavily as he walked. Nicole noticed for the first time that there were streaks of grey in his hair, which because of the breeze was slightly ruffled for once. No longer did he look so suave nor so distant, and Nicole had the strange urge to smooth his hair herself.

His voice broke rudely and most welcomingly into her thoughts. 'Would you hate so much to lose some of that fierce independence, Nicole, and belong completely to a man?'

She quickened her pace. 'The question has never arisen, nor ever shall. I shall never be in that position, shall I? I'm not a Greek peasant woman; I don't possess the qualities desirable in a Greek wife. I'm me and I can't do anything about it. I've been independent for too long.'

He had paused but now he hurried to catch her up. 'I am sorry if I offended you. I didn't mean to. The qualities you possess are most admirable. I woudn't deprecate them but I just wonder if it is what Paul needs in a woman.'

She made no answer. The villa was in front of them. She wondered what Paul had been doing while she'd been out and what he would think of this odd conversation if she were to tell him of it, which, of course, she would not.

'Alex,' she said thoughtfully a moment later, 'when Paul was arrested that time, do you think they hurt him very badly?'

He frowned. 'He hasn't told you anything about

it, has he?' She shook her head. 'If you mean, did they hurt him physically, he wasn't in custody for long enough, but there are mental scars even now. They will not fade so easily. Paul has a great deal of sensitivity. He had never known deprivation before and there it was, all around him. No more glory; just sordidness.'

'Don't scorn him for it, Alex. He had to make his protest.'

'It did no good.'

'You can't judge that. It was public opinion that rid the country of what it hated. Didn't you hate what was happening in your country?'

'Naturally I did.'

She knew he hated the topic of conversation too but she had to go on. Suddenly she wanted to know this man although she doubted if it were possible.

'You had a great deal of power to wield against them with your newspaper.'

He stopped to look at her. 'Do you think so? All my newsprint came by way of the government.

'So you played safe.'

She started to walk away from him but he caught her arm and pulled her back.

'I started selling newspapers in the street and by the time I owned the most successful one in Greece I wasn't going to jeopardise all that by foolish gestures. I could have done very easily and there were times when I was tempted to exercise power through print, but if I had the paper would have been closed down and I would have been deported. What good would that have done? I stayed and I was in a position to help in other ways, as I was able to do when Paul was arrested. And he wasn't the only one.'

'I'm sorry,' she said with a sigh. 'Paul keeps telling me I don't know anything about it too and you're both right.'

'There was more to it than just the suppression of free speech, you know. The living standards of the Greek people rose for the first time since the war. No one ever seems to mention that.

'Do you know anything about the people Paul was involved with before his arrest?'

She shook her head. 'He never spoke about it all to me.'

'They were determined to overthrow the government and replace it with a regime every bit as repressive, if not more so. Their policies seemed miraculous to Paul but he bitterly regrets that involvement now. My parents died fighting the Communists during the Civil War. Paul is too young to remember it, but I am not. It would have been an exchange of one evil for another, and perhaps one not so easily eliminated.'

Nicole hardly knew what to say. 'You've seen a great deal of suffering in your country.'

'But it's over now, and we will talk about something else.'

91

She sighed with relief as they walked towards the villa.

'You must forgive me for being Paul's champion. I still feel that it's right that he had his own beliefs, however misguided. But I'm glad you explained it to me. I had a lot of misguided ideas myself.'

'You are certainly not alone in that, Nicole.

When the villa came into view someone was just coming away from it, a girl whose hips swayed seductively as she walked. Sofia. As she approached she slowed her pace.

'*Herete*,' she greeted Alex, but only flashed a defiant and triumphant look at Nicole as she sauntered past.

'I wonder if she managed to see Paul,' she murmured as Alex continued to watch the girl.

He didn't answer her question but there was a pause and as he turned back to her he said in a calculated voice, 'What have you and Paul decided about the future?'

Startled she said nothing for a moment and then she had to look away from that searching gaze of his. 'We haven't decided anything as yet.'

'That seems hard to believe after all those hours you spent together on this island. Are you going to marry him?'

'As I said, no decision has been made yet.'

'You must have felt very strongly about him to come all the way to Greece.'

'I do feel very strongly about him, in more ways than one,' she answered meaningfully.

'Then I am sure you must have made up your mind one way or another. I think I have come to know you well enough to be sure of that.'

She drew a sigh. He was very persistent and she should have known he would be. They had come to the villa's gardens and a few more yards would bring her to Paul again.

'Yes, I suppose I have, but I have no intention of telling you what I have decided until it has been fully discussed with Paul, and certainly not while we are here.' She laughed unevenly. 'I'm going to wait until we're on neutral territory.'

He was still eyeing her steadily and it was no less disconcerting. 'There is no such thing where emotions are involved.'

She made to move away from him, but once more he caught her arm and drew her back towards him. 'Nicole, all I ask is one thing; that you don't marry him unless you love him very much.'

She stared at him for what seemed to be a very long time, and then she withdrew her arm in a deliberate gesture of separation. 'In my world, Alex, there can be no other reason.

'I'm sorry you don't approve, but I think you must agree that it's what Paul and I feel about each other which really matters.'

'I don't disapprove of you, Nicole—you must be-

93

lieve that—but I don't believe you would make a suitable wife for my brother. Or perhaps it is really the opposite which is true.'

She knew he was trying to make some kind of appeal to her, but she just turned on her heel and ran towards the villa, almost bumping into someone who was coming out at the same time. Nicole gasped and pulled back to see that it was a woman whom she had cannoned into, the same woman she had seen in Alex's flat in Athens.

'Oh dear, what a hurry,' she said, laughing gaily as Nicole tried to catch her breath.

'I apologise,' she said breathlessly.

She glanced back to see that Alex was coming on to the terrace. He was leaning on the stick again and his face was grave. He was so preoccupied he didn't see the woman until he had reached the verandah steps.

'Alex!' she cried.

He looked up then and his face cleared. Nicole had never seen such a transformation come over anyone, nor had she ever seen him look so delighted. The woman ran down the steps to greet him and he took her hand in his.

'What a wonderful surprise! When did you arrive?'

'Only about half an hour ago. What a nice welcome, Alex. I'm so glad I came now.'

Nicole moved away. She felt that they had forgotten her presence anyway, but before she could disappear quietly Alex said, 'You haven't met Nicole yet, Xenia.'

They came up the steps, arms entwined. Xenia Adrianou smiled and held out her hand. 'We have met before, I think, but this time I know who you are.' To Nicole's surprise she then kissed her on the cheek. 'Paul has been telling me all about you and you are every bit as delightful as he says. I couldn't be more pleased for you both.'

Nicole dared not look at Alex. 'I must go and find Paul. He'll be wondering where I am.'

'Oh, don't rush away so quickly.' Xenia Adrianou waved one hand in the air. 'Paul is in his room getting ready for dinner. He needs plenty of time. Demetrius helped him.'

Nicole smiled hesitantly. 'The walk from the village was rather a dusty one. I think I'd better go to my room and wash too.'

She knew Alex was watching her and hurried away before she was forced to stay.

Dinner that evening was easier than Nicole had imagined it would be. On previous evenings at the villa she had been one girl between two men, and knowing Alex's opinion of her was not conducive to her comfort. Now they were far more evenly balanced. Paul was already using his walking stick and he was able to get around much more easily. Nicole had no idea what his relationship with Xenia hap-

pened to be—from their earlier conversation she had
suspected he did not like her—but to her surprise she
soon discovered they were on excellent terms, unless,
of course, Paul's inveterate charm hid any dislike he
might feel towards the woman. In fact there were
moments that evening when Nicole felt a little left
out as they chattered, almost continuously, about
friends Paul had not seen for years. As if sensing
it in her it was, surprisingly, Alex who drew her back
into the conversation.

Chloris, their cook, made a special effort that evening with the food, and Xenia kept them all entertained with stories of her activities in Athens, recounted in a very amusing way. The verandah doors
were left open and a cooling breeze floated in. The
scene was set for an enjoyable evening, so Nicole
could not understand why her spirits were so
dampened, but it was so despite Xenia's kindness
towards her, and Alex's surprising attempt to behave
civilly—almost warmly. Perhaps, she mused, he was
aware of this confusion in her mind and sensed that
victory was near.

The men remained in the dining room to finish
the dinner wine whilst Xenia drew Nicole into the
other room.

'Let's go on to the verandah for a few minutes,'
she suggested and Nicole was glad to agree.

The air was like wine that night and the noises
which started up at dusk, the insects in the garden,

were comforting somehow. Xenia leaned against the balustrade. In the soft light from the room behind them her hair burned darkly and she looked as stunning on this primitive little island as she had in Athens. Nicole, as she watched her take a cigarette case out of her bag, marvelled at the fact. Nicole resented having to wear more than shorts and a sun top. Xenia dressed as she would for dinner at the smartest restaurant in Athens.

In a leisurely way Xenia lit her cigarette and as she replaced the lighter in her bag she surveyed Nicole carefully.

'I have never known Paul so keen on any girl,' she said at last.

'Has he known so many?'

She smiled. 'You know Paul. He's very attractive to women.'

'Oh, I know. I met one of them. Chloris's daughter.'

Xenia laughed. 'A delightful child, isn't she? You mustn't mind though. Some men do need a great deal of female company, but I have spoken to him and I can assure you it is you he really cares for.'

'I'm flattered.'

'You needn't be. Don't underestimate your own charms, my dear. When I saw you in Athens I thought, "What an attractive girl. I wonder who she can be?" I do approve of his choice. It is time he settled down.'

It was Nicole's turn to smile. 'You may approve, Xenia, but Alex certainly does not, and it's something I must consider. They aren't just brothers; there's a much closer tie than that.'

Xenia leaned her head back on the post and laughed again. It was a gentle sound and had an almost feline quality about it. In fact, everything about Xenia Adrianou was smooth and slinky. There were no rough edges to this woman, but there were certainly hidden depths which Nicole could not begin to fathom. In that respect she was very like Alex; there was a side to him Nicole would have loved to have known.

'Haven't you realized yet that Alex is over-anxious about everything concerned with Paul? It's almost a lifelong habit now and I doubt if you—or I—will be able to break him of it, so I suggest you get used to it.'

Nicole stared out at the darkened pool. 'I'm not sure that I can. A possessive mother I could have coped with; there's a wealth of advice about that kind of a problem. To make matters worse I have to admit Alex never makes a wrong decision regarding Paul.'

Xenia looked at her earnestly, 'Alex isn't really possessive. As I say, he's just over-anxious, and you might not know it but Paul has given him plenty of cause in the past.'

Nicole looked at her but the other woman had no

intention of elaborating. Instead she said, 'It doesn't matter at all, because you love Paul; that's all you have to think about. Your marriage will be the making of him, and Alex will be able to concentrate on his own life. It's about time he was able to.'

Nicole had the feeling that this was Xenia's prime concern and she could not blame her for it. It must be irksome to be in love with a man who was constantly absorbed in his brother's affairs. It irked Nicole too.

Xenia stubbed out her cigarette in an ashtray, which was on the verandah table, and then took Nicole's arm.

'Come, we shall join the men. It would be wonderful,' she continued without making a move, 'if you and Paul were to be married here on Kyros.' Nicole began to demur but Xenia gave her no chance. 'It's called the Island of Love. Did you know that?'

'No I didn't. I suppose it's because of Aphrodite's temple.'

'I fell in love here years ago.' She sighed at the memory and Nicole wondered if she were thinking of Alex. He would not be an easy man to love.

'Have you been to the temple dedicated to the Goddess of Love?'

'Yes, I went with Paul a few days ago. That is where he hurt his ankle, on the rough stones jutting out of the ground.'

'Oh dear,' the other woman laughed, 'that isn't a

very good omen.

'I feel that Kyros is my island. I discovered it quite by accident one year and fell in love with it. It has a beautiful church. Have you visited it yet?'

'Not yet.'

'Well, Paul has no interest in works of art; it would be just another church to him, but this one is Byzantine, and it has the most wonderful mosaics. Do you like works of art, Nicole?'

'Yes, and I know Greece has an abundance of them.'

'Too many are ruins,' Xenia said wistfully, 'but even they are beautiful.'

'Perhaps Paul and I will have a chance to see them together before I go back.'

Xenia beamed. 'That would be a wonderful idea, but Kyros is the most marvellous place for a wedding. Wouldn't you love to be married here?'

Shortly Nicole answered, 'I hadn't thought about it.'

Without waiting any longer she went inside. Paul was sitting on the settee, his stick by his side, and Alex was standing in front of him with his back to the windows.

'Do you think he is serious?' he was asking.

'Yes,' answered Paul, his voice no more than a whisper.

'Then we have little choice; the police will have to be told.'

'No! We've discussed this before, Alex. . . .'

Nicole came in and Alex turned round on his heel. 'What's this about the police?' she asked, looking from one to the other.

Alex smiled and he was as relaxed as ever, but she did notice that Paul was watching him fearfully.

'You are mistaken, Nicole. No mention was made of the police. We were talking about Paul's future employment.'

Paul relaxed and beckoned so she went to him. Xenia had followed her inside and now linked her arm into Alex's.

'It's such a lovely evening, Alex. It's a pity to spend it all indoors. Shall we go out for a walk?'

He looked more than a little reluctant to go at that moment, glancing at Paul hesitantly, but Xenia was pulling gently at his arm so he went with her and Nicole looked down at Paul once more. There was no sign of that fear now, but it had been there. She was certain of it.

Chapter Six

Nicole found that she did not sleep well that night. Her mind searched constantly for answers to the questions that were plaguing her, but none came. All she knew was that Paul was in some kind of trouble. Whether it was because of Alex or not she was no longer sure. It was feasible that it might be; Paul was not one to make enemies, but his brother certainly was, but it was fear she had seen in Paul's eyes and somehow she felt that Alex would be a lot more worried if he were the cause of it.

At last, when the first fingers of light began to poke through her shutters and the birds had begun their daily serenade, Nicole gave up trying to sleep and slipped out of bed. She opened one shutter and looked out on to the olive trees, which marched side by side up the hill towards Aphrodite's Temple.

It came to her then that it was only since her visit there that everything had changed. Because they had to be constantly in Alex's company now? Nicole asked herself. She didn't know, but she was aware that her week of happiness in Paul's company—the certainty of her feelings for him—no longer existed. Uncertainty plagued her once more.

Now she had found Paul and knew that he was safe she was determined to leave him for a while so that her feelings could become clear again. She did not doubt that she loved Paul—what girl would not?— she just couldn't think clearly in so close a confinement with two as unfathomable people as Xenia and Alex. Far from helping matters, Xenia's anxiety to see them married could only complicate it. Nicole had less of a mind to allow Xenia to rush her into marriage than she had to let Alex part them.

Nicole decided there was no point in going back to bed—she was more wide awake than ever now. She dressed quickly and as quietly as she could tiptoed down the stairs and through the villa. Chloris at least was also awake. Nicole could hear the clattering of the pans in the kitchen as she began her preparations for the day, but it would be quite some time before everyone else would assemble for breakfast. This was normally an informal meal although Nicole now suspected Xenia might turn it into something as formal as a gala dinner.

She had decided to go for a short stroll beyond the villa; walking was always such good therapy for exercising perplexities. She might even walk as far as the village and watch the fishing boats put out to sea. But she got only as far as the verandah, for there in the pool someone was swimming, and as she paused in surprise, wondering if it could be Demetrius stealing a clandestine dip before everyone else awoke, Alex emerged from the water, tanned, dripping, and looking like some god from the myths of antiquity.

He saw her too before she had a chance to slip away, and he swam to the edge of the pool.

'*Kalimera*,' he greeted her.

'Good morning.' She went down the steps towards him. 'I was certain I would be the first one up today.'

'If you get up early every day you would be sure to see me because I always swim first thing in the morning when I'm here.'

'I prefer to sleep late when I'm on holiday. It's something I can't enjoy normally.'

'I am not on holiday.'

Nicole ignored the insinuation in his voice and asked, 'Do you ever swim in the sea?'

'Not here. There are very strong currents around Kyros and even for a good swimmer it can be dangerous. Why don't you come in and join me now you are here?'

Nicole looked upwards. The sun wasn't even appearing over the horizon yet. She hugged herself, shivering slightly in the cool early morning air, and laughed.

'I don't think I'm hardy enough for that. I shall

just sit and watch and admire!'

'Don't be such a coward,' he chided. 'You'll enjoy it once you're in.'

Nicole stepped back a pace, laughing again. 'All right. I'll go and get changed.'

She turned and fled back into the villa but she had put on her costume and was back within five minutes. After only a moment's hesitation and urged on by his chiding remarks she plunged in. The shock of it almost took her breath away but he wasn't too far from her and she was determined not to show how badly she felt the cold. She swam away from him and before many more minutes had passed she no longer felt the cold at all and began to enjoy her unexpected dip. There was something almost wicked about swimming before the sun was even up.

At last he called to her to indicate that he was getting out of the pool and she followed him. As she wrapped a robe around her shivering body she gasped, 'That was very invigorating.'

She knew he was amused by her even though his face did remain serious. 'You should do it more often, every day if you can. It's good for you. Perhaps one day we shall swim together again, by moonlight this time.'

Nicole turned away from him. She never knew when he was being serious or when he was mocking her. As she wound a towel around her dripping hair, he said, 'Ah, here is Chloris with our coffee—right on time! I should think you will be ready for a hot drink.'

At that Nicole laughed and followed him on to the verandah where the plump Chloris had put the tray. As she poured the coffee Nicole was more than glad to find that it was steaming hot. Once that was done she sat back in the rattan chair, clasping the cup in her hands for warmth. She stared ahead of her, to the pool where now no ripple blemished its surface. In the water she had felt equal to him; now they were on firm land again and she was once more uneasy in his presence, uncertain of him. Paul was so much easier to get on with, it was hard to believe they were brothers.

'Look,' he said after a moment, 'the sun is coming up now. It's going to be another fine day.'

'Of course. Are there any other kind?'

'I expect so, but we choose our time of the year to visit Kyros.'

She leaned forward, no longer feeling cold. 'It's quite a magnificent sight,' she murmured as the sky began to turn red. 'Strange to tell, I've never seen it happen before.'

'It's no wonder ancient people worshipped the sun. Apart from needing its warmth, its reappearance must have been like a daily miracle to them.'

Nicole sat back and looked at him. She had not considered him capable of such profound thoughts; even though he had spoken lightly she had realized the simple phenomenon of the sun rising impressed him.

He turned to her then, looking directly into her eyes. She couldn't look away. It was as if the moment was frozen in time. Then he said, 'Would you be so kind as to pour me some more coffee?'

Her hand was shaking as she did so. What had she seen there in that glance? she asked herself. Not mockery, not derision, and it certainly was not amusement. It had been something quite different, almost shattering her composure.

'Paul tells me he intends to remain in Greece,' she said, deliberately not looking at him.

'It was always intended that he should. He will work for the newspaper at first and then we shall see.'

'But he already had a job in London.'

'It's not an important one. By no stretch of the imagination can it be considered *that*.'

His face had become closed again, inscrutable, shutting her out completely. It was just question and answer now. There was no communication between them. That searching and intimate look, that easy comaradie in the water, might never have been.

'If he works for you, Alex, there would be no incentive for him to succeed. He knows he'll be the boss one day and he'll have nothing to strive for.'

His eyes met hers again but there was nothing but coldness in them. Nicole felt bereft. It had been good to be on friendly terms with him. How good she was only just beginning to realize.

'Is that such a bad thing, Nicole?'

'I think so. Everyone thrives on a challenge. Here, you have done it all for him. You had the challenge and you met it. Why don't you encourage Paul to do it too?'

He was stirring his coffee, round and round thoughtfully in the cup. 'You are talking about me—and, I suspect, about yourself. But Paul is quite a different person. Left alone he will not amount to anything. If you think about it objectively you will realize it.'

Nicole put her coffee cup down. She was growing angry again, but she tried hard to hide it, not quite successfully.

'How do you know what he can do on his own unless you let him *try*?'

He drew a sigh. He was speaking very softly which, to Nicole, seemed to underline his determination. Alexander Stalis need never raise his voice to win a point in an argument. That was one of the things that annoyed her about him.

'Believe what you will about Paul; I am not forcing him to come back to Greece, but you cannot blame him for wanting to.'

'I blame you, Alex,' she said quietly. 'Two weeks ago Paul was happy in London. He wouldn't hear of coming back to Greece when I suggested it to him.

Now, since talking to you he's given up his job and he's decided to stay here.'

He continued to stare across the garden. 'If that is what you believe, try to persuade him to return to London with you. You will not succeed.'

'Naturally I won't be successful,' she retorted, unable to keep the bitterness out of her voice. 'My will isn't stronger than yours. My influence isn't nearly so deeply entrenched.'

He smiled then, sadly, she thought. 'I sometimes wonder about that. But,' he went on, more briskly this time, 'doesn't life here as the wife of a successful man appeal to you rather than what you would have in London?'

She turned away from him then. 'Success to me isn't measured by the size of a man's bank balance.'

'I think you are the type of person who would enjoy the romantic ideal of starving in a garret with some impoverished fellow who has glorious ideals and very little else.'

She started to get up, but he caught her wrist and held her there. Her eyes blazed into his but he held her there firmly.

'Listen to me, Nicole. Paul wants to come back to Greece because of *you*. He wants to be able to give you everything, as any man would who loves a woman.' She began to protest but he went on regardless. 'I am in agreement with him. Ideals are all very well but you can't eat them. It has given me a great

109

deal of satisfaction to look after Paul and to see that
he never went cold or hungry, and I am not going
to let you undo all that because of a few foolish
whims. They only amount to a little bit of inverted
snobbery after all.'

He let her go and she fell back into the chair, rubbing at her wrist which still bore the imprint of his
fingers. He was no longer looking at her when he said,
'I apologise for that Nicole. I didn't mean to hurt
you.'

'Men like you never mean to hurt,' she answered
resentfully. 'It's just that you can't help it.

'I'm only sorry that you regard my behaviour as
subversive. It wasn't meant to be.'

'You really mustn't take every word I utter as a
personal insult. I wonder why,' he went on, turning
to look at her again, 'you think so badly of me?'

Nicole was in too heated a mood even to listen to
him. Heedlessly she went on, 'Paul may mean a great
deal to you, but believe it or not, I care for him too.
There is nothing wrong with wealth or a good position in life; I just think Paul should try for them
himself.'

'I think I have heard enough on the subject. You
seem to have forgotten one person—an intelligent
adult who can think, speak and decide things for
himself. We are discussing him as if he can't possibly
do anything for himself.'

Nicole knew her cheeks were growing red. 'Well,

Alex, *can* he?' she whispered.

He banged his fist on the table, causing the crockery to rattle about alarmingly. 'Enough of this! Before you continue to criticize my attitude towards my own brother I would like to point out that you are, as yet, in no position to do so yourself. He is still my brother and no relation to you, and I would like to remind you that you are enjoying my hospitality here on Kyros.'

Nicole jumped to her feet. 'Enjoying is not the word I would use, but one thing I can do is remove my unwelcome presence. Thanks for the hospitality but I won't impose on it any longer, Mr Stalis.' He looked up at her and there was alarm in his expression now. 'Will you kindly ask Demetrius to take me back to the mainland?'

His eyes narrowed. 'You really want to go?'

'Obviously. I can hardly remain here now.'

'Because I happened to tell you what you already know to be quite true? I never imagined you to be so faint-hearted?'

He was mocking her again. Victorious. 'I have no wish to remain in the company of someone who obviously cannot abide me.'

Softly he said, 'But you are here to be with Paul, not me.'

'But it is your hospitality.' Her eyes flashed with anger again. 'I can see Paul elsewhere, which frankly would be best for all our sakes.'

111

He shook his head. 'I am afraid it won't be convenient for Demetrius to take you to the mainland. He is very busy at the moment.'

'There must be some form of public transport. . . .'

'If you intend to take the island steamer it only calls once a week and it came yesterday.'

Nicole began to feel a tremor of fear behind her anger. 'How can I get to Athens then?'

'You can't.'

'But I must! I shall ask Demetrius myself.'

'He takes orders only from me.'

In a casual way which angered her all the more he selected a peach from the fruit dish on the table and began to eat it unconcernedly.

'You can't keep me here against my will!'

He laughed. 'Certainly, I can't. I shall be leaving at the weekend myself; you can come with me. I shall see you safely to the mainland.'

Four more days!

It was Nicole's turn to laugh. 'Don't be ridiculous. If I want to leave here you can't keep me.'

He looked up at her, from beneath his long dark lashes. 'From a personal point of view I have no wish to keep you, but you mean a great deal to Paul, more I think than he means to you.' Her laughter died and she was about to protest, but he gave her no chance. 'If you remain Paul will be content to be here with you, and I mean him to stay here for now. And, remember; it was your idea to come here, not mine.'

112

There was no mistaking his determination and, choked with frustration, Nicole turned on her heel and ran back into the villa. When she reached the stairs Xenia was just coming down and Nicole paused momentarily in her flight. Xenia looked fresh and cheerful and she bade her a bright, 'Good morning.'

Nicole murmured 'Good morning,' in reply, noticing Xenia's look of surprise as she excused herself and started immediately up the stairs again. When she reached her room she slammed the door thankfully behind her and, throwing herself on her bed, she burst into tears.

'He refused to let me go, Paul! He won't hear of it so you must speak to him.'

Paul was dressed and sitting on the edge of his bed, staring dolefully at his sandals. He picked one of them up and turned it over in his hand.

'Do you think I can get these on today?'

Nicole put her hands to her cheeks. They felt hot and her temper had not been cooled by that outburst of almost despairing tears. She had taken off her wet costume and now wore a cotton sundress. She had considered getting ready to leave and sitting with her suitcase on the verandah until transport was provided for her, but recalling that look of determination on Alex's face she decided against it.

Now she sincerely hoped that by the time she helped Paul into the dining room for breakfast both

Xenia and Alex would not be there. She had been so distressed at the time she had hardly noticed Xenia, but now a picture of the woman burned into her mind. Her dark auburn hair had been caught up in a canary yellow ribbon which matched her silk shirt and slacks.

'Will you listen to me, Paul? I *must* go back to London, and your brother,' she said it witheringly, 'refuses to order Demetrius to take me to the mainland.'

Paul looked up at her and frowned. 'Why all the rush to go back all of a sudden?'

'It isn't all of a sudden. I've been here for more than a week and Sally has been coping all that time on her own. It's not right that I should stay here indefinitely while she is running my business!'

'No one has said you were going to stay for good, but you are on holiday and you've not been away for a fortnight yet. You're entitled to at least that, and I know Sally well enough to realize she won't mind in the least.'

'I'm determined to go. You can join me later if you wish. There's no reason why you shouldn't.'

His answering laughter did nothing to calm her wounded pride. 'I might not be able to join you for some time, but I'm still confined more or less to the villa and enjoying your company, so I'd be silly to give that up easily.'

'You're as mad as he is.'

He started to put on his sandals and Nicole was glad to see that his ankle had returned to more like its normal size.

'If you had a good enough excuse for leaving I'd be willing to intervene, but all that's happened is that you've had a difference of opinion with Alex again and your pride is hurt.'

'That's not true!'

'It is. You can never hide your feelings from me, Nicky, and I saw it in your face the moment you came in.'

'Well, what if I have? You know he and I can never agree on anything, but it has nothing to do with my wanting to go. I've been thinking of leaving for the past day or two.'

'Think again,' he said mildly. 'You can't really intend to leave here while I'm still an invalid. You'd never be hard-hearted enough to leave me in such a weakened state.'

She couldn't help but laugh at his mock outrage.

'Don't play on my sympathy, you fraud! You're almost better now.'

He stood up, using his stick, and tested his foot on the floor. 'Much better,' he agreed, 'but not quite fully recovered.'

He limped over to her and put one hand on her shoulder. 'If you can't get on with Alex, and there are times when he annoys me too, try not to punish me for it, darling.'

Her eyes darkened with pain, 'Oh, I wouldn't do that, Paul!'

'But by leaving now, while we're having such a good time, that is exactly what you would be doing. And if Alex does want to part us he's being very successful, isn't he?'

'If I wait until the weekend will you come too? At least as far as Athens. We could have a few days together there; you can show me all the sights.'

He couldn't hold her gaze any longer. His hand dropped from her shoulder and he shuffled away from her.

'It's impossible just now, Nicky.'

'Why, Paul? Because of this man who was following you?' He didn't answer. 'Please tell me what all this is about. Explain to me just what this man has threatened you with and why. Why are you so afraid?'

He laughed harshly. 'I'm not afraid, and I've already explained to you what it's all about.'

She stared at him and he put his hand out to her. 'Come on; help me. I'm hungry and we're late for breakfast.'

Sighing with resignation she went to take his arm, although now he was recovering well and had the stick she felt he really didn't need support any longer.

To her relief the dining room was empty when they went in, and two places were set for them. Chloris came bustling in with fresh coffee and Paul

116

conversed with her in Greek for a few moments.

'You have no need to worry,' he told Nicole when the woman had gone. 'Alex and Xenia will be out all day.' Nicole started to relax. 'They've gone out in the boat—fishing. Alex is very partial to fishing. We shall probably eat the catch.'

As Paul chattered happily Nicole almost choked with vexation. Demetrius was too busy, he had said. Too busy with a fishing trip to take her to the mainland! To her annoyance she felt tears of frustration pricking at her eyes.

Chapter Seven

It was easy to avoid contact with Alex the next day. Xenia, who possessed a very forceful personality, was Nicole's unwitting ally in that. She was anxious, it seemed, to have Alex to herself and also to afford the young couple as many opportunities to be alone as was possible. It appeared that she was in earnest in her desire to see Paul married and Alex thus freed of his responsibility towards him. Nicole somehow doubted if the matter would be so easily resolved. Lifetime habits were notoriously difficult to break.

But, seething with resentment against both Alex and Paul did not make Nicole a good companion and soon after lunch the following day she tackled Paul once more.

'So it seems you've definitely decided to stay in Greece.'

'I thought I'd made that clear to you the other day,' he answered in some surprise.

'I wasn't sure it was definitely decided—by you

anyway. I realize that Alex decided a long time ago what your life was to be.'

He laughed. 'Oh, don't blame old Alex, Nicky. I did make up my own mind. Remember, London was only temporary.'

They were sitting in the garden in the shade of the orange and lemon trees and at any other time Nicole would have found it idyllic. 'I somehow imagined, now that I'm involved, you might have discussed your future plans with me first.'

'What is there to discuss?' he went on, in that same air of bewilderment. 'It's a wife's place to go where her husband works, not the other way around—not yet anyway!

'You knew my home was in Greece when we met. Oh Nicky, what kind of a job did I have anyway?'

'A real one, which is more than the one Alex will create for you.'

He laughed again and she shot him an angry look. 'Well, why not? What's so marvellous about work anyway? We shall have lots of time to be together while he earns the bread. He does it so much better anyway.' When she didn't respond he said in a cojoling way, 'This move will be for your good too. We can have a really splendid home in Athens and even a villa like this one on one of the islands. We'll be very wealthy, Nicky. You won't need the headache of owning a boutique or doing any other job for that matter. You'll have everything you've ever wanted.'

And be beholden to Alexander Stalis for it! Nicole thought sourly, and this she realized at last was the basis of all her objections. The truth had finally come to her and it was shattering.

She swung her legs to the ground and stood up. 'Do you mind if I go for a walk, Paul? I'm getting stiff sitting here.'

He was watching her anxiously. 'I don't mind, only,' he glanced at his watch 'isn't it a little early yet? It's still quite hot for walking.'

'I'll keep in the shade.'

As she made to pass him he caught her hand. 'You're not angry with me, are you?'

She smiled down at him. 'No, I'm not angry with you, but, but I am angry with myself. I haven't been thinking at all straight about this matter.'

This much she knew was the truth too. She didn't blame Paul any more. What he wanted was very natural; Alex was his brother, and accepting all he had to give would be natural, but Nicole could not contemplate a lifetime of doing so, and the knowledge angered her. Any sane girl would rush to accept what Paul had to offer.

Although she had intended to take only a short walk, she soon found herself entering the village. There weren't many fishing boats moored in the harbour at this time of the day and only a few nets lying across the cobbles, drying in the sun. She did notice a smart cabin cruiser which looked out of place

120

on the island. The sight of it surprised her, for she had been told it was too early for casual visitors.

There were a few shops in the main street facing the harbour and Nicole always found them fascinating. One in particular was of great interest and seemed to sell every kind of hardware, with tin pots strung up from the ceiling and mops and detergents intermingling with cheese and sausages.

As Nicole approached the shop, Sofia was coming out. Nicole automatically stopped. The girl carried a basket full of groceries and when she saw Nicole standing there her bland expression gave way to one of fierce hatred.

Nicole said, '*Kalispera*, Sofia,' but the girl simply tossed back her dark hair and passed by without speaking. Nicole regretfully watched her, wishing she could know what Paul's relationship with Sofia really was; it would be too naive of her to believe it was entirely innocent and this set up another doubt in her mind—could she be happy married to a man who attracted women to him so easily?

Sofia had turned into one of the narrow alleyways so Nicole dimissed the matter from her mind and walked on towards the shop. At the front of the window was a small display of gifts which she had admired before. The pottery was very attractive but Nicole decided at last to buy a beaten copper jug to take home for Sally. It was just as she was coming out of the shop, carrying her purchase, that she saw a man emerge from the *taverna* a few doors away. Something about him made her stop and stare at him. It was purely an involuntary move and not based on reason. He was dark-skinned with black curly hair, and quite young—in his twenties, she guessed—with a very powerful build.

He was walking away from her, towards the quay, and therefore could not see her, but even so she drew back into the shop doorway in order to see him better unobserved. It could have been a coincidence—or even a mistake—but she was certain she had seen that man before: in the car outside Alex's apartment that first night in Athens.

The man climbed into the boat and a moment later its engine spluttered into life, but it wasn't until the cruiser was well out to sea that she emerged from the shop doorway. Nicole kept on watching the boat, biting her lip. She had no idea what she should do now. Could this be the man who had threatened Paul? Or was she being foolish?

It seemed providential that as she hovered there indecisively Alex and Xenia came strolling towards her, arm in arm. Nicole knew no hesitation then. Alex, for all his faults, would know what to do, and she began to run towards them.

'See that boat heading out to sea,' she said breathlessly without preamble.

Both of them followed the direction of her gaze. 'The man in it . . . I'm sure I saw him outside your apartment. He followed you that night I was in Athens, after I'd been to see you.'

Alex's eyes narrowed and Xenia looked at him with interest. 'Are you quite sure, Nicole?'

'As sure as I can be.' She described him as best she could whilst Alex listened in silence, his face set into an expressionless mask. 'He came out of the *taverna* and got into the boat.'

Alex looked at her at last. 'Did he see you?'

She shook her head. 'I hid in the doorway of one of the shops until he had gone.'

'Wait here' he said tersely. 'If he came out of the *taverna* Gregori will know what he wanted, if, indeed, he wanted anything,' he added quickly. 'I shall go and ask.'

Nicole started to follow him, calling, 'Alex . . .'

But he shouted, 'Wait there,' over his shoulder so firmly that she did go back to where Xenia was standing.

It was then that she realized that she was breathing unevenly. 'Xenia, do you know what this is all about?'

The older woman smiled. 'I'm afraid I don't.'

Nicole looked at her disbelievingly. 'But you've lent him your villa for Paul to hide in!'

Xenia continued to smile but her eyes remained on the door of the *taverna*. A few elderly men had emerged from their homes and were sitting at the outside tables where they would remain until it was time for them to go home and to bed.

'I never 'lend' it to Alex; it is always at his disposal. He never needs to ask or to explain.'

'Aren't you at all curious?'

'Naturally, but I have known Alex long enough to realize he will tell me nothing until he wants to, and pressing him is of no use. Believe me. Of course,' she went on. looking at Nicole now, 'I can have a shrewd guess what it's all about, and I would probably be right.'

Nicole became alert. 'What do you think it is?'

'Possibly at some time in the past Paul has compromised some girl and her closest relative has come to find him, to revenge her shame.'

She said it with such dramatic relish that Nicole was forced to laugh. 'Surely not.'

Xenia's eyebrows went up a fraction. 'This is Greece, remember. That sort of thing is still taken very seriously because the vast majority of our people haven't yet woken up to the fact that we're in the twentieth century. It would be a matter of honour to them, otherwise a whole family could lose face to the village they live in.'

'If what you surmise is true, Xenia, it would mean that this man followed Paul to London and then back to Greece again. Is that really possible for merely compromising a girl?'

'He would follow him to the ends of the earth if need be for a matter of family honour. I have known of it before. Time and distance mean little.'

Nicole's mind was in a whirl. Could it be? In England it would be a farce even to contemplate, but in Greece. . . . It *was* possible. The note said 'Remember Maria'. It would account for Paul's reluctance to admit why he was being threatened, and possibly he had made Alex promise to remain silent on the subject in order to spare her feelings.

'What could Paul have done?' she asked.

'Not necessarily very much, I should think.' She laughed. 'To be alone with a girl would be enough. And,' she went on, 'don't think we have seen the last of this fellow. He will be persistent.'

'What will he do if he does find Paul?'

Xenia smiled. 'I should think he would try to bully him into marrying the girl. If I were you, Nicole, I should marry Paul as soon as possible. It's his only hope.'

Nicole drew in a sharp breath. Alex was coming out of the *taverna* so she was saved the trouble of replying, for in truth she did not know what to say.

As soon as she saw him she knew that whatever he had been told it was not bad news.

'Gregori tells me the man was asking about Paul and myself, but as he knew we were here for privacy he told the man there was no one of that name on the island.'

'He must be visiting all the islands,' Nicole suggested, 'and asking the same question.'

'I dare say he is.'

She waited for him to elaborate further, but he kept on looking at her and then went on to say, 'There is nothing to worry about so I think it best if we keep this little bit of information from Paul.'

It wasn't a request and Nicole knew it, however mildly he had spoken, and although as ever she resented taking orders from him she had no intention of telling Paul about the man. Now she was certain in her mind what the trouble was about she had decided it wasn't her concern. The only thing that mattered now was for her to find a way to leave the island.

Xenia and Alex continued their interrupted stroll and Nicole started on her way back to the villa.

'There is nothing to worry about,' he had said, but Nicole suddenly had the feeling that, for a time, he had been very worried indeed.

Chloris once again surpassed herself in preparing dinner that night, and Nicole suspected that Xenia, since her arrival, had taken charge of the domestic arrangements at the villa.

But, despite the excellence of the meal, Nicole found she had no taste for the food set before her. In order not to draw attention to herself she did eat some *dolmades*—minced meat wrapped in vine leaves—which had been served as hors d'œvres, but as the others talked companionably it was all she

could do to pick at the *barbounia* that Alex and Xenia
had borne home triumphantly from their fishing trip
the previous day.

As far as Paul was concerned, he had made it clear
enough that he had no intention of aiding her attempts to leave the island sooner than necessary, and
Alex, who angered her far more, seemed intent on
behaving as if their exchange of words or their meeting that afternoon had never happened.

'Do you always rise so early?' Xenia asked as the
interminable meal drew to a close.

Four more days, she thought. It would seem endless.

'Not usually,' she replied. 'I couldn't sleep last
night for some reason so I decided to get up and go
out.'

All the time she was talking Alex was watching
her whilst Paul was preoccupied with peeling some
fruit.

'You are obviously not used to the heat.'

Nicole gladly seized on such an explanation. 'Yes,
I expect that is the reason.'

'I'm never alive until mid-morning,' Xenia went
on, laughing, 'although I thought I was doing very
well today—until I saw Nicole, that is.' She leaned
conspiratorially towards Paul. 'You will have to
hurry and get your ankle better, you know, or Nicole
will soon grow restless.'

She had spoken lightly but Nicole sensed a certain

amount of acidity on the woman's part and it came as something of a surprise for her to realize Xenia hadn't liked the idea of that morning swim. The revelation almost made her laugh out loud. It was incredible to believe that so sophisticated a creature was actually unsure of her man, so unsure as to resent any woman being near him. But this was exactly what had happened. Of course, Nicole reasoned, Alexander Stalis was a man of whom no woman could be certain, and far from admiring Xenia now she actually pitied her.

'Do you enjoy fishing?' Nicole asked of her when they were having coffee.

She laughed again. 'How little you know me! I may go along for Alex's sake,' she shot him a smile, 'which is an indication of my devotion, but I sunbathe while Alex and Demetrius do all the work.'

'Fishing isn't usually a woman's sport,' Alex observed as he poured some brandy for himself.

'I've never fancied sitting on the bank of a river,' Nicole answered, 'but I should imagine fishing in these waters in a boat could be very exciting.'

Alex turned round, glass in hand, and looked as if he were about to say something when Xenia winked conspiratorially at Paul.

'Need she say more? You will have to take her out in the boat when your ankle is better, Paul.'

'You don't have to worry about that, Xenia. I'm going to make these past few days up to Nicole just as soon as I can.'

'You don't have to make anything up to me,' she retorted, rather irritably.

'That's a very sensible attitude,' his brother said as he sat down, facing Nicole. 'It's as well you don't expect unflagging attention because once Paul is back in Athens he will have little time to waste.'

There was a subtle stress on his last word as he looked in Nicole's direction and immediately she got up and went to find the playing cards.

'Let's play rummy,' she said to Paul, drawing a table up to the settee where he was sitting.

Xenia leaned forward to touch Alex's hand. 'And do you know what I would like to do?'

Alex seemed to have been deep in thought, staring down at the floor. Now he raised his head slowly to look at her. 'You had better tell me, Xenia; I have never yet learned to read a woman's mind.'

She laid her head back on the settee, rubbing her hand over the arm. 'It's such a beautiful night. I thought it would be rather nice to walk to the temple.'

To her chagrin he started to laugh and she sat up straight again, looking furious until he said in a gentle tone of voice, 'Will you be satisfied with a swim in the pool for now?'

Her look of vexation turned into a smile. 'Only if you don't turn on the lights. There's a beautiful moon out tonight. We may as well use it.'

Alex inclined his head. 'It shall be just as you wish,

my dear. A swim by moonlight it is.'

He was looking at Nicole and she knew he was recalling their swim together and his reference to swimming by moonlight on that occasion. Only lovers, she thought, would swim by moonlight.

Xenia got to her feet and held out her hand to him and when they had gone Nicole drew a sigh of relief. The atmosphere was easier now they had gone. The conversation would hold no hidden meanings.

'Do you wish you were out there swimming too?' Paul asked in a soft voice.

Nicole was startled out of her thoughts. She looked at him wide eyed. 'What do you mean?' she asked in a breathless voice. For some reason her heart was pounding madly.

'I thought you might be regretting that I can't join in with all these activities.'

She immediately relaxed and smiled at him. 'Don't be such an idiot. Shall I deal first?'

Nicole lost almost every game despite Paul being, in normal circumstances, an indifferent player. On this occasion her mind, to his delight, was not on what she was doing. Paul claimed his victories with all the delight of a child, whilst from outside shouts and laughter could be plainly heard coming from the swimming pool. Each burst of laughter jarred on Nicole's already taut nerves.

After a while when Paul said, 'It's no fun winning tonight, Nicky, because you are clearly not on form,' she rubbed her eyes and answered, 'I must be tired. I awoke rather early this morning.'

'And you're not used to dawn swimming.' She was about to agree with him about that when he went on, 'And I'd advise you not to become involved in arguments with Alex in the future. They can be exhausting and you just can't win.'

'I'm beginning to realize that, and obviously so have you,' she told him wearily.

'I wish you could get on with him, but even if you can't it doesn't make any difference to us.'

Nicole could have argued that point with him but was too tired. Instead she said, 'Do you mind if I go to bed now?'

'Of course I mind, but,' he added in a gentler tone, 'you do look tired. I might as well come too. Xenia will keep Alex out there for ages yet. This week hasn't turned out as I'd hoped.'

'You can't forsee accidents, Paul.'

She helped him to his feet and he limped with the aid of his stick to Alex's study, which had quickly been converted into a temporary bedroom for Paul. At the door instead of relinquishing his hold on her he drew her close and kissed her with something like the ardour that had been missing of late. At last she drew away and he smiled down at her.

'You really are an old-fashioned girl, aren't you?'

She disentangled herself from his embrace at last and stood a little way apart from him. 'What makes

131

you say such a strange thing?'

He leaned his back against the door. 'I was just remembering all those times in London, when I begged you to stay with me and you always refused, as I knew you would. I was glad in a way that you did. It was the thing that set you apart.'

'What makes you think about it now?'

'It occurred to me that if I could persuade you to spend the night with me, I could really be sure you would marry me. You wouldn't have any more doubts, you know.'

She couldn't help but laugh. 'Is that your standard procedure?'

He was suddenly very serious. 'There has never been anyone quite like you, Nicky, believe it or not. I've never wanted to marry anyone before, and I'm far from sure of you.'

'Perhaps it's only because no other girl has refused you so consistently, and if that's the reason it's no basis for marriage.'

She stood on tiptoe and kissed his cheek, avoiding his lips, and before he could restrain her she hurried away. But by the time she had reached the sanctuary of her room tiredness had gone. She didn't even attempt to undress, for she knew she would not sleep. Instead she went to the window and pushed open the shutters, allowing herself to be cooled by the fragrant night air. Against the velvet sky the one remaining pillar of the temple stood outlined, lonely and strangely beautiful, in the moonlight.

For a while she just stood there, her chin resting on her hands, gazing out into the night.

'*Don't marry him unless you love him very much,*' Alex had said, and it had been more than a plea for his brother's happiness. Perhaps far more than even Alex had realized, for one thing her stay on Kyros had taught her was her need to love Paul very deeply before she could contemplate marriage.

It would take all her love and devotion to give up the boutique now, when success was in her grasp, to come and live in this beautiful country which was, nevertheless a strange one. She couldn't even speak the language.

And lastly there was Alex. Nicole didn't stop to wonder why he loomed so large in her mind; the fact remained that he did. To marry Paul was to be involved with Alex. He was implacably against their marriage, but in the clever way which was typical of him he had not chosen to dissuade Paul and thus, perhaps, incite his resentment—hatred even. No, he had known it would be best to work on Nicole herself, and, she realized, he had very nearly succeeded in persuading her that marriage to Paul would not work. But not quite. Nicole's feelings for Paul hadn't changed at all; she still loved him as before. His brother had not yet found a way of altering that.

Nicole knew that if she decided to stay she must grow accustomed to being a silent voice where Paul was concerned, for it would always be Alex who would be heard.

Nicole sighed to herself. It would not be easy.

She gazed up towards the temple. Would Aphrodite have been able to give her an answer to her dilemma? she wondered, for it was a difficult problem. For some other girl, happy-go-lucky Sally perhaps, there would have been no question. She would accept Alex—and Paul—for what they were. But then Paul could have chosen such a girl and at that moment she wondered if, unwittingly, he had picked someone who might prove to be a buffer between Alex and himself.

After a while, Nicole straightened up. There was something else she had forgotten. Emotions were running high, even Xenia's in her anxiety to see Paul married and so have Alex to herself at last, but there was something else—the real reason Paul was here instead of Athens. Until that little mystery was solved nothing could be decided.

Nicole still felt wide awake. Impulsively she went to the door and listened. There was no sign of anyone else up and around, which didn't surprise her as it had been quite some time since she had come up to her room.

She went downstairs and paused before going into the living room; but no one was there. Chloris had cleared away the coffee cups and there were two glasses on the coffee table which showed that Alex and Xenia had returned here after their swim. The verandah doors were closed but never locked at night and Nicole was able to let herself out with no trouble.

She had only intended to have a short walk in the hope it would induce sleep when she returned, but she found herself wandering in the direction of the Temple of Aphrodite. There was something about the place which drew her to it and even when the going became hard Nicole didn't turn back. The path was well lit by moonlight but even so, recalling Paul's accident, she stepped carefully. It would be so easy to trip over a stone or one of the cistus bushes which pushed their way through the hard ground. She had no wish to lie here, helpless, until someone came along to find her.

She didn't even feel tired when at last she reached the ruined gateway. She felt elated from the effort of her climb and it was worthwhile. She just gasped with pleasure at the sight of the old stones, gleaming white in the moonlight, and after a few moments she went further to the edge of the hill where she could see the water which was all round. It looked like a sheet of silver. Nicole turned away from the cliff edge and gazed around her. Some of the larger, upright stones looked almost like mortal beings. It was no wonder people of long ago believed in the power of romance in this place when the moon shone.

She began to feel the power of its loneliness too,

and it was not a comfortable experience. She was almost afraid, for there were thoughts running through her mind that she wished she could exorcise. Unwilling thoughts of Paul and herself, of Alex and Xenia.

Nicole suddenly realized it must be growing late and started back towards the path. Suddenly she was anxious to be away but she had gone only a few paces when a noise stopped her. She listened and it was unmistakably the sound of someone coming up the hill. A goat, she told herself, for there were so many of them on the island. But goats moved in silence. It was human footsteps she could hear. There was no doubt of it. Someone was coming along the path towards her, only the hill hid him from sight.

Nicole froze, realizing how isolated it was there and the foolishness of telling no one where she was going. It was just that she hadn't imagined anyone else would come here so late at night.

A shadow appeared in the gateway. 'Who is it?' she asked, her voice breathless with the fear she had come to feel.

'Nicole?'

He came towards her. Belated fear caused beads of perspiration to break out on her forehead but she relaxed now a little.

'Alex, what are you doing here?'

'The same as you, I imagine; seeking fresh air and solitude, perhaps solitude more than anything.'

She recognized the irony in his voice. He knew of

her conflict where Paul was concerned; he knew because it was he who had caused it.

'I. . . . I won't intrude on your solitude.'

She would have gone past him, glad to be away, but he caught her hand in his. 'Don't go just yet. Stay with me a while. Solitude is fine, but companionship is much better.'

'Xenia wanted to come here earlier, but you wouldn't accompany her.'

'At that moment I preferred to swim. Now,' he added, sounding regretful, 'she is too tired to come with me.'

Nicole hesitated and then let him draw her over to the olive tree. 'If you stand here you cannot see any buildings, only sky and sea all around. It's an odd sensation. Terrifying almost. Just imagine if the world were only sky and sea, and one rocky island.'

Nicole could say nothing in reply. She felt as if it were all unreal, that she had stayed in bed and this was only a dream. From here he could toss her into the sea and no one would ever know how it had happened. There would be no problem any longer. But she was not afraid, only bemused.

'It's one of the most beautiful places I have ever seen.'

'Sometimes when I am here I feel as if I am the only man in the world.'

'I feel that too,' she turned to look at him, 'but why should you want to?'

137

He laughed softly. 'At times it would be nice, less complicated if I were.'

'But any man would envy you. You have everything a man could possibly want from life.'

He looked at her then and his eyes were very dark. She backed away against the gnarled trunk of the olive tree which felt hard against her back.

'Have you heard the legend about this place?'

'Yes,' she whispered.

'Do you believe it?'

She shook her head and he came closer. She tried to back away but it was impossible. She was trapped between him and the tree. Her heart was beating fast as his lips came close to hers. As they met she closed her eyes, savouring the moment. It was as if everything she had ever said and done and wanted was leading only up to this moment of truth.

'It has nothing to do with the legend,' she murmured as he enfolded her in his arms.

'Must you argue even at a moment like this?' he asked, but there was no irritation in his voice, just tenderness.

She laughed softly and wound her arms around his neck. 'I must be wrong. I'll believe anything true in this place. There's magic in the very air we breathe here.'

There was no longer any conflict in her mind; now she knew why it had been there in the first place. As she had suspected Aphrodite had solved her problem as she had done for those people who lived so long ago, and solved it in the most unexpected way. And yet, Nicole mused, perhaps it wasn't so unexpected. Looking back it was inevitable; angry feelings between them had always been so easily aroused. . . . anger and love.

His lips explored her neck until they reached her lips again and by that time Nicole didn't care if she were there until dawn, or even for ever as long as he was with her.

At last he drew away from her slightly, saying deliberately in a soft voice close to her ear, 'You must tell Paul you don't want to marry him. You understand that now, don't you, Nicole?'

She stared back at him in the darkness, his eyes boring relentlessly into hers. He still held her tightly, his voice breathless, his lips close to her cheek. Her mind was still bemused by the suddenness of her awakening from dreaming to reality again, but there was no doubt that the dream was over now. She had realized too late what he had been about while the moonlight bewitched her. She backed away from him, saw the question in his eyes.

'Nicole . . .?'

'You've won, Alex. Of course I can't marry Paul now. You know that already, don't you? Your methods, I think, however. . . . dirty,' she almost choked over the word, 'never fail. You're a very determined man.'

'Nicole!'

She turned and began to run down the hill with is voice echoing in her ears. She ran as if the Furies pursued her until she could no longer hear his voice or his footsteps behind her. Ridding herself of the feel of his embrace which had thrilled her and had answered all her prayers, would not so easily be erased. It might, she thought tearfully, take a lifetime.

At last she reached the villa and it was only then that she realized she might have broken a leg in that mad headlong flight down the hill over that rough ground. If she had been aware of it somehow Nicole doubted if she would have cared.

No lights showed at any of the windows and she did not pause to switch on any as she ran through the villa. When she reached her room she slammed the door and took the precaution of locking it, standing breathlessly with her back to it.

She stood there for some few minutes until her breathing became more normal and it was then she realized that tears were streaming down her cheeks. She dashed them away with her hand and then, when she heard footsteps coming down the corridor, she stiffened, holding her breath. He knocked on the door and she moved away from it, as if she could be burned by any contact.

'Nicole?' he said softly. 'Are you in there?'

She didn't answer, for the tears were beginning to

fall again, almost choking her. What irony to find she was in love with the one man who hated her above all others. She had committed the sin of challenging his authority over Paul and he would use any method of paying her back for it.

'Nicole, will you let me in for a moment? I must talk to you.'

Still she didn't answer. She was too busy sniffing back her tears and not for anything would she let him know she was crying. He rattled at the doorknob and she moved back even further into the room, almost falling over the bed.

'All right,' he said at last. 'If you won't talk to me now I can't do anything about it without waking up the whole house, but I'll see you first thing in the morning.'

She had the feeling he was standing out there waiting for some reply, and sure enough a few moments later came the sound of his footsteps moving away. Nicole waited until she could hear him no more and then she sank down on to the bed and burying her head in her hands she sobbed until no more tears would come.

Nicole didn't trouble to undress; she just laid down on the bed and stared up at the ceiling. Strange how she had never noticed before that there was a pattern of swirls painted on it. At last she closed her eyes but they felt hot and prickly, and sleep would not come however hard she willed it. Sleep meant forgetfulness but all she could see was his face close to hers and feel the tenderness of his kiss, his body pressed against hers.

He was a betrayer. Nothing would be sacred to such an unscrupulous man. No doubt he kissed her only so he could blackmail her. If she had insisted on marrying Paul, Alex could tell him of their meeting, make it appear contrived. He could make her look guilty of betraying Paul so easily. Nicole wouldn't be surprised at anything he did to achieve his own way. But he wasn't to know all it would achieve was prove she loved him and not Paul. How the knowledge would amuse him.

When she realized at long last she wasn't going to get any sleep that night she leaped out of bed. She stripped off her clothes, had a cold shower, and immediately dressed again, this time in a pair of slacks and a heavy sweater. After that was accomplished she began systematically to pack her clothes. It took her less than five minutes to strip the room of anything that indicated she had ever stayed there.

As she crept out of the villa, clutching her suitcase, no one came to stop her. At that time of the morning this wasn't surprising but Nicole didn't dismiss the possibility of Alex being up too.

Outside, the swimming pool was still, clearly lit up by the moon which still shone brightly, although it was now on the wane, the sky already lightening. Nicole felt a lump form in her throat as she gazed for the last time at the gardens and then she quickly hurried on. This was, after all, Xenia's house—probably bought for her by Alex—and Nicole could not even recall happy times with him without remembering that too.

It was with great relief that she reached the path which led to the village and automatically quickened her pace. The same moon which shone so magically on her at the temple only hours ago served to light her flight from the man she had then gone to so willingly.

By the time she reached the first house of the village her suitcase was beginning to feel heavy, and although she had walked this route so many times before, on this occasion it seemed to take so much longer.

The sky was now growing lighter by the minute. Nicole noticed that in many of the houses people were up, and it was with some relief that she saw most of the fishing boats had not yet put to sea. As she approached the quay she could see that some of the fishermen were loading their nets. Nicole paused to watch them and they glanced at her curiously as they went about their work.

At that moment she knew a momentary panic. What if none of them would take her and she was forced, in humiliation, to return to the villa? They could all be in the pay of Alexander Stalis and answer to him for everything. Perhaps he had even anticipated her flight and had given orders for them not to take her to the mainland should she be foolish enough to ask. Nicole deliberately shook the thought from her mind, for whatever he was, he was not a monster. His protectiveness towards Paul might seem misguided to an outsider, but it was certainly well-meant. She realized that in her bitterness her beliefs about him might have been getting out of hand, that in struggling against her growing attraction to him she might have been fighting much more than that.

Nicole then paused to wonder if all of her ideas about him might be wrong. If, perhaps, he was more sincere than she had assumed. After all, he *had* been right in thinking her unsuited to Paul. If he hadn't meant to compromise her last night . . . She glanced back as if measuring the distance between the villa and herself, and then, giving herself a mental shake, she walked forward again.

Some of the vessels moored against the quay were caiques used for sponge fishing and she passed them by. The other boats were larger, powered, fishing boats and it was at the newest of these that Nicole stopped.

Two men, one very young and the other approaching middle age, were loading up the last of their nets. Nicole took a wad of drachma notes from her pocket and and approached the older man. He paused in his work and gazed at the money she held out to

144

him. To her gratification he appeared impressed by it.

'*Athinai, parakalo,*' she said slowly, indicating the boat. '*Athinai.*'

Nicole hoped that it was clear what she wanted of them and that the money she was offering was far and above what they could hope to earn from their fishing that day. The two fishermen had a quick discussion and to her relief the older man nodded. The young one, who could not have been more than fifteen years old, took her suitcase whilst the other, who might have been his father, helped her aboard and ushered her into the smelly little cabin. The odour of fish was everywhere but Nicole did not heed it; sufficient that she was going to escape an unbearable situation.

When the engine started up it sounded rough but she supposed the fishermen knew its capabilities and a two hour journey was not beyond its range. As the boat puttered away from the quay she drew a sigh of relief. Escape at last. Alexander Stalis had misjudged her tenacity too.

She no longer feared pursuit. Indeed, why should she? she reasoned. Alex had played his part well and achieved what he set out to do, even if it wasn't quite in the way he had intended. And Paul would be sleeping as peacefully as a baby. By the time he was fit enough to be able to pursue her, he would know that their romance was over. There was nothing left to do now except return to London.

As the boat began to gain speed Nicole came out of the cabin at last. The boy smiled at her shyly and she smiled back although her heart was unbearably heavy. The sun was rising from behind the island, scattering the last of the stars and bathing the cottages of Kyros in a pink glow. Yesterday she had watched the sun rise with Alex and had marvelled at that miracle of nature. Yesterday. . . .

As the island grew more distant she could no longer see it so clearly for the tears which had come unbidden to her eyes and blurred her last sight of Kyros.

Chapter Eight

It was the insistent ringing of the telephone that woke her. Nicole had been so soundly asleep that she lay there for a moment, wondering where she was. In an instant she remembered. She was back at the Hotel Argos in Athens and it was as if more than a week had rolled away and that time on the island had never happened.

The telephone rang again, just as it had done then. Nicole hesitated to answer it, feeling that it might be Alex again, about to give her those complicated instructions on how to reach Kyros.

When it rang again she did answer it and the voice did not belong to Alex at all; it was the hotel receptionist at the other end of the line.

'Miss Carrington?'

'Yes. What do you want?'

There was a pause. 'You asked me to try and obtain a plane reservation for you.'

Nicole sank back into the pillows, running her free

hand through her tangled hair. 'I do apologize. I've been asleep and I didn't quite realize . . .'

'That is quite all right, Miss Carrington. Would you prefer me to speak to you later?'

'No! Did you manage to find me a seat on tonight's flight?'

'I am so sorry, Miss Carrington, but there are no vacancies at all on any flight to London until the day after tomorrow at the very earliest.'

The girl's voice was filled with genuine regret and Nicole was so stunned she couldn't answer for the moment. Then she protested, 'But there must be. I have to leave Athens as soon as I can!'

'I have tried every airline. They are very busy at the moment. There has been a music festival in Athens last week and many visitors are now returning home. It's possible that there might be a last-minute cancellation and I've asked them to let me know if there is.'

'Thank you. You've tried hard and I'm very grateful.'

'I wish I could have been of more help.'

The receptionist was about to ring off when Nicole said suddenly, 'I don't mind if I have to make a connection. I'll fly to Paris or Rome if necessary. Will you try that for me please?'

'Certainly, but I think you will find it will still be a day or two before you'll be able to get any flight out of Athens.'

Nicole put the receiver back into its cradle and sighed. She glanced at her watch. Evening had come. It had been a long day. The fishing boat had come in at Piraeus and from there she had taken a taxi to the Argos, which, luckily, had a room available. The journey from Kyros had not been a comfortable one. Unlike the *Melisande,* the little fishing boat was not equipped for either long or comfortable journeys and the time taken was so much longer than in Alex's cruiser, and much rougher despite a relatively calm sea.

By the time she reached her room at the Argos her two sleepless nights, her churning emotions and the effects of the sea journey had taken its toll of her and she had thrown herself into bed and slept almost at once.

Now she was faced with the prospect of remaining for two more days in the city which reminded her so painfully of what she sought to forget. Alexander Stalis was everywhere; he was in her mind constantly.

Despite her misery Nicole suddenly realized she was hungry, which wasn't surprising. She hadn't eaten at all that day, refusing the hard, black bread which was all the fisherman could offer her. Realizing that there was nothing more she could do except wait and hope a cancellation would occur, she had a shower, dried her hair and got dressed quickly, all of which made her feel a little bit better.

The nagging heartache remained but at least she felt fresher, deciding to have a light meal sent up to the room, for dining alone in public was something she could not face just now.

As she brushed her hair she caught sight of the hotel notepaper placed prominently on the dressing table. Guiltily, she realized she would have to write to Paul and explain that she had decided their marriage would not work. He would be hurt and upset for a while but she didn't doubt he would recover in time, as Nicole, herself, was determined to do. Gazing at her wan reflection in the mirror she doubted if it would be so easy to achieve in her own case.

There came a knock on the door. Nicole got to her feet; she had no doubt who it would be. The receptionist must have managed to get her a seat on one of the flights leaving Athens!

Excitedly she called, 'Come in!'

But it wasn't the receptionist who stood in the door and automatically Nicole backed away until the corner of the dressing table pressed painfully into her back.

'Alex, what are you doing here?'

He came in and closed the door behind him. Nicole felt panic-stricken and her mouth became dry. Never did she imagine he would follow her to Athens. There was no reason why he should.

'I came to find you.'

'Paul? Is he all right?'

A ghost of a smile crossed his lips. 'Puzzled, but otherwise all right. He's wanting to know why you ran away last night.'

'Did you tell him?'

'I couldn't. I didn't know myself.'

She turned away, to look out of the unshuttered window, at dusk falling like a purple cloak over the city. 'How did you find me?'

'It was easy. I guessed that you wouldn't go straight to the airport, and this I suspect is the only hotel you know of.'

'If you've come to make sure I've finished with Paul you needn't worry; I have no intention of seeing him again. You've had your way in this as in everything else.'

He came across to her then and put his hands on her shoulders. She stiffened beneath his touch, but she didn't move away.

'Don't blame me for something you knew in your heart had to be.'

'You didn't have to force the decision on me in quite the way you did.'

'You're still blaming me; you were biased against me before we even met.'

She lowered her eyes, for she knew he spoke the truth. If there had been conflict between them she was more than guilty of perpetuating it.

'You've been wrong about me, Nicole. Very wrong.

151

It's true I never wanted you to marry Paul. I don't deny that.'

'Why, Alex?' she whispered. 'What is wrong with me?'

A smile twisted his lips for a moment and then it was gone. 'There is nothing wrong with you, Nicole. At first it was because I realized you were wrong for him, or rather he was wrong for you. Paul can be charming and a wonderful companion, but he is a child, always at play and life isn't like that. He can't make decisions for himself and for someone like you the fact would soon begin to irritate. I think you have realized these facts for yourself, Nicole. Later, it was more than just those reasons that set me against your plans. Nothing so noble, I'm afraid. I simply wanted you for myself.'

She turned round slowly, looking into his face, searching it for insincerity, but there was none. There was only anxiety there, on his face, in his eyes; anxiety to prove to her that he really meant what he had said. She had doubted him so much.

She swallowed the lump that had suddenly formed in her throat. 'You had a very odd way of showing it.'

'I wasn't very proud of falling in love with my brother's girl. I've never hurt him in his life and I didn't intend to start.'

'What made you change your mind?'

'You did. It was when I began to realize you didn't

152

care for him deeply—in the right way—and I started to think it time for him to face some of the more unpleasant facts of life. He will recover but if you go now I will not.'

She let him draw her into his arms. In the past few days she had known so much confusion she wasn't sure this was real, but his kiss was real, and she had no more doubts.

'I was going to write to Paul from here . . .' she said, a little breathlessly.

'You have no need. He is in Athens too.'

Her eyes opened wide. 'Here?'

'He insisted on coming after you, but don't worry about him; he is safe at the home of a friend.'

Nicole did draw away from him then, gazing questioningly into his eyes. 'Safe? Then there is danger.'

He sighed. 'Yes.'

'From whom?'

'If I told you the name it would mean nothing to you.'

'Then tell me why he wants Paul.'

'It is for Paul to tell you himself when you see him.'

She frowned. 'Why can't *you* tell me?'

He smiled slightly. 'Because I love you and you don't love Paul any more. But he doesn't know that yet, so you're going to have to tell him when you see him. I still want to be on good terms with my brother; I don't want him to think I've influenced you against

153

him in any way.'

She turned away from him. 'So it is something that is detrimental to Paul's character.'

His arms went round her waist. 'Some might think so; I don't but it is for you to judge for yourself. That will be tomorrow. Tonight is ours, Nicole. Put on your best dress and we'll go out and I can show you my Athens.'

She whirled round on him, her momentary delight dying. 'We can't, Alex. I haven't anything to wear. . . .'

To her surprise he laughed. 'A woman's lament that's as old as time itself.'

She wasn't laughing though. 'I meant that I have nothing smart enough for the places we'll be going to. I didn't come equipped, you see.'

He gazed at her seriously. 'You have no idea where I am taking you. So far you have always looked wonderful—to me anyway and surely that is all that matters now.'

She went into his arms again. 'If only I'd known.'

'I had to let you decide for yourself about Paul, with no outside pressures from me.'

She laughed unevenly. 'Oh Alex, how little you know!' She bit her lip as she drew away from him slowly. 'What will happen about Xenia? Paul told me. . . .'

'Xenia and I have been very close for many years—I won't deny that, but my happiness to her, as hers is to me, is of the utmost importance. Leave Xenia

154

to me. She will understand.'

Nicole thought it remarkable how blind men so often were where women were concerned, even women they knew very well indeed. But she would not waste time feeling sorry for Xenia. She would have been glad to see Nicole married to Paul for her own selfish reasons, and she, like Paul, would survive this disappointment and love again.

'It will take me only five minutes to get changed,' she told him, her mind at last relieved of the terrible burden of Xenia Adrianou.

How different tonight would be from the lonely meal she had envisaged so short a time before.

He squeezed her hand. 'I'll wait for you downstairs. Don't keep me waiting too long.'

Nicole couldn't do anything for excitement. Her personal happiness was almost too great to be borne after so much despair, and could not be blighted even by thoughts of Paul. She hugged herself delightedly and wandered across to the window. The sky was inky black now, sprinkled with stars, and the ruins on the Acropolis hill were bathed in the golden glow of floodlights.

The sight of it reminded her of the view from Alex's apartment—her home-to-be after it was redecorated, of course. Nothing of Xenia's would remain except for the sculptures, she decided. After a moment or two she laughed out loud at her own thoughts and hurried over to the wardrobe to find something suitable to wear. At last, after a great deal of deliberation over what was a very narrow choice, she decided to wear a yellow silk trouser suit and began to fling off her clothes.

She sang happily to herself as she dressed carefully and was downstairs in no more than the promised five minutes. His car was waiting outside and they drove towards Piraeus through the straggling Athens suburbs.

Never had Nicole spent a happier evening. The future was settled and when Alex asked her to marry him and remain in Athens she would agree immediately. There were no doubts on this occasion. To be with him for ever was all she asked, and if it meant giving up the boutique she would do so gladly.

They had dinner in a little *taverna* overlooking the harbour of Turcolimano, from which they could watch the yachts and fishing boats moored there. Every boat was lit up against the inky darkness of sea and sky, turning the little harbour into a fairyland of light.

The *taverna* was an unpretentious place with fishing nets masking otherwise bare walls, but the food was delicious—*souvlakia,* the Greek equivalent of shish kebab—and the proprietor knew Alex and welcomed him warmly.

Afterwards he drove her back to Athens, to another *taverna* in the Plaka district, the old part of the city which lies at the foot of the Acropolis. Its bal-

conied buildings and steep cobbled streets hadn't
changed for centuries.

This *taverna* was quite different to the one at
Turcolimano. Here was a place no larger, but it was
crammed with people who had only come to dance
or to listen to the music, which went on continuously,
echoing Nicole's own feeling of happiness.

They listened to bouzouki music and danced, and
when the hour grew very late they wandered hand
in hand through the steep cobbled streets of the Plaka
back to her hotel in the modern part of Athens close
by.

'I wish this evening need never end,' she said
happily as he unlocked her bedroom door for her.

He kissed her briefly on the lips. 'This is only the
first of many. You realize that, don't you?'

'It will never be as perfect as this one.'

His eyes met hers and then she was in his arms
once more. At last he released her. 'I think it's time
I was leaving now. I'll see you tomorrow.'

Uncertainly she said, 'When shall I see Paul?'

All evening she had deliberately shut out all
thoughts of Paul, of having to see him and tell him
she was in love with his brother. It was a task she did
not relish but one which she must face, and the
sooner the better.

'Tomorrow. He knows I have come to find you
tonight and he will be waiting impatiently for my
return with news of you.'

'You're not going to tell him about us, are you?'

'I think it would be best for you to tell him.'

'Then you'd best arrange for me to see him.'

'In the morning I'm going to see the police and get some advice. I have a friend there who will help me. After that I'll come here and take you to where Paul is staying.'

She nodded slowly, saying, 'Be truthful with me, Alex. How serious is this business?'

He sighed. 'It could be very serious.'

'And it must be to do with the trouble he was in before he left Greece.' He nodded. 'I don't understand it at all, Alex. That's all over now.'

'For Paul, I'm afraid, it isn't. You will know more about it tomorrow. I will make sure he tells you.' He bent and kissed her again and she held on to him tightly. 'And then,' he whispered, 'we can discuss our own future.' He drew away from her. 'Sweet dreams, my darling.'

'They would be. Everything would be perfect if only I were not so afraid.'

'You have no need to be.'

'But I have. If Paul's in danger . . .'

'He will be protected. I'm going to ensure that he is. Go to bed and try to think only of me.'

He smiled halfheartedly and she tried to respond. 'You know he tried to make out it was someone with a grudge against you. . . .'

He nodded slowly. 'That is one thing I must tell

158

you. However much our relationship has changed there is still one area of contention which might cause us trouble in the future. . . .' She looked at him questioningly. 'The matter of my relationship with my brother. This idea you have that I want to dominate Paul's life, make all his decisions for him. . . .'

'It doesn't matter now,' she said gently.

'It isn't true. If Paul wanted to make his own life away from me I would be only too pleased. I think you must know it isn't possible.'

'Yes,' she agreed, sighing gently. 'I've realized it. Paul has to have someone to lean on. I didn't want it to be me so I had no right to resent it being you. You must do whatever you can for him.'

He kissed her briefly and then was gone. Nicole went into her room. She was elated, and yet she felt fear too, for whatever it was that threatened Paul must certainly affect Alex and herself too.

Chapter Nine

A letter arrived from Sally the next morning, telling her business had been good whilst she'd been away and that she was managing fine with the help of her sister-in-law. Nicole warmed to the friendly, newsy letter from home and was happy that her absence had caused no hardship.

She was glad to know that life was going on as normal somewhere. Poor Sally would be staggered to learn she *was* getting married after all, but to a different man, one she hadn't even known two weeks ago. In all the six months since she had met Paul, Nicole felt she didn't understand him as well as she knew Alex now.

By the time she had finished reading the letter, the porter arrived with a basket of roses. There was no note with them, but as Nicole buried her face in their velvet softness she knew very well who had sent them.

She was thinking of going downstairs to wait in

the foyer of the hotel so she could see him the moment he arrived, when there came a knock on her bedroom door. She was glad he had come, for it was already growing late. Nicole had slept far longer than she had intended, but they had returned late last night and sleep was not quick to claim her. Her mind was too alive with thoughts of Alex, of their evening together, every precious moment of it. And then, of course, there was a worry too, a worry about Paul and what might happen to him.

Nicole rushed across to the door and pulled it open, her smile fading when she saw who was standing there.

Xenia said, 'May I come in Nicole?'

Nicole opened the door wider and then followed Xenia inside. She sat down in one of the easy chairs which stood by the window, mainly because her knees had gone so weak she could hardly stand. 'Sit down, Xenia,' she invited but the woman remained standing, towering over her.

It was obvious she knew all about Nicole's relationship with Alex. Nicole assumed, to be fair to Xenia, Alex had lost not time in telling her. But however understanding she might appear to him, at that moment she was beside herself with anger.

'Well, you are what is known, I believe, as a dark horse.'

Nicole stared down at her hands. 'What can I say, Xenia? It's so very hard to explain. I'm not sure

161

I really understand what has happened myself.'

She sank down into a chair opposite Nicole's and fumbled in her bag for her cigarette case. Even now, having undergone such a shock, she was only slightly out of control of her feelings.

'You needn't say anything.' She drew in a lungful of smoke and snapped out the flame in her lighter. 'What sickens me is the way you pretended concern for Paul, and all the time you were setting out to get Alex.'

Nicole's eyes blazed with anger now. 'I did not set out to "get" Alex, and I am concerned for Paul. I didn't mean to fall in love with Alex, or, I believe, he with me. I didn't dream he loved me until last night.' Her voice softened. 'Alex will be happy with me. Be glad for him.'

Xenia continued to gaze at Nicole steadily. Gazing back at her Nicole could not help but wonder why Alex had chosen her. Even having sustained what must have been a great shock and disappointment, this woman looked as cool and as elegant as ever. She had taken the time to dress in a smart grey two piece and to make sure her face and hair style were immaculately done. Nicole felt shabby by comparison and couldn't help but wonder if this, perhaps had been Xenia's main intention.

'I am sure in all this talk of love you haven't thought of the consequences of what you are doing—to Alex.'

Nicole looked at her appealingly. 'I know you've been acquainted with him for a great many years, Xenia—he holds you in such great esteem—but that isn't always a basis for marriage. I've known Paul for six months but even if I'd known him for six years. . . .'

She laughed harshly. 'You are so naive. You talk so glibly about love as if that is a panacea.' She sat back and crossed one leg over the other. 'My dear, I know everything about Alex. I understand him perfectly, know what his needs really are. What can you do for him? And before you answer "Love him" just what will it matter in six months or a year anyway? If I were at his side, I have so much influence, know so many of the people who can be of use to him in his work, which, let there be no doubt, is the most important thing of all to Alex. Once the honeymoon is over . . .'

She got to her feet and leaned over the table to stub out her half-smoked cigarette. Then she straightened up again and looked directly at Nicole. 'Think about it, my dear. Think about it very carefully and you will acknowledge that I am right. You will, I know, want what is best for Alex.'

Nicole watched her go. She had been so certain that the love they had for each other was all that mattered, but now she was shattered. What Xenia had said was so true.

She had little time to brood, however, for she did

163

then hurry downstairs, seating herself where she could see the door, and Xenia had been gone only a few minutes when Paul came limping into the foyer. She leaped to her feet the moment she saw him.

'Paul! You have no business to be here.'

'I've made it my business,' he said tersely.

'Did Alex tell you I was here?'

'Alex told me you were in Athens but he wouldn't tell me where! Wait until I see him,' he fumed. 'I want to know exactly what he thinks he is doing.'

'Don't blame Alex. He's only acting for your good—trying to protect you—and you should have done as he asked.' Her eyes narrowed slightly. 'If he didn't tell you, how did you find out where I was?'

'Xenia telephoned this morning to tell me. She thought I might like to know.'

'You'd better sit down now you're here. How is the ankle?'

'Fine.'

He eased himself into a chair and Nicole sat down too. She felt acutely uncomfortable now she was face to face with him. Looking at him now, at those flawless features that had thrilled her once, he seemed to be nothing more than a stranger. She couldn't imagine why she had ever contemplated marrying him.

'Shall I order a drink for you?' she asked quickly to hide her embarrassment.

He stared at her. 'Just tell me why you left, Nicole.'

164

She sighed. 'I had to go, Paul. Please understand . . .' He kept on looking at her. 'I thought we needed some breathing space,' she added lamely.

He flicked a non-existent fleck from his trousers. 'Why don't you just say you don't want to marry me? That is it, isn't it?'

She put her hand to her head. 'Oh, Paul, I'm sorry. I'm a coward and there isn't an easy way.' She did look at him then, appealingly, willing him to be understanding and knowing that was a vain hope.

'I've known it for a long while—even before you did, I think—all the time you were vacillating. But I kept on hoping.' He sighed. Anger would have been easier for her to bear. 'There are times, Nicky, when I wonder what is wrong with me.'

'Oh, there is nothing wrong with you, Paul! There are lots of other girls here in Athens, and all of them far more suited to you than I am.'

He smiled sadly and it tore at her heart. 'I suppose you'll be going back to London as soon as you can, to that boutique of yours. That is where your heart really is.'

'Did Xenia only tell you where I was?'

'She thought Alex might let you go away without letting me near you, and that I would want an opportunity of talking to you. She was right, of course. I was going mad there not knowing what was happening, what Alex was saying to you.' He paused. 'He is the reason you've changed your mind about me, isn't he?' He leaned forward. 'For a while you *were* mine; I know it!'

'We were never suited.'

'He was against you from the start,' he said bitterly. 'I thought it didn't matter, but to you it did.'

Nicole swallowed hard. 'It wasn't for the reason we thought, Paul. He loves me and wants to marry me.' He raised his eyes to hers slowly. 'And I love him too.'

There was no doubt the possibility had never occurred to him, just as it hadn't entered her mind either. Alex was not a man to give way to his emotions easily, nor wear his heart on his sleeve.

After a long moment of stunned silence, Paul cried, 'I don't believe it!'

'It's true. It happened very suddenly, Paul. That's why I left Kyros as I did. I was confused and unhappy—and I never wanted to hurt you. I'm so sorry it's turned out like this.'

'Sorry! You must be crazy! Alex will marry Xenia. Don't you see what he's trying to do to us? He wants to part us for good so he's doing it this way. It's irrevocable for us but once he has succeeded he'll find an excuse to drop you.'

Nicole stared at him with wide-eyed disbelief. 'You were supposed to be in love with me yourself, so why is it so impossible for Alex to be?' He didn't answer; he just glared fiercely at her and she said, 'You professed to love me and yet you saw a lot of

Sofia while we were apart.'

'She meant nothing to me.'

Nicole smiled then. 'Your logic is questionable, Paul. Alex does mean something to me and I suppose if I subscribed to your way of thinking that would be wrong!

'I think,' she went on in a gentle voice, 'you've never really been in love with anyone but yourself,' adding wearily, 'All this talking isn't going to get us anywhere. You really should go now, Paul.'

His hands were clenched into fists. 'Yes, I'll go. I'm going to find my precious brother and wring his neck!'

She leaned forward. 'No, Paul! He's terrified of hurting you. He's with the police now trying to arrange some protection for you. And speaking of that, it's time you told me what it's all about. It concerns a girl called Maria, doesn't it?'

He stood up and looked at her with eyes filled with smouldering hate. 'Didn't Alex tell you?'

'No. He wanted you to tell me yourself.'

He pushed his chair back with a jerk of his hand. He was smiling grimly, a travesty of a smile. 'I'll bet he does! Well, I'm not going to. There's no reason why I should. You're nothing to me now and he's nothing to me any more.'

Nicole jumped up. 'If I'm going to come between you and Alex I'd rather go away.'

'Oh, how noble of you, but don't trouble,' he said

contemptuously. 'I might have known he'd have you too. He's always had everything, done everything. I've never had a chance to equal him. Everything I do is wrong. He has a marvellous capacity for making me look a prize ninny! I can't compete with him at all!'

'You don't even try!' she protested. 'You've always leaned on him, turned to him, and he's always been there, cushioning you from each of life's little knocks. Who has ever cushioned Alex? You've always taken everything he's had to give; and not just material things. And now you resent any happiness he might find with me all because beneath all that hero-worship you're blindly jealous of him!'

'You're so right, Paul. You can't compete with him. He's a man and that is something you will never be!'

His face grew red and furiously he turned on his heel and rushed away from her, almost knocking over two old ladies who were just coming into the hotel. Nicole took no notice of the people who were staring at them; she hurried after him, calling his name over and over again. If he heard he took no notice, but she guessed that he was really deaf to everything at that moment except his own boiling hate and jealousy towards Alex and herself.

For once the road outside the hotel was not choked with traffic and so he didn't have to pause on the edge of the pavement. It was just as well, for he didn't stop to look right or left. Nicole hesitated on the

168

edge of the roadway., wondering whether she should go after him or wait to warn Alex of what had happened. She was hovering uncertainly when she caught sight of someone on the other side of the road, someone who was watching Paul—the man she had seen on Kyros the other day.

Paul hadn't seen him; he was still rushing, half limping towards him. Nicole shouted, 'Paul, look out!'

He stopped in the centre of the road when he too saw the man. The look of horror on his face was something she would never forget before he turned almost blindly, seeking escape, and began to run back towards Nicole, but by that time the traffic lights had changed to green and a great mass of vehicles surged forward. Paul seemed unaware of the blaring horns and flashing lights or of the deafening roar of their engines. He just dashed blindly into the path of the oncoming vehicles.

Nicole's eyes opened wide in horror and she screamed, 'Go back!' but he didn't hear her. She covered her face as a car bore down on him, unable to stop for the terrified man who had dashed in front of him.

There was a scream, the squealing of brakes and when she looked again Paul was lying beneath one of the cars. She gave a cry of anguish, of disbelief, and started forward, only someone pulled her back. She whirled round and saw that it was Alex who was at her side, his fingers biting into the soft flesh of her arm, but he was staring at his brother who was lying broken in the road.

'He was running away from that man!' she cried hysterically, and when she looked again a moment later there was no sign of him anywhere.

Nicole could not stop crying. She was lying on the black settee in Alex's apartment, sobbing her heart out. Everyone had gone now, the police and reporters, and while they'd been present she had managed to keep calm. But now the room was silent again, except for the sound of her crying and that seemed very loud.

Alex came silently across the room and knelt down on the carpet by her side. 'Calm yourself, Nicole,' he said gently. When his words had no effect on her he stroked her hair but she still kept her head averted from him. 'If you continue to cry so much you will make yourself ill. Here, drink this brandy. It will do you good.'

She shook her head and he said, 'Then please stop crying—for my sake.'

'I can't . . . help it,' she sobbed. 'It's all . . . my . . . fault. If I hadn't . . . rushed away . . . from Kyros and come to . . . Athens . . . Paul wouldn't have . . . followed me . . . and that man . . . wouldn't have found him. . . .'

He put his arms around her and drew her unwilingly towards him. 'The blame is no one's. You must understand that or you'll go mad. The blame could rest equally with Xenia for telling him where he could find you, or with me for not being with him every minute of the day. I could go on finding excuses, Nicole, but no one can have such responsibility for another human being. This is something I have learned, and you must realize it too if you are going to find any peace of mind at all. Paul will be all right. He'll be in hospital a long time, but he *will* be all right in time.'

He got up to sit beside her on the settee and she allowed him to hold her as if he were cradling a child. 'It was all so horrible, Alex. To see it happening and not be able to do anything to prevent it.'

'No one could.'

'And it was worse because we'd had words. I said some very hurtful things to him.'

'No doubt they were both overdue and deserved. You have never spared me your tongue. At the moment it doesn't even occur to you that you've hurt me, but if I were to be badly hurt, or die tomorrow, you would soon remember and regret all that's been said between us.'

'What,' she asked, dabbing at her eyes, 'will happen to the man? He was gone when I looked for him again. It was almost as if I'd dreamed he was there, only Paul saw him too. . . .'

'Andreas Constantin,' he said heavily. 'Nothing will

171

happen to him. I doubt if we shall ever see him again. He has avenged his sister.'

'But he caused Paul's accident. It's a miracle he isn't dead. He must be found and punished!'

When Alex looked at her his eyes were bleak. 'Punished for what, Nicole? He didn't even touch Paul. Technically he is innocent of everything. Paul's own fear caused his accident, nothing else; that and the guilt he has had to bear for so long. Perhaps when this is all over, when he is well again, he will know peace at last. I think he will realize he has paid dearly for what he did.'

'Will you tell me about it now, Alex? The whole story.'

'It goes back a long time.' He drank down the brandy he had brought for her. 'I have been guilty of great omissions where Paul is concerned. When he was a child whatever he wanted he was given. I took great pride in that because the novelty of being able to give was so new to me, but the trouble was he grew up believing everything he wanted he could have, and nothing he did would have any serious consequences. Life was only a game.'

'Now who is blaming himself?' she said softly.

He smiled sadly to himself. 'That is something which will never change. I will have to bear that guilt all the time when Paul is painfully mending and afterwards too. I must learn not to burden you with such thoughts though.

'The trouble began while he was at university. He has always been a bright boy and he did well for a while. He had no head for politics. What did it matter to him which government ruled the country? But then he met a girl called Maria Constantin, who was also a student at the university although she came from quite a different background to Paul. She was a very lovely girl. I had to agree with him there. In fact, she looked rather like you. I noticed that the day I first met you, but I wasn't surprised; Paul had been besotted by her at the time and haunted ever since. He must have chosen you quite unconsciously because of the resemblance.'

Nicole stared down at the carpet as he went on, 'The girl was mixed up with a reactionary group within the university, and her brother was the leader. Paul has always been easily impressed and it wasn't long before he was heavily involved in their activities. It was probably a deliberate ploy, in the hope that my newspaper could be of help to them at some time. I doubted that Maria was as in love with Paul as he was with her—she was altogether too hard a case to let her emotions become too much involved.' He sighed. 'Perhaps I am wrong. I don't really know.

'The result was that his work suffered and he was mixing with dangerous people.'

'Didn't you try to talk to him about it?'

'Oh yes, on many occasions. He understood my attitude and even sympathized with it, but the problem was, he thought, I was too ignorant and out of touch! He saw himself covered in glory, as the liberator of an oppressed people, never realizing that those who would liberate us would put Greece in the grips of a worse dictator.

'The others were clever but Paul was not so discreet about what he was doing. He never guarded his tongue, and it wasn't long before the police arrested him at a student meeting.'

'As soon as I heard, I set about having him released from custody, but it took a few hours. Naturally Paul didn't know of my efforts on his behalf and he must have felt very much alone and terrified. It was the first time he had been in a situation so grave or so potentially dangerous. They didn't hurt him physically; there was no need to. All they had to do was tell him what they would do to him if he didn't tell them who he was associated with.' He sighed. 'You know Paul as well as I do, Nicole; he told them everything they wanted to know.'

'The others were arrested?'

He nodded. 'And Paul was released. I decided it would be best to send him away, out of harm's way for a while—to London as it turned out.'

'Surely this man, Constantin, couldn't bear a grudge for such a reason for all this time.'

'The political police were not renowned for their gentleness, Nicole, and those he associated with were far tougher than Paul, committed to their cause to a very great degree. They didn't confess so easily, as Paul, deep in his heart knew very well would be the case. But it wasn't until later that I discovered at some time Maria had died in custody.'

Nicole felt ill. 'How dreadful! Oh, poor Paul. He must have been wretched, but he wasn't to know what would happen to them.'

'To be honest about it he would have closed his mind to it; but he did know, to say the least, that their imprisonment would not be a comfortable one. The burden of guilt in the affair wasn't easy for him to bear.'

'But it has been a long time.'

'Constantin remained in custody until a few months ago, when, as you know, the junta collapsed and all political prisoners were freed. One of them came to warn me that Constantin was going to find Paul and exact some kind of revenge for what had happened to Maria.

'Naturally, I wrote to warn him not to return to Greece, never imagining that Constantin would discover where Paul had gone and follow him there. I don't know what he intended to do. Perhaps he wanted to terrorise him before taking any other action. He probably wanted Paul to do exactly what he did— panic and return to Greece. I don't believe now that Constantin ever intended to harm Paul physically himself; that would have put him at risk too, put him back in prison. We really don't know what were his plans, only that he was ruthless and was capable of anything. He must have been very tenacious to find Paul as he did. He had only his own resources, but he managed to find him all the same, follow both you and myself at various times, and come very close to finding him on Kyros. I tried to have him traced myself but he was elusive too.'

'He must have been fanatically dedicated to track Paul down. It probably took him months.'

'Fanatic is the right description.'

'Oh. I wish I'd never come here!'

He looked down at her for a moment and then, putting his finger beneath her chin, he raised it until she was looking at him. 'Just think what we would have missed.'

'But Paul. . . .'

'He will mend and he will find happiness of his own. You know, I have the feeling all of this was inevitable. One way or another Constantin would have found a way even if it took him years, and Paul would have been reduced to a mental wreck before long.

'All that remains now is for us to make a future together. This mustn't be allowed to interfere with that.'

'Alex, if we do . . . well, Paul was very bitter about us. He'd never forgive you as long as I was there to remind him, and apart from that I would always remind *you* of what happened today. . . .'

'I don't particularly want to forget.

'What we decided about each other last night has nothing to do with this tragedy, Nicole. I know we're of different countries and we've already realized that our ideas differ, but that doesn't alter the basic fact—we love each other.'

'But Paul. . . .'

'He will get used to the idea. By the time he has half recovered he will have realized it is you and I who were meant for each other and he probably had a lucky escape.' He looked at her. 'I'm asking you not to leave me now, Nicole.'

'I don't want to, Alex. I don't doubt that you love me, but perhaps you would be better marrying someone who can further your business interests.'

'Xenia, for instance?' he asked gently. She didn't answer. 'I have known her for fourteen years. She's been a good friend and yes, perhaps I would have married her if I hadn't met you, but I don't want a wife who will be an asset to me. I have enough assets already. I just want someone like you, who will be here to welcome me home when I come back at the end of the day. That is what most men want, isn't it?'

'You are not an ordinary man, Alex.'

'But I am.' His hand tightened over hers. 'I assure you I am. There were no doubts in your mind last night,' he reminded her and then turned her round so she faced him. 'The only way you can be free of me is if you tell me you don't love me after all.'

Her eyes filled with tears. 'I can't,' she whispered. 'It wouldn't be true.'

He drew her close and kissed her gently. 'That is all I wanted to know. I can't promise that the immediate future will be idyllic, but at least we shall face it together.'

Ride to
Romance

Ride to Romance

Romance

Joan Murray

Poor little fellow, he looks neglected and half starved, she thought compassionately, as she saw his bare feet and a bleeding scratch down one leg. Then the door of the nearest caravan was opened and a shaft of light fell on his face.

"Mark! Mark darling, it's me, the taxi lady."

In five seconds he was in her arms, clinging to her as if he would never left her go!

CHAPTER 1

SHOPPING basket over her arm, Jill Railton reached
the end of Chapel Road and paused at the corner of
Castlebridge's main shopping street, looking up and down
with interest and satisfaction. It seemed incredible that
any place within fifteen miles of the Sussex coast could
have changed so little in ten years. There was the same
display of assorted frocks, blouses and stockings in the
window of Gales on one side of her and the same, rather
unenterprising arrangement of slightly faded cards advertising properties for sale in Bluett the estate agent on
the other. Across the High Street she could see the little
town's biggest garage, with the van of Mr Mead the
butcher taking in petrol, while the fourth corner of the
crossroads was still occupied by the tea room run by Miss
Lovelace and her sister. She could see Miss Jenny Lovelace now, in her flowered overall, laying the small tables
in the windows, and looking not a day older than she
had when nine-year-old Jill had gone in there with
Nanny for the real cream ice which was the two ladies'
speciality.

Glancing at the list Nanny had given her, she turned
up the street towards the grocer. Now she found changes.
The old stationer's had gone, replaced by W. H. Smith,
and Boots the chemist stood in the place of the queer,
old-fashioned premises of Mr Josiah Need—founded
1795. Woolworths was there, too, and a big supermarket

filled the space formerly occupied by a grocer, a sweet shop and a shoe repairer. With a sigh she joined the stream of women passing through the open doors, picked up a wire basket and started round the stalls. It was much more sensible, of course, and probably much cheaper, too, but she could remember quite clearly the day—her fourth birthday—when old William Funnell, with his gold-rimmed spectacles and grey overall, had taken a little pink sugar mouse from a box on the shelf behind him and given it to her as he was handing Nanny her change.

Thrusting such vain regrets out of her mind, she concentrated on the task in hand, and soon filled her basket and took her place in one of the queues making their way towards the pay desks. Evidently Friday morning was a very busy time, as there were at least a dozen women in front of her and most of them had brimming loads.

It was then that she got a less pleasant reminder of the past. A tall, angular lady, neat and prim, stood beside her at the end of the other procession. This was Miss Gregory, who lived opposite Kilkenny Cottage, and her presence and disapproving frowns had been the one disadvantage when Jill had spent her holidays there as a child. She and her closest friend, the widowed Mrs Meadows, who lived in a little house next to the chapel where her husband had been a deacon, were well known in Castlebridge for their scathing comments on people in general and their gossip about the inhabitants of their own small town in particular.

Suddenly Jill realised that Mrs Meadows was standing just in front of her, and she wondered whose character the two women would tear to shreds while they were moving up their respective queues. She soon found out!

"There you are, Hilda. I've been hoping to see you. Such goings on, you'll never believe." Miss Gregory drew a little closer, so that her words were only audible to the people nearest to her.

"Oh, what has been happening?"

"It's that Miss Williams who lives opposite to me. It's difficult to credit, but do you know she has actually got young Jill Railton staying with her. I'm surprised that she can dare, after all the disgrace and scandal.'

Jill went first red and then white. What should she do? But Miss Gregory went on eagerly and she had no option but to hear or move out of her place in the queue.

"I knew she'd got somebody coming when I saw her taking down the curtains in the spare bedroom for washing yesterday and cleaning the windows. I had a word with her while she was hanging them out, but she didn't say anything although I dropped a hint or two. But later on Doctor Mayhew called and she walked down her path with him. I happened to be cutting a few flowers in the garden near my gate and I overheard him saying to her: 'Now, Miss Williams, you let young Jill do the work for a while. It won't do her any harm and the rest will be just the thing for you.' So then I knew."

"Well, I suppose she is sorry for the girl. Mr Railton gave her the cottage she lives in, didn't he?"

"Dear me, no! It was Mrs Railton who left the cottage to Miss Williams, who had been her nanny when she was a child and then had looked after Jill. Don't you remember the story? Mr Railton was just a clerk in the office of Sir Martin Greening, who was a barrister and very wealthy. Sir Martin had only got one daughter and she was a delicate girl, rather plain and ordinary-looking. Ernest Railton was one of those very handsome men—glowing with health and charm

7

—and he set his cap at her and swept her off her feet. Then he used all the money he could get from her to set up on his own. She didn't live long, her health deteriorated after Jill's birth, and she died when the child was nine."

"Was that when Miss Williams came to live at the cottage?"

"Soon afterwards, though she and Jill had been down there for holidays quite often. I don't think she got on with Mr Railton; I suppose she could see through him; and as soon as he could after his wife's death he gave her the sack and sent the child to boarding school."

Jill boiled! She opened her mouth to pour out an eager defence of her father but then closed it again helplessly. Like so many other ill-natured remarks, there was too much truth in these statements for her to deny them. Daddy had married Mummy partly for her money. Her mother had been plain and delicate. But love had come afterwards; love and a tender concern for his ailing wife. This was shown clearly by his refusal to consider remarriage after her death, though Jill could think of at least a dozen women who would gladly have become her stepmother if her father had given them the slightest encouragement.

But Mrs Meadows was eager for more information. "What was the child like? Did she take after her father?"

"No, poor thing! I've never seen a plainer child— straight fair hair and eyes that looked far too big for her face. You'd have thought her father could at least have given her his looks, wouldn't you, although one hopes for her own sake that she hasn't inherited his character!"

"Has she arrived yet? Have you seen her?"

"I've seen her car—a great flashy thing—big enough

for a taxi! Wouldn't you think, Hilda, that with her father going bankrupt, and ruining hundreds of poor people at the same time, and then shooting himself to avoid facing trial, that his daughter would at least have the decency to be unostentatious. But there! I suppose as she is going to marry that young Lord Someone-or-other she feels that people will overlook anything she does."

Now it was Hilda Meadows' turn. "Mavis, didn't you know? I saw it in the paper a week or two ago. 'The marriage which has been arranged, etc., will not now take place.' It's rather amusing really, isn't it? The father marries for money, and it looks as if the daughter was going to be married for the cash she would bring with her. If seems as if there is some justice in the world after all."

Jill didn't listen any more. In her mind she re-lived that scene with Alastair and heard his embarrassed voice. "You know how it is, old thing. The family name and all that sort of stuff." She had pulled off the big ring and handed it to him without a word and had left him as soon as she could. At the time it had seemed only one more blow following a battering which had left her numb and shattered, and now, three weeks later, when the first shock had worn off, she found herself wondering rather vaguely how she felt about it. Heartbroken? No, certainly not that. Hurt? Well, a little perhaps, but not badly. Angry? No, not even that. Alastair had been kind and attentive and she had been fond of him. But, looking back over the past three months, twelve miserable weeks in which she had grown older by almost as many years, she realised that they had had little in common. She had really consented to marry him more to please her father than for any other reason. Their years together would have been friendly ones, and they would have gone their own separate ways, but surely there was more in marriage than that.

She was recalled to the present by finding herself at the pay counter. She waited until the girl had checked the goods, paid the bill and walked slowly out into the sunshine. All the joy she had felt in being back again in Castlebridge had gone, banished by the conversation she had overheard. She had hoped to find peace and security here. Nobody would know her and nobody would connect her with the events of the past few months. Now that illusion was shattered.

What should she do? It seemed rather cowardly to run away, but if she stayed it might cause unpleasantness for dear old Nanny. On the other hand, Nanny would definitely be glad of her help, both financially and with the work of the cottage.

As she stood irresolutely on the pavement, her other errands forgotten, two young women who had been behind her in the queue came through the doors.

"My word," said the taller one, "the Castlebridge Cats were in good form today, weren't they? Did you hear them? I wonder who the girl is. I'm sorry for her anyway, living right opposite Miss Gregory. She won't get much peace."

"Oh, I shouldn't think she would stay. You read the case in the papers, didn't you? That man Ernest Railton was practically a millionaire until he started the speculating which ruined him. I expect the girl has got plenty salted away. I wonder what she is like. One of those useless creatures, I suppose; finishing school in Paris and never done a hand's turn of work in her life. Well, I must get on. 'Bye for now."

Jill boiled again. So that was what people would think

10

of her. Well, she hadn't got a lot of her father's money "salted away". She hadn't kept a penny of his. She had a small income from investments left to her by her mother, but she would need to earn more somehow. Unfortunately that wretched girl was right in one way. She was useless. She had never been trained for anything. But she wouldn't run away. She would stay right here in Castlebridge and find a job. She would help Nanny run the cottage and pay her enough to make sure the old lady's money troubles were over. In the meantime she had shopping to finish. Settling her basket more firmly on her arm, she strode up the street in search of Mr Mead the butcher, Mr Cherrill the greengrocer and Mr Pease the pork butcher, whose sausages were, in Nanny's opinion, the best in the whole of Sussex!

CHAPTER 2

HER shopping finished, Jill set off home. Instead of retracing her steps and going down Chapel Road she took the slightly longer route which passed the station and then crossed the Castlebridge recreation ground. For a while she sat on one of the wooden seats watching a group of boisterous youngsters from the primary school, whose buildings backed on to the park. A young man was putting some thirty or forty boys through a course of exercises. This was obviously a new experience for the children and they had no idea of keeping time with each other. In vain the teacher counted and shouted. One boy would touch his toes five times while the one next to him touched his twice!

Why on earth doesn't he do it with them? Jill looked with some irritation at the teacher, who was standing behind one of the seats and resting his hands on the back. Then he called the boys to a halt and brought three of them to the front. He put these through the exercise until they were doing it in unison and then increased the number until the whole class had got the hang of what was required of them. He seems to have plenty of patience, she thought grudgingly, even if he is too lazy to do the exercises himself.

Her attention was distracted by the gambols of a small girl and a puppy, and the next time she looked at the boys they were forming into line to march back into school. As the last ones passed him the teacher took his place behind and Jill felt her cheeks blazing. He was terribly lame! No wonder he had been supporting himself by the back of the seat. It was a marvel that he had not taken the exercises sitting down.

Glancing at her watch, she got to her feet to continue her walk, and her mind went back to the immediate problem of finding some kind of employment. It would be no good asking Nanny. She, dear old soul, would insist that they had plenty of money between them, and if she helped in the house that would be all that could be expected of her. Jill was determined to show Miss Gregory that she was not just sponging on Nanny, but was making her own way.

She left the recreation ground and walked down a long road of small houses. She paused beside one where an elderly man was working in his little garden, hoeing the beds which were ablaze with sweet williams and snapdragons. This was Mr Wood, who ran practically the only taxi in the town. Jill remembered him well from the times he had driven her and Nanny from the station to Kilkenny Cottage for their holidays.

"Good morning, Mr Wood! It's nice to see you again."

The old fellow straightened his back at the sound of her voice, but for a few seconds he looked at her in a puzzled way. Then he gave her a beaming smile.

"Why, it's little Miss Jill! I reckoned I knew your voice, but I'd never have known you. My goodness me, Miss, you are a regular ugly duckling turned into a swan, aren't you."

He opened the gate and insisted on taking her basket and showing her round his garden. At the back of the cottage was a slightly larger patch than the one in front,

13

and here he had rows of lettuce and peas and a small bed of strawberries, just ripening.

"Let's see if we can find you a nice one, Miss," he said, and Jill couldn't help smiling as she realised that he had spoken just as he used to do when she was a small girl.

"Ah, there's a beauty!"

"Lovely!" She bit into it appreciatively. "It's funny how much nicer they taste when you eat them straight from the plant. How is the taxi going, Mr Wood? Have you still got the same old Humber?"

"Well, I have, just for one week more, Miss Jill, but poor old Hannah Humber is getting very old—like her owner—and the chap at the garage told me he didn't think she'll pass the test again. The Insurance Company is getting a bit difficult, too, owing to my age, so I've decided to give up and take my pension. I'm sorry to do it in a way—there's folk who depend on me—but what with one thing and another it seems best."

"Oh dear, what will people do? Does anyone else run a taxi in Castlebridge now?"

"Yes, there are two chaps who have hackney carriage licences. They usually meet the trains and that kind of thing. I suppose most of my regulars will have one or the other of them. Of course, there isn't the taxi business there was when I started, most folk have their own cars, but there are a few who'll miss me for a while."

"I'm sure they will. Dear old Hannah Humber! She always meant the beginning of my holiday for me." Back at the gate Jill took her basket and turned to go. Then she stopped. "Mr Wood, I've just had an idea. I need a job badly. Couldn't I run a taxi and take over your regulars?"

14

"You, Miss Jill? But you are only a child. Have you got a driving licence?"

"Goodness, yes! I got that more than a year ago, and last January I passed the advanced driving test. I often drove my father. He used to say that he'd got too much else to think about and couldn't concentrate on the traffic, so when Bale, his chauffeur, wasn't on duty I drove instead. I know quite a bit about upkeep, too. I've always been interested in engines, and last winter I went to the Technical School and took a car maintenance course."

"But what about a car? One of these little Mini things wouldn't be much use, and though I'd willingly let you have old Hannah, she wouldn't do either if she failed the test."

"I've got a car—a big Rover. I heard Miss Gregory talking about it this morning and she said it was big enough for a taxi. Daddy gave it to me for my nineteenth birthday because I used to enjoy driving it so much."

A lump came into her throat as she remembered her birthday morning. It was the first occasion on which she had had a suspicion that things were going wrong for her father.

"I was going to give you a little Mini for your own use, Poppet," he had said, "but things are a bit tight at the moment."

She had been thrilled. It was such a splendid car, big and powerful, and it had been one of her father's fancies to have his cars especially enamelled in royal blue and silver, so she had the satisfaction—or so she had felt at the time—of knowing that her Rover was unique. Now she could wish that it was dark green or grey or some commonplace colour which would not be so noticeable, but it didn't really matter. The main thing was

15

that it would hold five or six people, counting one or two in the front beside her.

"Tell me, Mr Wood, what do I have to do to become a taxi driver? Do I have to have a special licence or something?"

"Not unless you want to be registered as a hackney carriage. I never bothered with that myself; I just took private hire jobs; but if you wanted to take your place outside the station or tout for jobs in the street you'd have to have hackney carriage plates."

"Oh, no, I shouldn't want to do that. I shall need some time to help Miss Williams with the house and the garden. So what do I do? Just put up a notice on the gate, something like yours, saying 'Taxi for Hire'?"

"No, you'd have to apply to the Council for permission first. But as I'm giving up I should think you'd get that all right if you produced your advanced test certificate. Let me know how you get on, Miss Jill, and when you are ready to start and I'll tell my regulars about you. Oh, there's one other thing. I have a trip every morning —Monday to Friday—in term-time, taking six youngsters from here to the main road at Cinder Cross. They have to get there by eight-thirty to catch a bus into the Grammar School. The Education Authorities pay for that one—quite well, too—but you'd be wise to make sure before you apply for the job that your Insurance Company will cover you for carrying six children. Your policy probably says how many passengers the car is allowed to hold."

"Thank you so much. It will be splendid if I can fix it. I have been wondering all the morning what kind of job I can do. I'd hate to have to work indoors all day, even if I was qualified to do anything, which I'm afraid I'm not."

Old Mr Wood nodded sympathetically. Obviously he was quite familiar with her circumstances, but with the natural courtesy of his kind he forebore to comment. Jill shook hands with him and hurried home to Kilkenny Cottage, where she found Nanny getting rather anxious at her long absence.

"I'm sorry I've been such ages, Nanny. You didn't want any of the things for lunch, did you?"

"Only the bananas. But what happened, Jill? There wasn't any—any trouble, was there?"

"None at all—unless you count having my character described by Miss Gregory as trouble." Jill's laugh was slightly forced and she hurried on before Nanny could comment. "Then I stopped in the park for a while watching some of the schoolchildren. The man in charge of them was lame. I should have thought that it was rather a silly career to take up unless you are absolutely fit."

"That would be the new man. He is only temporary. Old Mr Bean, who has been at the school for the last twenty years, was taken ill suddenly at the beginning of the term, and Mr and Mrs Lipton were at their wit's end trying to find somebody to fill in."

"How many teachers do they have at the school?"

"Four. Mr and Mrs Lipton, one more man and one more girl. I meet Mrs Lipton sometimes at the Townswomen's Guild and she tells me about it." Nanny laughed suddenly. "They changed their junior lady teacher last Easter, too, and had such a job to find somebody that Mrs Lipton actually asked me if I'd like to do it! She said that at least I'd be able to keep the small ones in order. Of course, the Education Authorities wouldn't have allowed it. You have to have some kind of qualification to be teacher these days."

Mention of the Education Authorities gave Jill her chance to tell Nanny of her plans. She chattered on gaily, painting her prospects in rosy colours, but, as she expected, Nanny was horrified.

"Jill, you can't! Just think what your dear mother would have said. There's your grandfather, too. He lives at Haime since he retired, and that's only five miles away. Suppose he was to hear about it."

"Nanny, I don't honestly think Mummy would have disapproved. If she had been terribly conventional she would never have married a clerk from her father's office. I have a feeling that she would far rather know that I wanted to pay my way, however I did it, than that I should just be helpless and useless. As for Grandfather, I don't care what he thinks! I'd be glad if he did hear, and feel ashamed to have one of his family driving a taxi! He's never taken the least notice of me or of Daddy all these years. I expect he has done his best to forget my existence. No, I've made up my mind. I'm going to try to get this job. It will give me plenty of time to help you as well—I don't suppose I'll get very many trips until people begin to know about me and trust my driving—and there's heaps I can do here. It's time you had a holiday. That's what your doctor said, isn't it?"

"However did you know that?"

Nanny sounded so much astonished that Jill laughed and repeated the conversation she had overheard in the grocer's. Already her indignation against Miss Gregory was almost forgotten. In fact, if that good lady had been instrumental in suggesting a job she could do, Jill had good reason to be thankful to her.

Partly convinced by Jill's reasoning, Miss Williams raised no more objections to the plan. That afternoon the girl went to the local council offices, and, after being passed on from one person to another for half an hour, and then having to show her certificates and give details of her considerable driving experience, she was at last given the permission she needed.

The next few days were busy with correspondence and other planning. Jill went to the local printer and had some cards done, and Nanny, who by this time was determined to do her best to make the venture a success, took them to various shops where she was well known and asked to have them displayed. The Insurance Company agreed to allow her to carry six children and the Education Authorities were willing for her to take over the Cinder Cross trip when Mr Wood gave up.

So it happened that one Monday morning, ten days after her arrival at Castlebridge, Jill and her gleaming Rover left Kilkenny Cottage at eight five to pick up six children at the War Memorial outside the parish church.

*   *   *

Five of her passengers were waiting when she arrived. Two eleven-year-olds were passing the time scrambling among the branches of the huge old chestnut tree which overhung the memorial, two big boys were lounging against a fence, deep in conversation, and one of about thirteen was looking anxiously along the road, evidently awaiting the arrival of his particular friend. Jill pulled up, and as they obviously did not realise that this brightly coloured vehicle was their taxi she took the opportunity to study them carefully.

The small ones seemed to be typical young ruffians— they would have to be squashed if they started to rampage round in the car—but they looked nice enough children. The big boys would probably be more difficult

19

to handle. Jill looked with disfavour at their long hair—carefully unkempt—their exaggeratedly tight trousers and their general air of superiority. For the first time a twinge of doubt came into her mind. Was she wise to have undertaken this trip? But she forced the thought away. If they didn't behave she would have to threaten to report them to their headmaster or their parents, but probably she was being unnecessarily pessimistic. The fifth boy, who had now been joined by a breathless redhead of about his own age, looked a very different type. His hair was short and his shoes were shining; and although his blazer had leather patches and was bound with the same material at the bottoms of the sleeves, he contrived to look neat and—what was the word—wholesome.

She leant across and opened the near-side front door of the car. "Are you the boys for Cinder Cross?"

For a moment they gazed at her in amazement, then with a whoop which would have done credit to any Red Indian, one of the smallest ones leapt from the tree to the ground and rushed over.

"Bags I go in front! Come on, Jimmy!"

This suited Jill very well. They were better under her eye. The other four packed into the back, fitting easily on the wide seat, and they set off for the junction with the main road, three miles away.

After the first excitement shyness overcame the boys beside her and the first few minutes of the trip were silent. Then, as they were passing a small cluster of cottages beside the road, one of them nudged the other and pointed.

"Mr Davidson is late this morning. He'll never get to the school in time unless he gets a lift."

Jill looked in the direction indicated and saw the lame

young man who had been taking the boys of the Primary
School for their exercises on the morning she had crossed
the recreation ground. He was using a stick and was
obviously trying to move faster than his bad leg allowed.
He looked hot and uncomfortable.

"Does he walk all the way to the school near the
station?" she asked.

The reply came from the redheaded boy in the back.
"Yes, he teaches there. My brother Tim says he's grand,
much better than old Mr Bean, who used to teach me
when I was there. Mr Davidson has travelled a lot and
he tells the chaps interesting things about places; not
like an ordinary geography lesson at all. He was out in
a school in Persia last year, and in the holidays he went
to Israel and Pakistan and India. Tim says he's going
to work in the Persian oilfields when he leaves school."

"I'm not!" This from the freckled Jimmy, sitting
beside her. "I'm going to be an astronaut. I reckon by
the time I'm old enough people will be travelling to the
moon quite easily, and I'll be the first man to reach
Saturn or Jupiter or one of the other planets."

A lively argument followed, which lasted until they
reached the main road, where the boys tumbled out and
she swung the car round and started back towards Castlebridge. Soon she sighted ahead of her the lame man the
boys had called Mr Davidson. He was still at least three-
quarters of a mile from the school and it was obvious
that he would have quite a job to reach it in time, so
she pulled up just ahead of him, leant across and opened
the door.

"That's very good of you." He hobbled a few paces
to the open door and then started back as he caught
sight of her. The pleasant smile disappeared and he
looked at her as if she was some kind of poisonous

21

reptile! "Thank you for your offer, but it is good for me to walk."

Jill flinched as if from a blow in the face. There was only one possible explanation for his behaviour. He had recognised her from the plentiful photographs which had appeared in the papers at the time of the scandal, and he found it preferable to be late for school rather than to accept a lift from the daughter of Ernest Railton!

For a moment she felt utterly forlorn. Then she squared her shoulders and her head came up. If that was the kind of man Mr Davidson was, then he certainly did not deserve any sympathy from her in his lameness. Accelerating with quite unnecessary violence she swept off up the road, and some seven or eight minutes later she reached Kilkenny Cottage.

"Well, Jill, did that go all right?" Nanny came bustling into the kitchen.

"Yes, thank you, Nanny. They seem a nice lot of boys." She managed a little laugh. "You should have seen their faces when they realised that they were going in such a grand car. But I thought we arranged that you were going to take it easy and let me help with the work, and here you are nearly finished with the washing up."

"That's all right, dear. I'll go easily as I promised. But I can't be completely idle, I should be bored to death. And I've just taken a phone call for you—another order. Mrs Mayhew, the doctor's wife, wants to visit a friend over in Shepley and she said would you pick her up at eleven and fetch her at three. The doctor was going to take her, but he has to go to a conference in London today and she can't drive a car herself."

Shepley was ten miles away and an awkward journey from Castlebridge except by car, as the railway and bus routes meant going round two sides of a triangle. Jill cheered up a lot. Twenty miles twice and two school trips; not bad for her first day. She flung herself energetically into the housework and then went out to give the car an additional rub up with a soft cloth, to make sure it was looking its very best.

CHAPTER 3

BUT if Jill was happy Nicholas Davidson certainly was
not. His injured leg was improving slowly and now he
could walk fairly painlessly as long as he did not hurry.
But any attempt at speed brought back all the old throbbing, and that morning his landlady's alarm clock had
failed to go off and he had been three-quarters of an
hour late. He had wrenched his leg trying to come down
the stairs quickly and he had bolted his breakfast and
gone without his usual toast and marmalade. The car
pulling up to give him a lift had brought a wave of relief
flooding over him, and then he had caught sight of the
driver. Fair hair, blue eyes, utterly lovely—at first glance
she might almost have been Vivienne Bartlett herself!
Small wonder that he had recoiled and felt that it was
impossible to enter the car. But all the way to school,
which he managed to reach with just two minutes to
spare, and at intervals through that day, he was haunted
by the girl's expression. He could have understood if
she had been annoyed by his refusal, but she had looked
so dismayed—so hurt.

By four o'clock he was exhausted. Perhaps because
of the pain he was suffering he was less patient than
usual with his pupils, and in consequence the dull ones
seemed ten times duller and the naughty ones twice as
bad, while even the clever, hard-working ones struck him
as a lot of young hypocrites, currying favour for the sake

of winning a prize or getting a good report. When the
last pair of shoes had clattered across the playground he
went back into the classroom, sat down at his desk and
rested his head on his hands.

"Tired, Nick?"

Mr Lipton's voice made him sit up with a jerk. It
would never do to let the headmaster think that he was
going to pack up.

"It's nothing. Just a bit fagged for a moment."

"I noticed that you were more lame than usual. Come
and have a cup of tea with my wife and me before you
start home. You are too valuable for us to run any risk
of your going sick. Barbara was saying only yesterday
that she has never seen such an improvement in the
behaviour and bearing of the boys as there has been
this term."

Nicholas glowed with gratitude. It was the first inkling
he had been given that Mr and Mrs Lipton were pleased
with his work. He accompanied the older man over to
the nice little house next door to the school and spent
a pleasant half hour chatting to them over tea. Mr
Lipton even offered to get the car out and run him back
to his lodgings, but Nicholas refused, saying that he was
rested now and the walk would do him good.

He found his landlady getting quite anxious about him.

"Are you all right, Mr Davidson? I've been that
bothered all day, wondering if your leg had been very bad.
I bought a new alarm clock this morning; I'll see that you
don't get a late start again."

Nicholas laughed and reassured her. Then he went
out into the little garden behind the cottage, sat down
on an old white seat which stood under the spreading
branches of an apple tree and let himself think.

For the last six months he had deliberately driven all

thought of Persia, the Gachsaran school and Vivienne from his mind. He had determined to forget all that had happened and make a completely fresh start. Now he wondered if he had been wise. Hiding a wound from view did not necessarily heal it.

Left an orphan at an early age, Nicholas had no home ties and no dependants. His only sister—a year his junior —had married when she was twenty and now lived in Canada. His own ambition had always been to see as much of the world as possible. His tutor at Oxford had been responsible for his getting the job as one of the masters in the school for English and American boys whose fathers worked in the big oilfields round Gachsaran and he had loved it there. The pay was very good and enabled him to travel extensively in the holidays, usually in the company of Jeremy Peel, another bachelor teacher of about his own age. The thought of old Jeremy brought a warm glow to his heart. What a good pal he was and how furious he had been at the way things had turned out.

Although, with the exception of the head, the masters were all unmarried, they had not lacked female society. There were a number of young wives whose husbands worked for the oil company and also several single women in secretarial positions. There were tennis and dancing, bathing and riding, and the younger masters were always in demand to make up the company in some party or other. Jeremy had fallen in love at last, with an American girl who acted as secretary to her uncle, but Nicholas had remained heartwhole. Heartwhole, that is, until the arrival of Vivienne!

She had come to the school at the end of the previous September to stay for a month or two with her aunt, the headmaster's wife, and right from the start it seemed

to fall to his lot to be her escort. He could see her now
—so eager, so alive, so thrilled with everything. She had
wanted to see all that there was to be seen, and soon it
had become the accepted thing that he would hire a
car at the week-ends and drive her out to the oilfields,
or that they would go by air if the distance was too far
to drive. It was the air trips which had caused him some
slight uneasiness. Vivienne took it for granted that he
would pay both the fares, and soon he found himself
getting somewhat short of money. He had spent his
accumulated savings on a trip to Pakistan during the
summer holidays.

He grinned ruefully to himself as he remembered
what had happened when he had tried to tap Jeremy
for a loan.

"My good lad, for Heaven's sake be your age! Can't
you see that she is just using you? That young madam
has gold-digger written all over her! You take Uncle
Jeremy's advice and suggest that you go dutch for the
future."

He had been furious. Vivienne was so wonderful, and
if Jeremy was too thickheaded to see it, then the more
fool he. Vivienne was worth a thousand of his precious
Mary Youngs. All the same, he was still out of cash.
He managed to put off the trip they had planned because
the tennis club dance coincided with it, but ten days
later another jaunt came into view.

"Nick darling!" Vivienne caught up with him as he
was going in to afternoon school. "Nick, what do you
think? I met Captain Barclay this morning and he says
he will take us out to Kharg Island in his ship on Saturday if we can get down to Bandar Rig by two in the
afternoon. We can stay at the club there on Saturday
night and he will bring us back after tea on Sunday.

There are lovely bathing beaches on Kharg Island—almost as good as the South Seas, he told me. Won't it be fun?"

Nicholas agreed enthusiastically. He had always wanted to see Kharg Island, where the big loading terminal for the oilfields had been built. But then his straitened finances came back to his mind. Presumably Captain Barclay wouldn't want fares for the voyage, but they'd have to hire a car to take them down to the port of Bandar Rig and he simply couldn't run to it. The night on the island would also cost a certain amount, even if it was only drinks and food, though he'd have enough for that if it wasn't for the car trip.

On Thursday evening he saw Vivienne sitting in a deck chair outside Mr and Mrs Bailley's bungalow. He did not like to enter the headmaster's garden uninvited, but he waved and she came out to join him.

"I'm going along to the swimming pool," he said. "Would you like a dip?"

"Oh, lovely! I'll just get my things."

The staff at the school were all members of the local club, with its tennis courts and swimming pool, and Nicholas and Vivienne spent a pleasant hour in the water and basking in the sunshine. Several times Nick tried to think of some way of introducing the topic of the weekend, but in the end it was Vivienne who opened the subject.

"Nick, I'm longing for Saturday. Have you got everything fixed?"

"Not yet." He shifted uncomfortably and then decided to go full speed at the hurdle ahead. "I don't know how we can get down to Bandar Rig, Vi. I'm broke! Can you run to the car fare?"

She looked at him in astonishment. "Broke! But I

thought you got an absolutely fantastic salary at Gach-saran. Uncle Hubert is always complaining about the costs of running the school, and he said you were rolling in money."

Her voice had a sharp note which made him wince, but having started he felt that it would be better to make the position clear.

"We do get good pay, but I've nothing except that, and it won't run to living the way we have been doing in the last few weeks. I'm sorry, Vivienne darling, but unless you can meet the bill for the car this time I'm afraid we shall have to call off the trip."

For a long minute there was silence. Nicholas wished afterwards that he had kept his eyes on the girl beside him; her expression might have given him some warning of what was to come; but in his discomfort and unhappiness he gazed only at the water of the swimming pool.

She spoke at last. "Well, I'm not going to give up this trip. I've wanted to see Kharg ever since I came here. Don't worry, Nick, I'll arrange the car. Now I'd better be getting back. I promised Aunt Katherine that I'd go to some sherry party with her this evening."

Thankful that she seemed to have taken it so well, Nicholas sprang to his feet. "Come and have a quick one in the clubhouse before you go, darling. I'm so glad you understand."

On Friday evening he got a scribbled note from her.

"Okay about the car. I'll pick you up at your bunga-low at one o'clock. Vi."

But when she arrived, ten minutes late, he was astonished to see her at the wheel of the headmaster's car; a new one which was Mr Bailley's pride and delight.

"Goodness, Vivienne, however did you persuade your

uncle to lend you this? I didn't even know that you could drive."

"Of course I can drive. And he couldn't very well refuse, could he, as he and Aunt Katherine are away for the week-end. Come on, Nick, we shan't have any time to spare."

Mr and Mrs Bailley had flown that morning to spend the week-end at Shiraz, so Nicholas thought no more about it. In fact, after about ten minutes one thought occupied his mind to the exclusion of all else. Vivienne had said she could drive, but it was pretty obvious that she had never before handled a car as powerful as this one. She took the corners too fast, and on more than one occasion nearly had them off the road altogether.

"Hey, take it easy, darling! We've got plenty of time to get to the landing stage by two. Look, would you like me to drive? I'm more used to the bends on these roads than you are."

"No, I shouldn't. I've wanted to drive this car ever since I came and Uncle wouldn't let me. Now I've got the chance and I'm not giving it up for anyone." She swooped down a short steep hill and roared up the other side. Then she gave a laugh of sheer excitement. "Wouldn't he be furious if he could see me!"

It was several seconds before the full significance of what she had said dawned on him.

"Vivienne! You haven't taken the car without his permission? He'll skin you alive! And me too; he's sure to think I put the idea into your head."

"Well, so you did. You said I'd have to get the car if we were to go to Kharg and this was the only way I could do it. It's entirely your fault for deceiving me. You've spent money like water ever since I came and I thought you were rich. Now everyone takes it for granted that you are my boy friend and none of the others offers to take me out. If I'd known I'd have picked up somebody else right from the start."

Nicholas was furious. "So you made up to me just because you thought I was the one with the most money? Well, when we get back from this trip I'll see that people soon know that you aren't my girl friend, and then you can take your choice of the others. Why not try for Bill Cotton? He's rolling!" Bill Cotton was one of the engineers at Gachsaran. He was very clever and consequently extremely well paid, but a most unpleasant character and by far the most unpopular man in the place. "For goodness sake, girl, slow up! Even a good driver would take these corners carefully."

"And I'm not a good driver? Is that what you mean?"

To his horror she put her foot down on the accelerator and raced towards the next corner—a hairpin bend—at seventy miles an hour. Then the brakes screamed, the huge grey car rocked violently, there was a crash and he knew no more.

*   *   *

Neither of them was killed. In fact, miraculously, Vivienne escaped with surface cuts and bruises, though he suffered severe concussion in addition to his badly broken leg. But when some weeks later he was passed fit for visitors, he found that he was out of a job. Vivienne had told Mr Bailley that it was he who had been driving the car and that he had led her to believe that the headmaster had given him the keys. Vivienne herself had returned to England, and since it happened that nobody had seen them driving away from the school he felt that there was no chance that his story would be believed. Looking back afterwards he realised that he had been a fool not to stick to his guns and try to prove that the borrowing of the car had been none of his doing, but at the time he had felt so ill and so angry that it had not seemed worth while.

As soon as his leg was sufficiently healed to allow him to leave the hospital he had returned to England, and here his troubles had begun in earnest. Mr Bailley had given him a very restrained reference—damning with faint praise—and with his lameness as an added disadvantage the first half a dozen headmasters to whom he had applied had turned him down politely but very promptly. He was getting desperate when he received a letter from Colonel Furneaux, his godfather, who lived just outside Castlebridge and was one of the school managers, which had resulted in his getting his present job until old Mr Bean was well enough to return.

Hearing Mrs Pelman's voice, calling him in to supper, Nick rose to his feet and limped towards the house. His earlier despondency had vanished and he was feeling quite cheerful. Evidently it had been a good thing to go over in his mind the events of the past few months. And, equally obviously, if his love for Vivienne had ever been more than a mere obsession, it had gone now.

If only he'd got himself straightened out before that regrettable episode with the girl in the Rover. It was improbable that he'd ever see her again, and if he did she certainly wouldn't offer him a lift. He had an unreasonable desire to explain his action. There must have been some good reason why she had looked so much hurt, almost as if he had slapped her in the face! Bother the whole silly business! Then Mrs Pelman called again, and he left the sunny garden and went in for his meal.

CHAPTER 4

NICHOLAS had made up his mind to think no more about the unknown girl in the blue and silver Rover, so he was decidedly annoyed with himself when he realised that he was constantly looking over his shoulder on his journey to the school the next morning. Silly ass! In any case he'd been late on the previous day. Even is she did pass that way regularly, if eight forty-five was her usual time there was no reason why she should overtake him at eight twenty.

He was approaching the War Memorial when he saw the car and gasped in astonishment. The girl was picking up the boys for the Grammar School! He'd known that the old fellow was packing up the taxi business, but he'd had no idea that his successor would be a girl.

For the next few mornings he met her at different places on the route, but she never seemed to be looking in his direction. Gradually his awkwardness over his behaviour on the previous Monday faded from his mind and by Friday he had almost stopped looking out for the car. But then something happened which reopened the self-inflicted wound. After the physical exercises in the park he found himself walking back to the school beside nine-year-old Tim Grey, whose brother was one of the taxi passengers.

"I say, sir, did you know about the new taxi driver? It's a girl, and Jimmy says the car is a beaut!"

33

"Yes, I've seen it, Tim. It doesn't look much like a taxi, does it?"

"No. I heard Mum and Dad talking about it yesterday. The taxi lady used to be rich—or at least her dad was—and then something went wrong and he lost all his money, so he bumped himself off. Now she's driving her car to get enough money for clothes and food and things like that."

Nicholas laughed. "Are you sure you've got it right, Tim? It sounds more like a story you've heard on the television."

"No, honestly, sir, it's true. She is living right opposite to my dad's Aunt Mavis, and she came round yesterday afternoon. Old Cat! That's what Mum calls her."

Having heard something of Miss Mavis Gregory's reputation, Nick made no comment, but later on that day he asked Mrs Lipton if she knew whether there was any truth in Tim's story.

"Yes, poor girl. You probably saw the case in the papers. That financier, Ernest Railton, who committed suicide when things got too hot for him. But all the same, Miss Gregory really ought to be stopped. The damage she can do with that acid tongue of hers is unbelievable. Miss Railton is staying with Miss Williams at Kilkenny Cottage, and I've promised to put any business which comes to my notice in her way. Miss Williams gave me one of the cards they had had printed. So if you hear of anybody needing a taxi, you might give them her number."

She produced the card from her handbag and Nicholas made a note of the phone number. As he walked slowly back to his lodgings he thought over the story he had heard. Evidently the girl was the plucky type who wasn't going to allow the scandal to get her down. Suddenly he stopped and his face flamed. No wonder she had looked so stricken when he had refused the lift she had offered. She must have thought he had recognised her and wouldn't ride with her on account of what had happened. This was awful!

All kinds of wild ideas passed through his mind. Should he ring her up and apologise? Should he try to waylay her and beg a lift? Should he write? He rejected them all. The only way he could excuse his conduct was to explain that he had found her too much like the girl who had let him down, and that seemed just too futile for words.

As it happened he needed to do none of those things. When he reached his lodgings he found a letter waiting for him. It was from Joyce Barlow, who before her marriage had been Joyce Furneaux, the daughter of his godfather.

"Dear Nick," she had written,

"I expect you know that Dad has invited Michael, the children and me to spend the next fortnight, while he is in France, at Fir Lodge. We'd got everything fixed up, including seeing Mark and Mary's school teachers to get them leave of absence, and now Michael has to go to Scotland for the firm for a week. This means that the kids and I will have to come by train. We'll need a taxi from the station and I can't remember the name and address of that old chap with the big Humber, who, as far as I can recollect, is practically the only one available. Would you please book him for me, to meet the four fifteen. We shall have masses of gear, as usual, but I think he'll be able to fit it all in. I hope we shall see you often while we are there. In fact, if you are free on Saturday afternoon, you might like us to pick you up on our way and you could help us to get settled in! If so, perhaps you'd fix it up with the taxi man. Mark is longing to see you and to hear some more stories of your travels.

In haste,
Joyce."

While he had his meal Nick debated with himself about the advisibility of accepting a lift in the car, but decided against it. It might make things awkward to meet Miss Railton in front of Joyce and the children. He'd walk out to Fir Lodge. It was not much more than a mile and a half from his digs and he could take his time. In the meantime he'd better phone and book the car. His landlady wasn't on the phone, but fortunately there was a call box just along the road.

* * *

"Is that you, Jill?" Miss Williams called from the kitchen as Jill came in from putting away the car. "I've just booked a trip for you for tomorrow afternoon. It's to meet the four fifteen train and take a Mrs Barlow and her children out to Fir Lodge. The man who phoned said you'd easily recognise them as there is a boy of seven, a girl of five and a toddler, as well as a lot of luggage."

"That's good, Nanny. I'll be almost full up tomorrow now. Where is Fir Lodge? Do you know?"

"Not exactly, but you turn off to the left about a mile before you get to Cinder Cross."

"Oh, yes, I know. I've noticed that turning and wondered where it led. I'll finish that ironing for you, Nanny. You really shouldn't be doing my frocks at all. I'm supposed to be saving you work, not making extra for you."

Miss Williams laughed. "All right, dear, but you

36

mustn't make me too lazy. Doctor Mayhew dropped in this morning and he said I was much better already. And he told me, too, that his wife was very pleased with your driving. She had been a little nervous, but you didn't give her any frights at all!"

*   *   *

The four fifteen train was packed to the corridors on Saturday afternoon, but almost all the passengers were bound for the coast and only a sprinkling alighted at Castlebridge. Jill sighted her customers at once, as their compartment was just in front of the exit. A youngish woman got down first and lifted out a lively-looking toddler. A bit too active, perhaps, as she darted away along the platform as her mother turned to assist a bigger girl, pale and limp, with bedraggled hair and a dirty, tear-streaked face.

"Tilly, come here!" The harassed woman caught the pickle by the arm and pulled her back. "Stand still, for goodness sake! Mary, can you hold on to Tilly while we get the things out? Oh dear, I hope the cases have been put out of the guard's van."

Jill, who had been waiting outside the barrier, slipped through and hurried to her side.

"Can I help you?"

"Oh, thank you so much. If you could take the things out of the compartment for me I could look after the bigger baggage."

With one child on each side of her she hastened away, and Jill turned to take various packages from the boy who was still standing in the carriage door. Three baskets, a zipp-topped bag, a school satchel and an assortment of coats were pressed into her arms before the boy descended. Leaving the child to carry two of the baskets, she slung the coats over one shoulder, the satchel over the other and took the third basket and the bag in either hand. The train pulled away and the woman, who had now parked the lively toddler in a small folding pushchair, came along the platform accompanied by the station's only porter with a loaded barrow.

"Thank you so much. I don't know how I should have managed if you hadn't come along. I was expecting a taxi man to meet me but I can't see him. I do hope he got the message."

"Mr Wood, you mean? I think you are Mrs Barlow? Old Mr Wood has given up work and I have taken over his regular passengers. That's my car there."

"Ooo, a taxi lady! But it doesn't look like a taxi. Mummy, may I ride in the front?"

"I don't know, Mark. We'll have to see how the luggage fits in, and in any case you must ask Miss— Miss—"

"Miss Railton. I expect we can arrange things so that Mark has room in the front if you like."

The Rover's capacious boot took almost all the luggage, so Mark got his wish. Mrs Barlow sank back against the comfortable upholstery with a sigh of relief.

"Of all the journeys! It's so long since I had to travel by train that I had forgotten how hectic it can be." She sat Tilly on one side of her and put her arm round the bigger girl on the other side. "There, Mary darling, you'll be all right now. We'll soon be at Grandad's."

"Mary felt sick in the train." Mark's voice was scornful of such weakness. "I like trains. We had to change in London and I went to look at the engine."

Mary was already recovering. "It wasn't because of the train that I was ill. It was that funny cake thing we had at the station in London."

"Of course it was, darling. But another time, if anything tastes funny, don't eat it." Mrs Barlow was also getting over the difficulties of the journey. "Take my advice, Miss Railton. If you ever have to take small children on a journey, bring all the food you need with you."

"I never eat much myself when I go by train. I used to be a very bad traveller when I was small." Jill reached into the pocket of the car and produced a screw-topped jar which she handed over her shoulder. "Perhaps Mary would like a barley sugar. It's a great help if you are feeling a bit upset."

The rest of the trip passed quickly and, following the directions given to her by Mrs Barlow, Jill drove up a short drive, bordered by the fir trees from which the house got its name, on to a beautifully kept sweep of gravel in front of a pleasant modern house. As the car stopped the front door was opened and an elderly woman came out, accompanied by a young man. Jill glanced at them and then looked away, dismay and embarrassment bringing a flush to her cheeks. It was the lame school teacher!

"Uncle Nick! Mummy, Uncle Nick is here." Mark shot from the car like a rocket, rushed across the intervening space and flung himself at the young man so energetically that he almost toppled him over.

"Hey, steady on, young fellow! Elephants aren't in it. Joyce, my dear, it's lovely to see you." He glanced at the pile of luggage which Jill was beginning to unload. "Travelling light as usual, eh! Hold on a minute, Miss Railton. I'll carry those."

Jill took no notice except to stiffen as he called her by her name. So, as she had thought, he had known who she was that morning. The Barlows were involved

39

in excited greetings with Colonel Furneaux's old house-keeper and were all chattering at once, so she just went on quietly with the unloading, carried the cases to the front door and then got back into the driving seat to wait until Mrs Barlow was ready to pay her.

"Just a minute, Mrs Deane. I'll settle up with Miss Railton. Now where did I put my bag?" She found it under the pile of coats, produced a note and Jill gave her the change. "Thank you so much for all your help. I'd have been in a frightful mess on the platform if you hadn't come to my assistance. Look, my husband expects to join us next Saturday with the car, but until then we shall be dependent on taxis if we want to go any-where. Are you very booked up?"

"No, I'm only just starting in the business. I have a trip each morning, taking boys to Cinder Cross for the school bus, and I have to pick them up again at four thirty, but apart from that I've nothing regular booked. My number is Castlebridge 4278, if you should need me."

"4278, I'll remember that. Now come along, children. You must get cleaned up. Mrs Deane has tea all ready for us. Say goodbye and thank you to Miss Railton."

"Goodbye, Miss Railton. Thank you for letting me ride in front."

"Goodbye, taxi lady." Mary came over and stood beside Jill's door. "Thank you for the sweet. May I ride in front with you next time?"

"I can't promise, Mary. If I do drive you again you must ask your mummy."

Small Tilly was not to be out-done. "'Bye, taxi lady. Tilly 'ide in f'ont, too."

Mrs Barlow laughed and shepherded them away and Jill started her engine. Then she realised that the lame man was still standing near the front door. As the Barlow family went indoors he limped over to the car.

"Miss Railton, I feel that I must apologise for my rudeness that morning when you offered me a lift. I should like to explain—"

Jill's chin went up. "There is no need either to apologise or to explain. Your attitude was quite natural. No self-respecting person would accept a favour from the daughter of Ernest Railton."

Even as she spoke she let in the clutch, and in two seconds she was round a bend in the drive and out of sight!

As she drove back to Kilkenny Cottage her thoughts were a jumble of amusement with the children and their name for her—taxi-lady sounded rather nice—and annoyance with their uncle and his duty apology. She found Nanny waiting tea for her and she entertained the old lady, as had become the custom, with a description of her passengers and journeys for the day.

CHAPTER 5

AFTER the strain of the past week Jill was glad to take things easily on Sunday morning. She and Nanny got up late—too late to get to church on time—and spent most of the sunny hours lazing in the garden. At about half past five Miss Williams roused herself.

"I think I will walk along to church this evening as I didn't go this morning," she said. "But don't feel that you have to come with me if you'd rather not, dear. The quiet rest might do you more good."

She moved to pick up the tray on which they had carried out their tea but Jill jumped up quickly. "I'll take that, Nanny," she said, "but I think, if you don't mind, I'll skip church until next week. I've got such a lot to think about; I'm sure I couldn't concentrate on the service."

"Of course, my dear. Oh, there is the telephone." They went indoors and she hurried through into the sitting-room and picked up the receiver. After a few moments she turned to Jill. "It's for you, Jill. Mrs Barlow."

"Oh, good! Good afternoon, Mrs Barlow. Jill Railton here. . . . Oh, what a shame. Of course I'll come out. . . ." There was quite a long pause and then she continued in a very different voice; what Nanny called her 'Jill Railton—Taxi' voice "Yes, Mrs Barlow. I quite understand. If he is there I'll wait for him."

42

She turned to Miss Williams. "Mrs Barlow has asked if I'll go out there and discuss trips for the coming week, Nanny. She has twisted her leg and is having difficulty in walking, and she hopes that I'll be able to take them for some outings so that the kiddies can enjoy their holiday. I don't suppose I shall be long; perhaps I can pick you up outside the church when the service is over. Or, look, why don't you come with me instead? I'm sure Mrs Barlow wouldn't mind."

"No, thank you, dear. I didn't go to church this morning and I don't like to miss all day. But I should be glad of a lift as far as the church as time is getting on. Don't worry about bringing me home if it doesn't fit in easily. I am quite used to walking that far."

"All right, Nanny." Jill washed up the tea things while the old lady went up to tidy her hair and put on a hat. As they were driving to the church she went back to the subject. "I expect I'll be glad of an excuse to get away, so I shall tell Mrs Barlow I'm picking you up. You get out at about half past seven, I expect, don't you?"

Miss Williams was puzzled. Jill had sounded so glad to have an opportunity to see and talk to Mrs Barlow, but now she seemed almost loath to go. Was it something to do with the last part of the telephone conversation?

"You'll enjoy this, dear, won't you?" she said. "Mrs Barlow sounded such a nice friendly person, and it will be good for you to have somebody young to talk to."

"Ye-es. The trouble is that she asked me to stop on the way and pick up Mr Davidson who lives in Tindal; you know, that little hamlet with a couple of shops and a dozen or so cottages, about a mile along the road from here. He isn't on the phone, so I've got to see if he is home and, if he is, ask him to come with me."

"Well, that won't bother you, will it? I expect he is a friend of Mrs Barlow."

"Yes, I expect that is it. He was at Fir Lodge when they arrived yesterday and the children called him Uncle Nick, but if her maiden name was Furneaux he can't be her brother. He is the lame schoolmaster at the Primary School, and I just can't stick him. He is stuck-up, self-opinionated, pompous and prejudiced!"

Perhaps it was fortunate that they reached the church just then and Miss Williams was not obliged to reply. Jill dropped her by the Memorial and drove away, leaving the old lady looking after her with very mixed feelings. It was unlike Jill to take violent dislikes to anybody. What had the young man said or done which had upset her so badly?

Meanwhile the big Rover had reached Tindal and come to a stop beside the little whitewashed cottage with the green gate. A woman answered the door and the girl explained her errand and went back to the car to wait. As she saw the young man come limping down the path she got out and opened the rear door for him, her expression so forbidding that his nervous smile faded. He took his seat, she closed the door, went round to her own place and drove off. They reached Fir Lodge a few minutes later without exchanging a single word, and it is doubtful which of them was more uncomfortable!

*   *   *

Mark Barlow heard the car pulling up and came dashing to meet them. "Hello, Miss Railton! Hello, Uncle Nick! Mummy is just putting Mary to bed. She told me to tell you she would be down in a minute."

"I'll go up and see her." Nicholas was glad of an opportunity to get away from the stony-faced girl in the driving seat. "Take Miss Railton into the sitting-room, Mark."

But Mark ignored the command and jumped into the seat beside Jill instead, asking innumerable questions about the car, and it was not until Mrs Barlow appeared on the doorstep that Jill left her position and went to meet her.

"Good evening, Miss Railton. It is good of you to come out on a Sunday evening."

"That's all right, thank you. I hadn't anything special to do. I am sorry about your leg. What have you done to it?"

Mrs Barlow, who was walking with a stick and limping as badly as Nicholas, smiled ruefully. "It was the silliest thing. I injured this leg badly three years ago—a skiing accident—and it has always been a bit weak. Then this afternoon Tilly was running round the garden and fell, I jumped up quickly to go to her and somehow I twisted it. I had to telephone to the doctor—fortunately the man who looked after us when we were children—but he says there is nothing that can be done about it. I've just got to rest it as much as possible and use a stick to take my weight as far as I can."

She led the way into the sitting-room and sat down thankfully. "Now, Miss Railton, what I'd like would be for you to give us as much time as you can spare this week. I've lots of friends who live within a few miles of us, and I thought perhaps you could drop us with one of them during the morning and pick us up again later in the day. And if you have any days which are not booked at all except for the school trip, perhaps you could drive us to the sea and spend the day with us.

I know it is asking a lot—and of course I'd pay you for the time as well as the trip—but I do want the kiddies to enjoy themselves and not just have to stay in the garden here."

Jill got out her diary and they were busy making plans when Nicholas, who had been putting Mark to bed, came down to join them.

"Joyce, where is Mrs Deane? I looked in the kitchen and she isn't there."

"No. It never rains but it pours, as old Aunt Adelaide used to say. Late yesterday evening she got a phone call from her brother-in-law. Her sister has been taken ill and rushed to hospital and Mrs Deane had to go off there first thing this morning to take care of the children. She has fixed up with a friend—Mrs Pullar, from one of those cottages at Cinder Cross—to come in by day, but she can only come while her children are at school —quarter to nine until quarter to four."

"Does that mean that you'll have to be alone in the house at night?" Joyce bit her lip and nodded. "But you can't, Joyce. You'll be a nervous wreck before the end of the week. Why don't you ask somebody to come and keep you company?"

"I've been considering that, but I can't think of anyone who wouldn't be more bother than she was worth." She turned to Jill. "I suppose it sounds cowardly and foolish to you, Miss Railton, but I'm nervous of being on my own at night. We had a burglary at home last year and—well, I interrupted the man and he turned —rather nasty." She broke off, remembering the unpleasant episode all too vividly.

"Of course I understand. You ought to have someone here, oughtn't you, in case your leg stiffens up more and makes moving too difficult."

"Look here, Joyce old thing, I'll come out and spend the nights here this week. I wouldn't be very early, but at least I'd be here in time to put Mark to bed. I can doss down on the settee here."

"Oh, Nick, that would be wonderful. It would make all the difference. How about letting Mrs Pelman know? And how could you get to school in time in the mornings? There is no bus, is there? If only we'd got the car, instead of Michael having had to take it."

Jill had a brief battle with herself. Much as she disliked the thought of helping Nicholas Davidson, or of risking another snub, she realised that it would solve Mrs Barlow's main difficulty, and she couldn't help being sorry for her, with so much to contend with.

"I can go in to your lodgings with a message on my way back if that would help," she said rather curtly. "And I have to be at Cinder Cross tomorrow morning at eight thirty, so I shall pass the end of this road at about eight thirty-five on my return journey. If you care to be there by then, I will drive you as far as the Memorial. I usually reach there by about quarter to nine, so that should give you time to get to school."

There was an uncomfortable silence for a few seconds, while Nicholas tried to think of some appreciative way of accepting an offer so grudgingly made.

"Perhaps that would be best. I'll pay you your usual fare of course."

He couldn't have chosen a worse sentence!

"No thank you! My licence does not allow me to tout for jobs. It's a free lift or nothing. Mrs Barlow, I must be getting back. I'm picking Miss Williams up after church. Please don't bother to come out with me. I hope so much that your leg will be better in the morning. Goodbye!"

She almost fled from the room, shot into the car as if pursued by demons, and was down the drive almost before the amazed Mrs Barlow had had time to reach the front door.

CHAPTER 6

WHEN her alarm awoke her the next morning Jill lay
for a minute or two wondering why she should be
looking forward with dread to the day ahead. It was
Monday and she would be picking up her pleasant crowd
of schoolboys at the Memorial as usual. She liked them
all, especially the exuberant Jimmy Grey and the quiet
thirteen-year-old, John Allen. Even the two shaggy-
looking big boys gave no trouble. They had looked her
over once or twice with a calculating eye which had
made her slightly apprehensive, but had obviously dismissed her as too old—or possibly too much of a square
—she didn't mind which—and now regarded her just
as the driver of the car.

As she jumped out of bed she remembered. She had
offered to pick up Nicholas Davidson and bring him
back to Castlebridge. Why did he have to keep cropping
up? Out of all the inhabitants of the district, why did
their paths have to cross continually? She wished now
that she had accepted his patronising apology instead of
acting so childishly. That would have closed the incident
of their first meeting and things would not have been so
strained. Oh well, it was all in the day's work!

After the first few mornings she had persuaded Miss
Williams to stay in bed until later. She took the old lady
up a cup of tea from her breakfast pot and Nanny got

up at her leisure after Jill had gone out. That morning
the phone rang as she was putting on the kettle.

"Miss Railton? I'm sorry to ring you so early, but I
had to catch you before you started for Cinder Cross.
I'm Rita Shelton, the junior teacher at Castlebridge
Primary. I usually come to school on my scooter, but
this morning I can't start it. If I catch the bus which
takes the children into the Grammar School and get off
at Cinder Cross, could you possibly take me into Castlebridge?"

"Of course, Miss Shelton. I'm glad you rang, as I
usually just drop the boys without waiting for the bus.
I will see you later."

As she ate her breakfast her heart sang. Now there
would be no difficulty. Miss Shelton would probably
decide to sit beside her in the front of the car and she
wouldn't have to talk to Mr Davidson at all.

So it came about that Nicholas Davidson, waiting at
the corner of the road, all strung up and determined
once and for all to straighten out the muddle which
existed between himself and the wretched Miss Railton,
was thwarted again.

"Good morning, Mr Davidson." Jill opened the
car door in her approved taxi-driver style—slightly
exaggerated, if the truth be told—"I hope it was a quiet
night at Fir Lodge?"

"Absolutely peaceful, thank you."

And that was all! Jill went back to the conversation
she had been having with Miss Shelton about the possible
causes of the trouble with her scooter, and ten minutes
later the Rover pulled up outside the school.

"I'll pick you up here at about ten past four then,
Miss Shelton. Goodbye. Goodbye, Mr Davidson. I must
fly. I've got another appointment at nine fifteen." Jill

smiled at the girl and drove away, leaving a frustrated
and annoyed young man standing on the pavement!

*　　　*　　　*

That Monday morning was a pattern for the rest of
the week. Nicholas spent each night out at Fir Lodge
and every morning he waited at the end of the road,
hoping against hope that he would be the only passenger.
But Rita Shelton's scooter needed a major repair and
every day he found her in the seat beside the driver.

Miss Railton was perfectly polite to him, bidding him
good morning and goodbye and answering courteously
if he broke into the conversation with a remark, but he
was a passenger; a stranger who it was her job to transport from one place to another. Even more annoying,
her attitude to the Shelton girl was friendly and gay;
they laughed and chattered like magpies on the short
trips to and from Cinder Cross. He also knew that she
was very friendly with all the Barlow family. Apparently
he was the only person with whom Miss Railton would
not unbend. He told himself fiercely that such an
obstinate, unforgiving nature was a very bad trait in
a girl, and he was much better off without her friendship, but it didn't do the least good. He wanted to be
friends. He wanted her to know that he hadn't refused
her kindly offered lift that morning because she was
Ernest Railton's daughter, but because he had been fool
enough to fall in love with another blue-eyed fair-haired
girl who had let him down, and he knew he wouldn't
be satisfied until he had told her.

Jill was having a lovely week. She liked Rita Shelton
and felt that their friendship would last even after the
scooter was repaired. She was also thoroughly enjoying

51

the time she spent in the company of the Barlow family. Joyce was a wonderful person. She asked no questions about the reason for Jill's unusual occupation; made no effort to pry into the girl's past; but at the same time she was genuinely interested in all the day-to-day happenings of Jill's life. They might have been cousins, or even sisters, and Jill, bereft of all close relatives, appreciated her attitude more than she could say.

On Monday and Wednesday she picked up the family at Fir Lodge during the morning and drove them, once to Shepley and once to a village five miles from Castlebridge, picking them up again after tea, but on Tuesday and Thursday, having no other trips booked, she drove them to the sea at Wittering and spent the day there, returning in time for the school journey. She went into the sea with them, ran races with them, and helped to dress them afterwards. She loved them all; the quicksilver Tilly, the quieter Mary and the boisterous Mark. Mark was the biggest handful; being the eldest he had been somewhat spoilt and Jill felt that he needed his father's supervision. But he was a most lovable imp and soon forgot his annoyance when he was prevented from doing something on which he had set his heart.

There had been the business of the circus for example. There were posters in Wittering advertising Bamer's Circus in Chichester on Friday and Mark at once demanded that they should all go.

"No, Mark, I'm afraid not. Tilly is much too young, and we should not be able to get home afterwards because Jill would have to go back to Castlebridge long before the show was over."

"Why can't we come home by bus? I would like to see the circus. Look, Mummy, there are elephants. I would like to see the elephants."

Mary had joined in then, also demanding to see the elephants and Joyce, tired and in pain, was rather short with her persistent young son.

"Now just stop it, Mark! We are not going to the circus and that is flat. If you are very good until Daddy comes I will ask him if he will take you to the Bertram Mills Circus in London next Christmas. That will be much bigger than this one."

Jill glanced at her watch. "We ought to be starting back in ten minutes, please, Mrs Barlow. Who would like an ice before we go?" And the circus was forgotten!

On Friday the weather broke, the rain came down in torrents and Joyce Barlow telephoned to cancel their outing. Jill, after the previous busy days, was not sorry to have a few hours to spare to help Nanny in the house. At about half past three the rain stopped and at four o'clock she pulled up as usual outside the school.

Rita Shelton came running out to the place where Nicholas Davidson was already waiting.

"Miss Railton, I shan't be going back with you this afternoon after all. Mummy phoned earlier in the day. She wants me to join her on the four twenty-five train and go to London with her. She has got tickets for Blue Narcissus, and now Daddy can't get away to go so I'm going instead. And she says that the garage have phoned to say that my scooter is ready, so I shall be all right for next week. Thank you ever so much for taking me as you have done. I do wish you'd accept your fare though. I feel so mean—as if I'd been cadging. I know you say that you get paid for those trips already, but you've come out of your way to drop me and pick me up here."

"I've enjoyed your company. I hope you will let me know any time if you need to come by the bus and that

53

you'll enjoy the show. I believe it's grand. Oh, it's going to pour again. What a day!"

Jill jumped out of the car, avoiding a big puddle, went round to the near side where Nicholas was standing and made a move to open the rear door for him.

"I want to ride in front with the taxi lady! It's my turn today!" He spoke in childish tones, reminding Jill of the endless argument which went on between Mark and Mary each time she took them out.

She stiffened and hesitated. During her trips with the Barlows she had heard a lot about Nicholas. Uncle Nick was a great favourite with the children and almost like a brother to their mother. Amongst other things she had learned that his injury had been caused by a car accident and that the car had been driven by his girl friend.

"I never saw her," Joyce Barlow had said, "but Nicholas sent me a snap of her. Very attractive in a way, I should think, with colouring rather like yours, but she looked a bit too artificial to be my cup of tea." Then she had laughed rather ruefully. "But there, I suppose I'd find something wrong with any girl with whom Nick fell in love. Didn't W. S. Gilbert say something about sisterly jealousy?"

For a few seconds they stood facing each other—two sensitive young people, both longing to be friends but finding it difficult to break the ice.

The ice was broken for them by a big lorry laden with sand. It came roaring along the road without noticing the water on the surface and sent a sheet of spray into the faces of both of them! Fortunately they were wearing raincoats and the water wasn't muddy— the road surface had been cleaned by the earlier rain —but they looked so comical that they both started laughing. It was the best thing which could have hap-

pened. You couldn't go on being stiff and frosty while
you were shaking with giggles. Jill shut the rear door,
Nicholas slipped in beside the driving seat and half a
minute later they were off.

"My goodness, I'm a bit late! That was stopping to
talk." Jill waited until she was clear of the built-up area
and then put her foot down. Suddenly she remembered.
"Oh, I forgot! Does speed worry you?"

"Not in the ordinary way. Certainly not like this."
He paused. "I suppose Joyce told you about my accident? And about the driver?"

"Well, a bit about the driver. I gather that I look
like her?"

"At first glance, but not really. Vivienne is older than
you and more—more—I suppose you would say more
sophisticated, but I hate that word."

Jill felt a sudden pang—a tug on her heart strings.
She could picture that other girl—lovely, poised and
desirable—in fact, all the things she herself was not.
And seeing her suddenly in the driving seat must have
brought back a bitter memory of the accident and the
danger Vivienne had been in. She wanted to ask more
but Nicholas continued before she had a chance.

"I'm sorry I was such an ass," he said, "especially
when one of the kids in school told me your name and
I realised what you were bound to have thought."

"That's all right. We are all square anyway. I was
beastly rude. Let's call it quits. Here we are." She
stopped at the corner leading to Fir Lodge. "I'm so glad
Mr Barlow comes tomorrow."

"So am I. Goodbye, Jill. Very many thanks for the
lifts."

Jill nodded and sped away. After all her hurry she
had plenty of time as the bus was late, but after waiting

ten minutes, chatting with Mrs Pullar and hearing of the events at Fir Lodge through that day of bad weather, she saw it coming. Her six passengers took their places and they set off for Castlebridge.

As she was passing the lane leading to Fir Lodge she glanced idly in that direction, then put her foot hard down on the brake. Through the rain, which was now coming down hard again, she saw small Mary running at full speed towards her, while Nicholas was hurrying along behind her as fast as his limp would allow.

Not wishing to let the child rush into the road in case another car should come along, she backed into the lane. "Hello, Mary! Did you want to see me?"

"Yes. Mark has gone and we can't find him. We've looked everywhere."

Jill, remembering Mrs Pullar's tales of a bored and rather difficult small boy, who, in the woman's words, would be the better for a good spanking, smiled reassuringly.

"I expect he is hiding, Mary, just for fun." She waited until Nicholas reached her and raised her eyebrows enquiringly.

"He has disappeared completely, Jill. Joyce has hunted everywhere, even in the garden, though it's so soaking wet out there that I think even he would hesitate. Joyce is in an awful state, feeling helpless because of her leg. I hate to bother you, Jill, and to make the boys a bit late back, but could you possibly go back to Cinder Cross and ask Mrs Pullar if she knows where he is? Joyce felt that he might possibly have walked back with her."

"No, he isn't there. I've just been talking to Mrs Pullar. Is Mrs Barlow sure he isn't in the house or garden?"

"Yes, they've been over the place with a fine tooth

56

comb. Joyce has worn herself out. Little monkey! Which way can he have gone?"

Jill shook her head helplessly. "Look, Nick, I must get the boys home. I'll drop them and come straight back. And we'll keep an eye open for him along the road, although I can't think of any reason why he should have gone to Castlebridge. Do you know what he was wearing?"

Nicholas glanced at Mary, who brightened up at the prospect of giving some information. "The same as he had on yesterday," she said promptly. "That blue and white thing."

Jill smiled her thanks, let in the clutch and swung back on to the main road. "Keep an eye open, all of you, will you, please. Mark Barlow is seven, with dark hair, and wearing a blue and white shirt. But with all this rain I should think he would have been bound to take cover, even if he is on this road."

The boys scanned the route eagerly but there was no sign of the sturdy little figure. Jill dropped them at the Memorial, turned the big Rover round and roared off again, carefully enough in the built-up area but touching sixty on the open road beyond. Less than a quarter of an hour after she had left Nicholas and Mary she was back at Fir Lodge. She hoped against hope that the child would have returned, but one glance at Joyce's haggard face told its own story. Where, oh where, could the boy have gone?

CHAPTER 7

"Oh, Mrs Barlow, don't worry so! He can't have come to any harm, can he, even if he has decided to go off on an expedition of his own? He is very good about looking before he crosses the road, and he has got lots of sense."

"That's what I keep telling her, Jill. Now look, Joyce, we'll take Mary and Tilly, and you sit down and put your leg up. Come on, kids! Never mind the rain; the car is just outside."

Tilly, ready for anything, ran out into the downpour at once, scrambled into the driving seat, because Jill had left that door open, and ensconced herself firmly alongside the driver. In spite of her anxiety Jill couldn't help smiling. She turned to Mrs Barlow.

"Would you please telephone to Miss Williams for me, Mrs Barlow, and let her know what is happening? She will be expecting me back."

"Yes, I'll do that. And are you sure I shouldn't phone the police, Nick?"

"Not yet. After all, it is only a bit over an hour since he was with you. If we can't get a clue we'll come back and then perhaps you'll have to, but they won't thank you for alerting them yet. Come on, Mary, we'll go in the back and you can look out one side while I watch the other. I'll give you sixpence if you see him first."

His light-hearted tone had its intended effect and

Joyce managed half a smile as Jill started the engine and turned into the drive.

"Which way, Nick? I've been to Cinder Cross without seeing him and also to Castlebridge. Where else can we look?"

"We'll go along the lane here. He might have gone to the farm. I was talking about it yesterday evening, and telling him about the pony Joyce and I used to ride."

But when they turned in through the farm gate and he enquired from the farmer's wife she shook her head.

"No, sir, I'm afraid not. My 'usband might have seen 'im though." She called over her shoulder. "Will, there's a gennelman 'ere looking for a small boy, Colonel Furneaux's grandson, that's staying at the lodge. 'Aven't seen 'im, 'ave you?"

There was the sound of scraping chair legs and the farmer, a big burly man, joined them.

"Don't think so, Maggie. I seen some kids splashing along the lane 'bout 'alf an hour ago, just as I was coming in, but I didn't take much notice of 'em, being in an 'urry like. Two of 'em were the Jevons kids—I saw young Sally's red pigtails 'anging down 'er back—but, now I come to think of it, there was one I'd never seen before—little dark-haired boy—'bout six or seven I should think."

"That could easily be Mark. Thank you so much. Where does the Jevons family live? I'd better see them."

"About half a mile along; where the lane joins the main road. There are two cottages and Bob Jevons is in the first one."

Nicholas thanked them again and went back to the car. "It may be a false alarm, Jill," he said, "but it is worth trying."

But as they rounded the last bend in the lane they

were brought to a halt. A big elm had fallen across the road, blocking it completely. Two men armed with a petrol saw had taken off some of the branches, but it was obviously going to be a long job. As Jill stopped, the younger of the two came up to the car.

"Sorry, ma'am, I'm afraid you'll have to go back. The rain washed a bit of the bank away and brought this old chap down."

"Oh, dear, what an awful job for you in all this weather. Tell me, have any children been along this way since you came? We are looking for a little boy."

"Only the pair from the cottage on the corner, ma'am, and one other nipper with them. We lifted them over the tree."

Jill questioned him eagerly, but he had not really taken much notice of the children and still they had no real proof that the third one was Mark.

"How far is the cottage from here?" she asked.

"Only about a hundred yards, ma'am." He looked at Nicholas. "I could give you a hand to get over if you'd like to walk along there, sir."

"No, Nick, you can't; not with your bad leg. I'll go."

Nicholas opened his mouth to protest, but she was obviously right and he had to let her go. The two men helped her on to the trunk of the huge elm and down the other side and she disappeared from view.

After what seemed a long time, but was actually only five minutes, she reappeared, jumped down from the tree trunk and came running towards the car.

"Nick, I believe it was Mark. The Jevons' cottage was locked up, but a woman in the adjoining one heard me knocking and came out. She said she had seen a small boy standing at the gate when the Jevons children went in. He was wearing a navy blue raincoat but nothing on his head. He had brown eyes and dark hair and he was wearing muddy white socks and brown sandals. But that's not all. She says the Jevons family have all gone to the circus in Chichester! Mary, has Mark been talking about the circus today?"

"Oh yes, lots and lots of times. Mummy got cross in the end and told him he wasn't to say any more about it."

"And then these other kids probably told him they were going." Nicholas broke in eagerly. "But I wonder why he came this way. You'd have thought he'd have gone to Castlebridge. That's the quickest way to the coast."

"We came back this way from Wittering yesterday. Mrs Barlow said it was a short cut and it did save about two miles. But, Nick, how would he think he was going to get there? Oh, if only we could get through!"

"I know. We'll have to go back, up to Cinder Cross and then along the main road until we get to the junction with the Chichester road. But we'd have to go back to Fir Lodge to tell Joyce what has happened and to drop the girls."

There was a wail of protest from Mary, but Jill backed the big car until she reached a gateway in which it was safe to turn and then roared away along the lane to Fir Lodge.

They found that Joyce, unable to bear the suspense any longer, had got on to the police constable in Castlebridge and was expecting him out at any moment. Nicholas told her what they had found out, delivered the protesting small girls into her charge and he and Jill set off again.

It took them twenty minutes to reach the corner where

the Jevons' cottage stood and then they started watching carefully on either side of the road as the miles rolled away. The rain was still teeming down in sheets and it seemed impossible that any seven-year-old would go on walking through it towards a goal so many miles away.

Nicholas was silent now; anxious and troubled. Mark was so young—so vulnerable. Suppose he had accepted a lift? One read such horrible stories. And Colonel Furneaux was a well-known man; a Deputy Lieutenant and wealthy. Suppose Mark mentioned his grandfather. Nicholas shivered and then made an effort to pull himself together.

"Chichester, one mile," he said, as they passed a signpost. "What shall we do when we get there? We can hardly ask the circus people if they have seen a small boy."

Jill tried to smile, though she was not far from tears. "I suppose we'd better go in and try to get into a position from which we can look at the audience. It's funny really; I hate circuses. The trapeze acts frighten me to death and I can't bear seeing animals doing tricks. But of course I shan't be looking at the acts this evening."

But when, some ten minutes later, they walked up to the ticket office, their plans received a check.

"Sorry, sir, full up!"

In vain Nicholas explained the position; the woman was adamant. The authorities were very strict, and taking too many people was forbidden.

"Don't you see, there's a copper standing by that car, and he's got his eye on you now. I'm sorry, sir, but I can't do anything."

Jill and Nick looked back towards the Rover. Suddenly Jill's spirits rose with a bound.

"Nick, perhaps he's been told to look out for the car.

Perhaps Mark has got back and Joyce has asked the police to let us know. Oh, I do hope that's it."

Leaving Nicholas to follow at his own speed, she rushed across the muddy field. "This is my car. Were you by any chance looking for me?"

"Miss Railton?" She nodded. "I've been asked by Castlebridge to contact you and give you any assistance I can, Miss. I take it you haven't found the small boy?"

"No. I hoped you might have come to tell us he was home. But you can help us, Constable." She went on to explain the difficulty about getting into the tent. "Of course she is only doing her duty, but couldn't you tell her that it would be all right to make an exception this time and let us in? We can't just wait until the show is over. If he is in there we might miss him in the crowd who will be coming out."

"All right, Miss. Leave it to me." He crossed to the pay desk and returned three minutes later. "I've fixed it for one of you to come in with me. There are gangways every twenty seats, so you should be able to see the boy if he is there."

"That's fine, Constable. I'll go, Jill. You get a bit of rest."

Jill wanted to protest that it would be too much strain on his leg, but he gave her no time. He and the policeman disappeared into the big tent and she got back into the car and tried to relax. Although the rain was easing to a drizzle now, and it was only seven o'clock, the clouds were so low that it was already dusk. Lights were blazing from the windows of the caravans which bordered the field and she could also see that the tent which adjoined the big top, and which was presumably the place where the artists waited their turns to perform, was also brightly lighted.

Half an hour passed—each leaden minute seeming an eternity—and she could not wait in the car any longer. The rain had quite stopped now, and despite the mud she started walking towards this second tent, wondering whether it would be possible from there to see into the big top and perhaps catch sight of Nicholas and the policeman.

She was half way there when she heard a man's angry voice.

"You again, boy! Get out! It's time you were in bed. D'ya hear!" There was the sound of a blow and a child's squeal. "Now get away. If I catch you prowling round here again I'll give you a real licking."

In the half light Jill saw the child come rushing out, tripping over one of the ropes and falling headlong. He picked himself up and moved slowly towards the caravans and she wondered what his mother would have to say to him. He was plastered in mud from head to foot.

Poor little fellow, he looks neglected and half starved, she thought compassionately, as she saw his bare feet and a bleeding scratch down one leg. Then the door of the nearest caravan was opened and a shaft of light fell on his face.

"Mark! Mark darling, it's me, the taxi lady." She hurled herself across the grass towards him, and in five seconds he was in her arms, clinging to her as if he would never let her go!

CHAPTER 8

"THERE's the paper boy coming now, Joyce. I wonder what they've got to say."

"I'll get it, Uncle Nick." Mary popped down from her chair before Mark, rather sleepy that morning, could forestall her. She ran out into the hall and came back with the folded paper. "Does it say something about Mark?"

When the Rover had reached Fir Lodge on the previous evening—Nick having already telephoned to Joyce to allay her anxiety—they had found the local reporter for the *West Sussex Gazette* awaiting them. Mark had been bathed and put to bed and they had given the man the bare outline of the story.

It had been so simple after all. The small boy, bored with being cooped up all day in the house, had put on his raincoat and had slipped off for a walk on his own. In the lane he had fallen in with the Jevons children and had learned of their coming visit to the circus, which had added fuel to the flames of his own longing. He had made the journey to Chichester in the boot of Mr Jevons' old car, which, fortunately for the boy, he had not locked when he reached his destination.

It was not until he was actually approaching the pay desk that he had realised that he had no money! Poor Mark! He was too honest to try to slip in undetected among the groups of children, and he just hung about unnoticed as the crowds surged past him. He was soaked to the skin, his sandals were hurting and he took them off and put them on the ground beside him. Then one of the circus hands, suspecting him of planning to gate-crash the show, chased him away, and he could not find his way back to the place where he had left his shoes.

He had roamed round the ground, growing hungrier and more desperate as time passed, and had finally been attracted by the light streaming from the tent adjoining the big top. There he had had his one piece of good fortune. He had seen the elephants being brought through to do their act. He had been gazing at them in fascinated awe when the same man had sighted him again. Then Jill had come and his troubles were over.

The reporter had done his job well. The story, which was on the front page, was headed "A Chip Off the Old Block!" It recalled the exploits of Colonel Furneaux when, as a young sub-lieutenant in the First World War, he had made his way undetected behind the enemy lines, and it painted the adventures of the Colonel's small grandson in almost equally glowing colours.

The last paragraph reported the chase by Miss Jill Railton, the enterprising lady taxi driver of Castlebridge. Nicholas grinned as Joyce read it aloud. This was a piece of good, free advertising for Jill!

When Joyce and the children had left the dining-room Nicholas took the paper again and read the article more carefully. Jill! The name suited her. He smiled as he thought of the different expressions he had seen on her face since their first, most regrettable meeting; hurt, angry, gay and grave; but always her blue eyes had looked honestly and fearlessly into his. How plucky she was, too. It couldn't have been easy for anyone brought up in the lap of luxury, as she must have been, to take on the job she was doing; to be at the beck and call of all types of passengers.

How could he—even for one fleeting moment—have thought she was like Vivienne! He tried to picture that spoilt young woman in similar circumstances, but his imagination was not good enough for the task. Of course Vivienne would not have thought of doing any such thing. She would just have wound her tentacles firmly round the first eligible male and expected him to look after her. And the wretched man would have done it, too! He himself had good reason to know that.

How soon could he see Jill again? He'd have no excuse for spending the nights at Fir Lodge any longer, as Michael Barlow would be here. Could he think up some message which would necessitate his calling her on the phone? Would she come out and have a meal with him one evening? There wasn't much doing at Castlebridge, but perhaps they could go up to Town and do a show. She had sounded rather wistful when Rita Shelton had been talking about the Blue Narcissus. Anyway, he would see her again somehow and go on seeing her. And then, when he got himself fixed up with a permanent teaching job—which he would have to do, as old Mr Bean would be returning to Castlebridge Primary next term—he would ask her to chuck being a taxi driver and be a school teacher's wife instead.

He had got that far with his daydream when Mark came bursting into the room.

"Uncle Nick, we've found an old swing in the garage. Will you come and fix it up for us?"

"I'll have a shot, Mark. I think I remember that swing. Your mother and her brother used to use it when they were small, and I did, too, when I was staying here with them."

The ropes were rotten and quite unsafe, but Nicholas remembered seeing a bundle of new sash cord rope in the scullery. Some of it had been used to repair the clothes airer. Nick sent Mary to beg for it and, accompanied by all three children, made his way to an old oak tree in the garden.

"There, you see that branch which sticks out straight? The swing used to hang from that."

It took half an hour before he would pass the finished article as safe for use. Then he gave small Tilly a gentle ride before leaving the two bigger ones to take their turns. He was going back to the house when an old but beautifully kept Rolls Royce swung up the drive and pulled up before the front door. The chauffeur got out and assisted his passenger to alight. He was a tall man, white-haired and upright, but he wore very dark tinted glasses and walked with a white stick. Nicholas hurried forward.

"Good morning. Can I help you, sir?"

The man looked towards him. "Thank you. I have come to see Colonel Furneaux. Are you young John? If so, I think we have met before. But your voice does not sound familiar."

"No, sir. My name is Davidson. Colonel Furneaux is my godfather and I spent a lot of time here when I was a boy, but I don't think we have met?" He put a slight query into his voice.

"No, I don't think we have, though Colonel Furneaux has often spoken to me of you. My name is Greening —Martin Greening—and I came to live at Haime two years ago when I retired."

Nicholas looked at him with interest. Sir Martin Greening, Q.C., one of the most respected barristers in

London, well known for his defence of anyone who he considered might have had an unfair deal.

"Colonel Furneaux is away just now, sir. He is on holiday in France. Joyce—Mrs Barlow—is here with her children. Would you like to see her?"

At that moment Joyce, who had seen the car from the window, came hurrying out.

"Sir Martin, how nice to see you again." She took his outstretched hand in hers. "Dad wrote to me about your sight. I was so sorry. Is it very bad?"

"It's not permanent, my dear; at least, I hope not. The surgeons have to wait until a certain stage is reached before they operate on the cataract. It's just unfortunate that both my eyes are affected at the same time. At present I am almost blind. I can just see that someone dressed in blue is standing in front of me. But Mr Fern hopes to operate in September and he says he sees no reason why my sight should not be almost as good as new."

"I'm so glad. We are just going to have some coffee. Andrews, if you'd like to go round and see Mrs Pullar you can pick out that blue mug you are so fond of!" She gave her arm to Sir Martin to lead him into the house. She settled him in a comfortable armchair and put a small table by his side before handing him his cup.

"Was it something special you wanted to see Daddy about, Sir Martin? He'll be home at the end of next week, but he is travelling round in France and I can't get into touch with him."

"No. It was really to find out about you and your family that I came. I can't read the newspapers now and I hate having them read to me. But Andrews tells me that there is an article in the *Gazette* about your son getting into mischief, trying to see the circus, and having half the constabulary of West Sussex searching for him."

"Well, it was not quite as bad as that," laughed Joyce, and she and Nicholas recounted the whole story. He listened carefully; his head turned slightly sideways, as if by catching every inflection of their voices he might make up to some extent for his loss of sight.

"Fortunately Mark seems to have got over it completely this morning. In fact, I have a feeling that he sees himself as quite a hero. Little pickle! What Michael will say when he hears I can't imagine."

"And this woman who drives a taxi? Tell me about her."

"Jill? She is a splendid person—not much more than a child. I believe she is nineteen and she holds the certificate from the School of Advanced Motoring, but she doesn't look her age. The children are very fond of her—and of her car! It is an exciting-looking vehicle to be a taxi, silver and blue. I understand that her father gave it to her for her last birthday. He died shortly afterwards, and as she is not too well off she decided to make her living with it."

"Blue and silver, eh? Am I right in thinking that her surname is Railton?" Surprised at his interest, Joyce said it was, and he continued: "Do you know anything about her father? How he died, for instance?"

"No, I never asked her."

"I do." Nicholas thought it would be best to confirm the barrister's suspicion. "Her father was Ernest Railton, the financier. Do you know anything about him, sir?"

"I should do—he married my daughter. So your taxi driver is my grand-daughter. I haven't seen her since her mother died—some ten years ago—and not very often before that. Her father and I—well, we didn't exactly get on together. She was a scrawny little object the last time we met."

"She is lovely now." Joyce spoke thoughtfully. "Of course that's it! I've often wondered who it was that she resembled. If you put her into the same costume, she could have sat for that portrait of Lady Greening which you have in your sitting-room, Sir Martin. You'd like her, I know. She is full of grit and doesn't let anything get her down."

"I must make her acquaintance. Perhaps when Andrews has his day off I might need a taxi."

"I thought your invaluable Horace drove you then?" Joyce looked at him quizzically. "How is he, by the way, and dear old Mrs Greeves, too?"

"Oh, of course, you didn't know. Horace had a brother who went to New Zealand as a young man, and he died last year leaving everything to Horace. So six months ago he and Sarah went off to take possession of their inheritance. I heard from him last week. He says it is a wonderful country, and he wants me to go out and pay them a long visit. He doesn't know how much worse my sight has got."

"Poor Sir Martin, I can't imagine your house without Mr and Mrs Greeves. How are you managing?"

"I had a dreadful time at first. One or two couples answered my advertisement, but either they didn't like the country or the idea of having to act as valet to a man who is almost blind seemed too much like work. For a while Andrews was doing everything for me and his wife came in to run the house. But then came the Easter holidays and the children were home from school, which made things very difficult for her. I was almost desperate when I had a letter from a great nephew in Australia; the grandson of my sister Rachel, who married

an Australian soldier in 1918. I lost touch with that
branch of the family when Rachel died, and I was
delighted to hear from Edward Blake."

"How nice for you. Is he—Edward—in England
now?"

"Indeed he is, Joyce. He is a splendid fellow, who is
at present acting as my valet, secretary and indeed as
my right hand. I think he has led rather a wild life—
his parents died when he was only a boy and he had to
fend for himself—but his wide experience is a great help
to me. I understand that his varied jobs have included
manservant, receptionist in a hotel in Melbourne and
assistant purser in a passenger ship, so he says he finds
it child's play to look after one old man, even if he is
almost blind."

"I'm so glad you've got someone to help you," said
Joyce warmly. "But surely he can't manage to run the
house and do the cooking as well?"

"No, that would be too much. But he had met a young
woman—also Australian—on the plane coming to
England. She was hoping to find work in this country,
so he got into touch with her. I must admit that her
cooking doesn't quite equal Sarah's, but it is adequate,
and of course I don't entertain much at present."

Nick's thoughts were still on Jill. "But, Sir Martin,
if you have this Mr—Mr Blake—surely he can drive
you if your chauffeur is off duty?"

Sir Martin shook his head. "No. I suggested that, but
he had to admit that his licence in Australia had been
suspended. I told you that he had been a bit wild, and
I gather that a certain rather hectic party was responsible. But of course that bars his getting a licence over
here. So when Andrews is away I am very awkwardly
placed." He put down his coffee cup and rose to his

feet, a commanding and dominant personality in spite of his affliction. "I shall be most glad to get in touch with Jill. I had no idea what had become of her. I was at a clinic at the time the—the tragedy occurred, and did not know anything about it until it was too late even to try to express my sympathy." He put his hand on Joyce's shoulder. "Come over and see me if you have time to spare while you are here, Joyce. And you, too, Mr Davidson. I know that living in digs can be dreary at times, so if you feel like coming out to keep an old man company for the week-end, just give me a ring."

Nicholas thanked him and shook hands, and as Joyce accompanied Sir Martin to his car he heard her giving the barrister Jill's phone number. He stood at the window watching the Rolls running smoothly down the drive and his heart felt like lead. Gone was his daydream of asking Jill to share the life of a schoolmaster. As Sir Martin Greening's grand-daughter she was as far above him as the stars. He could guess what would happen. Sir Martin would get into touch with her and persuade her to give up the taxi business, and in no time at all she would be making her home with him. Then, when he had had the operation on his eyes, he would go to New Zealand for a long visit and take Jill with him, and he—Nicholas—would see her no more!

CHAPTER 9

JILL had gone up to collect Nanny's breakfast tray and they had just read the article in the *Gazette* when the telephone rang. She ran down and answered it.

"Castlebridge 4278. Miss Railton—taxi."

"My name is Mrs Younge. I live at the Old Vicarage at Shepley and I want to be driven to Petworth. Are you booked up this morning, or can you do the trip?"

"Yes, Mrs Younge, I can fit that in. What time do you wish to get to Petworth?"

She made a note of the instructions and rang off. Before the time came to start for Shepley she had booked two trips for that afternoon and three more for the following Monday. There was no knowing how long it would last; probably it would be only a nine-days-wonder; but she might as well make the most of it.

Miss Williams was rather unhappy about this sudden rush of orders. "I wish you had only to take trips for people you know something about, Jill. You may get some most unpleasant folk who will take advantage of you and keep you hanging about until late at night. I don't like it."

The same idea had flashed across Jill's mind, but she had pushed it into the background. She was running a business now and personal likes and dislikes must not be allowed to enter into it.

"You needn't worry, Nanny. I'll take care. But I'll

tell you what I'll do. I'll always keep enough small change on me to be able to telephone you if I'm going to be later than I had expected. Now I must fly. It would be a bad start to my newly acquired rush of work if I was late. I shall go straight from this first trip to Mrs Younge at Shepley, so I shan't be back until lunch-time."

In actual fact she wasn't back until teatime, but to allay Nanny's anxiety she telephoned to Kilkenny Cottage from Petworth. When she got back from the last run that afternoon she sank into one of the comfortable little chairs by the open window in the sitting-room and smiled gaily at the old lady.

"Nanny, it's quite fun being a celebrity! Mrs Younge gave me coffee and Mrs Baker gave me lunch, and they both wanted to know all about what they called my hair-raising adventures. I'm getting quite used to it now. I've concocted an exciting story which doesn't really tell them a thing which wasn't in the *Gazette* this morning and they seem quite satisfied. But apart from the publicity, everyone I have driven today has approved of me and the car, and has promised to employ me in the future, so Mark Barlow and the circus have done me a good turn."

"That's splendid for you, dear, but I still wish you didn't have to do it. But perhaps you won't need to earn your living for much longer. This afternoon your grandfather telephoned to me. He didn't know, until he heard the story this morning, where you were living. He wants you to come over and visit him as soon as you have a free afternoon. Perhaps he will ask you to live with him. He must be rather lonely."

At the mention of her grandfather's name Jill's expression hardened. Gone was the happy, excited girl, making a success of her job, and in her place was a serious-looking woman—firm and determined.

"He'll have to wait a long time before he receives a visit from me, Nanny. In all the years since Mummy died I've hardly had a word from him. If Daddy could have gone to him for help it might have made all the difference, and at least you'd have thought that, if he really cared at all about me, Grandfather could have got into touch with me when Daddy died. No, he had to wait until all the scandal had died down and people had forgotten that I am Ernest Railton's daughter, so now he can jolly well do without me. Now, what about to-morrow? Would you like to go out somewhere for the day, Nanny? Or would you rather go to church in the morning and then we could take our tea and have a run somewhere in the afternoon?"

"I'd like to go to church, dear, but it would be nice to go out in the afternoon, if only to get away from that old telephone. There it goes again!"

But that time it was only a wrong number and for the rest of the evening they were left in peace.

*   *   *

On Monday morning Jill picked up the Grammar School boys as usual and looked out for Nicholas when she reached Tindal on the return journey, hoping to give him a lift and hear how the Barlow family were getting on.

But Nicholas had made up his mind that the less he saw of the girl who had so completely captured his heart, the better it would be for him. He had discovered that there was an alternative though slightly longer route which led from his lodgings to the school and had left early enough to go that way, and although each morning and each afternoon on her trips to Cinder Cross Jill kept watch for the halting figure, she was doomed to disappointment.

So, although from the point of business it was a most satisfactory week, by Friday evening she was feeling flat and unhappy. She told herself firmly that it was just reaction. She couldn't expect life to go on being as exciting as it had during her first days of taxi work, and of course it would be much too exhausting if it did. She would not admit, even to herself, that Nicholas was at the root of her unhappiness. What difference did it make to her if she never set eyes on him again? They were friends, and it was no use crying for the moon. But she sighed heavily as she washed up the tea things on Friday and went out to check over the car in preparation for a busy Saturday.

*   *   *

Nicholas, too, had had a dull week. Joyce Barlow had given him an invitation to join them at Fir Lodge on any evening he liked, but by the time he got back to his rooms he was too tired to walk the extra distance. The bigger boys at the school had tests coming up shortly, and this meant a lot of extra work and a bit of coaching for the less bright ones. By Friday evening he was worn out and disheartened. His leg did not seem to be improving at all. He couldn't hear of a single vacancy for the coming September which appealed to him in the least. He found himself wondering dismally if he was doomed to spend the rest of his teaching life moving from one part-time job to another; always living in digs and permanently lame.

How was Jill getting on, he wondered? Perhaps he had been foolish to try to avoid seeing her. After all, it couldn't do her any harm, and it would brighten his days a little, just to start the mornings sitting by her side in the Rover, watching her sure touch on the wheel and sometimes stealing a swift glance at her lovely face.

He wondered if she and her grandfather had been in touch with each other yet. Perhaps she would be spending some time with the old chap during the coming week-end. Suddenly he remembered the invitation he himself had received to go along to Haime Grange at any time when he felt the need of a change. That was an idea. He'd telephone to Sir Martin and see if he could go the next day, and he'd ring Jill and book her to drive him there. He finished his meal, called through to Mrs Pelman to say that he was going out and limped along to the call box.

Sir Martin answered the phone himself and sounded genuinely pleased to hear from him.

"Splendid! I shall be glad to have you, my boy. Bring some things and spend the night here, won't you? Andrews can drive you back to your digs on Sunday evening. Would you like him to come over and fetch you? It's too far to walk."

"That's good of you, Sir Martin, but please don't bother. I'll get your grand-daughter to bring me. She has given me a lift so often and refused payment that I shall be glad to have a chance of hiring her for a trip for a change."

There was silence and then Sir Martin laughed rather ruefully. "Well, you'd better not let her know your destination until she has agreed to take the trip. I've tried several times during the last few days to get her to come here and I have failed. In fact, I haven't even spoken to her yet. Old Miss Williams always seems to answer the telephone and—although she doesn't say so in so many words—I gather that the child has no desire at all to renew acquaintance with me."

Nicholas's heart leapt! So Jill didn't want to be just Sir Martin's grand-daughter; a member of a rich man's family; a lady of leisure. Perhaps, after all, she wasn't so utterly beyond his reach. Then his conscience smote him as he remembered the old man's blindness. Perhaps Jill didn't know about that.

"Thank you for the warning, Sir Martin." He spoke as lightly as he could. "I'll not tell her where I want to go. Will you expect me sometime during the morning then, please; whenever Jill can fit in the trip. She is bound to be busy as it is a Saturday."

He rang off and dialled 4278. Miss Williams answered and told him that Miss Railton was outside cleaning the car and could she take a message.

"I was wondering if she could find time tomorrow morning to pick me up at my rooms—she knows where I live—in Tindal—and take me over to Haime. I'm staying there for the week-end with a friend of my god-father's."

"I'll go and ask her, Mr Davidson. Will you hold the line, please."

"Right. Oh, and, Miss Williams, will you please make it clear to her that I am booking her for this journey —not begging for a lift. She has been far too generous to me already."

Nanny laughed. She had never met Nicholas Davidson but she had heard a lot about him in one way and another. Now she decided that she liked the sound of his voice. It was a good thing that Jill had found at least one young friend in Castlebridge. She smiled to herself as she remembered Jill's first description of the young man; she had revised her opinion now!

She hurried out to the yard and returned to say that Jill would pick him up at ten o'clock, if that would be convenient. She needed to be back in Castlebridge by ten forty-five, to meet a train, but that should fit in all right.

Nicholas hung up and returned to his rooms. His depression was gone. His leg wasn't hurting so badly! A good job would be sure to turn up! And he was going to see Jill tomorrow!

Punctually at ten o'clock the Rover pulled up outside Mrs Pelman's house. Nicholas was waiting by the gate and he came out quickly, threw his week-end case in the back of the car and took his seat beside Jill.

"Which way do we go? I haven't been to Haime yet."

"The best way from here would be to go along that lane where the tree was down last week. Now tell me how you've been getting on since then. What does it feel like to be a celebrity?"

Jill told him a few of the funny experiences she had had since their last meeting, and a quarter of an hour later they emerged from the lane into the main road and a hundred yards farther on turned left towards the village of Haime.

"We go past the church and then turn right," directed Nicholas, "and Haime Grange is about half a mile along on the left."

"Haime Grange? Isn't that where Sir Martin Greening lives?"

"That's right. He is an old friend of Colonel Furneaux, and he called at Fir Lodge last Saturday to get the story of young Mark's adventures. He invited me to come out and see him when I had a week-end to spare."

There was an awkward silence, broken at last when they reached the gate of Haime Grange.

"Nicholas, would you mind if I dropped you here? You probably don't know it, but Sir Martin Greening is my mother's father and I—I don't want to meet him."

"Why not, Jill? Yes, I had heard that he was your grandfather and that he is longing to get to know you better. Apparently he had had no idea that you were in this district until that article came out in the paper last week."

"That's why I don't want anything to do with him! As far as I know, he was the one man who could have helped my father when he was in such trouble. Grandfather must be rolling in money, and if he had offered a loan then Daddy might have been able to—to get through. But for all the notice he took of us he might have been the other side of the world."

"He was! Not actually as far away as that, but quite out of touch with things which were going on. It was about six months ago that—that it happened, wasn't it?" His tone was embarrassed, but Jill nodded impatiently. "Well, it was just then that his sight deteriorated suddenly, and he said that he spent some weeks in a clinic. He knew nothing about your father's trouble until it was far too late to be of any use. He is practically blind now, you know, although he told Joyce that the ophthalmic surgeon hopes to be able to operate soon."

"Oh, Nicholas, I didn't know. Poor Grandfather! I don't remember much about him; I only saw him very rarely when I was a small girl; but I shall never forget his lovely garden in Richmond and the way he used

to walk about among his roses, looking at them and
touching the buds as if—as if to caress them."

She restarted the engine and drove up the short
curling drive, coming to a halt in front of the steps
leading up to the front door.

"My word, what a lovely place." Nicholas looked
round him in admiration.

Haime Grange was quite small but beautifully pro-
portioned. The roof of hand-made brown tiles swept
down in a graceful curve, broken in the middle by a
dormer window, and extended in an almost horizontal
sweep to cover a wide loggia and big bay windows on
either side. On the left of the house—the west side—the
garden fell away in beautiful terraces, and Jill saw that
Sir Martin still retained his love of roses. Sheltered from
the north by a tall barrier of immaculately kept poplar
trees, they blazed from their beds in every conceivable
shade of red, pink and yellow.

But they had no time for more than a quick glance at
the garden before their attention was drawn to the man
who got up from a long chair on the sunny side of the
loggia.

"Is that you, Mr Davidson?" Sir Martin moved
forward, stick in hand, but paused at the top of the wide
steps.

"Yes, Sir Martin, here I am." Nicholas got out and
limped up to shake hands. Then he turned to Jill, who
had taken his bag from the back of the car and come
up to his side. "Er—do I introduce you or what? It
would be a bit odd, wouldn't it?"

"Of course you don't. Grandfather, I didn't know
about your sight or I would have been over to see you
before. And now I can't stop for more than a minute

as I have another appointment. May I come over again sometime, please?"

"Any time, my child." He held out his hand and she took it in both hers. "I wish I could see you. Joyce Barlow tells me that you are like your grandmother. Have you time just to slip into the living-room and look at her portrait?"

He led the way into the room on the left and stopped before a painting in an oval frame, which was hanging on one side of the fireplace.

"Of course, I remember this picture now. Yes, I think it is a bit like me, but I'm not nearly so nice looking."

"Rubbish! Sorry, that sounded rude, but honestly, Jill, it's amazingly like you." Nicholas looked from the pictured face, with its hair style of forty years ago, to the lovely one beside him, and for a moment, had Jill been looking in his direction, she would have seen the unmistakable light of love in his eyes. She, however, was still studying the portrait, and only Sir Martin, accustomed for years to noting the slightest inflection in the human voice, read his tone aright.

Oh, so that is how the land lies, is it, he thought, but wisely kept his own counsel. "That's splendid," he said. "Now I shall be able to picture you easily, until the time comes that they can remove the shutters and let me see again. How about something to drink, my dear, before you go? It wouldn't take more than a few minutes to make a cup of coffee. And you must meet Edward. He is a second cousin of yours—my sister Rachel's grandson—and lives with me at present."

"I'd like to meet him, Grandfather, but I really mustn't stop now. May I come one evening next week? Tuesday or Wednesday?"

"Tuesday would be fine. Come as early as you are free."

"All right. Then I'll be over on Tuesday at about six. I'll look forward to that. Goodbye for now, Grandfather. 'Bye, Nick!" She hurried away and the two men heard the sound of the Rover's engine as the car slid away down the drive.

CHAPTER 10

IT WAS nearly eleven o'clock when Jill got back to Kilkenny Cottage on Tuesday evening, opened the door quietly with her latchkey and crept upstairs.

"Is that you, Jill?"

"Yes, Nanny. I'm sorry if I woke you."

"You didn't, dearie. I've only just got in. There was a nice concert on the television and I didn't come up until half past ten. Did you have a good time?"

"Lovely, Nanny. Grandfather is a darling and he is so brave and uncomplaining. He is so—so interested and alive, in spite of scarcely being able to see at all. I've promised to go over again on Saturday afternoon and spend the night there."

"And the young man who is living with him? What is he like?"

Jill giggled—a girlish sound which made old Miss Williams look at her curiously.

"He is not a bit what I expected," she said. "Nick didn't like him a bit and somehow I got the impression that he was rather a bounder. You know how it is sometimes with people who have had to make their own way in life and haven't cared how many people they hurt in achieving their ambition. But Edward isn't a bit like that. He was charming to me and so gentle and courteous. I can only think that Nick was jealous of him."

"Why should he be jealous?"

"Well, Edward is tremendously good looking; tall and broad-shouldered and sun-tanned." She hesitated and then went on with a little rush: "It's really Edward's fault that I'm so late back. When Grandfather had gone up to bed we sat chatting. He told me something about his life in Australia and wanted to know all about Father and my taxi business and everything. He says that, if Grandfather can spare him, he would like to take me dancing one evening soon. He is so fond of Grandfather, Nanny, and so good and patient. He isn't servile, but he is always there—an arm for Grandfather to lean on."

"How old is he?"

"I don't know. Thirty to thirty-five, I should think. He said that his grandmother—Grandfather's sister— was married when she was twenty, and his parents were both very young, so it is natural that he would be years older than I am, although we are the same generation."

"I'm glad Sir Martin has got him. What about the Australian girl who does the cooking and runs the house? Did you meet her?"

"Yes." Jill frowned. "Her name is Selina—Selina Lester. I didn't care much for the look of her, but I must admit that the supper was very well cooked and served and the house is beautifully kept. I got the impression that she thought I was an intruder. Perhaps she has visions of my going there often and making a lot of extra work for her. Never mind. As long as she looks after my grandfather properly it doesn't matter what she thinks of me. Nanny, I must get to bed. To-morrow is also a day."

*   *   *

"Good morning, Jill!" Nicholas limped forward

quickly as the Rover pulled up alongside him. "Did you enjoy your evening yesterday?"

"I had a lovely time. Grandfather is a darling, isn't he. I'm going out again on Saturday and spending the night, and he told me to say that you would be very welcome, too, if you have nothing better to do."

Nicholas was about to accept eagerly—the prospect of being with Jill for a whole week-end was an entrancing one—but then he remembered Edward.

"How about the nephew-valet-general factotum? How did you get on with him?"

"Edward? I liked him, Nick. He is tremendous fun. I am sure you'd think so, too, if you got to know him better."

So the blighter was fun, was he? Nicholas immediately felt that he himself was old and humourless—a dull schoolmaster, crippled and useless—an object of pity. He writhed.

"Ugh! Well, everyone to his taste. Will you thank Sir Martin for his kind invitation, Jill, and tell him that I'm afraid I can't manage next week-end. No, perhaps I'd better write. It was decent of him to ask me."

A little distressed by this—she, too, had looked forward eagerly to having a few hours with Nicholas instead of a mere five minutes between Tindal and the Memorial —Jill pulled up. "I expect Grandfather would like to get a letter," she said. "See you this afternoon, Nick."

Before going back to Kilkenny Cottage she stopped at the post office to buy some stamps. As she came out she heard her name being called and looked round. Edward was walking quickly towards her.

"Good morning, Jill. I came in early to do my shopping today as I got a lift from the laundry man who calls on Wednesdays. I've nearly finished my list now. How about coming to that little café on the corner and having a cup of coffee or something before I start on the long trail back? This not having a driving licence is a menace. Andrews usually brings Selina or me in for the shopping, but today he is driving Sir Martin to visit an old friend in Winchester."

"Haime is an awkward place if you haven't got a car, isn't it. I can't stop for coffee, I'm afraid, Edward, as I've got to meet the next train. But that trip will only take a short time. If you like to wait about half an hour I could run you out to Haime. My next job isn't until eleven."

"Jill, you are a life-saver! I hate trudging along with a basket full of shopping. I'm thinking of asking Sir Martin if I can keep a horse! At least you don't need a driving licence for that, and I'd feel much more at home. It's a man's way of getting about."

In her mind's eye Jill could visualise the tall, sunburnt figure mounted on a frisky horse, controlling the spirited animal easily with firm but gentle hands. Her own upbringing had not included much contact with horses and she was slightly afraid of them.

"Did you ride a lot in Australia?" she asked.

"Naturally. I could stay in the saddle almost as soon as I could walk." He looked at the pretty, slender girl before him and Jill found herself blushing at the admiration which showed so clearly in his eyes. "Oh, Jill, how I'd like to show you my country one of these days. You'd love it, I know. It's so wide and unrestricted. Who knows? Perhaps sometime in the future, when Sir Martin has got his sight back and doesn't need me any more. But I mustn't keep you and make you late for the train. Where will I see you? At the crossroads?"

"Yes, that would be best. I'll pick you up there at about half past nine."

She hurried back to the Rover and drove back to Kilkenny Cottage to make sure that there were no more orders, then to the station yard, excited and eager. She had never met anyone like Edward before. Of course she didn't like him as much as she liked Nicholas. She couldn't imagine being friends with Edward as she and Nick were friends. He was too—she tried to put her thoughts into words—too forceful. No, that wasn't right; that suggested a domineering character. Too manly perhaps. No, that wasn't right either. Nick was manly, too. Then the train came in and she thrust her turbulent thoughts away and turned her attention back to Jill Railton—Taxi!

*   *   *

The next few weeks were some of the happiest ones she ever remembered. She had just enough work to keep her occupied while still giving her time to help Miss Williams in the cottage and the garden. To her joy Nicholas accepted a lift to school on most mornings, and although she knew that they were just friends and could never be more because Vivienne had all his love, his companionship for those few minutes brightened her whole day. In fact, although she was unaware of it, the same was true of him. He had more or less resigned himself to acceptance of the knowledge that he could never ask Jill to be his wife, but he had decided that even a small slice of cake was better than nothing.

Of course there was Edward Blake! Edward! Whenever she thought of Edward Jill felt her heart beginning to thump uncomfortably. He was an exciting person, but when she was alone with him she was somehow conscious of being close to some hidden force which could easily get out of control. It was as if she was at the foot of a volcanic mountain which might erupt at any moment.

It was partly for this reason that she had avoided going out with him. On one or two occasions he had suggested a dinner and dance at Petersfield, but she had made an excuse; an early engagement the next morning or tiredness after an extra busy day. Edward had accepted the flimsy excuses with a smile and an uplifted eyebrow, but Jill had a feeling that he would not wait much longer before making a chance to tell her that he loved her. Not that she needed to be told. It showed so clearly in his every word and action.

She sighed. It would be so suitable in every way, and she was sure that Grandfather would be pleased. But she didn't love Edward—she loved Nicholas. And Nicholas loved Vivienne. Why did things have to work out so queerly? Why couldn't she give Edward a love to equal his own?

Perhaps the greatest cause of her happiness was her relations with her grandfather. Her admiration for him and for his courage grew at each meeting and she had taken to visiting Haime Grange for an hour or so in the evening two or three times a week, much to Nanny's satisfaction. To Miss Williams' surprise Sir Martin made no effort to persuade Jill to give up her taxi business. He obviously admired her enterprising spirit and realised that financial independence was most important for her in view of what had happened to her father. Sometimes she would pick up Nicholas and take him with her and those were the happiest evenings of all. When Nick was there Edward usually took the opportunity of going out; he liked Nick as little as Nick liked him. They would sit out among the roses and Jill would listen while the two men talked. Nick would speak of the places he had visited, although she noticed that he always steered off any conversation about the school in Persia, and Sir Martin would tell them about some of the interesting cases which had come his way. Jill loved it all.

One Friday, about half way through July, Sir Martin telephoned to her at lunchtime.

"I thought I might catch you at home at this time, Jill. Tell me, my dear, are you very much booked up for tomorrow morning?"

"Not terribly, Grandfather. I've a trip at nine thirty and then I have to meet the ten five train. But that one is only to take people about two miles, so I should be free by ten thirty. Did you want me to do something for you?"

"If you could. I heard this morning from Mr Fern, the ophthalmic specialist. He will be in Brighton tomorrow morning, and if I can get there any time before noon he would like to check up on my eyes. He knows I don't really like going to London at present; I find the noise very trying when I can't see what is going on. I could get Andrews to take me, but I promised him this week-end free, as his son is visiting them. I know he would forfeit the time willingly if I asked him, but I don't want to do so if it can be avoided."

"Of course not. That's his eldest son, I suppose; the one who has just joined the merchant navy?"

"That's right. He's seventeen now and a splendid young chap."

"Well, if I pick you up at ten forty-five we should reach the Eye Hospital in Brighton by eleven-thirty. Will that do?"

"Admirably, my dear. How about asking Nicholas to

come along, too, if he is free? I've told Edward to take a day off while he has the chance. Nicholas can keep you company while you are waiting for me and we'll all have lunch together afterwards. I hope you don't have to hurry back?"

Jill consulted her diary for the next day. "No, as long as I'm back by three thirty that will be all right. I'll try to waylay Nick when I do the Cinder Cross trip. Good-bye for now, Grandfather. I'll see you tomorrow."

The weather on the next morning was glorious—a perfect day. Jill and Nicholas left Sir Martin at the hospital and went down to the beach for a bathe. Jill was not much of a swimmer but Nicholas was really good. He moved through the water with deceptively easy-looking strokes, covering three or four yards to every one of hers.

"My word, this water feels icy after the Persian Gulf! I'm going to sun bathe, Jill. Are you coming or are you hardier than I am?"

"No, I'll come. It's my first dip this year and I'm getting chilly, too." They went up the warm sand side by side, found the place where they had left their clothes and lay basking in the sun. "Nick, do you find that your limp doesn't worry you when you swim? I've sometimes heard that swimming is wonderfully good for that kind of thing."

"It's odd that you should say that. I just didn't notice my leg at all. I wonder what the orthopædic fellow I have to see in Town would say to that. 'I told you so!' probably. Unsympathetic blighter!"

His voice was so disgruntled that Jill laughed. "You sound as if you don't like him at all. What did he say which annoyed you so much?"

"He as good as insinuated that I wasn't really trying

to get better. If I'd forget my leg and concentrate on doing my job I'd jolly soon walk as well as I'd ever done. Tommy rot! How can you forget a thing which hurts like—like anything?" Jill laughed at the rather lame substitution for the word he had nearly used, and Nick continued : "If the chap only knew how much depended on my leg. My next job—my whole future—my whole life!"

"I know. He doesn't sound a very understanding person. Let's get dressed, Nick. It's quarter past twelve already and I want to look at one or two shops before we go back to Grandfather. It's Nanny's birthday next Wednesday and I must find her a nice present."

Ten minutes later they were strolling side by side up from the beach towards the shops. Somehow the talk they had had about Nick's disability seemed to have drawn them closer together. Jill had always avoided the topic before, fearing to make matters worse, but now she realised that she had been wrong. He slid her arm through his as they sauntered along the promenade and she felt her heart beating a little faster. There had been something in his tone, too, as he had spoken of his future. Could he possibly have been including her in his plans? Of course there was still Vivienne somewhere in the background, but their friendship had grown so rapidly in the last few weeks that she was almost beginning to hope that the unknown Miss Bartlett was fading from Nick's memory.

"Hello, here's one of those 'photographs while you wait' places." Nicholas steered her towards a small booth "How about a memento of a happy day?"

"Nick, I'm looking a sight! You have yours done while I try to tidy my hair."

"Okay, but don't run away." Nick entered the booth

while Jill got out her comb and tried to remove the traces of her bathe, then she took her turn in front of the camera.

"Twenty to one. Just time to get your little present, come back for our wonderful likenesses and get to the hospital by one o'clock. Tell you what, Jill, how about buying a frame and giving Miss Williams one of the photos? I'm sure she'd like that more than anything."

Jill laughed. She didn't think it would be really suitable as a birthday present, but it would do as an extra. Nanny had asked her only a few days before if she had a photograph of herself which she could spare. They found a small shop and chose a little wooden frame in the size to take the snaps.

Nick got his first. He looked at them and roared with laughter. Two of them were frightful, but the third was a very good likeness.

"Oh, I like that one."

He separated it from the others and handed it to her with a bow. "Madam, may I offer you my image to carry next to your heart!"

His words were spoken jestingly but Jill took the little square photograph and slid it into the centre of her handbag, wishing she could indeed put it in a locket to hang forever close to her heart!

"Thank you, Nick. I dread to look at mine. I always photograph badly, even in a proper studio."

But as it happened all three of these had come out beautifully. The gay face, the sparkling eyes, the curls which were slightly tumbled from her bathe, the camera had reproduced them all.

"Jill, they are jolly good. I wonder which one Miss Williams will want. May I have second choice, please?"

"You can choose now. Nanny won't mind which it is."

94

He studied each one carefully, comparing it with the original before him, and finally picked out the first. "I'll have that one, please. I've seen you looking like that so often. Now, in the dead of night, when I can't sleep, I shall be able to take it out and write sonnets about your beauty and charm! Not that I could write a sonnet if I lived to be a hundred, but the thoughts will be there even if I can't put them into words."

Her colour rose at his tone and she changed the subject quickly to hide her confusion. "Come on, Nick, we mustn't keep Grandfather waiting. It has been fun this morning, hasn't it?"

"It surely has. I haven't enjoyed myself so much for months, and somehow you have often given me the impression that you haven't had all that much fun in your young life. We must plan some more outings together. Perhaps we could go up to Town one evening and take in a show. Would you like that?"

And then, when she was about to accept his offer enthusiastically, his expression changed. They were passing the entrance to a big shop—still arm in arm—and he swept her inside and behind a display stand.

"Nick, whatever is the matter?"

"I believe I saw Vivienne! Just coming along the road towards us. My word, I hope she didn't see us!"

Completely unaware of the effect his words would have on the girl beside him, he peered stealthily from his hiding place.

"That's all right, she has gone by, and now I'm not sure that it was Vivienne after all. Flap over! I've an idea though that we might be nearer to the hospital if we went out on the other side of this shop. Let's ask, shall we?"

Without waiting for her to agree he turned to the

95

nearest assistant and enquired. "Yes, I was right. We come out opposite the main entrance. I'd hate to keep Sir Martin waiting, just because we are having such a good time."

Were having a good time, thought Jill bitterly. Oh, how utterly beastly life could be! And what a fool she was! The mere thought of Vivienne seeing them together was enough to make Nicholas forget all the pretty speeches he had been making to her. For a moment she longed to say that she could find her own way to the hospital and didn't need his company any more. But of course she couldn't do that. She would have to drive him back to Castlebridge, and it would only make things horribly awkward if they had a row. Really it was her own fault for being so easily deceived—for indulging in wishful thinking. She and Nicholas were friends and that was all. She had decided to accept his friendship and there was no reason why the last wonderful hour should make any difference.

Sir Martin was waiting for them in the sunshine outside the hospital. Jill left Nicholas to limp the last few yards and ran to his side.

"Grandfather, you are looking very cheerful. What did Mr Fern say? Was he pleased?"

"Very pleased, my dear, and so was I. I have had my sentence reduced by one month! Mr Fern will operate at the beginning of August."

"Dear Grandfather, I am so glad." She squeezed his arm affectionately. "Then you will be fit to go and visit Horace before the winter sets in. New Zealand must be lovely in November and December, especially in the part where Horace is."

"Yes, I must admit that I am looking forward to it. You had better come with me, my dear. I shall need a companion on the journey." Then, sensing her indecision, he added : "But you don't have to decide about that yet. There will be plenty of time. Did you enjoy your swim?"

Nicholas winced. It was just as he had expected but dreaded. Jill would go off to the other side of the world and pass out of his life. She had been so wonderful that morning, too, and he was beginning to dare to hope that, after all, her friendship might ripen into the love her felt for her. Ah well, there was still a week of this term. He would contrive somehow to see her each day. Even a crumb was better than no bread at all!

So two foolish, reserved young people were very quiet for the rest of that afternoon and only Sir Martin, rejoicing at the prospect of an early release from his blindness, enjoyed the return trip to Castlebridge.

CHAPTER 11

ON MONDAY morning Jill picked Nicholas up just out-
his lodgings.

"Thanks awfully, Jill. I'd be in a mess this morning
if it wasn't for you. I got a letter from Jeremy Peel, my
best friend at Gachsaran, and spent more time than I'd
realised reading it."

Then he fell silent and didn't say another word until
she reached the corner where she usually dropped him.
He looked pale, she noticed, and he was frowning.

"Is there anything wrong, Nick? Is your leg hurting
you more than usual?"

"Eh? No, I think it is a bit better." He pulled himself
together and tried to smile at her, but it was rather a
half-hearted effort. "No, old Jeremy's letter has made
me green with envy, and has also brought home to me
the rotten position I'm in. I'll be one of the unemployed
at the end of this week, you know, and finding another
job is going to be a grim business."

Jill started the engine again. "I'll take you as far as
the school today. I haven't another trip until half past
nine. With the whole summer holidays to come, Nick,
isn't there any chance of your being fit enough to go
back to Gachsaran next term?"

"Great Scot, no! There's no question of that. But
Jeremy is leaving at the end of this term, too. He is
getting married to an American girl and going over

there. The two schools he mentioned were both out there; at least, one was in the States and one in Canada. He doesn't know which one he wants. Lucky blighter! I'd settle for either."

"Canada sounds wonderful. It is a country I've always wanted to see. Daddy and I were supposed to be going over for a holiday once, but then some business deal prevented it. What part of the country is the school in?"

Nicholas took the letter out of his pocket and pulled out the closely written sheets. A snap had been enclosed and slipped unnoticed to the floor while he scanned the pages.

"Here it is. 'The Canadian school is in Ontario, only a mile or so north of Lake Ontario and less than a hundred miles from Toronto. It is a big boarding school and I gather they have tremendous fun—winter and summer—on the lake. On the whole I prefer that to the American one, but Mary may feel that she'd rather be in her own country.' "

Nick refolded the sheets and stuffed them back in the envelope. "I should think it would be a good part of the world. My sister—practically my only relative—lives not far from Quebec and she loves it there."

Jill pulled up outside the school and stooped to pick up the snap. It was a group of four people dressed for tennis.

"Oh, thanks. That's old Jeremy and his girl. It's quite a good likeness."

Jill looked at the man to whom he was pointing. "He does look jolly. Is that his fiancée? She is very lovely."

"Lovely? Mary? Do you think so? Oh, I see. That's not Mary—she is on Jeremy's left. That's Vivienne Bartlett. She is the niece of the headmaster's wife, you know, and she is staying out there again, so it couldn't possibly have been her I saw on Saturday."

"Oh, Nick, how could you ever have thought that she and I were alike?"

"Eh? Oh, I forgot I had told you about that. Of course there is no comparison between you really; it was just at first that your colouring reminded me of her." He looked at the girl beside him and frowned. He longed to tell her of some of the differences between her and the lovely, painted lady of the snapshot, but bit off the words which sprang to his tongue. Once he started he would have to go on and—more than ever since he had realised that morning how poor his prospects were—he just mustn't do it. "My word, I must rush. The bell will go in five minutes and I've never been late yet. Goodbye, Jill. Thanks for the lift."

He hurried away as fast as his limp would allow—and he seemed to be even more lame that morning than usual—and Jill sat looking after him. She could feel tears pricking her eyes and she blinked them away furiously. She had known all along that she couldn't come up to Vivienne's standard, but somehow she had fooled herself into thinking that perhaps—in the end—he had seemed so much more than just friendly lately —he had liked being with her—she—he—they—

"Jill, you fool!" She took herself to task firmly. "Go on home. Nanny will be waiting for you. And count your blessings, can't you!"

But when she got back to Kilkenny Cottage she found Nanny in tears.

"Ah, there you are, dearie. I've just taken a call for you from Mrs Mayhew. She wants you to drive her to Horsham this afternoon. Her appointment is at two thirty, so you'll be back in good time for the school trip."

While she was speaking she folded her letter, pushed it into her pocket and tried surreptitiously to brush off a tear which was trickling down her cheek.

"That's fine. I like driving Mrs Mayhew. What's wrong, Nanny? That looks like Miss Clapton's writing. It isn't your sister, is it?" Miss Williams's only sister—a widow with one daughter—lived near Bournemouth. She was only sixty-five—ten years younger than Nanny —but Jill knew that she was rather delicate.

"I'm afraid it is. She got a cold somehow and it has turned to pneumonia. Sheila says she is in hospital and is asking for me. It's odd really, as I haven't seen her for ten years now, and Sheila does everything for her, but I used to look after her when she was a little girl and I suppose her mind has gone back to those days. Poor Mary! I wish she wasn't so far away."

"But Bournemouth isn't that far away. Could your niece put you up? You could have your sister's bed, couldn't you? You put your things together, Nanny, and as soon as I'm back from the school trip we'll have a quick cup of tea and get off. You could send Miss Clapton a wire to say that you are coming, if you think that would be better."

"But, Jill dear, how would you manage? There would be nobody to look after you and cook your meals. And what about answering the telephone?"

"Never mind about that. I can always open a tin of something for midday and cook some eggs in the evening. As for the phone, if people want me enough they'll ring again."

"But what will Sir Martin say? You are going out there this evening, aren't you?"

"Oh, yes, I forgot that. I'll give him a ring and explain."

Miss Williams opened her mouth to protest further, but Jill pretended not to notice. She had quite a long conversation with her grandfather and then turned to Nanny in triumph.

"Now you needn't worry any more, Nanny. Grandfather wants me to go and stay at Haime while you are away. He says I can have the phone calls put over to his number—like doctors do when one of them is off duty—and he or Edward can take messages for me. Now I must go or I'll be late. Don't worry, Nanny dear. It's bound to do your sister good to see you and you haven't had a holiday for years."

So at ten thirty that evening Jill swung the big Rover up the drive at Haime Grange and ran it into the garage beside her grandfather's Rolls. She was walking towards the front door when she heard Edward's voice and, without thinking, paused to listen.

"Now hold your horses, Selina," he was saying. "You knew how you'd be placed when you took on the job. You can't back out now. She'll be out most of the day. She won't give any trouble. Think what it means and have some sense, girl."

Jill's cheeks blazed in the warm darkness. Through the weeks of her visits to her grandfather's house she had been more and more conscious of the house-keeper's dislike and animosity. Now obviously the idea of having to cater for Jill and wait on her had brought things to a head, and Edward was trying to persuade her not to give notice.

Oh well, it wouldn't be for long, and she must do her best to make as little extra work as possible. She ran lightly up the steps and through the open front door.

"I'm here, Grandfather!" she called from the hall, and then, opening the door of the sitting-room, she crossed to his chair. "You shouldn't have waited up for me. I believe you were dozing."

"I think I was half asleep, but I've only just turned off the radio and I don't usually go to bed until about eleven. How has the day gone? Wait a minute, I'll get Selina to bring you some food. What would you like?"

"A cup of tea would be lovely, Grandfather, please, but I don't want anything else. But don't bother Selina. I'll slip into the kitchen on my way to bed. I had a meal with Nanny and her niece before I left there."

"How is Miss Williams's sister?"

"Very bad, I am afraid. Miss Clapton said her mother hardly recognised her when she visited the hospital this afternoon. I hope that seeing Nanny will help her, or anyway that she will know her. Nanny will be so hurt if her sister is too ill to benefit from her coming. Sheila Clapton promised to phone here tomorrow and leave a message for me." She tried to stifle a yawn. "Sorry, Grandfather, I'm dead beat tonight. It's been quite a day."

But later on, lying in the comfortable bed in the spare room, after having a cup of tea in the kitchen with Edward and a Selina who was obviously doing her best to be pleasant, she found that sleep eluded her. She got out again, drew back the curtains and stood looking down into the rose garden, now bathed in moonlight. A honeysuckle was trained to a trellis below her and its fragrance soothed and comforted her after the stress and strain of the day. The road to Bournmouth had been thronged with traffic, and for parts of their journey their passage had been complicated by convoys of slow-moving military vehicles. Coming at the end of a long day, and having Nanny beside her looking so worried and sad, it was no wonder that she was more weary than usual. But although she would not admit it, even to herself, it was none of these things which was coming between her and sleep. It was the look on Nick's face as he compared her with the memories of Vivienne which had been aroused by that snapshot!

CHAPTER 12

THAT Monday was a busy one for Nicholas as well as for Jill. Final preparations were being made at the school for the Speech Day on the following Thursday. All the best of the work the children had done was to be exhibited, and in addition there was to be a display of singing games, country dancing and physical exercises, and the smallest children had been practising hard to render a performance of well-known tunes with a recorder band and a percussion group. So it was not until he got back to his rooms and was sitting relaxing in a chair in the garden that he remembered Jeremy's letter and took the time to read it properly, instead of just skimming through it as he had done at breakfast.

As befitted a man whose main subject was English, Jeremy wrote well, and his descriptions of events at Gachsaran brought back vividly the days they had spent together there. But he wrote that things hadn't been the same since Nick left. The new master was elderly, precise and entirely lacking in imagination. Altogether Jeremy would be glad to be away from it and to try life in the New World.

Then he got to Vivienne. "As you will see by the enclosed snap, Madame Vivienne is honouring Gachsaran with her presence again. I rather gather that her latest victim—a young Oxford undergraduate who will in due course inherit a title—saw the red light in time and got himself engaged to someone else. Of course, Madame doesn't put it like that. According to her version he was infatuated with her but she decided that he was too young, so he is consoling himself with a silly little girl who worships the ground he walks on and is blind to all his faults. Madame has decided that she prefers men who have had more experience of the world. She now has her sights on old Tom Tescaneau. You remember him, I expect; forty-five if he's a day but rolling in money. It would serve her right if she hooked him. No doubt she imagines that she could get him to retire and take her to the Riviera and all the other places where the idle rich congregate, but I rather think she would find she'd met her match in him. Anyway, time will tell."

Nicholas chuckled to himself as he finished the letter and folded it up. How Jeremy loathed Vivienne! Then he noticed that the back page, otherwise empty, held two postscripts.

"P.S. Mary and I are bidden to a final farewell dinner with the Head and Mrs Bailley next Monday. No doubt congratulations to me and commiserations to Mary, together with the usual cruet or butter dish! But if Madame is there I have the germ of an idea. I'll let you know if it works out.

"P.P.S. The Canadian school is also advertising for a master for languages. Wouldn't it be great if you and I both fetch up there. But don't apply yet—see above."

And that was all. With a sigh of longing Nicholas got up and went into the house. Whatever crack-brained scheme Jeremy had, he didn't see how it could help him to a job in Canada. It was no good his applying with only a recommendation from Mr Lipton for his work at Castlebridge this term, and the testimonial he'd had from Mr Bailley wouldn't cut much ice with any decent headmaster. Ruefully he sat down with the educational supplement of *The Times,* and started to read through the list of situations vacant for the following term.

*   *   *

On Tuesday morning he finished breakfast punctually and walked slowly down the path on his way to school. Leaving as early as this he would be almost at Castlebridge before Jill overtook him on her way back from the Cinder Cross trip, but perhaps it was as well. He was afraid she might have realised from his expression on the previous day, when he had been comparing her with Vivienne, just how he felt about her, and if she was friendly he might be carried away before he could stop himself.

To his surprise the Rover, going in the direction of Castlebridge, stopped at the gate just as he reached it.

"Nicholas, I'm so glad you are early. I was afraid I might not see you. Get in and I'll take you as far as the Memorial."

As they went she explained briefly about Miss Williams being away and about Sir Martin's invitation to make Haime Grange her headquarters during Nanny's absence, so that there would be no difficulty about telephone calls.

"I don't think Selina is too pleased about it," she said ruefully. "I gave her and Edward my timetable as it stands for the next few days, so that they could book any trips which fitted in, but she didn't seem exactly enthusiastic. I hope she won't go and give notice. She's a good cook and works very well in the house, and I'd hate it if my being there disrupted Grandfather's arrangements."

She dropped him then and picked up her usual six boys. When she had taken them to their bus she drove to Kilkenny Cottage to see if there was any mail for her or Nanny, and after that she had several short trips booked, so she didn't get back to Haime until lunchtime.

Sir Martin had been still in bed when she had left the house shortly before eight, but now he was sitting in his favourite place in the loggia. She ran up the wide steps and kissed him.

"Good morning, Grandfather. I hope I haven't kept you waiting for lunch. Is there any news from Nanny yet?"

"Yes, my dear, she, or rather her niece, telephoned at about eleven o'clock."

She could tell by his tone that the report was not good.

"How is Nanny's sister? Is she worse?"

"She died last night, quite peacefully, in her sleep. But Miss Clapton said she and Miss Williams were called to the hospital to see her at about nine o'clock and they were told then that there was very little hope of her lasting through the night. She said her mother knew Miss Williams and was obviously very glad indeed to see her, so old Nanny will feel well rewarded for having taken the journey."

"Poor Nanny! What will she do, Grandfather? Did Miss Clapton say when she would like me to fetch her? Will she stay for the funeral?"

"Yes, she will. Miss Clapton discussed it with me and I said I thought it would be best. Then she hopes to come back to Castlebridge with Miss Williams, but she will telephone again in a day or two and let us know."

"That is all right then. Now I had better go and tidy up. I wonder if Edward or Selina has booked any other trips for me. If not I shall have a free afternoon until I pick up the boys."

As she passed through the hall she looked at the pad on which she had written out her timetable. Selina came out of the dining-room at the sound of her footsteps.

"I put in one journey for you this afternoon, Jill. A Miss Gregory has some friends arriving by the three o'clock train and wants you to pick them up at the station. She said you'd know the address."

"Only too well, thank you, Selina! That will fit in nicely. I can pick up Nicholas Davidson and drop him at Tindal on my way to Cinder Cross."

She reached the school a little early and pulled up to wait.

"Hello, Jill! It seems ages since I saw you. How's the taxi business?" Rita Shelton, whose infants finished a little earlier that the other children, came over to her car.

"Quite well, thank you, Rita. How's the scooter? No more trouble?"

"No, it's been running beautifully. Nicholas was telling me about your being out with Sir Martin Greening. He is a darling, isn't he? My father is his solicitor and I've met him several times. He had a wonderful couple called Horace and Sarah Greeves. Daddy used to say that Horace should have been called Jeeves instead."

"They have gone to New Zealand now." Jill told her about Horace's inheritance and the coming of Edward. "It was just when Grandfather was getting desperate that Edward happened to write and say that he wanted to see England and was there any chance of his getting a job. And it was Edward who found a cook house-keeper, too; Selina Lester, another Australian. She came over on the same plane."

"Goodness, I've met her! But no, it can't be the same one. There was a Selina with a surname something like Lester at the Teacher Training College during my first year, but she decided that she wasn't cut out to be a teacher and she gave it up to get married."

Jill laughed. "I sympathise with her. I don't think I'd have the patience for teaching either. But as you say, it couldn't have been the same Selina. Ah, here's Nicholas. I had to come up this end, Nick, so I thought you'd like a lift."

"Thanks awfully, Jill. I'll be glad to get back and put my feet up. End-of-term fever is possessing my little fiends already!"

He gave her a few illustrations of the fiendishness as they drove to Tindal and then she went on to Cinder Cross, took her usual car load back to the Memorial and returned to Haime Grange. There was a strange car outside the front door and as she was coming towards the front door steps she heard her grandfather's voice from the sitting-room.

"That's all, Philip. How soon can you let me have it for signature? There's no immediate rush, but I want to get everything settled before I have this operation. Jill has been through so much; I want to be sure that her future is secure."

Jill wished she hadn't heard. Darling Grandfather! Evidently he was making a new will in which she was to be included. Of course it was wonderful of him to care for her so much, but surely there was no danger in this eye operation? He couldn't die? A cold hand clutched her heart.

She ran up the two shallow steps and in to the hall. Her light shoes made no sound and Selina, who was rearranging the big bowl of sweet peas by the sitting-room door, looked up with a start.

"Must you creep about like that, Jill? You made me jump and now I've messed these up again."

Jill bit her lip. Selina was really objectionable at times. But she didn't want to quarrel and upset the smooth running of the house.

"I'm sorry, Selina. Look, I'll finish those. Don't you bother."

She picked up three pink blooms and one white one, which had fallen on the floor, and started to tuck them back in the bowl, and Selina, after a moment's pause, went away. A few seconds later the sitting-room door opened and her grandfather came out, accompanied by a short, nicely dressed man of about fifty.

"Ah, there you are, Jill my dear. I'd like you to meet Mr Shelton, who deals with all my legal business. I think you know his daughter, who teaches at Castlebridge."

"Yes, I do." Jill shook hands warmly. "In fact I was talking to Rita this afternoon."

"You've been very helpful to her, Miss Railton. She would have been awkwardly placed when her scooter was out of action if it hadn't been for your assistance. Well, goodbye, Sir Martin. I'll be along on Thursday evening some time, but probably not until about nine o'clock. Oh, how about a witness? I can sign, of course, but neither Miss Railton nor Mr Blake should do it. Would you like me to bring somebody with me, or will Andrews be available?"

"Oh, don't you bother, Philip. I'll find somebody."

Jill, not liking to appear to be listening to their words, withdrew across the hall towards the open door of the dining-room. As she reached it she saw the other door, which led into the kitchen, being closed very gently and a flash of a green overall in the gap. Selina, curious as most women are, was obviously interested in Sir Martin's business with his solicitor. Probably the arranging of the sweet peas just outside the sitting-room door had been for the same purpose. She smiled and then frowned. There was something rather unpleasant about this eavesdropping. But it wouldn't be for much longer. If Sir Martin's eyesight improved, as it should after this operation, he would probably go to Mr Shelton's office if they had any business.

Having waited by the door until the car had driven away, Sir Martin turned towards Jill. "Edward is out this afternoon, Jill, so we won't wait tea for him. Touch the bell for Selina to bring it, will you, please."

Jill obeyed and they went into the sitting-room and sat down by the open french windows looking out on the terraces. She chattered as gaily as usual, trying to think of some amusing things which had happened during the day, but when Selina had brought in the tea trolley and left the room Sir Martin leant forward and put his hand on her arm.

"What's wrong, Jill?" he asked quietly.

"Nothing, Grandfather. At least—well—" She paused and then told him what she had overheard. "It isn't really dangerous, is it? The operation, I mean. Nothing could go wrong, could it?"

"No, my dear, I don't think so. Of course it may be unsuccessful, in which case I suppose I shall be quite blind." Jill drew a sharp breath of pain. "But Mr Fern holds out every hope of success. No, my dear, it is just that I wish to be sure that I have done everything in my power to make your future happy and secure. You are my only direct descendant, Jill, and therefore you should naturally be my heir."

Jill had taken less notice of this part of the conversation between Sir Martin and his solicitor than of the reference to the operation. Now a sudden thought struck her.

"Grandfather, I suppose I shouldn't ask, but, if you hadn't—if we hadn't got to know each other, who would have—"

He smiled at her faltering words and helped her out.

"I made a will soon after Edward came to live with me, in which I left everything to him, my dear, because there was nobody else. But he knew nothing of it, so he will have no cause to feel cheated. In any case I am leaving him a thousand pounds, as a reward for his kindness to me during these difficult months. But Edward is a man, Jill, and it is better for him to have to make his own way in the world. Just forget all about it, my dear. Mr Shelton is bringing the will for signature on Thursday evening and that will tidy everything up. But I see no reason why I should die for many a long year yet."

"I hope not." She left her chair, slipped her arm round his neck and kissed him gently. "We can do such a lot of things together when you get your sight back. And you are going to visit Horace and Sarah, aren't you? Oh, I'm longing for next month to be over."

CHAPTER 13

"NICHOLAS, you go out to Sir Martin Greening's house sometimes, don't you?" Rita Shelton came over to him while they were supervising the children's mid-morning break.

"Yes, quite often. Why?"

"Well, I was talking about the place to Jill yesterday and she mentioned the woman who is cook house-keeper —Selina Lester. Have you seen her? What does she look like?"

"Oh, I don't know. I'm not much hand at describing women. Reddish hair—medium height—a bit freckled —not outstanding in any way. Why are you interested in her?"

Rita told him of her conversation with Jill. "I've got rather a 'thing' about remembering people's names and I was pretty sure that the girl I knew was called Lester. So yesterday evening I phoned a cousin who had been at the college with me but had started a year earlier, and would therefore have had more time with Selina. Her name was Lester and she was Australian. I'm sure it was the same person. But our Selina left to get married and this woman is still calling herself Lester. And Jill said she had only just come to England, on the same plane as Edward Somebody-or-other."

"It sounds like the same girl. But I suppose the proposed wedding never came off, or else it went on the rocks. I don't care for her much—she seems rather bad tempered—and to be quite honest, I can't stand the sight of him—but they seem to suit Sir Martin all right. I wonder what the idea was; pretending she'd never been in England before. I'd like to know the name of the man she was marrying. I suppose your cousin didn't tell you that?"

"No, but I'll ring her again this evening and see if she knows. Ah well, back to the grindstone!" She rang the big brass bell and she and Nicholas shooed their pupils back to their classrooms.

*   *   *

Wednesday was always Jill's busiest day, with several standing engagements including one forty-mile trip, taking an elderly lady to visit her even more elderly sister, and having lunch in a café there before bringing her back to Castlebridge. So, as she left the house before Sir Martin was up, she did not see her grandfather until she returned at tea time. It was a lovely sunny day and they sat with Edward among the rose bushes drinking a cup of tea and chatting happily.

"Have you ever been to Pine Hill, Jill?"

"Pine Hill? I'm not sure, Grandfather. Is it very steep, with a pool at the bottom in the middle of some woods? If so, I believe Mummy took me there once for a picnic when I was small, but I can't remember more about it than that."

"That is the place. I asked you because I had a letter this morning from an old friend who lives close to the bottom of Pine Hill. He wrote to ask me if I could possibly call to see him tomorrow afternoon at about half past five. I thought, if it did not interfere with any other trip you have booked, you might care to drive me there. We could take my car instead of yours. I'm sure you would like to try your hand at driving it."

"Oh, I'd love that. As a matter of fact the Rover hasn't sounded quite right once or twice today. I'm going to have a look at the engine later to see if I can spot the trouble. I don't want it breaking down on me. I've nothing booked tomorrow after Cinder Cross and that will be the last of those for about two months. The boys are getting very excited."

After tea she changed into a pair of old jeans and went round to the garage. It took her an hour to locate a small fault in the wiring and then she came up against an obstacle—a small nut which defied all her efforts to turn it.

"How are you getting on? Can I help?" Edward had come quietly over the grass and was close to the garage before she was aware of his presence.

She had done her best to avoid being alone with him while she was staying at Haime Grange, fearing that he might ask her to marry him and that her refusal would make the position difficult for them both. But now she was thankful to see him.

"Please, Edward. I can't unscrew this. Wait a second though; I'll wipe the handle of this spanner. I'm in such a mess and you don't want to get your hands dirty if you are going to help Grandfather later."

"Yes, you look a sight! There is a smear of black grease on one cheek and your hair is standing on end." He took the spanner she held out to him and then caught both her grimy hands in his. "But still you look wonderful! Oh, Jill, I've never met a girl like you. I've knocked about all over the world; I've talked to all kinds of women, from—from Prime Ministers' daughters to bar-

116

maids in rowdy water-front pubs; but I have to come to a little English backwater to meet the girl of my dreams. Darling Jill, I'm not fit to clean your shoes, but I do love you so. When will you marry me?"

Jill tried in vain to pull her hands away. "No, Edward, please. Oh, do let me go—you'll get filthy. I do like you, but, honestly, that's all. I'm not in love with you at all."

"But you could be, Jill. You like me—that's something. I know I'm not much of a chap—I've done all sorts of jobs in my time—some things I hate to remember —but if you married me you could change all that. I'd work as I've never worked before, and I'd do everything I could to make you happy."

The sun, which had been hidden for most of the day, came out at that moment, and a shaft of light fell on them. It brought out Edward's wonderful good looks. But that was not all. It also showed quite clearly the lines round his mouth and eyes; lines which Jill thought had probably been caused by all the worry and trouble he had had to face.

Suddenly she felt a wave of overwhelming pity for him. Poor Edward, what a difficult life he must have led, always struggling to make his own way without help of parents or other relatives. No wonder he was glad to have found a home where he was welcome.

Sensing her sympathy he let go of her hands and slipped his arms about her. "I knew you loved me! Darling, think how happy Sir Martin will be. We are his only two living descendants and our union will be just perfect."

For a moment Jill was tempted. Grandfather was so good and it would be just right. And, after all, Nicholas didn't want her. He wanted his Vivienne and nobody

else would do. For three or four seconds she stayed
quietly in his embrace, but as he bent his head to kiss
her she knew it wouldn't do.

"No, Edward, I don't love you. Please let me go."
Then, as his clasp only tightened, she started to struggle.
"Let me go! Let me go, or I'll scream and Grandfather
or Selina will hear."

"You little—" He swallowed the word but his arms
fell to his sides. Then he gripped her by the shoulders
and his fingers bit into her flesh like steel claws. "I see
what it is. While I was the old josser's heir you were as
sweet as honey. Now he is changing his will, so you've
no further use for me."

She opened her mouth to protest but he gave her no
chance.

"Don't count your chickens too soon, my fine lady!
That will isn't signed yet. Maybe it never will be signed."
She looked at him, puzzled by his knowledge of the new
will and he, misunderstanding her bewildered expression,
added hastily: "If I tell Sir Martin how you have reacted to the thought of becoming heiress to his fifty
thousand he may have second thoughts."

"It has got nothing to do with Grandfather's money.
I just don't love you. I used to like you a bit, but now
I can't think why I did."

It was a reckless thing to say. His face flushed and
his eyes blazed as he glared down at her, and for a
moment she was terrified. Then came an interruption.
Footsteps crunched in the gravel on the path from
the garage to the back door and Edward loosened
his grip as Andrews, Sir Martin's chauffeur, came into
view.

"Trouble, Miss Jill? Sir Martin said the Rover wasn't
running too well."

Edward, who had stiffened at the first words, relaxed again.

"It's all right, thank you. Miss Jill has found the fault."

Andrews ignored this and came to look at the engine. "I see, Miss. That's easily replaced. If you'd like to get on into the house I'll fix it for you."

"That would be lovely if you could. I've hardly had towards the back door and then, just round the corner any time with Grandfather today." She turned to go of the garage, she paused at the sound of Andrews' voice. The chauffeur, not realising that she was still within hearing, put his hand on Edward's arm.

"You are on to a soft job here, Mr Blake. If you don't want to lose it then keep your hands off Miss Jill. If Sir Martin had seen what I saw as I came round from the back there you'd be out of here tonight. Ah-ah! Temper!" Jill caught her breath as Edward's clenched fist swung towards the older man's head, but Andrews was on the watch and the blow missed. "No, sir, just keep your distance. I served in the Commandos for five years. I'm no defenceless girl."

Edward scowled and for a moment Jill was afraid he was going to start a fight. Then discretion evidently prevailed. He turned on his heel and walked quickly away.

CHAPTER 14

ON THURSDAY morning Jill found Nicholas waiting at his gate as she came along.

"May I beg a lift today, Jill? It's going to be pretty hectic, and I shall need all my energy."

"I should think you would. Look, Nick, Grandfather said if I saw you this morning would I ask you to come over this evening, and spend the week-end with us if you haven't got anything better to do. If you'll say when you can be ready I'll fetch you. That is, if you'd like to come."

"I'd love to come. It will give me some much-needed refreshment before I settle down to the grind of finding another job. What time would suit you best?"

"Well, I'm taking Grandfather to see a friend near the bottom of Pine Hill. He has to be there at five thirty, so I expect we shall leave Haime soon after five. He says I can drive his Rolls for that. I'm longing to see what it feels like. I could pick you up just before five and you could come too, and keep me company, if that isn't too early for you. Otherwise it will have to be when we get back. That, I suppose, means about six thirty."

"It had better be the six thirty. I may be late home from school and not ready by five. 'Bye for now, Jill. See you this evening."

He hurried as fast as his leg would allow on the rest of his walk to the school, where he found an unusual

120

ustle everywhere. Boys and girls, most of whom
enerally arrived about ten seconds before the bell, were
ready running round in the classrooms, making sure
nat their own paintings, clay models, handicrafts objects
nd other exhibits were either in position on the walls or
andy for putting out on the tables.

"Please, sir, I can't find my model of the Concorde."

"Please, sir, the animals we stuck on the African
orest are all falling off again!"

"Please, sir, can I put my picture of New York up
n the wall? You said it was very good."

Nicholas was thankful when the bell went for morning
rayers. Obviously ordinary classes were out of the
uestion, but somehow the rest of the morning had to
e occupied and the fever of excitement reduced to a
ightly more normal level, but what to do he had no
lea. However, Mr Lipton was accustomed to last-day-
f-the-school-year excitement. He stopped Nicholas as
ne children were going towards their classrooms.

"Unless you've got anything special planned for this
norning, Nick, you might like to use these. Give them
fteen minutes for each paper and then let them change
ver and check each other's, which will take about
nother quarter of an hour. That will keep them busy
or the next hour and then, after break, we'll have a final
un through for this afternoon."

Nicholas thanked him and took the sheaf of papers,
rhich he found were tests—though fairly easy ones—
overing the syllabus for the past term's work. All the
nswers required were short ones and had to be inserted
n the paper itself. It was the kind of thing the children
oved and the time passed unexpectedly peacefully until
ne bell for mid-morning break.

The final rehearsal for the afternoon's entertainment

121

went as badly as such things almost invariably do. I
the P.E. display two boys turned left on the comman
to turn right, four more got hopelessly lost and forgo
the order in which the movements were to be mad
and the counter-marching, with two files crossing th
playground diagonally, became a complete muddle an
ended in hopeless confusion.

Nicholas was in despair, but he need not have worried
In the afternoon everything went like clockwork. Th
parents and friends who thronged the whole buildin
and admired whole-heartedly the exhibits of their ow
offspring, and more or less enthusiastically—according t
their characters—those of their classmates, seemed de
lighted with the whole programme.

By three thirty it was all over. The last pupil ha
departed, laden with his belongings, and the whole schoo
resembled Hampstead Heath after August Bank Holi
day! Mrs Lipton came into the big classroom and
laughed at the expression on Nick's face.

"Amazing, isn't it? Never mind, the cleaners will ge
down to it tomorrow morning and Hugh and I will b
on our way to Cornwall for three blissful weeks. Com
and have a cup of tea, Nicholas, if you can spare th
time. Hugh wants to talk to you and it won't take fiv
minutes to boil up a kettle."

"Nicholas, I've been hoping to see you before I left."
Rita Shelton waylaid him as he made his way towards
the Liptons' house. "I just wanted to say goodbye and
wish you luck. It's been fun this term, working with you,
and I wish you were staying permanently."

"Thanks, Rita. So do I in many ways. Oh, by the
way, could your cousin give you any more news of our
mutual friend Selina Lester?"

"No. I rang yesterday evening but she was out. I left

a message with Aunt Alison asking June to ring me if she knew anything more about the wedding, but I didn't hear so I suppose she didn't. I must fly, Nicholas. I'm off to Norway on Saturday with a party of friends and I've masses to do before I go."

They shook hands and she sped away, and Nicholas limped over to the schoolmaster's cottage. The interview with Mr Lipton was most satisfactory. He said how much he wished he could keep Nick permanently and told him to write without hesitation if there was any way in which he could help. He gave him a splendid testimonial and wished him the best of luck.

All fine and dandy as far as it goes, thought Nicholas ruefully, as he made his halting way out of the building and set off for Tindal, but just not enough. Oh well, it's no good crying over spilt milk!

Back at his rooms he stopped to chat for a while with Mrs Pelman, then went into his own sitting-room, where he found three letters lying on his table. Two were air mail letter cards, and he saw with some satisfaction that one was from his sister and one from Jeremy. The third was a long, business envelope at which he did not bother to look.

Sitting down in a chair by the window he slit the sides of Jeremy's first. To his amazement the paper was almost blank; in fact the whole letter consisted of one brief sentence.

"It worked!
Jeremy!"

CHAPTER 15

It was not until some time later that Nicholas learned what had happened on that Monday evening in Mr and Mrs Bailley's bungalow.

The party was not a big one; just Jeremy and Mary, Vivienne and the school matron and two other masters. They had a festive meal and then took coffee and drinks out on to the verandah. Mr Bailley waited until everybody was comfortably settled and then rose to his feet and made a short speech. He thanked Jeremy for the hard work he had done while he was at Gachsaran and wished him and his fiancée all success and happiness in their life together, wherever they finally decided that this should be. He ended by producing a small leather case which he handed to Mary.

Jeremy breathed an involuntary sigh of relief. It wasn't a cruet! Then Mary opened the case and they both exclaimed with pleasure. Inside were six silver spoons, antique and most beautifully made. The case was new and bore the name of one of the best-known jewellers in Teheran.

"Oh, Mr Bailley, they are lovely. Thank you both so much." Mary looked from the headmaster to his wife with a grateful smile.

"Speech! Speech!" This came from the other four guests.

Jeremy rose to his feet reluctantly. "I'm afraid making

speeches isn't in my line, but I should like first of all to add my thanks to you, sir, and to Mrs Bailley for your lovely present. I don't feel that I deserve half the nice things you have said about me, but I can say quite truthfully that when we use our lovely spoons I shall be reminded of some very happy times here. No doubt, in the future, when we are either shivering in Canada or stopping our ears to the roar of traffic in the U.S.A., we shall think longingly of life in Gachsaran and wish ourselves back among you all."

He tried to think of some witty phrase with which to finish, but his mind remained infuriatingly blank and he sat down abruptly. The others applauded and smiled and then, much to his relief, the formal part of the evening seemed to be at an end.

This left him with time to try to put his plan into action for the unmasking of Vivienne, but somehow the opportunity seemed impossible to create. Every topic under the sun was discussed and it was not until it was nearly time to break up the party that the matron gave him the opening he needed.

"Where will the wedding be, Jeremy? And where are you going for your honeymoon?"

"We are being married in a little village in Buckinghamshire, where Mary's parents are living at present. He is working at the American Embassy in London. We are going to tour by car for our honeymoon; probably in Scotland, as neither of us has ever been there. Mary's father is giving us a car for a wedding present."

"It's wonderful, isn't it," said Mary. "But Jeremy and I will both have to brush up our driving. Neither of us has driven since we've been here. These roads and these hairpin bends are quite terrifying."

The science master—a Scot—laughed. "You'll have

just as bad corners to cope with in Scotland, and you'll have to remember to drive on the left, too."

"Yes, we shall. But as we haven't got used to driving on the right that part won't be difficult." Mary turned casually to Vivienne. "You don't drive, do you, Miss Bartlett?"

Her tone was slightly patronising and Vivienne reacted to it immediately. "Certainly I drive! I've taken a car through the Scottish highlands, too. There are some difficult corners, but they are all right if you just keep your head and use your common sense."

"There you are, darling!" Jeremy gave his fiancée's arm a squeeze. "Completely crushed! It's a pity you never tried driving out here, Miss Bartlett, then you could tell us how you thought these roads compared with the ones we shall be using next month. But of course it does take a really experienced driver to negotiate the hills and corners of this district."

"And you don't think I should be good enough? Well, let me tell you, Jeremy Peel, that I have driven here and I managed perfectly well—"

She stopped, realising what she had said. But, unfortunately for her, indignation had made her raise her voice and Mr Bailley had overheard her remark.

"But, Vivienne, I thought you did not hold a licence to drive in Persia? You remember I told you it was necessary when you wanted to drive my car." There was a pause as the girl tried to think of a way out of her dilemma and then the headmaster continued: "Whose car did you drive?"

"Mr Tescaneau's, Uncle Hubert. He took me out last Friday and let me try. He said he'd risk my not having a licence."

"Lucky girl!" Jeremy sounded envious. "Which one was he driving—the Jaguar or the Renault?"

"The Jaguar. It's lovely and it goes beautifully."

"But he hasn't got a Jaguar. His big car is a Daimler. You are a rotten liar, Vivienne Bartlett. You know quite well that the only time you've ever driven a car on these roads was when you borrowed Mr Bailley's last year, smashed it up and then planted the blame on Nick Davidson."

Silence! Vivienne went first white and then red and finally burst out indignantly: "What rubbish! You know it isn't true, Uncle Hubert. Nick borrowed your car and it was he who drove it all the time."

Before anything more could be said Mrs Bailley broke into the conversation. "Well, don't let us spoil the evening by having an argument. We've had such a happy time."

The guests took the hint and made a move. Mr and Mrs Bailley went with them as far as the door and she detained Jeremy and Mary until the others had gone.

"You fixed that well, Jeremy. I've always been puzzled about that afternoon. It seemed out of character for Nicholas to do such a thing. But why didn't he deny it?"

"I don't know, Mrs Bailley. I think it was just that he was feeling too wretchedly ill, and he knew that Mr Bailley was bound to take your niece's word in preference to his."

"I see. Don't go yet, Vivienne." This as the girl came in from the verandah and moved as if to go to her room. "Now that the others have gone, let us have a final drink with Jeremy and Mary."

Unwillingly Vivienne joined them. Mr Bailley refilled the glasses.

"Just one thing, Hubert, before we drink our last

toast. Vivienne, how did Nicholas Davidson know where your uncle kept the keys of his car?"

Defiantly the girl threw back her head and gulped down her drink. "All right! I took the keys and I drove the car! Nick didn't know the first thing about it; he was far too law-abiding to think of such a thing. He actually thought Uncle Hubert had lent it to me! But I wanted to go to Kharg Island and Nick would not get us a car, so it was the only way. Now you know—and I'll go and pack!"

She swept out of the room and her uncle and aunt let her go. Mr Bailley was looking very grave.

"Why didn't you tell me before, Jeremy?"

"Nick made me promise not to, sir. He said it wouldn't do any good, as Vivienne would never corroborate my story, and it might end with my losing my job, too."

"Well, I am glad the truth has come out at last. I am afraid I have been guilty of a grave injustice. I will write to Mr Davidson if you will give me his present address."

Jeremy supplied it and soon afterwards he and Mary took their leave. "Wasn't that wonderful, darling. You played your part splendidly; just the right disparaging tone to put Madame's back up. Old Hubert was the personification of the Victorian schoolmaster, wasn't he? The phrase 'grave injustice' just rolled off his tongue! I'd love to see his letter to Nick."

*   *   *

Having cogitated for a while over Jeremy's cryptic message and cursed his friend for not being more explicit, Nick turned to his sister's letter. It was the usual cheery babble. He could almost picture her as she wrote it in her sunny garden with his small godson, Nicholas junior, whom he had not yet seen, playing in his sand-pit beside her.

Having given him all her news and commented on his last letter, she wrote: "Nicky dear, why don't you chuck England when you've finished this job at Castlebridge and come out to Canada? I'm sure Bill or his parents could pull some strings and get you a better position here. Your French would be a tremendous asset, as so many of the people speak only that. Even if you don't find a job straight away it would be so lovely to have you, and I'm sure you could do with a holiday."

Nicholas folded the flimsy sheet with a grateful smile. Dear old Sue! But it wouldn't do. He would have barely enough to pay his fare to Canada, and with his wretched limp he probably wouldn't be able to get any other job if he couldn't find an opening in a school.

Finally he picked up the foolscap envelope and saw that this one, too, had come by air mail from Persia, so it was probably more important than he had thought. There were two sheets—a covering letter and an enclosure—and he whistled with surprise as he saw the signature. Hubert S. Bailley!

The letter was formal and rather stiff; the writer was not a man who found apology easy; but it was none the less a sincere expression of his regret. And the enclosure was a glowing testimonial to Nick's character and his teaching ability; a recommendation which could well make any headmaster feel that he was getting a treasure! Nick's fingers trembled a little as he returned the papers to their envelope. The possibilities which the letter opened up were unending. A good job in England? Perhaps a school in France, teaching English as well as languages? What about that place in Canada which Jeremy had mentioned? Most important—far and away the most important of all—the main barrier had now been removed between him and his greatest desire—Jill!

He looked at his watch. Five o'clock. He wished now that he had arranged with Jill to be picked up at the earlier time and gone to Pine Hill with her. He remembered the place well. He had picnicked by the pool on numerous occasions when he and Joyce and John Furneaux were children. He smiled reminiscently as he had a fleeting recollection of the three of them going hell for leather down that ghastly hill, disdaining the use of brakes and surging over the slightly hump-backed bridge at the bottom so fast that their bikes left the road and leapt as much as four feet before landing again just in time for them to take the sharp left-hand bend. Looking back, he marvelled that none of them had gone head first over the handlebars into the hedge ahead. They had worked their guardian angels hard during those distant summer days!

But his thoughts passed quickly from the hill to the pool; a golden spot where they had sat on deep piles of pine needles and dabbled their feet in the water. If he and Jill could sit there, surely the words he longed to say would come easily. Oh, Jill! Jill!

He had reached that stage in his daydreams when he heard the slam of the small gate and light footsteps hurrying up the path. Perhaps Jill had been passing and had stopped to see if he was ready. He reached the window in time to see Rita Shelton standing at the front door, and a few moments later she was in his room.

"Hello, Rita, I didn't expect to see—is something wrong?"

"Yes, I think so. Nicholas, what did you say is the

name of that Australian cousin of Jill's? It's Edward Something, isn't it?"

"Yes. Edward Blake. Why?"

She pulled a piece of paper out of her pocket. "When I got home this afternoon I found June there. She didn't phone yesterday because she realised that for some reason I was attaching a lot of importance to this business. But this afternoon she visited another ex-student of the college—Maud Grey—a girl who had been very friendly with Selina. This is a photo of Maud and her boyfriend and Selina and her fiancé. His name was Edward, but Maud couldn't remember his surname."

It was a very good likeness. "That's Edward Blake all right. So all that stuff he wrote to Sir Martin about wanting to see England for the first time was a lot of hooey. But I wonder what was the idea of concealing the fact that Selina is his wife."

"She isn't! Three days before the date fixed for the wedding he was arrested for obtaining money under false pretences and went to prison for two years!"

CHAPTER 16

JILL's principal trip that morning was a long one. An elderly lady—a patient of Doctor Mayhew—had decided to take a short holiday in a boarding house in East-bourne, and as she had plenty of money and disliked travelling by train, she had booked Jill to drive her there. Unfortunately she was one of those irritating people who have absolutely no idea of time. She kept the taxi waiting for half an hour before she was finally ready to go, and then decided to stop at a nice looking café about half way through the journey because she felt sure that she would faint if she did not have some nourishment.

"You know how it is, Miss Railton," she said. "I eat so little, especially at breakfast. My woman simply will not arrive before ten o'clock and I have to get a meal for myself. And this morning I felt that I couldn't manage anything except a boiled egg and some toast. You will come and join me, won't you?"

Jill, whose usual breakfast was an egg and a piece of toast, and who considered that quite sufficient to last her until lunch, agreed reluctantly and they took their seats at one of the small tables on the terrace. Mrs Donahue ordered coffee and biscuits, but the place was busy and it was not until fully threequarters of an hour later that they finally got back to the car to continue their journey, and it was twelve o'clock before she left her passenger at the big boarding house overlooking the sea.

My goodness, I'll have to step on it, she thought to herself. Grandfather does like his meals punctually and I've never been late yet.

But misfortunes seldom come singly. She went back to the car to find that she had run over a broken bottle as she pulled in to the kerb and both the near-side tyres were flat! With only one spare wheel this necessitated the assistance of a garage—fortunately quite close by— and she left Eastbourne at last at twenty to one. While she was waiting she had telephoned to Haime and spoken to Sir Martin, but the episode had annoyed her and she hurried into the dining-room feeling decidedly hot and bothered.

Her grandfather accepted her apology amusedly. "My dear child, don't worry. You are fortunate not to have your plans upset more often. Selina has kept your meal hot for you and you can tell me all about your morning as you eat."

"Grandfather, you are a darling! I'm afraid I have rather a 'thing' about punctuality." She looked across the table affectionately but rather unhappily. "I almost wish I wasn't quite so busy. I'm having all the advantages of living here with you and being waited on hand and foot and you don't get anything in return."

He took the hand she had held out to him and kissed it gently. "You've given me more than you'll ever know, child. I was becoming a very lonely old man and—in my lowest moments—beginning to wonder whether it would not be better if the surgeon's knife slipped a little next month. But now I've got somebody to live for and I'm impatient to have the operation over so that I can see you properly. You mustn't worry about me. Colonel

Furneaux is coming over this afternoon. I haven't seen him since he came back from France."

Selina's entry with the coffee put an end to the conversation and as soon as she had gulped down her cup Jill set off for the four short trips which filled her afternoon.

During tea Sir Martin entertained her with tales of the latest exploits of the Barlow children, at whose home Colonel Furneaux had just spent a few days. Mark had decided to be a detective when he grew up and was investigating the affairs of all his neighbours and finding a crook round every corner, but it was small Mary who had seen the only actual crime which had come their way. Shopping with her mother in the local supermarket, she had noticed a customer slipping nylon stockings from the stand into her handbag. The grateful store manager had rewarded her with a huge box of chocolates.

"I understand that young Mark felt distinctly aggrieved," he said with a chuckle. Then, noticing the house-keeper waiting in the room : "Yes, Selina?"

"Sir, I was wondering if it would be all right for Edward and me to go out this evening. I know Mr Davidson is coming, but his room is all ready for him. The meal is laid in the dining-room and it's a cold one this evening except for the soup. I wouldn't ask, sir, while Miss Jill is staying, but I haven't been out for a week and this is a special occasion."

"I can easily heat the soup, Grandfather. What is the special occasion, Selina? Your birthday?"

"No, Miss Jill." Jill's lips twitched as she contrasted Selina's respectful tone in Sir Martin's presence with her abrupt and familiar attitude when they were alone. "It's a racing event at Goodwood which is being organised for charity—for the blind actually—and I know someone who is taking part. If we could go out as soon as I've cleared up the tea we'd probably be back at about eleven."

"Certainly you may go, Selina. I hope your friend wins his race." Sir Martin waited until she had shut the door and then turned to Jill. "I can't quite fathom the relationship between Edward and Selina. Of course I never see them together or it might be easier. I understood from Edward that he had never met her until the time they travelled to England together and happened to get into conversation. She has a neat enough figure as far as I can see, but she sounds rather less well educated than he. Is she pretty?"

"No, I don't think so. In fact, to me she looks very plain. Of course I've never seen her dressed to go out —she might look nicer then—but she seems to take very little trouble over her appearance."

She sat quiet then, trying to remember how Edward and Selina had acted on the few occasions when she had seen them together. One tiny incident, which had passed almost unnoticed at the time, came back to her mind. Edward had suggested that he and Jill might have a walk together after dinner on a Saturday evening when she had been spending a week-end at Haime Grange, and Selina had come into the dining-room while he was trying to persuade her to agree. The Australian girl had just looked at him without speaking and had rubbed her finger across her lips, and Edward had changed his mind, murmuring something about having remembered that he had some letters to write. At the time she had been so glad to avoid the walk without giving offence that the strangeness had escaped her notice. Now she wondered. Anyway, it was all too vague to recount to her grandfather.

"I expect he just wants to keep her happy," she said. "She is a good cook, and it must be a bit lonely for her here if she hasn't any friends in England. I think we'd better be getting on if you are ready, Grandfather. We don't want to have to hurry, and I think you said your friend is expecting you at half past five."

"That's right, my dear. Don't bother to bring the car round. I'll come to the garage with you."

Side by side they left the house and walked round to the big double garage, where the Rolls and the Rover were standing side by side. Somewhat to Jill's surprise Edward was rubbing up the chromium with a soft duster.

"I thought I'd better have the Rolls looking her best for her new chauffeur," he said lightly. "You keep the Rover so beautifully, Jill, that it wouldn't do to damage your reputation by having a spot of dust anywhere."

Sir Martin, apparently not noticing anything amiss in his words, laughed happily, but Jill, detecting the mockery in the tone, flushed awkwardly. Since the scene on the previous evening she had managed to avoid being alone with Edward. Ruefully she began to wonder if she would have to leave Haime Grange before Nanny came back from Bournemouth.

Slipping through the big doors she took her seat in the Rolls, started the engine and drove carefully out on to the sweep of gravel. After the Rover she was very conscious of the extra width of the bigger car, and although it seemed wonderfully easy to handle, she was suddenly beset with doubts.

"Grandfather, I'm wondering if we'd better go in the Rover after all. I don't want to make you nervous."

"Whichever you prefer, my dear."

"Jill, I don't think you ought to take the Rover." Edward looked at her with a frown. "You know you were having trouble with it yesterday. I thought you were supposed to be an experienced driver. Surely you can manage a Rolls? I've never been in the fortunate position of having a chance to drive one, but I guess if I did have an opportunity I wouldn't funk it!"

"You have no right to speak to Jill like that, Edward." Sir Martin's voice was sharper than Jill had ever heard it before. "Reasonable care is not cowardice. Perhaps if you had shown a little more caution you would now hold a driving licence and be able to take the Rolls or the Rover down Pine Hill."

Edward shot him a furious glance which, fortunately, he could not see, but Jill reacted to Edward's taunt as any self-respecting person would.

"I wasn't really funking. I just wanted to be sure of not giving Grandfather a jolt. But I expect I'll soon get used to the Rolls, and then I'll hate the thought of going back to the Rover. Will you ride in front with me, Grandfather, or would you rather sit at the back?"

"With you," he replied promptly, and Edward, as if to make amends for his rudeness, opened the door for him and steadied him as he took his seat. Then he carefully fastened the seat belt, stood back and closed the car door and saluted mockingly to Jill.

She tossed her head in annoyance. He was really impossible. But there was no answer to his behaviour unless she wished to have a row with him, so she started up and drove away. As she was about to turn the corner and go down towards the gate she glanced in the driving mirror. He was looking after her with a queer expression on his face; a mixture of dislike, scorn and—and what was it exactly? It seemed almost like triumph, but then what had Edward to be triumphant about? He had made her look small and babyish in front of her grand-

father—her cheeks burned at the recollection of his jibe
—but he had earned a sharp rebuke and had not improved his position in the house. Ah well, it didn't matter.
She thrust the uncomfortable thoughts away and gave
herself up to the enjoyment of the lovely car and Sir
Martin's company.

"I looked up Pine Hill on the map, Grandfather, and
I think I turn right about three miles from Cinder Cross,
don't I?"

"Yes, I think that would be the best way for us today.
There is a shorter route, which cuts off about four miles,
but it is narrow and twisty and I think I might find it
difficult to direct you. The wider roads are more comfortable for me at present, too. When one cannot see it
is startling to have the brakes applied suddenly."

"It must be. Oh, Grandfather, I'm so longing for you
to be able to see properly. We'll go to some of your
favourite places, shall we?"

"I shall look forward to that. But I don't need my
eyes to picture Pine Hill and its woods. It was there
that I asked your grandmother to marry me."

He sat quietly after that and Jill knew he was back
in the old days. As she turned smoothly into the minor
road, and travelled along it at reduced speed so that
the poorer surface should not worry him with unexpected
jolts, she tried to imagine the scene. How long ago would
it have been? She knew that he had not married young,
and neither had her mother, and she herself was nineteen.
It must have been about fifty years ago that Grandfather
and Grandmother had married, not long after the end
of the First World War. She had studied costume at
school, and she tried to visualise the beautifully dressed,
dignified figure of Lady Greening as depicted in the
portrait in the sitting-room at Haime Grange, in the

loose, floppy, shapeless frocks of that period. And would Grandfather have been wearing those frightful Oxford bags?

She nearly giggled at the thought, but an abrupt change of scene banished visions of the past. They had rounded a bend and suddenly the valley lay in front of them. She stopped the car and looked at it delightedly.

"Oh, Grandfather, what a wonderful place! It's so completely unspoilt—just meadows and fields, with that little stream meandering through, and then that pine wood. The sun is catching the tops of the trees and making them look quite pink. And there isn't a house in sight. Oh yes, there is. I can just see the roof and chimneys."

"That would be our destination, Jill. My oldest friend lives there. We were at school together and then at university. We joined the army on the same day and crossed to France together. He was badly wounded at the Battle of the Somme and for the last thirty-five years he has been crippled. But his right arm still functions and he is now a well-known landscape artist. His name is Ian Macfarlane—you may have heard of him."

"Oh, I have! In fact, I've got two of his pictures stored away. They were in my bedroom at home. Of course! One of them is of this valley—that little bridge with the pine wood behind it. Mother gave it to me for my birthday when I was eight, and I remember she said she knew the artist." She glanced at her watch and restarted the engine. "We've just timed it nicely. It's nearly twenty-five past five. Oo—what a hill!"

She changed from top to third gear and put her foot hard down on the brake to take the first sharp corner. To her surprise, although the lower gear reduced the speed, the brake seemed to have no effect, and the big car took the bend at an uncomfortably fast rate and only just missed the hedge. Straightening up, she pulled on the hand brake, but nothing happened. Had she been driving the Rover she would have changed down again, but with the strange car she dare not risk it. To get into neutral and be unable to engage a lower gear would be fatal. With gathering momentum they approached the next bend.

"Grandfather, the brakes aren't working!"

Sir Martin pulled hard on the hand brake as they took this second bend, this time going on to the grass verge before they were round.

"It would seem that you are right, Jill." He was silent for a moment, and then in a tone of utter anguish: "Oh, Jill, my darling, not you! You are so young!"

They were round the last of the bends now and dropping like a plummet down a gradient of one in four towards the little bridge over the stream. Jill braced herself and sat like a rock. From the top of the hill she had seen the hazard in front of her—the narrowness of the bridge and the sharp turn on the other side—she could only do her best and pray for God's help. 'Trust in God and keep your powder dry!' The words flashed into and out of her mind and brought an involuntary smile to her lips as they rushed across the last ten yards of level ground and on to the bridge as she pulled the wheel hard over.

With the hold the Rolls had on the road, she might have got round if it had not been for the hump in the middle of the bridge. As it was the car was lifted off the ground, and the action of moving the steering wheel had no effect. There was a jolt, followed by a thunderous crash. Jill's head came into contact with the metal upright of the door and she knew no more!

CHAPTER 17

WHEN Rita had gone Nick's longing to see Jill had increased a hundredfold. It seemed almost unbearable to have to wait until six thirty. Restlessly he picked up his week-end case and limped down to the gate, looking in vain for a sight of the blue and silver Rover. It was past five o'clock now and obviously she and Sir Martin would have left already for his appointment at Pine Hill.

"Good evening, Mr Davidson. Going away?" It was Mrs Pelman's next-door neighbour coming out of his door to get his car from the garage between the two houses.

"Yes. Only as far as Haime though. I'd hoped that I might see Miss Railton passing after taking the Grammar School boys back to Castlebridge, but I'm afraid I'm too late for that now."

"Well, I can drop you at Haime if you like. I'm going to this big charity meeting at Goodwood, and it wouldn't be much out of my way."

"Would you, Mr Tanner? That's jolly good of you." He took his seat in the little red car—a sports model which was its owner's pride and joy—and less than ten minutes later he was dropped at the gate of Haime Grange. He paused for a few seconds to get his breath back, and to marvel that the car was still in one piece if that was Maurice Tanner's normal method of taking his corners, and then trudged up the short drive. At one point he could see the open garage with the Rover beside the empty space where the Rolls usually stood. Ah well, that was only what he had expected. He'd just have to wait until they returned.

The front door was open, and as he was nearing it he stopped abruptly. From inside the house he heard a woman scream! The sound was coming from the kitchen quarters and, his limp forgotten, Nicholas was across the hall and into the passage in something like five seconds.

Furious scuffling sounds were coming from the room on the right and he gazed aghast at the sight which met his eyes. Edward Blake was standing with his back to the door and his hands on the throat of Selina Lester! The woman was beating at him, but he was holding her at arm's length and her fists could not reach his face.

It was no time to be scupulous. With his limp he knew that he would be no match for the tall, strong Australian. The rolling pin lay on the kitchen table. In two paces he had reached it and a second later he struck the man a hard blow just behind his right ear; a spot where he had been taught in his youth that you could knock out an adversary without doing permanent harm. He had never put the teaching into practice before, but now he had proof of its worth. Edward released his hold and slid to the floor.

For a moment Nicholas was afraid that Selina was going to faint. She was greeny white and gasping for breath. But she staggered to the sink and splashed water on to her face. Then she turned to him frantically.

"Oh, Mr Davidson, it's Sir Martin—Sir Martin and Jill! They'll be killed—I know they will. Oh, what can we do? He said they'd be all right; he fastened Sir Martin's seat belt and Jill had one, too. He said he only meant to make them have a bit of a smash so that Sir

Martin couldn't sign the new will tonight. Oh, it's all my fault! I ought not to have told him about the will. What can I do? What can I do?"

Nicholas took her by the arm and pushed her into a chair. "Pull yourself together, Selina. What has Edward done?"

"It's the brakes—the brakes of the Rolls. Jill wanted to take her own car at the last minute and Edward teased her and said she was a coward so that she'd go in Sir Martin's after all. That's how I found out. He was laughing about it and I asked him what the joke was. He said he'd get all Sir Martin's money if the old will stood, and then we'd be married. And when I said I'd tell on him he said he'd marry me if I kept my mouth shut. Marry him! I told him I wouldn't marry him for all the money in the world. Then he laughed and said he might as well be hung for a sheep as a lamb!" Her hands went up to her neck, which was red and bruised, and she shuddered. "Oh, Mr Davidson!"

Nicholas pulled her to her feet. "Come on, Selina. We've got to stop them. How long ago did they leave?"

"About ten minutes, I should think. But I don't know where they've gone except that there is a hill."

"I do. Let's hope the key is in the Rover. Thank goodness I drove one like it sometimes when I was in Persia. But I'll have to remember to keep to the left." As he started the car and swept down the drive and through the little village, sounding the horn almost continuously to keep the road clear, he went on questioning the girl beside him. "What did Edward do to the brakes, Selina? Did he tell you?"

"Yes, but I didn't understand. Something about cutting a cable almost through so that some liquid would leak out slowly and then the brakes wouldn't work on

143

the hill. Mr Davidson, where are you going? You'll never get along here. Suppose we meet something."

"I must risk that. This way is quite a bit shorter and comes out at the top of the hill. Jill will have gone by the main road and she won't drive fast. We've just got to get there before they do."

Looking back afterwards to that nightmare drive Nicholas wondered how he had ever done it. He took that narrow lane at forty miles an hour, trusting blindly that the next corner would not produce an obstacle. Once the front wheels of a tractor were just emerging from a field gate when a furious blast of his horn brought the cursing driver to a halt and they scraped by with their off-side wheels on the grass verge, and at the time his only thought was one of thankfulness that the tractor was behind them and not ahead, blocking their way.

A hundred yards from the place where the lane joined the main road there was a gap where a hedge had been replaced by posts and wire fencing, giving a view of the valley and the hill. He looked that way and a groan burst from his lips. Sir Martin's Rolls was rushing downward at breakneck speed. He and Selina were too late!

It took every atom of his self control to make him change gear and take that hill at a reasonable speed, when his whole being was frantic with longing to reach the other car. But it wouldn't help Jill if he crashed the Rover. The speedometer needle swung back to twenty-five and then, as they reached the bridge, to twenty miles an hour. Then they were round and stopped, the doors were flung open and he and Selina were beside the Rolls.

The remains of the Rolls! The bonnet was crumpled and the off-side front wheel was buried in the hedge. Sir Martin, still held by his seat belt, was drooping orward and across the left side of the steering wheel and glass from the shattered windscreen was strewn on and ill round him. But where was Jill? Her door had burst open and the driving seat was empty. He scrambled on to the grass verge, which here was twelve to eighteen inches high, and looked round him, calling her name.

Then he saw her, and if he had been frightened before he was terrified now. Between the verge and the hedge there was a ditch and Jill was lying in this, with half her body and both legs hidden by the car. Was she pinned down? Was she alive?

"Jill! Jill darling!" Somehow he got down beside her, thrusting away the overhanging grass. Then he straightened his back and leant against the hedge, sick and dizzy with relief. She had been thrown clear and there was a gap of several inches between her and the nearest metal.

As he looked at her, trying to decide whether he should try to move her or go and fetch help, she turned her head and opened her eyes.

"Jill darling, keep still! Don't try to move. We'll get help soon."

"What happened? Oh, my shoulder hurts. Grandfather! Nick, is Grandfather all right?"

Selina's face appeared beside Nick's. "I think he is all right, Jill. He is out cold, but he's breathing and I can't see that he has broken anything. Oh, here is another car."

The new arrival—a small Hillman which had come out of the gate leading to Ian Macfarlane's house—pulled up abruptly. Nick breathed a sigh of relief at the sight of the man who hurried towards them. It was Doctor Mayhew.

"What's happened? That is Jill Railton's car, isn't it?

Phew, what a mess! Where is the girl? And where is the driver of Sir Martin's car?"

As he spoke he was already bending over the unconscious man, feeling his pulse and carefully removing fragments of glass.

"Jill was driving Sir Martin's car, sir. I came after her because—" he paused. It was obvious from the state of the Rolls that there would be no proof that the brakes had been tampered with, and perhaps, in any case, Sir Martin would not want to bring a case against his great-nephew, serious though the charge would be. "Because someone told me that Jill didn't know that the brakes were faulty, and I hoped to stop her before she got to this hill. Jill is in the ditch there. She has injured her shoulder, but she is conscious. Is Sir Martin bad?"

"I can't tell yet. There is probably some concussion, but no bones broken as far as I can see. Thank goodness he had a seat belt. Let's look at the lass now."

After a quick examination and a few questions he signed to Nicholas and between them they managed to lift her out and lay her on the bank.

"We shall need an ambulance," he said. "Will you go up to Mr Macfarlane's house, Mr Davidson, tell them what has happened and ask if you can telephone for one from there. Then ring the hospital, say you are speaking for me, and tell them that I shall want the small private room for Sir Martin and a bed for young Jill. Then you had better ring the police and report the accident."

Nicholas looked once more at the limp figure and pale face of the girl he loved, and then he and Selina got back into the Rover and drove along to the little white cottage where the artist lived. The phone calls and the conversation with Mr Macfarlane took some time, and when he returned to the bridge the ambulance had been

146

and gone and there was a note on the seat of the Rolls asking him to wait until the police arrived.

As they waited Selina looked at him curiously. "Why didn't you tell the doctor about Edward?" she asked.

Nicholas explained and she nodded. "I'm glad. He's a crook, of course, and he deserves to go back to prison, but he has had a very hard life. His father was a brute and his mother was weak and Edward seems to have inherited all the faults of both of them." She laughed suddenly—a short, bitter sound with no mirth in it. "It's queer that I can discuss him so—so dispassionately. I was madly in love with him once. Did you know?" Nick nodded. "When he told me he wanted me to take the job with Sir Martin, so that I could act as his spy if he needed one, I agreed readily. I thought he'd marry me when he had got everything he wanted. Then Jill came on the scene. She'd got everything; looks, liveliness, everything. And she was Sir Martin's grand-daughter. Edward turned his charm on her at once and I didn't see how she could resist him. How I hated her! Then the lawyer came and I listened outside the door while Sir Martin told him about changing his will, and I told Edward." She shivered. "If only I hadn't done it! What do you think will happen, Mr Davidson? I can't go back to that house with Edward there. He'll kill me!"

"No, you can't. At least, not by yourself. We'll go back together and see what is happening. Then you'd better collect some things and we'll find you a room for a few nights. Perhaps my landlady will know somewhere. Thank goodness, here's the police car. I can't wait to get to the hospital and find out how Jill is—and Sir Martin, of course."

CHAPTER 18

THE police constable, not knowing of any connection between the Rover and the damaged car, asked few questions, and soon Nicholas and Selina were on their way back to Castlebridge. When they reached the hospital they met Doctor Mayhew just leaving.

"How are they, Doctor?" he asked eagerly.

"Could be a lot worse. Sir Martin isn't fully conscious yet, but except for some bad bruises there is only the concussion. A few days' rest should put him right."

"And Jill?"

"Broken collarbone and two ribs and general shakeup. The bone has been set and the ribs strapped, so now all she needs is a good sleep. The nurse is going to give her a sedative."

"Could I see her for a few minutes?"

Doctor Mayhew looked at him doubtfully. "All right —just for five minutes. Don't excite her. Tomorrow is also a day."

He patted the young man on the shoulder and hurried away and Nicholas made his way to the bed at the end of the women's surgical ward. A nurse was just approaching with a trolley.

"Good evening, Nurse. Doctor Mayhew says I may see Miss Railton for a few minutes before she goes to sleep."

The nurse looked her disapproval, but when Jill added her pleas she relented, and then, seeing Nick's glance of

148

embarrassment at the next bed, she pulled the curtains.

"Just a few minutes then," she said. "Miss Railton needs some sleep."

Jill waited until she had closed the remaining gap in the curtains and then clutched Nick's hand feverishly.

"Nick, I don't understand. How did you get there? Why did you come? And how is Grandfather? Have you seen him?"

Nicholas looked at her flushed face. "The doctor says Sir Martin will be quite all right in a day or two. But he also told me I wasn't to let you get excited. Do you really want to hear about it this evening? It's all okay now."

"Yes, I do. I'll never sleep otherwise. Please tell me."

So then he told her, as briefly and dispassionately as possible, about Rita's visit, his journey to Haime, Selina's disclosure and the race to Pine Hill.

"Now I'd better go or the nurse will be after my blood. I promised Selina I'd take her back to Haime to fetch some things, so that she won't have any more trouble with Edward. You don't mind my taking the Rover back, do you?"

"Of course not. I didn't realise before that your leg would allow you to drive."

For a moment there was silence as it dawned on Nicholas like a bolt from the blue, that until that evening he certainly would not have been able to drive the Rover, or any other car with a clutch pedal which needed the use of his left leg. He sprang to his feet and walked quickly up and down the two or three paces which the space beside the bed allowed.

"Jill darling, it's gone! It's almost unbelievable. Talk about the influence of mind over matter!"

"What do you mean?"

"Well, first of all I suppose it was the need to get to you quickly that made me forget myself for the first time for six months. There's another reason, too, but perhaps I'd better not tell you about that tonight."

"Oh do, Nick. I'm not a bit sleepy."

"Well, very briefly, the trouble which caused my leaving Gachsaran has been cleared up. I had a letter from the headmaster there today, sending me a really first-class testimonial. Now I'll be able to get a job easily —a good one—even that one in Canada which Jeremy was talking about, if it isn't taken already, and you know what that means, don't you? All right, Nurse, I'm just going."

The nurse, pushing the trolley, came in firmly, evidently having made up her mind that it was the only way to get her patient treated.

"What does it mean, Nick? Do tell me."

Nicholas bent over her so that his words could not be overheard. "It means that I'll be able to ask the girl I love if she will marry me! Do you think she will say yes?"

On top of everything she had suffered, both mental and physical, during the last two hours, this was the last straw. All Nick's happiness, the curing of his limp, even the exuberance which had made him call her Jill darling —words which had brought a surge of joy to her heart— were because there was now no barrier between him and Vivienne. He could ask Vivienne to marry him! The "Jill darling" was just the overflow of his happiness, and perhaps a certain amount of relief that she, his friend, was safe.

Forcing back the tears which were pricking her eyes, she managed a smile. "Of course she will say yes, Nick. How could she say anything else?"

"You darling!" Nick bent over her as if to kiss her, but the presence of the nurse deterred him. "I'll be in tomorrow. Sleep well," and he was gone.

The tears overflowed then, but the nurse took no notice. She was accustomed to the reaction which followed experiences like the one this girl had been through. She prepared the injection, keeping the conversation to such safe subjects as Jill's work as a taxi driver and the question of whether the girl had seen a controversial programme on the television on the previous evening, and by the time she had finished Jill had got her feelings under control and was able to smile her thanks.

"That's lovely and comfortable, Nurse, thank you."

"Good. You'll be better in the morning. Now I'll bring you a drink and leave you in peace."

*　　*　　*

Peace! Not much peace for me tonight, thought Jill sadly, but when the drink came she took it obediently and settled down. Whatever it was which had been put in the injection was most effective. Less than five minutes later, the troubles and excitements of the evening forgotten, she was deeply asleep.

Meanwhile Nicholas Davidson had left the hospital with Selina and was on his way back to Haime. He was in the seventh heaven of happiness. Jill had promised to marry him! With that testimonial from Mr Bailley he could get a job anywhere. If Jill preferred it they would stay in England, but she might like the idea of seeing Canada or some other part of the world. He pulled up outside the front door and came back to the present day and to the frightened girl on the seat beside him.

"Now we'd better see where Mr Edward Blake is

lurking," he said in as light a tone as he could muster
"Just a minute, though. Perhaps I'd better be prepared."

He went to the boot of the car and extracted an eight
inch spanner from Jill's tool kit. Perhaps it was cowardly
but this was no time for recklessness.

In fact his precaution was unnecessary. The house wa
deserted. And not only deserted! Sir Martin's desk ha
been forced and the drawers in his bedroom had been
searched, evidently for money. Even the few pounds i
the house-keeping purse had disappeared. Selina shoo
it out and a folded slip of paper fell to the floor.

"Goodbye, Selina!" it read. "If you had been conten
to string along with me we should both have been rich
But you know the old saying: 'Hell hath no fury like
woman scorned!' Not that I ever cared a brass farthin
for Jill. I like my women tough—like you. My exit i
already planned, so it will be useless to call in the police
They'd never catch me. I'm sure Great Uncle Marti
won't begrudge me the few pounds I'm taking. He's no
a bad old codger! I hope he'll keep you on as his coo
house-keeper—it is all you are fit for.

"Goodbye.

Edward."

There were tears in Selina's eyes as she passed th
note to Nicholas to read. She had loved Edward for s
long in spite of his faults. Now she would never see hin
again.

For his part, Nicholas was thankful. Presumably th
fellow was well away and perhaps even already out o
the country. The note, he felt, was typical of the man
He could almost see the look on the handsome face a
he had written it. Selfish, unscrupulous and bad to th
core. Selina was well rid of him.

"Well, I shan't need this!" He put down the spanne

ith an attempt at a laugh. "Cheer up, Selina. Sir Martin
ill see that you are all right, I'm sure. I'll go round and
ck up while you pack a bag. I don't suppose you want
stay here on your own, do you?" A shiver was her
ily answer and he laughed again, more naturally this
me. Then, while she packed the things she needed,
e telephoned to Mr Shelton and gave him a brief out-
ne of the evening's events and then saw the house
roperly shut up before taking Selina to Tindal to find
room for the night.

This proved quite simple as Mrs Tanner had a spare
oom. Nicholas saw the girl fixed up and then went back
his own sitting-room next door. The rest of the evening
assed in a happy dream. How soon would Jill marry
im? Would she want to wait until after Sir Martin's
peration? Though that might well be over before they'd
ot everything fixed and the banns called. What a
arling she was and what pluck she had. Nine o'clock!
ot much more than twelve hours before he could see
er again!

CHAPTER 19

JILL awoke the next morning feeling as if she had bee[n]
put through a washing machine and then spin-dried f[or]
good measure! Sore, stiff, bruised all over and with [a]
mouth like a lime-kiln, she opened her eyes to a brigh[t]
sunny morning and closed them again in an effort t[o]
ease her throbbing head.

"Well, Miss Railton, awake at last? I'll bring you [a]
cup of tea." The nurse who had treated her on the pr[e]-
vious evening smiled sympathetically. "I expect you a[re]
feeling a bit like the morning after the night befor[e]
aren't you?"

"I am rather." Jill tried to smile in return. "Nurs[e]
how is Grandfather? Have you heard?"

"He is splendid. He awoke at about seven o'clock wit[h]
no ill effects at all, as far as we have been able to fin[d]
out. He will stay in bed, of course, until the doctor ha[s]
examined him, but they don't think he has taken an[y]
harm."

She bustled away and presently a younger nurs[e]
brought a tray of tea and toast. Jill looked at it wit[h]
distaste; she didn't want anything to eat; but when sh[e]
had been propped up and had taken a few sips of we[l]-
come liquid she discovered after all that she was ver[y]
hungry, and she remembered that she had eaten nothin[g]
since teatime on the previous day.

She was just finishing when the nurse returned.

"Here is Mr Davidson, Miss Railton. Sister says he mustn't stop for more than ten minutes as the doctor will be doing his round."

Jill drew a quick breath. She wished she had had more time to prepare for their next meeting. She wished she hadn't had to see him again ever—or at least not until she had got used to the idea of his marriage to Vivienne. She forced a smile to her lips.

"Hello, Nick. It's kind of you to come and see me. I thought you'd be too busy getting everything settled up. Have you seen Grandfather yet? The nurse says he is going to be all right."

"Yes, I've just come from him. He is wonderful, and only worried about you. But what did you mean, getting everything settled up? There's nothing I can do at Haime Grange. Mr Shelton is coming to see Sir Martin later today, and he will deal with anything that is necessary."

"No, I meant your own affairs. We didn't have time to talk about it yesterday, but I really am glad about your news from Gachsaran. I never actually knew what had happened there, but I gathered that there had been some trouble. Have you decided yet whether you will write to the headmaster of that school in Canada? Or shall you wait until you find out if your fiancée would like it?"

"But you—" Nick stopped, puzzled and tongue-tied. Then he came over to the bed. "Drink up that tea and I'll take the tray." He waited until she had finished, put the tray on the table and then came back. "Either you or I was more dopey than I realised last night. Do you remember what I said?"

"Of course I do. You said that now you could get a good job, and you would be able to ask Vivienne to marry you."

"Vivienne! Ask Vivienne to marry me? Jill—my own precious, wonderful Jill—you silly, ridiculous, beautiful girl—I wouldn't ask Vivienne to marry me if she was the only woman left in the world! Oh, I can see now. I was the idiotic one. I was asking you to marry me, and all night long I've been dancing on air because you said yes."

Suddenly he pulled the curtains round the bed, bent over her, slid his left arm round her shoulders and turned her face up to his. "I'd better say it again, quickly and clearly, so that there can be no possibility of misunderstanding. Jill, I love you. Please will you marry me?"

Colour swept into her cheeks and her blue eyes shone with joy. "Oh, Nick, yes! I think I was a bit idiotic too, but I've loved you for such a long time."

After that it seemed only a few seconds before they heard voices and looked round to see Doctor Mayhew smiling in at them through a gap in the curtains.

*   *   *

On a fresh morning in early September two people stood together on the boat deck of the S.S. Empress of Canada. Behind them the sun was rising over the Atlantic Ocean; in front of them was the mouth of the St Lawrence river. Nick's arm tightened round his wife's waist.

"Happy, darling? No regrets? No fears?"

"Happier than I've ever been in my life. Oh, Nick, what a lot has happened in the last few weeks. Grandfather's sight restored—even better than the surgeon dared to hope—and his setting off for the other side of the world. You do think it was all right for him to go alone, don't you?"

"Of course it was. Horace is going to meet him at

Wellington. And he won't be alone, as Selina is going to Australia on the same ship."

"Of course. I'm glad he has been so good to her, Nick, and that he was content to let Edward just fade away without taking any action against him. I suppose, strictly speaking, he should have gone to the police about him, but somehow I don't think Edward had had a fair chance in life."

"Perhaps not." Nicholas didn't want to talk about Edward. He went back to their earlier subject. "Then, when Sir Martin's visit to New Zealand is over, no doubt Horace will help him with the arrangements for his voyage to us. We'll have six months, darling, to get our little home ready for him. I'm longing to see it, aren't you?"

"I am, and to meet your friend Jeremy and his wife, too."

"Well, we'll see them in a week's time. But first I'm looking forward to showing Sue what a wonderful girl I've found." He chuckled. "I sent her a snap of Vivienne once, when I was so crazy about her, and Sue didn't approve at all. She'll find out that her brother has learnt some sense at last."

They fell silent then, watching the land ahead as the rising sun lighted it more and more clearly. Suddenly Jill laughed and Nicholas looked down at her enquiringly.

"What's the joke?"

"I was thinking of Miss Gregory. Do you realise, Nick, that if it hadn't been for her none of this would have happened? If she hadn't suggested that the Rover was big enough for a taxi I'd never have thought of using it that way. Then I'd never have met you, or the Barlows. And if it hadn't been for little Mark Barlow there wouldn't have been that article in the papers, and Grandfather wouldn't have known about me. It's like the house that Jack built."

"How pleased she'd be if she knew what an important part she had played in our lives. You'd better send her a card to thank her."

"I will. I must sign it Jill Railton, I suppose?"

"Oh no, you can't do that, Mrs Davidson! And she wouldn't know who it was if you put Jill Davidson."

"I know," said Jill. "I'll use the nicest name anyone called me when I was driving a taxi."

A week later Miss Gregory found among her mail a picture postcard of the parliament buildings in Ottawa. It was signed quite simply: "The Taxi Lady!"

Broken Vows

Christine Wilson

Broken Vows

Christine Wilson

For a moment the world rocked dizzily before it steadied again. Grey eyes held blue, with a depth of unspoken misery and meaning. She could see that he was just as shocked as she was.

'Sue! Oh Sue!' he whispered, his voice thick with emotion.

Chapter One

THE string of pearls snapped in Susan Mohr's impatient hands, sending a cascade onto the carpet and under the dressing-table. Tears in her eyes, she watched the rolling gems but made no effort to retrieve them. She blinked rapidly and muttered softly under her breath.

This was just about the last straw!

She was late for the party and still Glyn, her husband had not come home from the office at his father's enormous factory. Why, oh why had she accepted that invitation for tonight? Glyn had been furious when he found out about it. He was such a bear these days; nothing she did or said seemed to please him. He deliberately went out of his way to upset her, seeming to take some kind of fiendish delight in angering and hurting her.

What a fool she had been to think their marriage could work! Four months of being Mrs. Glyn Mohr, wife of the well-to-do heir to Edward Mohr, owner of a vast network of factories.

Yet she had tried, hadn't she? They had both gone into marriage knowing the difficulties that were besetting them. Why then had they failed so soon and so miserably?

Susan bent down to pick up the pearls. They lay in her palm . . . cold and unfriendly. She almost threw them down again in disgust . . . that was how she felt, cold and unwanted. At the beginning she had wanted jewellery and all the other many things money could buy. Glyn had promised her everything, yet now none of it held any more interest for her. She knew the broken necklace's worth but all she wanted to do was to throw it away and never see it again.

What was the matter with her? What was she searching for? Why did nothing interest her any longer? What did she want from Glyn?

Susan leant against the dressing-table chair and buried her face in her arm to weep. It was pointless in going on. She must make up her mind one way or the other. She had made a terrible mistake. It was useless not to tell Glyn. But when? After the party tonight? He probably wouldn't care if she left him.

The telephone bell shattered the silence.

Slowly Susan rose and went over to the bedside table to lift the receiver.

" Hallo, Susan Mohr speaking."

" Sue, it's me," Glyn's voice sounded harsh. " You'd better go without me. I shall be late home and probably unable to make the party at all."

Susan swallowed hard. It had been Glyn himself who had changed his mind so abruptly this morning and said that they ought to go tonight. He was so inconsistent!

" Why couldn't you have told me this morning?" she demanded angrily. " I know your working late is only an excuse. You never wanted to go to Janine's twenty- first party even though she is the daughter of one of your oldest friends. You've telephoned me now just to get pleasure out of knowing that I have gone to a great deal of trouble getting ready."

Glyn's chuckle came over the wire.

" What would you rather do? Enjoy yourself with our friends or dine alone at home with me . . . just the two of us . . . or does the thought of another dreary, silent evening with your loving husband sicken you?" he demanded fiercely.

Susan bit her lip.

"Glyn. Come home and get ready."

"Why?" the reply was quick and sharp.

"You can't afford to offend any more of your friends, you know."

He laughed bitterly.

"For one moment I thought perhaps you were going to tell me you missed me and wanted me with you."

Susan refused to be goaded.

"Glyn, I don't want to quarrel over the phone. I just want you to take me to Janine's party."

"My dear girl, why should I? Are you afraid of being a wallflower and that no one will dance with you?" he chuckled again. "Surely all your *admirers* will be there? They'll jump at the chance of finding an undisturbed corner in which to have a cosy tête-à-tête with you!" His tone was bantering then it altered, menacingly. "But remember, my darling, you're *my* wife for now and always, even if you don't behave like one."

Stung by the cruelty in his voice, Susan's reply was quick. How *dared* he say that to her! Heaven knows she'd tried hard enough to hide her dislike of being touched by him, but he had not understood her. Perhaps if she hadn't been quite so seasick during their awful honeymoon . . . but all that was past now. Here was the opportunity she had been waiting for. Take it now . . .

"Glyn, I'm leaving you."

There was a stunned silence before Susan went on rapidly. "It's no good. We should never have married. After the party I won't be coming back here."

He had found his voice at last.

"Don't be such a little fool! Of course you don't mean it. You're just saying these things to get me home."

"I do mean it!" she declared hysterically. "I can't go on. I'm fed up with your sneering, cruel remarks and the way you treat me ... like ... like a *chattel*."

"I love you, Susan," he said quietly.

"Pardon?" she had not caught the words.

"Damn it, woman, do I have to shout? I said I love you."

Susan laughed bitterly.

"No you don't. Neither of us loves the other, and that's where we've failed. Now I'm going to ring off. I'm late already. Even if it's the last thing I do for you, I will at least have the courtesy to turn up at the Hobblesons'. When I've gone they won't be able to say I had no manners."

She flung down the receiver. It was done now. Glyn hadn't believed her. Well, she'd soon change all that, she decided grimly, marching to the wardrobe and throwing it open. She tossed her suitcase on the bed and started to cram it full of clothes. She would show Glyn! When he came home tonight the house would be empty and she didn't care ... she didn't care.

Suddenly she began to cry. Long, racking sobs which left her breathless and red-eyed.

Ten minutes later she had backed her car out of the garage and was driving along the road to the hotel she knew to be five miles on the far side of the Hobblesons' large country house. She would book a single room for one night and make up her mind tomorrow where she would eventually go.

As she drove slowly along the winding roads her mind flew back over the past few months, wondering what had driven her to Glyn. Of course it had been That Dress!

The dress had been the star of Maître André's collection and Susan had so longed to be the one chosen to model it. Once again, Maître André had turned her down in favour of Gail. The tall, graceful, willowy Gail whose honey eyes and full smile seemed to win more orders for Maître André than any other model. Susan was very envious of Gail, but in her heart she knew she could never emulate her. Her own figure was excellent but there was something lacking in her poise and manner that she simply could not overcome. Maître André had been kind in his criticism and, although she had not wanted to admit to herself the truth, she knew she would always be one of the " also rans " . . . a girl whose face might appear now and again in the not-so-well-known fashion magazines but never, never in the top-class journals. No matter how hard she tried, she would not reach the standards she had set herself. If only she could conquer that feeling of lack of self-confidence which plagued her!

Susan watched Gail from behind the alcove. The clever lighting picked out every detail of the dress, sending shadows where the Maître wished them to fall and exposing Gail as an ethereal, beautiful, sylvan creature. Susan's heart sank. She ought never to have chosen modelling as a career!

There was a gasp of admiration from the crowd then a burst of spontaneous applause. Maître André beamed with delight. Susan watched the audience distastefully. There was the fat, overdressed and over-bejewelled duchess whose body bulged over the sides of her chair like an unset jelly. She ought to be home doing remedial exercises and keeping to a strict diet instead of sitting here wheezing, Susan thought rudely, adding that if *she* had all those jewels she would wear just one or two items at a time so that their full beauty could be enjoyed instead of being swamped by glitter.

Then there was the nervous bride-to-be sitting on the very

edge of her chair while her fierce-countenanced mother whispered and prodded her unmercifully. Next to her sat a benevolent old gentleman who always came to the Maître's Occasions although no one seemed to know why. Her eyes passed over the representatives from the British, French and American Press and on to Glyn Mohr who sat in his usual seat at the end of the front row. How he managed to obtain one of the best seats every time the Maître showed a collection, Susan could not imagine, for he was not known as one of the Maître's clients. She thought crossly:

With all that wealth behind him he can buy himself in anywhere!

Earlier today while she had been modelling one of the less exotic gowns, she had allowed herself the luxury of a direct stare at Mr. Mohr and, if there was venom in that fixed smile, then only he had seen it. His firmly closed lips betrayed no secrets and the clear, grey eyes were cool and inexpressive under heavy eyebrows that overhung his face like the thatched roof of a country cottage, thereby giving him an intense, forbidding look. He supported his chin in his clenched hand as the elbow rested on the arm of the chair and, for a moment, the long fingers had uncurled to move very slightly in salutation.

He looks more like the Devil than ever! Susan decided and giggled inwardly. How annoyed he would be to learn that she and the other girls had christened him " Old Lucifer ". Of course, that had been before he had spoken to Susan. Even now, when she knew him better, she still could not rid herself of the fitting name.

As she had turned before him, he had caught her eye again and given her a deliberate and broad wink which had annoyed her even more. If she had been standing but a little closer, perhaps she might have endeavoured to grind her heel into that elegantly polished toe-cap resting on the floor beyond the crossed legs. The Maître would never have forgiven her for causing an " incident " of almost international proportions during this, his most important collection.

Glyn never seemed to do any work at all! Susan resented this fact. Naturally, he did *have* a job: as one of the directors on the board of the big firm owned by his parents. When he was not making half-hearted attempts at work on the vast premises, he did nothing because, as he had told her months ago, there was absolutely no need for him to work at all. It appeared that no one worried if he did not put in an appearance in the executive offices for weeks on end. He had his father's permission to use his time as he wished.

Until the day five months ago when he had idled into the salon in company with his mother, Glyn had had no purpose in life. Now he was always hanging around the salon, attending every major and minor collection. He was always sitting there . . . in the same front seat.

The girls began to wonder about him but not for long. He soon informed Susan why he was there. There were no half-measures with a man like Glyn Mohr, as Susan had swiftly discovered. When he made up his mind to do something, then nothing and nobody stood in his way. From the start his main ambition had been to improve his acquaintance with Susan.

At first she had been a little afraid of the sudden attentions, then she was flattered and intrigued by them. He had lavished money and presents on her, while all the time she was uncomfortably conscious that he was doing so merely to sell himself to her. She had learned quickly that he was a man used to having everything the way *he* wanted it, regardless of whom or what stood in his way.

Naturally Susan had been bowled over by the promise of

riches. She loved being the centre of attraction and, after so many years of pinching and scraping, she welcomed Glyn's generosity. He was forceful and persuasive, and liked always to have his own way in the arrangement of the time they spent together. He had every minute planned and she was too busy enjoying herself to question his right of choice. In some way, his being there seemed to make up for her lack of success as a model.

On meeting Edward and Beatrice Mohr, Glyn's parents, the dislike had been mutual. Edward was a man in his late sixties, whose sole occupation and topic was the state of the stock market. Beatrice was an inveterate snob and Susan saw through her within five minutes of their introduction. Unfortunately, Edward had not had the courtesy or kindness to wait until Glyn had taken Susan out of earshot before saying to his blowsy wife:

" Really, Bea, how *could* you allow our boy to take up with that type of girl? Surely there are enough young females among his own set to satisfy him without lowering himself almost to working-class level?"

Susan's lips had tightened and she had the pleasure of witnessing Glyn's acute discomfort as he tried to gloss over his father's boorish lack of manners. Yet he need not have worried for Susan was used to remarks in this vein. After all, over the past years, she had had plenty of practice! She had never quite succeeded in eliminating that slight accent from her speech. It was a legacy from her early days in the working-class area where she had been brought up. Seven years ago, when she had been seventeen, she had won a beauty contest at a holiday camp. It had taken weeks and weeks of hard saving to pay for just one week's holiday away from Mackay's chain store. The prize money and later very fortuitous introductions had been just sufficient to enable her to give up her job as shop assistant and take up modelling. Admittedly, there had been some very bad days when she had not known where the next meal was coming from, but somehow she had managed: mainly by taking part-time and arduous duties as a waitress in a restaurant. Determination, however, had won, and she had come through safely. If it hadn't been for dear Mum who had contributed a small sum each week . . . a sum she could ill afford . . . she might have failed.

During the past three years everything had changed. Now it was she, Susan, who was sending home money to help Mum bring up her four brothers and two sisters. The smell of poverty and National Assistance still nauseated her. She had vowed never to be poor again.

Back in the changing-rooms, Susan rested her aching feet. She was dead tired and the thought of bed was enticing. She pushed weary feet into low-heeled shoes, knowing they were not particularly becoming but no one would notice at this late hour. She ran a comb through her unruly hair before cramming it willy-nilly under a saucy hat. Opening her capacious handbag, she thrust all her oddments into it and then prepared to leave the salon.

Now for a hot bath! she thought. Tonight she was too exhausted even to cook herself a meal. Biscuits and cheese and a cup of tea would have to do.

Outside the salon, a sleek grey sports car was drawn up.

How was it that *he* was always able to find a parking space?

She frowned. Tonight of all nights Glyn was waiting. She ought to have guessed he'd be there. If only she'd thought, she could have slipped out of one of the other exits. Hadn't she made it abundantly clear to him only last night that she would *not* be free tonight? But he was a man who would not be gainsaid.

She pulled back sharply, hiding in the shadows and hoping he had not seen her. With a little bit of good luck, she might be able to slip away in the opposite direction.

However, it was now too late. With the lithe grace of a panther, he had flung open the car door and his huge frame was now striding towards her.

" Where shall we go?" he demanded authoritatively. " I've booked a table at Alberto's, if that's okay with you." It was his choice of place, as usual.

" I'm sorry, Glyn. Not tonight, thanks. I thought I'd made that clear yesterday."

" Nonsense! Of course we're going out. You should know me well enough by now, my dear. Hop in!" He pushed her towards the car but she stood firm.

" Glyn, I'm dead beat. I want to go home. Really I do."

For a moment he stared at her, then he scowled, the sardonic devil's eyebrows meeting.

" I want you to come with me!" he protested.

" Oh, for Heaven's sake! Don't you ever think of what *I* want?" she demanded fiercely, and pushed him roughly aside. " If you'll excuse me, I'm off to catch a bus."

" Very well," he said pettishly. " If that's how you feel, I'll drive you home." Susan looked at him, distrustingly. " I promise," he went on. " First stop your apartment."

He helped her into the car and they drove off.

A sign post loomed ahead and Susan slowed down to read it, then she turned on her left indicator and swung the little car round the tight bend into a side road.

Chapter Two

SUSAN'S lips tightened as she remembered the further events of that evening . . . that fateful moment when she had so blindly turned her steps towards this path which was going to lead her straight to a single room at the hotel five miles further on . . .

Glyn swiftly negotiated the four miles to Susan's apartment building. It was set back in a quiet side street of unpretentious houses which all bore the sad look of decay. Inside the building there were dark passages and grimy wallpaper, but the two rooms Susan rented were clean and bright. She had purchased a gay material for curtains, and the small knick-knacks she had collected over the past four years served to give the rooms a warm, lived-in appearance. The rent was reasonable, and living here suited Susan admirably, for it meant that her busy mother had one less mouth to feed.

At the front door, Susan turned to thank Glyn for bringing her home but he was already at her side.

"Key, please," he demanded, and when she began to protest, he went on, "If you won't dine with me, then it's the least you can do to invite me in for a drink," he grinned. "Thanks for saving you your bus fare."

" You know I don't keep spirits! " she snapped. " Not even a beer tucked away anywhere."

He leaned closer.

" Did I say I wanted one, sweetheart? Tea or coffee'll do. Cocoa if you like. They're all nectar from your gentle hands."

The flatlet was cold and dark, and the meter empty.

" Good thing I came with you," Glyn commented as Susan fumbled in her purse for a shilling.

" I usually leave a couple of shilling pieces beside the meter in case it runs out at an awkward time, which is now. Bobs are in very short supply at the moment. If they don't come and empty this thing, I'll do it myself and blow the electricity company! " she declared, thumping the meter angrily.

Glyn pulled out a handful of silver from his trousers pocket and stood on the landing to hunt through it.

" You're in luck, darling," he said. " Four. These should help for a little while. No. No," he protested quickly as she gave him two florins in exchange.

Susan's eyes sparkled dangerously.

" You'll take these and like it."

" If I refuse?"

" Then it's the last time you take me out, or bring me home."

" Cutting off your pretty little nose to spite your face, eh?" he enquired lightly, although his eyes were unsmiling.

" Exactly," was her cool reply before she vanished into the kitchenette. " I haven't anything stronger than black coffee, do you mind?"

" I'd rather have white, *if* you can spare the milk," he replied sarcastically. Susan banged a tray onto the table and he grinned, knowing he had annoyed her. Then he joined her in the kitchenette where he leaned against the door jamb, hands in pockets, watching as she filled the kettle before plugging it in. She crossed the floor to the shelf beside him, reaching behind the curtain which cloaked her groceries. He was there before her. Their hands met on the tin of instant coffee. Suddenly he pulled her towards him and stared down at her. Their faces were only a few inches from each other and the air became still. Then, to her great surprise, he raised his hands and gently cupped her face in them, his fingers stroking her cheeks. She had an overwhelming desire to run away . . . and one to turn her head until her lips were buried in his palm . . . he had never touched her like this before . . . their relationship had been so formal and correct . . . until now.

Suddenly he released her and went over to the power point to switch on the kettle which she had forgotten.

His back to her, he said steadily:

" Susan, will you marry me?"

He was joking, of course.

" Why?" she asked cheerfully, matching his nonchalance.

" Why do people want to marry each other?" He turned to face her. His eyes were veiled but he was watching her closely.

" Because . . . oh let's stop this silly game!"

" I'm quite serious, Susan. Surely people marry because they're in love with one another, don't they?"

Susan turned from his intent gaze and began to make a great deal of clatter with cups and saucers.

" There's no need to get het up and red-cheeked," he continued, amused. " Surely it can't have escaped your notice that I'm in love with you?" His tone was light and bantering and she was uncertain whether to believe him. " What do you say?" he added.

She wanted to laugh. Of all the unromantic, brainless ways of making a proposal of marriage! Of course he must be joking. She stared at him and suddenly knew that he was indeed in earnest.

What *could* she say? Glyn was likeable, yes. Naturally he had plenty of faults, but so did everyone else, herself included. He often behaved like a spoiled child but this did not detract from his attractiveness. He was far too free with his money and liked getting his own way. However, he knew her background and even the sordidness of her past had not deterred him; he took her at face value and she enjoyed being pampered by him. No matter where they went or what they did together, she never had the dreaded fear that he was unable to pay for anything. And it wasn't as if she was a success at modelling. It would be irksome to admit defeat but to marry Glyn would be a means of bowing out gracefully.

Yet to love him! That was a completely different matter.

Uncannily, almost as if he was reading her thoughts, he broke in:

" I know damned well that you don't love me, Susan, but you need the things I can give you. Putting me aside for the moment, think of all the dresses, jewels, enjoyment and luxury I can give you once we are married. Everything you've ever wanted can be yours. A decent home, food and warmth, no need to wear yourself out each day at the Maître's. Think of it, Susan, think! "

Susan shuddered. An intense feeling of shame swept over her for he had exactly mirrored her own thoughts.

" You make it sound so horribly mercenary! " she said.

" I mean to be mercenary, darling! Do you think I haven't been wise to what's been going through that quick little brain of yours all these months? Admit it, darling, you wouldn't have looked at a man eleven years your senior if I hadn't had wealth, now, would you?" Susan was crimson with embarrassment. It was all so terribly true!

Glyn laughed gaily.

"Come on, own up! I know I'm no Don Juan, no Romeo to bring a flutter to the heart of every female who sees me. My nose is too big, my face hard and my hair's almost grey already. I don't profess to be the film star lover who will sweep you into his arms in an ecstasy of madness . . . although I *shall* teach you to love me, my girl!" He paused for a moment, then continued: "I also know that many people consider I'm not a particularly pleasant man to know. I'm selfish, I go for what takes my fancy, regardless of those in my way; I'm luxury-loving and I'm afraid I sometimes drink far more than is good for me. On the other hand, I'm just the man for you, although you haven't recognised the fact yet. You need me, my dear. You are struggling for the many things I already have. Let's say I'm Temptation Personified. All you have to do is to accept my proposal, and everything is yours. There'll be no need to wear yourself out at the salon any more and, be honest with yourself, my sweet," he added gently, "You aren't the top model. I'm going to stick my neck out and you can call me all sorts of names for telling you this, but modelling isn't *really* you, is it? A person of your type has either to be tops or nothing, isn't that so? Come on, darling, back out now while you can . . . by marrying me."

Susan turned off the kettle, speechless. Glyn could read her like a book!

"Whichever way you look at it, I'm not at all a bad proposition," he added lightly. "You're a lucky girl. I could give you the names of quite a few women who'd be only too pleased to get their thieving little paws on my father's fortune through me. I'm thirty-five, in good health, and have an almost limitless bank balance. Also, I happen to love you."

Never in her life had Susan conjured up dreams of a proposal like Glyn's. It was extraordinarily forthright, but honest. It occurred to her that she had heard doorstep salesmen explain their wares in similar manner, and, once again she wanted to giggle shamelessly. However, her conscience got the better of her.

It was all *wrong*! She must put an end to this before they went too far. Aloud she said:

"It wouldn't be right. You tempt me with offers of wealth, and everyone but a fool knows that money can't buy happiness. I don't love you and I have no wish to marry without love."

He laughed and came over to her. As he put his arms around her reluctant body, he said:

"My sweet, you are so right! I agree, it most definitely wouldn't be fair. However, you seem to be crediting me with very little sense, you know. At my age you don't expect me to be a novice in this game of love, do you? I assure you that in my skilled hands you could soon be taught to love me."

Susan shuddered, suddenly apprehensive.

"And if we fail?" she managed to gasp.

He put a finger on her lips.

"Fail? Don't you know me well enough by now to realise that I *always* succeed in getting what I want? Besides, who are you to talk of failure? Haven't you worked your way up from almost nothing, letting nothing deter you? Come darling, let's look on our marriage as just another problem to be solved. Problem, or battle if you prefer to think of it that way, and one we shall win together. *You* need feel no guilt. If I'm willing to take the risk, then surely that absolves you? From now on it will be my responsibility.

"*Will* you marry me?"

She pulled away from him and busied herself at the sink, panic-stricken. Part of her wanted to leap at the chance he had offered her yet somehow she had no wish to commit herself so quickly.

"Your parents don't like me," she hedged. "How angry they'll be! You could do far better for yourself, as I'm sure they'll tell you."

Glyn snorted.

"We needn't worry about them. This is *our* affair, not theirs. *I'm* the one to choose who is to become my wife. Enough of this arguing." He laid his hands on her shoulders and turned her towards him. She was drawn into his arms and kissed in a commanding, authoritative manner which she found a trifle distasteful, but felt obliged to acquiesce.

Oh yes, Glyn Mohr, you're certainly an expert in this! she thought grimly. The realisation both annoyed and disappointed her. His kiss had been so horribly . . . what was the expression? . . . business-like, that was it . . . What had she expected? The earth to open up beneath her feet or something equally melodramatic? He had told her he loved her, but that was obviously not true, not after such routine kissing. There must have been many, many women before her!

Should she accept? She wanted to do so, although she knew it could easily prove to be a hideous mistake. On the other hand, it was not as if she was deliberately deceiving Glyn, because he had recognised the pitfalls already bringing them into the open for them both to see. Therefore, if she said "yes" now, it would be equal responsibility if things didn't work as he had hoped.

She must never allow Mum to suspect that she was prepared to marry Glyn merely for his worldly possessions. Put in those words, it sounded terrible. Which, of course, it was. She was disgusted with herself.

Now Glyn had started to kiss her in a different manner, and the hidden passion frightened her. He was so masterful and possessive and she mustn't allow herself to be dominated. Remember what had happened to poor Mum because she had allowed herself to be ruled and mastered by Father. He had been a useless, conniving, hard and selfish brute, yet somehow . . . and this Susan could not bring herself to understand . . . Mum had loved Father passionately and had almost broken her heart the day he had been killed through his own carelessness at work. Twelve-year-old Susan had vowed then and there that never, never, as long as she lived, would she allow any man to beat, cajole, bully or dominate her so completely that she could never call her life her own. When she grew up, even if she loved someone to distraction, she would *not* permit herself to be mastered. *She* would dominate the man she married, not he her!

The man she married!

She was beginning to shake in Glyn's hard embrace and a strange whirl of feeling threatened to engulf her. She was suddenly terrified. She pulled her mouth away.

"Stop! Stop! Oh please stop!" she begged, pushing her hands against his chest. His eyes gleamed dangerously. "You're rough and you're hurting me."

He released her at once and watched her with a glint in his eyes. She bit her lip, thinking of that embrace. If she was to keep her part of the bargain, she must learn to put up with any distastefulness and try to participate, but it wouldn't be easy. She mustn't lose control of herself.

Drawing a big breath, she made up her mind.

"Yes, Glyn, I will marry you, and I promise I'll try to do as you wish."

He grunted with satisfaction and, to her surprise, lit a cigarette. It was exactly as if he had just completed a business deal to the benefit of both parties.

Hardly the reaction she had expected!

The entrance to the hotel loomed ahead of Susan and she drove into the car park. Inside the lobby, the receptionist greeted her with a smile and, within minutes, the bellboy was showing her up to a neat, clean single room. She flung her suitcase onto the stool at the end of the bed and sat down on the soft bedspread. She had done it! She was alone at last and the break had been made. At the party tonight she need say nothing. Glyn's friends would find out all in good time; she wished to do nothing to spoil Janine's great day.

She knew one couple who would shed no tears over the failure of her marriage! Edward and Beatrice Mohr.

Chapter Three

WHEN Glyn's parents were informed of the impending marriage, they were horrified and proceeded at once to tell their son exactly what they thought of the 'girl from the back streets'. Beatrice felt he was letting the family down badly, having conveniently forgotten her own background as a parlour-maid, while Edward took it upon himself to do everything in his power to dissuade Susan from marrying Glyn.

He did not realise, however, that each meeting with his future daughter-in-law served only to intensify her purpose. She was determined to surprise them all by the success of her marriage to Glyn. Edward Mohr eventually came straight to the point.

"I know your type. You're a scheming little gold-digger. You've tricked my boy into marrying you." His voice was sneering and his eyes snapped as Susan stared coolly back at him. "You aren't in love with my Glyn!" he accused. "You aren't worthy of him."

"I did not trick Glyn!" she retorted angrily, flushing. "We both know exactly what we are doing, Mr. Mohr. Surely you have sufficient trust in your son to give him credit for knowing his own mind? *I* should have thought he was well beyond the age of requiring parental guidance," she finished cuttingly. "I refuse to discuss the matter further. Anything else you have to say should be said to Glyn."

Mr. Mohr quivered with fury and wagged a finger at Susan.

"I warn you here and now, my fine Miss, that if there should ever be any trouble between you and my son, I will do my all to make certain *you* don't go unpunished."

This augurs a good beginning! she thought wryly.

A few days later, Glyn took her by car to pay one of her rare visits to her mother. Mrs. Onsworth was delighted to see them both and it was plain to Susan that she had taken an immediate liking to Glyn.

"Take care of her," she begged him, with tears in her eyes. "Love her well. She's been a good girl and a fine daughter to me."

"I will," Glyn promised, his throat suddenly dry.

Alone with Susan, Mrs. Onsworth accused:

"What are you playing at, child? You're no more in love with him than I am! It's as plain as a pikestaff to me, your mother. To think that a daughter of mine should agree to marry without love! And he so very much in love with you."

Susan looked up, startled.

"Is it so obvious?" she asked.

"Obvious he loves you or that you don't love him? Both. Maybe not everyone sees through eyes like mine. I loved the weak man who was your father with a passion I could not curb and therefore perhaps I notice more than those who haven't suffered. Haven't you thought what you will be doing to him by marrying him without love?" She gripped Susan's arm. "You'll destroy him. Tell him now, before it's too late! Be honest with him."

Susan smiled, bored with the subject.

" Mother, you're fussing. Hasn't it occurred to you that Glyn already knows I don't love him?"

Her mother stared disbelievingly at her.

" Then why is he going on with this . . . this masquerade?"

" Don't fuss, Mum! I'm not deceiving Glyn. We both know what to expect from each other."

Mrs. Onsworth was not to be placated. She allowed Susan to see how displeased and disappointed she felt.

" I don't think I want to come to your wedding, dear," she said before they left the house. Susan bit her lip but said nothing. Mum simply did not understand.

Later that night she cried herself to sleep.

Having temporarily got over her objections to the marriage, Mrs. Mohr decided to organise a large, flashy wedding to impress all her important friends. To her added annoyance, Glyn was dead against all flamboyance.

" What will all our influential friends think of us?" she wailed. " The Arbuthnots, the Courtenay-Hamptons, and those sort of people."

" Mother, I couldn't care less! Susan and I are not a peepshow. Besides, aren't you being hypocritical? You know damned well you're dead set against this wedding. Susan and I have decided we'd like a very quiet one."

Mrs. Mohr snorted.

" Oh, very well! " she snapped petulantly. " Have it your own way. You always did, so I don't suppose you'll change your habits at this late age. I only hope your . . . your *wife* will remember her duty to the family name and start producing an heir as soon as possible. You owe it to your father."

Glyn's mouth quivered with amusement.

" I assure you, Mother, Susan knows exactly what is expected of her."

" But do you?" his mother insisted. Glyn looked away.

" Yes, Mother. You and father have set your hearts on my having a son to perpetuate the family name. I promise that Susan won't fail in her duty."

The days before the wedding were occupied in finding a house on the outskirts of the town. Glyn eventually purchased a large Victorian monstrosity with three floors. Susan stared at it, aghast.

" How can I be expected to keep all these rooms clean and tidy?" she demanded. " And why do we need such a huge place?"

" We have to entertain, my sweet," Glyn soothed. " And I can certainly afford servants."

" If we can find any! " Susan retorted.

" That's all being done, so you needn't worry your head over that problem. Mother is finding them for us."

Susan bristled.

" Is your mother going to take over our lives?" she demanded bitterly.

Glyn laughed.

" Certainly not. I decided you need not have the bother of interviewing people, so asked mother to do it for you."

" What about furniture for this mansion?" she asked.

" Plenty of time for that. I've had some in store for years now. Stuff that was left me by my grandparents. I doubt if we need buy much, except carpets, of course."

Susan turned away, frustrated. So it had all been arranged for her as usual! A Victorian house, draughty and cold, and full of old-fashioned heavy furniture that took ages to dust. She would have liked to live in a new, modern house, complete with all the latest gadgets and simply-designed furniture, but that was not to be. Once again, Glyn hadn't considered it necessary to consult her.

The wedding ceremony took place early one cold autumnal morning. There were only four witnesses, all friends of Glyn's. Afterwards, Susan and her new husband left on a cruising honeymoon to the Canary Isles.

From its very beginning, the honeymoon was doomed to failure. As the liner left port, it was met by a cold and fierce westerly wind which steadily increased as the hours passed. Susan and Glyn stood side by side on deck, watching the swiftly vanishing coastline, until the cold and driven spray sent them seeking the warmth of their cabin.

Glyn had booked a first-class suite so that they might enjoy the utmost privacy. As they went down the companionway, the decks were beginning to roll sluggishly. Susan gripped the handrail and gulped hastily.

"Anything wrong, darling?" Glyn murmured in her ear. She tried to pull herself together, and smiled.

"No. No, of course not," came the gay reply.

Inside their suite, she began to remove her coat and scarf. The floor moved ominously beneath her feet, but Glyn seemed oblivious to this. He came over to her and folded his arms around her.

"Sweet!" he murmured. "At last I have you to myself." His lips travelled down her neck and, as he gently unbuttoned her new blouse, he whispered words she could not hear. Then his mouth met hers, hard and demanding, forceful and expert.

The floor moved again, this time more positively. The hum of engines could be heard somewhere in the distant part of the ship. With all her might, Susan thrust Glyn away and sat down hastily on the bed, her face white and drawn.

"Ooh, Glyn, I think I'm going to be sick!" she moaned.

The weather worsened into a force nine gale which kept up for three whole days. Susan cared little what was happening around her for she lay in bed, too ill to know whether it was night or day. The ship's doctor came to visit her often, with remedies for her seasickness, but nothing seemed to make her feel any different.

The liner pitched and tossed its way through angry, boiling seas. Well muffled against the cold and freezing spray, Glyn paraded the empty decks when it was safe to do so, or else haunted the almost empty public rooms. He brooded unhappily, wishing he had chosen to fly instead of taking Susan by sea. The ship's doctor had expressed the opinion that it would not be wise for Susan to travel often by sea as it had made her so desperately ill. Although he could have had his meals served in the suite, out of consideration for his sick wife, Glyn chose to eat in the main dining-room which was almost deserted except for a few stalwarts.

He felt totally alone, and had plenty of time to think as he watched the grey sea leaping across the ship's bows.

The gale died down but it was many days before Susan felt anything near her old self. It was not until they had dropped anchor in a quiet, sunny harbour that she came up on deck for the first time since leaving the English coast. Pale and shaky, she watched the bustling activity with disinterested eyes.

Now that she was better, Glyn began to assert his authority as her husband. She was disinclined for love-making, but knew what was expected of her and therefore resigned herself to the inevitable although she still felt slightly unwell. It was far worse than she had ever imagined. Glyn went about the whole thing with a selfish ruthlessness and lack of delicacy that terrified and completely revolted her. She almost screamed when he came towards her.

When at long last it was all over, he would roll away from her and fall asleep, one arm sprawled across her chest like an iron band and the other hanging over the edge of the bed. She looked at him . . . at the thick black hairs that crawled across his arms, and shuddered. It seemed to her that no sooner had he started to make love to her than he was asleep while she was left tense and terrified on her side of the bed.

In a very short time she began to dread the familiar overtures and found herself making all kinds of ridiculous excuses to avoid his proximity. She tried never to undress or change when he was in the room as this always aroused his passion.

It isn't as if he's inexperienced, she decided grimly, it's just that he has no thought or consideration for my share in the relationship.

He was a brutal, selfish lover, while she was merely the tool of his satisfaction. Listening to him snoring at her side, bitter tears welled up. He wasn't giving her a chance! Didn't he realise how ill she had been? She wanted to tell him he wasn't helping her, but lacked the courage. He'd probably laugh at her, and that was something she couldn't bear, not at this early stage. She needed gentleness and understanding but these she realised Glyn was totally unprepared to give.

She hated their intimate moments and naturally it was not long before Glyn noticed. His mouth twisted in an ugly grimace as he pushed her roughly from him. She clutched at the sides of the mattress to save herself from falling out of bed.

" Is it too much to hope you'll make up your mind to do better once the honeymoon's over and we're home?" he sneered as he rose from the bed. " Some honeymoon!"

"Where are you going?" Susan asked anxiously as he began to dress.

"Does it matter so long as you're on your own?" he snarled and slammed from the room.

She cried herself to sleep, after waiting in vain for him to return. Why, oh why couldn't he try to understand her difficulties?

They met next morning at breakfast. He was already seated when she entered their small dining-room.

"Good morning," he said. "I've ordered for you." There was no apology, nothing, and her intention of going to him to put her arms round him with an early morning kiss swiftly died. Right! She'd show him that two could play at that game.

The quarrel remained hovering between them.

In the days left, they walked the decks, joined in the games and dancing, laughing and talking as before, but when they were alone, there was a coolness that had not been there previously. Glyn did not attempt to make love to Susan again, neither did he kiss or hold her. Shyness kept her from him and she was too afraid of rebuff even to slip her hand into his.

The days dragged by and the dreaded return voyage was calm. Susan was not ill although she felt sick the whole time. At last the honeymoon had ended and they were in Glyn's car driving towards their new home. Its bleak and forbidding exterior came into sight as they entered the long, gravelled drive. Susan's heart sank. Would she ever come to like this monstrosity?

Chapter Four

AFTER the return from their honeymoon, life for Susan became one almost unending stream of parties and entertainment. All Glyn's friends and associates wanted to meet the new Mrs. Mohr and judge her for themselves. After her first initial qualms, Susan soon discovered, to her great surprise, that she was at once a tremendous success with both the men and the women. She was also gratified to learn that one or two of them had seen her picture in the many fashion magazines they ardently scanned at home.

All Glyn's friends were rich and influential and it came as rather a shock to Susan to find that although she was popular with everybody, she had nothing in common with any of them. The women were empty-headed and idle and usually completely bored with their narrow lives. They had servants to do their housework for them, and nannies to cope with their offspring. Everything and everyone seemed so artificial.

To outsiders, the marriage between Glyn and Susan was made to seem idyllic during those first few months, and only the two participants knew the truth. They had agreed to act normally in the company of others, no matter how difficult life at home had proved. Soon people began dropping sly hints about ' the patter of tiny feet ' . . . a phrase which nauseated Susan. There was a warning light in Glyn's eyes as he made a nonchalant reply:

" Plenty of time for that later, eh, darling?" his smile did not reach his eyes and the grip on her arm hurt her. She almost screamed aloud, but managed to look suitably embarrassed, to the delight of the questioners.

Under the bright façade of happiness, fear and resentment lurked. Glyn was impatient and very resentful of his wife's continued passivity and revulsion. On her part, no matter how hard she tried to pretend, she could not get away from the fact that Glyn made love to her solely to please himself. She willed herself to respond with some ardour but felt nothing. There wasn't even a flicker of warmth within her. She shuddered whenever he came near her, and began to dread even the lightest of his kisses, jerking her head away.

One late evening, while she was washing up the dishes, Glyn came into the kitchen.

" Surely those can be left for Mrs. Coombes when she arrives in the morning?" he demanded.

" I like to do them sometimes."

" Nonsense. You'll ruin your hands. Shall I buy a dishwasher instead? They say they're very good." He came behind her as she bent over the sink, caught her shoulders and began to run his mouth up and down her neck. She leapt away as if he had scalded her with boiling water.

" Damn you, woman!" he snarled, baring his teeth. " What the devil's wrong with you? You're cold, damned cold. Haven't you any spark of fire in you at all?" He seized her in hands that bruised and pulled her round to face him. She pushed wildly against him.

" Not now, I'm busy!" she protested, terrified.

" Damn it, I want to kiss you, and you'll like it!" He caught her head between hands that began to squeeze. Then he gripped her hair and pulled her face up to his. Tears of pain came to her eyes but his were hard and merciless as he brought his mouth down on hers, forcing her to cry out. The kiss was insulting, as he had meant it to be. She slapped him hard across the face.

He jerked back, hand to cheek.

" Please, Glyn, leave me alone! " she begged. " I've got a splitting head."

" ' I'm busy. I've got a headache,' " he mimicked cruelly. " Isn't there any excuse you haven't used? Were you born without the capacity to love?" he demanded angrily. His eyes fell on a pile of plates. He picked them up carefully one by one and then with a deliberate and vicious sweep of his arm, he flung them against the wall where they shattered noisily.

Susan cried out. Glyn stamped from the room.

" Where are you going?" she called after him.

" Out. Anywhere but here. To people who know how to appreciate me. Then perhaps I'll get blinding drunk, just for a change."

The front door banged and Susan was alone. She leaned against the draining-board and cried bitterly. What had she done? Why on earth had she agreed to this marriage in the first place?

Glyn was as good as his word. The following morning Susan was frightened to find him dead drunk on the settee, with the room reeking of spirits.

The invitations continued to pour in. Dances, dinner-parties and the theatre, to say nothing of the countless cock-tail parties. Susan's popularity with Glyn's men friends was an added bone of contention between them. With smoulder-ing glances, her husband would watch her as she laughed and talked to his friends, but he said nothing, which served to drive Susan further from him. She enjoyed male flattery and flirted outrageously, yet her heart was heavy.

No man can be patient for very long, and Susan's behaviour was rewarded by downright rudeness from Glyn, regardless of whom might be listening. She went red with mortification, an experience which gave Glyn a malicious pleasure.

"I say, old chap, take it easy!" one embarrassed young man was forced to blurt out after a particularly cruel and cutting remark Glyn had made concerning his wife. Glyn laughed sarcastically before replying:

"Take no notice of me, Charles. Susan's so much in love with me that she doesn't care what I say about her, do you, sweetheart?" he added, putting an arm around her shoulders affectionately and brushing her forehead with his lips. But his fingernails bit deeply into the upper part of her arm. She managed to keep a charming smile.

It was not long before Susan began to dread parties, but Glyn insisted on her accompanying him.

"Must show off my beautiful and *loving* wife!" he mocked. "Don't forget, it'll soon be our turn to entertain here." He leaned over her shoulder as she did her hair. "One day, my girl, someone is going to awaken you and show you what you've been missing. I pity the poor man, whoever he may be!" He pulled a lock of hair ungently. "And for heaven's sake put some colour on your cheeks to hide those ghastly rings under your eyes. You'll have people asking if you're pregnant," and he laughed bitterly.

Soon the tension could not be ignored by their friends. Pamela Bristow, the young wife of one of Glyn's co-directors, tried to draw Susan out to confide in her. They were alone in the bedroom, powdering their noses when Pamela urged her to unburden herself.

"Please don't think I'm prying, Sue, but any fool can see something's wrong between you and Glyn. Would you like to tell me about it? Naturally, I'll treat everything you say with the utmost secrecy, and nothing will go any further. But I can't bear to see you and him so miserable. I know Glyn well. He's been spoiled all his life, we know that, but he does love you!" Pamela sat on the bed and watched Susan renew her lipstick.

"I'd hoped people hadn't noticed what was going on," she began feebly.

"Glyn himself makes it so painfully obvious with his uncharitable remarks. So unlike him, too! Sue, it's useless trying to remain blind, isn't it? What's up? It's so soon after your marriage to be hating each other when all the time it's plain you're in love."

Susan replaced the top of her lipstick.

"I was a fool to marry him! We thought it might work out, but we were mistaken. And it's too late now. Oh, Pam, what can I do?" The plea was a cry from the heart. "Glyn's . . . well, he's . . . he's . . ." she faltered.

"Yes, Sue, I know what you're trying to say. He's going out of his way to hurt you. And doing so in the most childish way possible . . . in public. Poor old Glyn! He was never allowed to grow up properly. That ghastly mother of his mollycoddled him." She looked at Susan shrewdly. "Yet when we met before you two got married, I thought I'd never seen a man so much in love."

"You must have been mistaken," Susan declared coldly.

"Don't be silly, Sue. Of course he loves you, just as much as you love him."

Pamela just doesn't understand! Susan thought sadly.

"Is it the usual old story?" her friend went on gently.

"What are you getting at?"

"Oh, you're so naïve! Bed, and all that."

Susan got up.

" I don't want to discuss it further!" she said huffily, her cheeks crimson. Pamela sighed and slipped her arm through Susan's.

"Why don't you pop down to your quack's and have a little natter with him?" she suggested. "It's surprising what a short chat can do about putting things right."

Susan did not answer. Downstairs, Glyn was waiting, one hand on the newel post and a drink in the other.

Oh dear, I hope he isn't going to drink too much, Susan thought. She had seen her husband drunk once only and drunkenness terrified her. Her own father had often come home drunk . . . and Mum had always been red-eyed the following morning . . .

"Ah!" Glyn said loudly. "Here at last is my adorable little wife. Where have you been all this time? Surely such diminutive noses don't require all that attention?" he came up a few steps to meet her.

"Be quiet, Glyn!" she urged as people stopped talking to listen to the loud exchange of words. But on he went:

"Swopping wifely confidences, no doubt? Has my wife been telling you little anecdotes that can't be told in public?" He laughed scathingly, then pulled Susan's arm and thrust her towards a very surprised looking middle-aged man. "Here, George, you must dance with my darling Susan. She doesn't dance with me because I like to hold her too close and tread on her toes . . . in more ways than one," he added under his breath for Susan's ears only. He held his glass high and squinted at it through one half-closed eye. "While I partake of some more of this nectar. I think perhaps I'll get drunk tonight. Susan's scared of drunks, aren't you, darling? Like she's scared of lots of other things." He brushed past Susan and walked to the bar. She remained at the foot of the stairs, tears stinging her eyes so much that she could hardly see George in front of her. He, naturally, was acutely embarrassed.

"Forgive me if I don't accept your kind invitation to dance," she said to him, " but I'm a little tired. I think I'll go home."

Things couldn't go on like this, she decided. Life became worse every day. It was all her own fault. She had made Glyn like this, and now it was up to her to make amends, although she could not help feeling that a man of stronger character might have had the moral strength to surmount the difficulties.

Glyn was weak, weak. She was disappointed. She hadn't wanted to marry a man who would dominate her, yet, on the other hand, she had not wished to have a man who would permit her to grind him into the dust beneath her heel.

What *did* she want?

Glyn did not come home until very late that night, but she was already fast asleep.

When she awoke, he was standing at her bedside, a deep scowl on his face. She sat up, suddenly scared, and pulled the bedclothes tightly around her.

If only he would beg her forgiveness! The apology did not come. Instead he regarded her with anger in his eyes. She felt a flame of fury rise, threatening to choke her.

"A fine performance you gave last night!" she snapped.

"Indeed? And what of your own? You won't have a small drink with me, you refuse to dance with me, and you repel all my amorous advances." He sat down heavily onto the other twin bed and, leaning over, seized her wrist to twist it painfully. " What is it you want? Another man, perhaps, or a bigger allowance?" He released her, tossing her wrist roughly aside. "All right. You can have more money. I'll arrange with the Bank to increase your personal spending money. I don't care how much extra you want, as long as it makes you content and more pleasant to live with."

She reached for her dressing-gown and pulled it round her.

"I don't want your money! I don't need anything from you except perhaps a little courtesy and kindness once in a while. Oh God, it's all my fault. We've made a hideous mistake. I should never have married you without loving you."

He stood up and stared at her.

"I understand," he said in a slow voice. "We've been married only a few months and already you're tired of it. You hate everything about me, except my money."

"That isn't true!"

"Then what *is* the truth?" He went over to her and held her shoulders. "Do you know what I should do with you? Rip this damned dressing-gown off and toss you onto my bed, there to teach you the meaning of love." He dropped his arms. "But I won't. Somehow sex doesn't seem to matter any more," he went on sadly. "The battle's over, and I've lost. I don't need you physically. Well, does that please you?" He looked up. "Have I taken a dreaded load from your mind?"

That afternoon Susan heard from her bank manager that her allowance had been doubled.

Chapter Five

HERE she was, a week later, sitting on the bed in a hotel when she had been due at a party half an hour ago. Susan stood up and smoothed her dress. Then she opened her suitcase to take out the present she had chosen for Janine.

Most of the guests had already arrived, and many friends called their greetings to Susan.

Pamela bustled up to her, asking:

" Where's Glyn?"

" He couldn't come. Something to do with late work at the office." Pamela nodded understandingly and then a serious-looking young man came up to whisk Susan away for her first dance. As the evening progressed she was conscious of glances in her direction but no one else asked about Glyn.

It was a magnificent party. The entire ground floor had been emptied of furniture and carpets to provide ample room for dancing. One room at the end of the house had been set aside for games and the bar had been set up in the dining-room which opened into the enormous drawing-room. The conservatory doors were also open so that the orchestra could sit there. The plants and tender blooms had been removed earlier that day so there was plenty of space for everyone to dance and enjoy themselves. A marquee stood outside the open french windows of the dining-room and it was here that a running buffet supper was in progress.

Susan was glad that she had come to the party after all. Janine was so pleased to see her, and introduced her to the current boy-friend, a plain, tall and string-bean-like young man with twinkling eyes set under a shock of unruly carroty hair. His name was Frank.

Altogether there were about one hundred and twenty guests present.

Two hours after her arrival, as she was being led laughing and flushed back to her seat in an alcove after a dance, her eye fell on the immaculately dressed figure of her husband. He was at the bar, a drink in his hand. When he saw her, he raised his glass mockingly and then drained it at a gulp.

Heavens! Had he come here to get drunk? she thought wildly.

She wasn't going to take any risks. This was Janine's party. Glyn wasn't to be allowed to spoil it. Whatever his intention, she must try and get him away from the bar.

" Excuse me," she said to her young escort, and hurried towards Glyn. She guessed that he had come here to cause trouble . . . she must prevent it at all costs. She passed Pamela on her way. Pam's arm shot out as she hissed in Susan's ear:

" I tried to catch your eye when I saw him arrive, but you've been far too busy enjoying yourself."

Unfortunately, as she had almost reached the bar, Frank stepped in front of her and asked if he could have the next dance with her. She began to refuse, but Glyn said loudly:

" Go ahead, my dear, I can wait. What I have to say isn't important." She hesitated but allowed Frank to lead her onto the floor. Her feet stumbled as she kept looking anxiously back at Glyn who, his glass replenished for the third time, had now turned back to watch her every movement. He grinned mockingly. To her horror, he suddenly thrust his way through the dancers and reached her side.

" Young man, go find a partner your own age," he said rudely and pushed Frank away from Susan. She trembled and Frank had the good sense to leave them without protest. Glyn put his arms round her and pulled her close . . . too close.

" Glyn! You're tight! " she accused.

" Wrong again, my sweet. I may have had a few, one too many perhaps, but my mind is as clear as a bell. I want to talk to you and then I'll get drunk afterwards. Will that suit you?" His voice was loud and carried above the music. One or two couples turned to stare at them.

" Shut up, Glyn. Remember where you are! " Susan admonished, then turned round to search for a way out of this seething body of dancers. He noticed her anxiety.

" Scared of me?" he chided. " Come on, I want to talk to you. You've got some explaining to do." He dragged her roughly towards an open french window which led onto a terrace outside, with sloping lawns beyond.

" Now," he said, all banter gone. " When I reached home I noticed you had carried out your silly threat by packing some of your clothes."

" That's correct. I told you over the phone that after this party I wouldn't be going home, and I meant it. Our marriage is finished . . . for good."

He gripped her arms.

" You'll be back. You're just trying to goad me into losing my temper."

She sighed.

" Oh, Glyn, Glyn, why can't you recognise the truth when you see it. We *have* to part. There's nothing left for us. There never was anything at the beginning. Open your eyes! See life for what it is."

" You can't leave me! I won't let you."

She reached up and prised his fingers free.

" Stop it, Glyn, and pull yourself together. You *have* had too much to drink although you don't think so. If there's one thing I loathe, it's a man who can't carry his drink. I'm not going back to your house . . . ever. I've arranged everything." She laughed suddenly. " You know, it's really rather amusing. At long last I've actually managed to do something for myself without having to consult you first. I've made up my mind to leave you and it is now a *fait accompli*. Cheer up, you won't miss me. You said you didn't need me any more."

" Need you!" he growled. " My God, woman, if you'd only known the number of nights I've lain awake longing for the slightest indication that you were inviting me into your bed! I can't understand myself because you're now proving to me that you're nothing more than a . . ." and he used a terrible word. She gasped, then he swung back his hand and hit her with the full force of his arm. Her hand flew to her face and she fell back against the parapet. Lithe as a panther he was upon her, lifting her up by the arms and pulling her towards him.

" I won't let you go! I can't bear any more of this hell we've been going through. Sue, Sue, my darling, promise you won't leave me!" he moaned, his mouth on her throat.

Conscious that they could be seen by anyone passing the lighted windows, Susan knew panic.

" I hate you! I hate you!" she hissed and wrenched herself free. She fled from him across the lawn. Where was the drive? She had lost her bearings but if only she could reach the sanctuary of her car she might escape the man behind her.

Glyn was running close on her heels. She was too late to

reach the drive. If she could get to that clump of trees and bushes over there perhaps she could still escape him by doubling back through the tree trunks. Hope and fear spurred her on.

She had almost reached sanctuary and was pushing her way past branches that scratched and tore at her, when she heard his quick, gasped breathing. Then his hands were upon her. She choked back a scream knowing this would bring people out to see what was wrong. His fingers clutched her dress and there was a ripping sound.

" You've torn my frock! " she panted.

" Damn the dress." His hands were around her throat and he was shaking her. She began to feel faint. He was saying:

" This time you've gone too far. I'll teach you what it means to thwart me. A man can take so much but there always comes a time when he can take no more."

Dimly she heard the sound of music drifting out from the dance room three hundred yards away, then she lost her balance in a whirl of giddiness. Glyn toppled across her and, momentarily winded, she lay gasping for breath. She could see the tree tops etched against the night sky above her head, then they were abruptly blotted out as he bent to kiss her savagely. She tried to protest but the words would not come. His hands moved swiftly and expertly over her as he loosened the torn bodice.

" No, no! " she moaned softly.

" No one will tell *me* when and where I'm to make love to my own wife! " he declared. " Even if I have to half-kill you to make you submit, I *will* make you love me! " His lips travelled down from her throat and she shivered. Raising her hands to push him off, he caught them both in one of his and pinioned them behind her head.

" You flirt and make eyes at all my male friends, yet refuse to undress if I'm in the bedroom. You behave promiscuously with all but me. Now I'll teach you what it is to be made love to by a man who knows your true, scheming little mind."

Once again, he kissed her mouth, with searching, bruising lips that were ruthless and demanding. By now he had aroused in her all her instincts to fight against a dreaded Nemesis. She had never known him like this. His savageness was deliberate but, at the same time, Susan recognised something akin almost to desperation in his passion. Without first realising what it was, a great feeling of pity and remorse welled up in her. It was only now that she knew how deeply he must love her.

" You *will* love me! " he moaned against her mouth. " I can't go on being tormented like this. You're like stone. I need you to be warm and vibrant. I beg you, Sue, my only Sue, love me, love me! I love you so terribly."

Suddenly she wanted to accept him, wanted to give in to him, wanted him to dominate. She was tired of fighting on her own in the world. It was a woman's need to be loved and ruled by her husband. Here was a destiny far more powerful than any of the mental barriers she had so carefully erected around herself since her father had died. Glyn was too strong for her . . . and all at once she was glad . . . terribly glad. She wanted him to have his own way. There was something so different about him tonight. For the first time he needed to arouse her rather than gratify himself. A tide of wild emotion almost drowned her with its intensity. She cried out and pulled her arms away from his grasp. He paused, looking down at her in the dim light.

" I want to love you," she whispered and threw her arms round his neck pulling his face down to her. For a moment he stared down at her in disbelief, then he saw her gentle smile, which told him all he longed to know.

" I love you, Sue," he whispered.

She stopped fighting him and matched his passion with her own. She was being carried along on great waves of glory. She wondered if she could bear it. Then the world shattered into a thousand pieces.

" All hate gone?" she whispered aeons later. He raised himself on one elbow and gently stroked the cheek he had hit back there on the parapet.

" Forgive me, darling, forgive," and touched her lips with his. The kiss was gentle and suppliant.

The party was still in full swing when Susan and Glyn crept towards the drive. Glyn opened the car door.

" Don't you think I ought to drive?" Susan asked, as Glyn stumbled slightly.

" My dearest wife, I haven't had all that many drinks!" he protested. " I think I'm quite capable of driving you home in my own car."

" We could take mine," she urged, but Glyn was adamant. He got into the driver's seat but before he turned the ignition key he put his hand over hers and asked:

" You will come home with me?"

She nodded, astonished and delighted by the warmth of love she now felt for him.

" Please, if you still want me."

He laughed joyously. The car seemed to sway dangerously across the road as they left the large country house. Neither noticed nor worried. All Susan could think of was the exciting realisation that she loved Glyn after all. Whatever had held her back in the past, its fear had gone like a puff of wind. They had their whole future before them, and she meant to

make the most of it. There was so much to be said, but it
could all wait until they reached home. The memory of tonight in the garden was too close, too poignant.

She stretched out a hand to touch his as it lay on the
steering-wheel. His hand was so strong and no longer fright-
ening to look at as the wedding-ring she had given him
glinted in the light from the dashboard. In reply, he turned
to look down at her.

Too late she realised what she had done. Too late she saw
the sharp corner. In diverting his attention he had allowed
the car to swing across the road. His reactions must have
been slowed by the whisky he had drunk earlier, and he was
unable to correct the swerve. The corner flew to meet them,
Glyn fighting for control. The engine howled madly as the
car crashed into a tree.

Chapter Six

AT first Susan could not understand what was wrong. There were people moving about her, as if in a haze, and dim voices were speaking:

"Careful now, take her away while we try to get the other free . . . badly injured . . . where's that doctor with the morphia?" Then there was oblivion.

Hours later she opened her eyes. The ceiling above her head was white and it met a wall in which there was a door. Her eyes travelled past this door seeing the blood-drip-stand and restfully patterned curtains suspended over the bed in which she lay. Many pillows kept her in a semi-recumbent position. She lowered her eyes and started. Both her arms were encased in bandages, and she realised that to draw a breath was an effort causing pain. She tried to move, but the ache in her head and chest soon stopped her.

Suddenly there was a nurse at her side.

"Where did you come from?" Susan asked, her mind bleary. The nurse smiled.

"I've been here all the time, Mrs. Mohr," she patted the bedclothes and felt the pulse in Susan's neck. "You must lie still. Are you feeling a little more comfortable now?"

"Where am I?" Susan whispered.

"In a private room of St. Stephen's Hospital."

"What . . . what happened?" The drugs were preventing her from coherent thought.

" You were involved in a car accident just before midnight last night."

" What time is it now?"

" Almost five in the morning. Now you must go to sleep again."

Susan turned her head to the window where the early morning light was beginning to illuminate the world outside. Birds were singing gaily.

" Why are my hands like this?" she said disinterestedly.

" They were badly cut. The doctor said there was no need to worry as they'll heal very quickly. He'll be in to see you later today. Now, dear, try to drink some of this." She turned away to pick up a feeding cup which she held to her patient's lips.

Memory suddenly came flooding back, and Susan jerked herself up in bed, only to fall back in acute pain.

" Glyn! " she moaned. " My husband, how is he? Is he hurt too?" She had remembered now. It had been he who was driving. Then there was that dreadful bend and the terrifying swerve and that was all.

The nurse eased Susan back onto the pillows and held the cup for her. She said in a matter-of-fact voice:

" Your husband's in a room further along the corridor. He's also been hurt, but Doctor can tell you more about him, later."

Fear gripped Susan.

" He isn't . . . ?"

" Of course not, Mrs. Mohr! Like you, he needs as much rest as possible. Now you really must sleep."

Surprisingly, Susan fell asleep almost at once. When she re-awoke she discovered that it was almost two o'clock in the afternoon. The room was bright with the early May sunshine which helped her to feel very much better. Her head ached only slightly now but she was stiff all over. When the nurse came to tidy her bed, Susan asked for a mirror.

"I expect I look awful!" she said, smiling ruefully. "Am I in for a shock?" The nurse opened a drawer and withdrew a hand mirror which she held up in front of Susan's face.

"There, Mrs. Mohr. Believe me, it isn't all that bad."

Susan gasped.

"Oh!" A vivid bruise disfigured one cheek and the other was showing the beginnings of a magnificent black eye.

"I expect you banged your head against the dashboard," the nurse suggested. "It almost always happens. But don't worry. By the time you're allowed to leave, most of the bruising will have faded. It always looks far worse than it is for the first day or two."

Susan bit her lip. She knew what had caused the mark across her cheek. She had been too scared to realise at the time how hard Glyn had hit her.

"I'd like to see my husband." The nurse placed the mirror on the bed-table.

"Sister can tell you more than I. I'll let her know you're awake," and she hurried away, leaving Susan to lean her head back against the pillows. In the distance she could hear the bustle of the hospital and busy traffic somewhere a long way from the building.

A few minutes later Sister came into the room. She was a small woman, dressed in dark blue, with snow-white cuffs and a dainty lace cap on her head. She looked very young for such responsibility. At her side walked a stout, middle-aged man whom Susan rightly took to be the specialist. He looked her over thoughtfully, picked up the chart from the table near the door and then came over to her.

"You're feeling better? Good." His voice was gruff but

kind. He leaned over her looking into each eye in turn. "Headache almost gone?" Susan nodded. "Hands comfortable?"

He motioned to Sister who leaned over to undo Susan's pyjama jacket. It was an ugly article belonging to the hospital and its wearer vowed to have her own clothes brought to the hospital as soon as possible. The specialist examined the strapping that had been put round Susan's chest and then stood back while Sister rearranged the clothes.

"Now, Mrs. Mohr, you've had a slight knock on the head, but I doubt if the skull is fractured. Just to make certain, I will arrange for the portable X-ray unit to visit. At the same time I'll want your ribs re-X-rayed. There are three cracked ones which should mend in no time, and a few deep cuts and grazes on your hands and arms. Otherwise I think you'll live." He smiled engagingly down at her. "A couple of weeks in bed here and then you'll be able to go home. However, we'll review that some time next week."

"Please, Doctor, how's my husband?" she begged anxiously. The doctor scratched his chin thoughtfully.

"Ah, yes, Mr. Mohr. Now, Madam, I'm not going to beat about the bush. You'll be wanting the truth, naturally. Your husband's injuries are very much more serious than your own. I understand he was driving?"

"Yes."

"His left leg is fractured in three places, and we've put it in traction. You know what I mean?" Susan understood. "Later, when his general condition improves we'll attend to the fractures more thoroughly, but at the present time any operation is inadvisable. He had a very bad knock on the head, fracturing his skull in two places; fortunately, without depression. He's still deeply unconscious and all we can do is to wait until he comes round." He patted her bandaged hand soothingly.

" You mustn't fret, Mrs. Mohr. A lapse into unconsciousness is Nature's sole way of giving the brain the rest it so badly needs after damage has been suffered. There's nothing at all unusual in a patient remaining unconscious for hours, sometimes days, following a serious road accident."

" I must see him! " Susan declared frantically.

" My dear, it'll do neither of you any good. When he's come round, then we'll see if you can visit him, but for the time being it's better for you to stay in bed."

" Couldn't I just see how he is? Even if he doesn't know me, I don't mind as long as I can see him."

" No, Mrs. Mohr. You're far from well yourself, and it will only aggravate your own discomfort to allow you to move about too soon. Tomorrow? Well, we'll see how you are in the morning." He smiled again and turned to Sister. " If there's anything you need, Sister can get it for you. Goodbye for now, Mrs. Mohr, and sleep all you can," and the two of them left the room.

Two minutes later, the Sister came back.

" Mrs. Mohr, I'm sure you'd like some of your own things. If you care to give me a list and the name of someone in your house, I can arrange for them to be brought over here. Also, things for your husband."

Susan bit her lip.

" I . . . I have a room at the Three Cross Ways hotel, it's number fifteen, I think. My suitcase is there already. Perhaps you'd better contact my husband's parents to bring his personal belongings," she suggested, after a pause. " They'll have to be told about Glyn as soon as possible. Do you mind? " she looked helplessly at Sister who did not betray her surprise by a flicker of an eyelid. No doubt, thought

Susan, she was used to coping with awkward situations. She hoped Mr. and Mrs. Mohr would not ask to see her. She couldn't face them today. They'd be sure to blame her for the accident.

Less than two hours later, she heard the familiar voice of her father-in-law raised in anger just outside the door. Then the soft ones of Sister's, soothing and placating. Then the talking died away as footsteps receded. Susan was almost asleep again when the door opened and Sister said:

" Mr. Mohr would like to see you."

" No! " But it was too late. Edward marched into the room. He stopped at the foot of her bed, staring down at her, dislike and suspicion on his face.

" Well, what have you to say about all this? " he demanded. " What have you and my boy been doing to get the car and yourselves into such a mess? "

Susan explained as well as she was able. She told her father-in-law how they had left the party, and about the car swerving off the road.

" Have you seen Glyn? " he snapped. Susan shook her head.

" I'm not allowed to get out of bed yet."

" Well, I've seen him, and he looks terrible," Edward announced bluntly. " I insisted on seeing him."

At that moment there was a knock at the door and a junior nurse came in. She carried Susan's suitcase.

" The hotel have just sent this over, Mrs. Mohr. I'll come back later to unpack for you." She put it in a corner of the room and then hurried out. There was silence.

" Hotel? What hotel? What was she talking about? " Edward demanded. " Glyn didn't say anything about the two of you going away. Besides, I brought his things. Why weren't they with yours? "

Susan leaned back and sighed.

"Does it matter?" she murmured wearily.

"Not at the moment. I'll wait for Glyn to explain." He moved over to the window and looked out. "I suppose the young fool had had too much to drink at the party."

"No more than anyone else," Susan said.

"Of course he did!" Edward came towards her and wagged his finger at her menacingly. "Until you came into my son's life, he never once over indulged, but since you two married, at times he's had just a few too many. Oh, don't bother to deny it! Word gets around, you know. You can't keep juicy bits of gossip like that hidden for long. Some people delight in telling those who are nearest and dearest! I was one of the very first to hear about my son's shortcomings, never fear."

"He's only been drunk once!" Susan protested wearily.

"Nonsense! I've heard about the things he says to you in public. If that isn't alcohol in his veins, then what is it, eh? I brought my boy up with good manners and breeding. Of course it's too much drink that's been loosening his tongue! And I blame you."

Susan turned her head into the pillow. How could she possibly explain to . . . to this dreadful man the real reason for his son's behaviour? It *had* been partly her fault he had treated her so cruelly, but he wasn't a drunkard!

"It was *your* fault Glyn was drunk last night!" his father accused bitingly. "Your fault he crashed the car and almost killed himself."

"Please go away!" Susan had begun to cry. "Leave me alone. My head's hurting."

"You may cry now, my girl, but if our Glyn has to suffer because of you, then this won't be the last you'll hear of it. Not by a long chalk!"

With that Edward Mohr stamped from the room.

Susan fumbled blindly for the bell-push pinned within reach of her counterpane. A scared-faced nurse took one look at the sobbing patient and rushed away to fetch Sister. Sister soothed and comforted with words as she prepared a sedative.

" I don't want Mr. Mohr ever to come in here again! " Susan wept. " Please, Sister, I can't bear it! "

" I'll see that he doesn't upset you again, Mrs. Mohr. Now please calm down. We can't have visitors upsetting our patients like this, can we? "

Susan spent a troubled and restless night. Edward haunted her in her dreams, forever pointing his long, accusing finger at her as he leaned over the limp body of his son.

The following afternoon, Susan was allowed to see Glyn. Two nurses helped her into a wheelchair. It was quite an effort to move, but she managed it, protesting only slightly. Then she was wheeled along the corridor towards the room where Glyn lay. Outside the door a notice proclaimed:

" QUIET PLEASE. ABSOLUTELY NO VISITORS WITHOUT SISTER'S PERMISSION."

Inside the room, Glyn lay with closed eyes in a bed similar to the one Susan had just left. The blinds were down, shading the room. His left leg was supported in a cradle and traction ropes and weights overhung the foot of the bed. A blood- and saline-drip stood at the left-hand side of the bed, while a nurse sat quietly on the right-hand side, watching the patient.

Susan was wheeled over to that side of the bed, the nurse rising to make room for her. She looked down at her unconscious husband. His head was bandaged, one eye badly swollen and bruised, while almost his entire face was covered with cuts and scratches. His hands lay white and still outside the bedclothes.

"Glyn!" she whispered. The nurse bent over her.

"He can't hear you, Mrs. Mohr. He's still deeply unconscious."

Susan wanted to cradle one of those limp hands to her lips but her own were awkward and unwieldy, so she had to content herself with staring at him.

"Has he been like this all the time?" she asked the nurse. "I mean, ever since the accident?"

The nurse nodded.

Susan was allowed to stay for five minutes, after which she was wheeled back to her own room. She felt lonely and strangely depressed, longing only for Glyn to regain consciousness.

Chapter Seven

SUSAN was obliged to go through the formality of an interview with the local police regarding what she could remember of the accident. Sister had refused to allow the police sergeant to talk to Susan for two days but in the end her patient felt well enough to make her statement. Reluctantly she had to admit that they had been to a party but was emphatic that Glyn had not had too much to drink.

" There was a witness to the accident, Mrs. Mohr," the sergeant went on kindly. " He was coming out of a side turning and saw your car take the corner too widely and collide with that tree. He has made a full statement and, if it's any comfort to you, he doesn't consider the car to have been driven recklessly. There may be a case of driving without due care or control but I hope not one of driving under the influence of drink. You must realise that the hospital authorities say your husband was smelling quite strongly of spirits when admitted."

" But he hadn't had too many, officer! " Susan protested.

" I hope to be able to interview Mr. Mohr for myself when he's better, although, of course, I don't expect him to remember very much after head injuries and being unconscious so long." He put away his notebook. " We shall rely on the witness, and possibly your own testimony." He smiled as he rose to leave. " But you needn't worry, Madam, no steps can be taken until your husband is well enough to attend court."

He left Susan with plenty to think about. She had not known that those with head injuries often forgot what had happened. How much was Glyn to forget? she wondered, and made up her mind to ask the House Surgeon.

When he visited her that evening, and she put her question to him, he replied:

"Yes, Mrs. Mohr, it's usually the case with head injuries and concussion. A state of what we term ' retrograde amnesia ' occurs. This means that the patient can forget some of the events leading up to the actual injury. For instance, in slighter cases, such as that of a child falling out of a tree and bumping its head, he may not even remember climbing up in the first place, let alone tumbling off a branch! The more serious the brain damage, the longer the period of amnesia." He looked down at his hands. " It may be possible that when Mr. Mohr eventually wakes, he may not remember leaving the party or even going to it!"

Susan frowned.

" My father-in-law thinks Glyn had been drinking heavily, but he'd only had a few, doctor. Will that make any difference?"

" Depending on how well he can tolerate spirits, his memory might have been a little blurred already, which will put our time back even further." He looked at her. " Does it matter, Mrs. Mohr? Wouldn't it be better for him to remember little about the evening?" His suggestion was gentle and sympathetic.

" He *wasn't* drunk!" Susan cried aloud. " But no one will take my word. Oh, everything's so horribly muddled, I just don't know what to think!"

When she was on her own again, the problem whirled

round and round her mind. It was possible that Glyn would not even remember how they had fought, and the eventual, wonderful reconciliation. Hot blushes swept over her as she thought of that evening. Perhaps he might even have forgotten that she had threatened to leave him? If Glyn could remember only that they were living together under difficult conditions, forgetting the reconciliation and all that had led up to it, then she would have to act cautiously. Her spirits rose. When they were both home again, she could make it up to him! Especially if he had forgotten her threat to leave him.

The suitcase from the hotel! How could she explain that? Edward Mohr was certain to ask Glyn about it. Oh, no! She must stop him, but how? To raise the matter again was tantamount to arousing fresh suspicions in her father-in-law's mind. Better left alone and hope for the best.

If Glyn should ask her about the party, what then? She could not tell him the truth . . . it was too personal and poignant.

He ought to know, a small voice prompted her. Yet if she told him, he'd probably sneer at her, accusing her of pure invention and she did not think she would be able to face his scorn and derision quite yet.

It was not until five days after the accident that Glyn regained consciousness. Susan was wheeled in to see him again. The nurse placed the wheelchair at his side and left them alone. Her heart thudding painfully, Susan looked at her husband. His eyes were closed and he was lying very quietly in bed.

" Glyn! " she whispered and gently laid her hand on his. With a shudder he pulled his away, turning his head towards her and opening his eyes. Then he shut them again as if he was in great pain.

"Go away!" he whispered, then raised his voice. "Nurse? Nurse! Where are you?" Immediately the door opened and the nurse bustled in again.

"I'm here, Mr. Mohr. Is there anything you want?"

"Take my wife away. I don't want to see her. I've nothing to say to her and am certain she has little to say to me." His voice was hard and cold.

"Glyn, darling, I must talk to you!" Susan begged, tears welling up. She reached for his hand again but he jerked it away from her. "Why don't you want me with you?"

Glyn turned to look her full in the face.

"Don't hedge. I'm not dying, you know. You were leaving me and my head's aching far too much for me to argue about it now."

"No, Glyn! I'm not leaving you!" she protested.

"Why not? Because I've hurt myself?" He laughed, a hollow, mirthless sound in the back of his throat. "Don't be such a fool, Susan. I don't need you. Especially not now. It was all over before we crashed. Finished. Weeks and weeks ago. We can't use the accident as an excuse to carry on the ridiculous farce of the last months."

"Please, Glyn. I can make it up to you, I promise."

"Make it up? Why? Can't you get it into that pretty little head that I don't need you now? And for goodness' sake, stop snivelling, woman!" He put his hand to his head, and went on: "I've forgotten what happened that evening except that you told me you were leaving me, and I saw some of your clothes and hair brushes had gone. I remember that all right. It was the first thing I knew when I woke up today."

"It wasn't true!" Susan cried.

"Don't lie to me, sweetheart. You know damned well we can't live together. Shall I tell you something, my poor pathetic little wife? The first thing I realised when I came to was that I felt glad and strangely at peace with myself and the world. Do you know why I had that feeling? It was because my problem had been resolved. You and I were finished and I was glad . . . glad."

Chapter Eight

SUSAN was almost hysterical when she reached the privacy of her room, and Sister sent for the House Surgeon. A sedative having been prescribed and given, Susan lay back in bed, waiting for sleep to drown her unhappiness.

Glyn had forgotten everything but their bitter words, and her threat to leave him. The events of the party and afterwards were as if they had never been. As far as he was concerned, their married life was over, and he was profoundly glad. But she could not allow it to be so!

A small ray of hope shone forth. He was still very unwell. Later, perhaps, when they had both been discharged from hospital and at home again, she could bring him to realise that it *was* possible for them to live together. In another day or two, when he had regained more of his lost strength, he would be a different man.

Susan was too optimistic. In the meantime, Glyn's father had visited his son and told him everything, including Susan's hotel room. He had even gone so far as to check the register for himself for absolute proof. When Susan was wheeled into Glyn's room, he waved her away again.

" I refuse to continue quarrelling with you. My father has confirmed everything I wanted to be sure of. Nurse, Mrs. Mohr won't be staying. Please take her back to her room."

Later, from the gossip Susan picked up from the nurses, she learned that Glyn had insisted on being moved to a room on a lower corridor, to be away from her. The nursing staff seemed to know what had happened and Susan found their compassion almost too much to bear. No doubt they discussed both herself and Glyn at great length behind her back, but she did not care.

The specialist told her quite calmly and kindly that he was afraid he was unable to permit her to visit her husband, as he had threatened to discharge himself unless his request to refuse Susan access to his room was carried out. Reluctantly, the medical staff had agreed to concede. Susan, however, was not placated by the specialist's explanation that Glyn needed rest and quiet and on no account was he to be upset or excited.

All through her illness, Susan had received many gifts of flowers and fruit from Glyn's friends and their wives, but she refused to see anyone. Not even Pamela.

Edward and Beatrice sent her nothing, although she had one further visit from the former.

" My son has told me everything," he began. " It's just as I expected. I knew this marriage was a dreadful mistake, and I've been proved right. He has told my wife and I that you had left him and we all agree that it was the best thing you have ever done."

" I'm not leaving him now! " Susan protested hotly.

" Oh? Changed your mind? Why? Are you afraid you won't be able to get your greedy little paws on Glyn's money?"

" How *dare* you! " Susan was quivering with fury. " I don't want money. I want Glyn."

" Unfortunately for you, my dear, he doesn't want you," her father-in-law snapped viciously. " He and I have discussed what must be done. He has to remain in bed for many weeks yet, but, with my wife's help and that of a trained nurse, we've arranged for him to be cared for at our house. He'll be given expert care and attention . . . also love, a commodity which you have proved sadly incapable of giving," he added harshly. "The front door will be barred to you, Susan, at Glyn's personal request. The Mohrs don't want you. Have I made myself quite clear?"

"Perfectly," Susan replied, with the light of battle in her eyes. "But I'm warning you all, don't expect me to give up Glyn just because you've ordered me to do so, because I won't. Glyn's my husband, and I mean to keep him, whatever you say."

Edward Mohr laughed softly.

"Oh, my dear girl, how foolish you are!" he said and then left the room. The laugh and the pity in it frightened Susan far more than the threats and scorn.

Three days later she was discharged from hospital and returned to the bleak house she knew as home. It stood dark, drear and impersonal, and suddenly she hated it with an intense loathing. It had never been what she could call a proper home, and neither of them had tried to make it one. Even their own personal effects around the place looked awkward and out of character.

Susan knew that Glyn was being transferred to his parents' home in four or five weeks time, despite Edward Mohr's assurance that it was to be sooner . . . Glyn had needed further operations on his fractured left leg, and the medical staff in charge of his case advised him to remain under their care until these operations had been completed.

During this time Susan did not visit the hospital, although she wanted to very much. Instead, she stayed at home, reading and watching television, but the place was quiet and tomb-like. She had no inclination to go out and enjoy herself, but Pamela called on her regularly, bringing her magazines and the latest titbits of gossip. Unfortunately, it seemed to Susan that the whole world knew about her parting with Glyn. Pamela's sympathy was almost too much to bear. Susan remained listless and disinterested. Her doctor prescribed a tonic to buck her up but she was not to be enlivened.

Somehow the weeks passed. She rang the hospital and learned that Glyn was being discharged the following day. Immediately she put on her hat and coat and rang for a taxi to take her to St. Stephen's.

She found Glyn sitting by the window of his room, his left leg encased in a plaster and propped up on a stool. He turned to look at her with a complete lack of emotion, and her heart sank. She came to stand beside him and noticed for the first time that his hair had become more grey during the seven weeks he had been in hospital. The sunlight danced on it and she longed to run her fingers through it.

" Glyn, I've come here today to beg you to change your mind and come home with me tomorrow," she began shakily. " Your place is with me. I can give you the care and attention you need." He shook his head.

" No, Susan, that part of my life has finished. I've made all the necessary arrangements with my parents. I'm far too tired and disinterested to live and quarrel with you."

" But we needn't quarrel! Not any more," she protested, reaching for one of his hands. He removed it slowly and stared up at her.

" No, Susan, it's too late. Our marriage has died; long, long ago. Almost before it began," he added sadly.

" Glyn, do you remember anything at all that happened the night of the accident?" she urged but he shook his head.

"Very little. A few days previously you and I had quarrelled bitterly, then the evening of the party I rang up to tell you I wouldn't be going. You then said you'd leave me. I was furiously angry and decided to go to Janine's after all. When I got home to change, you'd already left, complete with packed bag, bound for some hotel or other, I presumed. I am told, however, that when I got to the party, we had some sort of scene. Father says I possibly drank too much because I was so angry with you. True?"

"Yes and no. We argued just like all the other times in public except . . ."

"Don't bother to go on," Glyn interrupted. "I can well imagine what happened afterwards. We went on quarrelling; there's no need to deny it because everybody knows we left the place busy arguing. Everyone knows everything . . . except me, of course," he added bitterly.

Clutching desperately at a straw, Susan cried:

"They don't know *everything*!"

"My friends have tried to make light of it, but I must have behaved abominably, only they're too good natured to admit it. Because I was tight . . ."

"You weren't."

"I must have been. Why else should I drive into that confounded tree?"

"Glyn, if we were quarrelling, haven't you wondered why we were both in your car?" Susan pressed urgently, reaching for the opening he had given her.

Her husband shrugged his shoulders disinterestedly.

"I can't imagine, and I don't particularly care now. We were in my car which hit a tree. That's all there is to it."

Susan turned away. She just couldn't bring herself to tell him at this moment! He was in one of his stubborn moods when she knew he certainly wouldn't listen to her.

" Can't we start afresh?" she whispered. " Please, Glyn? Give me just one more chance!" She sank onto her knees beside his chair and looked up at him beseechingly. His eyes were scornful.

" For heaven's sake, get up, Susan! I loathe people who come crawling to me. There's absolutely no need to indulge in these histrionics. I'm too weak and tired to make the effort to start afresh now. All I want is to be allowed to live in peace and quiet without the eternal bickering and tension. We never had anything in common after all, did we? You were right. We shouldn't have married. It was then that I had the misfortune to be in love with you . . . no, don't interrupt . . . but now even that has disappeared." His face was pitying. " What's left?"

Susan rose and went to the window so he should not see her grief.

" I was foolish, Susan. I'd hoped you'd come to love me when all the time I was so blind I couldn't see it was only the glitter of wealth you loved."

" Glyn, you're wrong, so very wrong! It's *you* I love!" she protested in a choked voice.

" Bah! Funny way you have of showing it, my dear! At the moment all you feel for me is pity because I've been injured physically. I'm an invalid who needs careful attention, and you pride yourself on being the one most suited to the task." He turned sharply in his chair and raised his voice. " I don't want you or your pity. I want to be left alone, understand?"

" Don't you care at all what I do?" she asked going to his side.

" As we're being frank with each other this afternoon, then I'll give you a frank answer. No. I'm beyond both love and hate. I'm just completely disinterested. Oh, I'll see you're well provided for and want for nothing financially, never fear."

She leaned over him, her eyes snapping.

"I know who's behind all this! Your father's been at work. He's talked you into 'buying me off'. Well, you can tell him this, Glyn Mohr, I wouldn't touch a penny of your filthy conscience money, not even to save me from starving. I'd rather steal than accept money from you or him!" She marched to the door where she paused to fling back at him: "I wish you joy while living with your parents. I've heard of women running back to Mother, but never of a man!" and she slammed the door hard.

Chapter Nine

Susan toyed with the idea of going to see her mother, whom she had not visited since before her marriage. She had meant to see her soon after their return from honeymoon but as life with Glyn had not started smoothly, she had decided to put it off until things were a little happier between herself and her husband. As the time passed, she had become more apprehensive. Her mother's disapproval of the intention to marry a man she didn't love had shamed her deeply and she had not dared to admit how true her mother's prophecy had proved. Now that the marriage was over, she found she could not take the step. Kinder to let her remain ignorant of the truth, Susan decided. Fortunately there had not been very much publicity given by the newsapers to the accident. Now, if she had been an ex-top model, how they might have splashed it across their pages!

As far as Mrs. Onsworth was concerned, the less she knew the better.

Susan had a far more important and immediate problem to consider now. What was she to do? To continue living in this mausoleum was entirely out of the question. She must find a small apartment, and perhaps the Maître would give her back her old job. There were great doubts about that, however, because there were plenty of other models of her standard. Still, she'd try, but not today. She did not feel up to making the effort of calling on her former employer, and the rigours of modelling were a little too much to consider at the present time.

She had not felt at all well since the accident. She was listless and tired easily, probably all due to having fractured her ribs, she decided. And her back had begun to ache almost incessantly. By the end of a morning she was quite glad to lie on the settee and sleep. Idly, she looked at herself in the long mirror beside the dressing-table.

Mm! she thought ruefully. Some strict dieting needed here if she was to resume modelling. Too much flesh had been added since her marriage, especially around the hips. Before she even asked the Maître to take her back, she would have to start getting rid of this excess.

Two days after Glyn left hospital, the weather became abominably hot, making Susan feel very ill. She was giddy with the heat, and food nauseated her. The first afternoon she felt unwell, she put herself to bed in a darkened room where she slept fitfully. After a restful night, she arose feeling more like her old self again, yet halfway through breakfast she had to push the food away and dash wildly for the bathroom. White and shaken, she emerged a quarter of an hour later. Obviously she must have eaten something that had gone off in the heat, because hot summer days had never afflicted her in this manner.

When the same thing happened again on the next two mornings, she was obliged to sit down on her bed and think carefully. A great suspicion had grown in her mind. This was no food-poisoning! She stared at Glyn's empty bed and the more she thought about it, the more it seemed possible.

How many weeks since the accident? Eight? Nearly nine? One by one the little pieces of jigsaw slipped into place. Of course! The listlessness and backache and general feeling of *malaise* that she had put down to the after-effects of the car smash. She rose and looked at herself in the mirror. Yes, the thickening around the hips . . . she was going to have Glyn's baby!

Her flushed and excited face stared back at her. How thrilled Glyn would be to learn the truth! She knew he had always wanted a son, and the elder Mohrs had made no pretence of their eagerness for a grandson to carry on the family name. Now that there was a baby on the way, Glyn would forgive her for everything that had happened and they would make a fresh start together.

A sudden doubt assailed her.

Could she tell him the truth? He might not believe her. After all, why should he? As far as he knew there wasn't the slightest possibility of Susan being pregnant for they both knew he had not sought the warmth of her twin bed for at least three months before that fatal evening. It was perfectly possible that he would accuse her of promiscuity with another man.

Even if she told him exactly what had taken place during the period of time which was now a blank spot in his memory, she doubted whether he'd believe it to be true. Far more probable that he would accuse her of fabricating the whole story, to cover her own sins.

What *was* she to do?

She turned the problem over in her mind for a very long time and came to the conclusion that she should do nothing towards telling Glyn until she had ascertained for herself whether she was pregnant. She was almost positive but a visit to the doctor was clearly indicated.

I mustn't see our own G.P.! she decided suddenly, for he might inadvertently let slip the truth to Glyn, and that she did not want. If anyone was to tell him, then she was the person.

Later that morning she went to a pharmacists in the High Street to enquire the names of any doctors prepared to take private patients. The assistant was very helpful, consulting lists that were kept in the office, and then gave her the names and addresses of two doctors. She thanked the girl, and then went to the phone-box. Her appointment was for two o'clock the following afternoon.

The intervening twenty-four hours passed very slowly, but Susan used them to plan her campaign. She decided not to use her married name, as the Mohrs were a familiar one in the city, with their great factory spreading across many acres on its outskirts. Her maiden name, perhaps? No. Better to use the word " Moore " . . . same name, different spelling. Nothing to connect her with Edward or Glyn now. She would tell the doctor that she had only just moved to the city and had not yet had time to find a house or a local G.P. That would prevent him from following up her case, and she would be the only one to know the truth until she had found some easier way of breaking the news to Glyn.

The doctor was kind and Susan wished she did not have to deceive him. He made a brisk examination and while she was getting dressed again, he said:

" Yes, Mrs. Moore, I think we can put the date of birth in January. Late January. I'll look in my book and give you a more approximate date in a minute. Of course," he added, smiling, " we can never say for sure which day baby will put in an appearance, because they like to arrive when they want to! Especially first babies. Would you like me to arrange for you to go into one of the private nursing homes for your confinement? Arrangements have to be made early, you understand, and I can give you the names of two who would

take you as a paying patient. On the other hand, if you prefer to use the very excellent facilities offered by the Health
Service, either in a hospital or having the baby in your own
home, then I suggest that you find a panel doctor in the
district you're hoping to live. He can make all the arrangements for you, and look after you during the very important
pre-natal period." He smiled again. "Having a baby as a
paying patient can be an extremely expensive business, Mrs.
Moore."

"I understand," Susan replied. "I'll discuss it with my
husband and I expect we'll join a National Health doctor's
panel."

"Splendid! Now, I'll write a letter for you to give your
new doctor. Just sit down, and I won't be long."

Five minutes later, Susan emerged into the bright sunshine, the promised letter clutched in one hand, and a receipt
for the consultation in the other. She walked blindly towards
the bus stop. It was true! There was no doubt about it. She
was going to have Glyn's baby. The knowledge gave her a
warm, comforting feeling. Whatever happened now, she
would always have something of Glyn's. No one could ever
rob her of this part of him.

At home she ordered tea which Elsie, the maid, brought
into the lounge. As she drank the refreshing liquid, she
pondered her next move. It was essential that she spoke to
Glyn. It was ridiculous to hope that he might open his arms
and draw her to him . . . the past forgotten.

It was possible that he didn't want either her or the child.
In that case, she certainly had no intention of placing him
under any kind of obligation to her. She still had her pride,
if nothing else.

For over half an hour she sat looking at the telephone,
wondering whether to ring him or go round to see him in

person. The disadvantage of calling at his parents' home was the question of whether they would allow her to speak to him alone. On the phone she might have a little privacy. Whichever method she used, she had to speak to Glyn.

At last she took the plunge and lifted the receiver, dialling her in-laws' home number. The maid answered and she asked to speak to Mr. Glyn Mohr.

"One moment please, Madam. Who is calling?" Susan gave her name and the maid put down the receiver. With heart in mouth and almost sick with apprehension, Susan waited. She played a childish mental game: the longer I wait, the more likely it'll be Glyn who comes! She strained her ears for the sound of a limping man but soon, all too soon, she heard the swift treads of a heavy walker. The receiver was snatched up and Edward's gruff voice bellowed in her ear:

"Now look here, Susan, Glyn and I have asked you to leave us alone, and that includes telephone calls."

"I'd like to speak to him, please," she requested firmly.

"Well you can't. He doesn't want to speak to you. Tell me what you've got to say, and make it brief. I'm a busy man."

"Does Glyn know I'm on the phone?" Susan persisted.

"Naturally. The maid knows her duty. However, my son has refused to accept your call. What do you want?"

Susan knew when she was beaten.

"It's nothing, Mr. Mohr. Nothing important," she murmured quietly and replaced the receiver in its cradle. Then she sank onto the settee and cried as if her heart would break.

It was useless . . . quite useless! Glyn didn't care what happened to her. Therefore it would be better for him to remain in complete ignorance about the baby. There was really no need for him ever to find out because she would go far, far away, and cut herself free from the chains that held her. She must make a new life for herself and the baby. She must eject Glyn from mind and memory, and live only for *her* baby! It would be hers and hers alone. She need never share it with anyone . . . not even her own mother.

Half an hour later there was a ring at the front door bell. Susan heard Elsie cross the hall, and wondered who could be calling at this time of the late afternoon. She hoped it was nobody important because she did not feel up to seeing anyone. Then she heard Elsie's soft voice and deeper tones, arguing. The door was thrown open and Edward Mohr pushed past the protesting Elsie. He flung his hat down on a chair and kicked the door shut with his foot. He leaned over the back of the settee glaring down at Susan's startled face and began:

" I'll not beat about the bush with you, young woman. Neither will I tolerate you phoning my house and upsetting my son, who is still far from well, as you should know! I think he's told you in no uncertain terms that he'll have nothing further to do with you, which includes phone calls and personal visits. I wasn't prepared to discuss the matter over the telephone for my servants to overhear, that's why I'm here now." He put his hand inside his breast pocket and drew out a folded piece of paper which he opened in front of her. She saw it was a cheque.

" I presume you wanted to discuss money with Glyn, so I'm here in his stead. Look at it!" he ordered. " I've made it out to a sum to keep you in sufficient comfort for a few years." He waved it under her nose. " Go on, girl, look at it! Or isn't it enough for you?" he added cruelly. " Don't pretend this amount is unsatisfactory."

Susan recoiled, horrified.

"I . . . I," she began, then closed her mouth firmly. Under ordinary circumstances nothing on earth would have made her even consider accepting such an enormous amount of money from anyone, least of all Edward Mohr. Between yesterday and today, everything had undergone an abrupt change. The future had been clearly mapped out for her. She was expecting Glyn's child, and naturally she would need money for it. The two of them had to live and eat and she could not now return to work. She had a very small sum of money that Glyn had settled on her; in addition there was the large amount he had put into the bank a week before the accident. She could leave that where it was, with a Banker's Order to continue the regular payments to her mother which she had not stopped after her marriage.

Accepting money from Edward was a different matter. In an inexplicable way, she felt obliged to accept it, because he had been instrumental in wooing Glyn away from her. He owed her more than he could ever give.

Calmly she stretched out her hand and said:

"Very well, Mr. Mohr. I'll take this. But not for the reason you think. If it gives you any satisfaction to feel you've 'bought me off', as I believe the saying is, then I trust you'll enjoy the pleasure it gives you. However, it's possible the day may arrive when you realise exactly what you've done by offering me this money."

"I very much doubt it!" Edward sneered, and a grim smile spread across his heavy features. "Just as I'd always expected. It was our money you were really after, not our son. He's well rid of you." He picked up his hat and prepared to leave, adding:

"You realise, I hope, that now you have money, you can't continue to live on here?"

The futility of Edward's words struck Susan as being

very amusing. She threw back her head and laughed.

"Believe me, Mr. Mohr, the sooner I can leave here the happier I'll be!"

Edward snorted angrily and showed himself out.

Well, she had done it now! What was the next move? There was little time to waste.

Chapter Ten

SUSAN'S most immediate problem to be resolved was the question of finding somewhere to live. She wanted to leave the city. The possibility of meeting either Glyn or his friends was too great, and she needed to forget him completely. Some small country town, perhaps? A place where she was unknown and had never visited.

The morning after Edward's visit Susan went out and bought copies of as many national newspapers as possible, and any women's magazines containing likely advertisements. She spent the remainder of the day poring over the closely printed pages. She had almost given up in despair when she came across something which seemed the very answer to her prayers:

" Wanted urgently. Suitable tenant. Three-year lease. Coastal village cottage. Two beds, living, kitchen, all mod. cons. Owner going abroad. Swift settlement imperative.—Box 5978."

Susan went to the writing-desk and wrote to the number given in the advertisement. She hoped there would not be too many applicants and wondered where the coastal village was situated.

Three days later, her query was answered. A letter came from a small Cornish village that Susan had never heard of previously. Hastily she took out the road maps Glyn kept in the desk, and found it tucked away between high cliffs about ten miles from the nearest market town. Then she read the letter. It was warm and friendly, asking her to call at the address given as soon as it was convenient.

As soon as it was convenient! That would be tomorrow. Excitement surged through Susan. She must book a seat on the Paddington-Penzance express which stopped at the station in this city, and make arrangements to spend at least one night away from home. She doubted if it would be possible to do the two journeys in one day as she did not wish to overtax herself during the early stages of her pregnancy.

The train was half-full, and she found her seat easily. On reaching her destination she found that there was a bus waiting to take her, and the people who had travelled into the market town to do their shopping, back to the village. A deeply sunburned old man helped her lift her light suitcase aboard, and then assisted her into a seat near the door. The bus was full and everybody seemed to know everyone else. During the journey, purchases and prices were discussed and compared. Also relatives' complaints, and the latest additions to families both in the village and the town, and who was planning to take in summer visitors and who was not.

Susan was deeply interested. They seemed a happy, care-free group of folk; a community, in fact. Many cast quick glances at her, nodding a salutation with a smile. Just before she reached the village, she asked the conductor if he could recommend a hotel where she might stay overnight.

"There's only the 'Pinhay Arms'," he said. "We'll be stopping right outside, Ma'am, so you shouldn't be 'aving any trouble finding it. Bob Slater's the landlord. Course, it isn't exactly an hotel, jes' the local inn, but they say the beds are wonderful."

Susan was enchanted with the inn. The ceilings were low and oak-beamed. Everywhere brass shone, and the doors had latches instead of handles. Bob Slater showed her to a small room overlooking the harbour, where blue cornflowers in a glass vase embellished the wide window-sill. The curtains were gaily coloured and both windows were open wide to welcome the sunlight. The murmur of the sea and the lazy cry of the gulls drifted in from outside.

Downstairs, Susan asked to be directed to the cottage.

" Ah, you'm be coming to live there, may be?" Bob Slater nodded his head knowingly. " The Baileys be sailing next week and I know them to be keen to find someone quick-like. Haven't found anyone to their liking yet, so I'm told." He wiped the back of his hand across his mouth, and said: " Go outside the door, Mrs. Moore, then turn right. Walk about 'undred yards till you gets to the cottage with the blue door. Mrs. Gerraty's white cat'll be sitting outside. Always does, so there won't be any mistaking the place. Then walk on till you comes to the gate leading to the field where Farmer Buse keeps 'is cows, and Bailey's cottage be the second one to your left."

Susan thanked him demurely, although she badly wanted to laugh. She doubted if she would ever find her way after such directions. To her amazement, everything was as Bob Slater had said, even to the somnolent white cat.

The Baileys' cottage was small and set a little way back from the road. A creaking gate which needed oiling opened onto a crazy-paving path edged with green glass globes. A wide arch of honeysuckle tumbled over the front door. Instead of a knocker, there was a large ship's bell. All the windows upstairs and down were wide open and, from inside,

Susan could hear the strains of music. The radio, probably.

Almost at once the front door was opened by a small, fat woman with a smiling, suntanned face who greeted her:

"I'm Mrs. Bailey. You must be Mrs. Moore. We received your postcard this morning. I'm so glad you could come. Did you have a good journey down? Not too crowded, I hope?" Susan answered each of the questions and found herself being ushered through a small hall towards a large room overlooking the garden at the back of the cottage.

She gasped with pleasure. It was a beautiful room, with two sets of french windows opening onto the well-kept garden which sloped gently away from the house towards the cliffs so that a good expanse of the harbour and surrounding district could be seen. The room itself was comfortably furnished, with good quality mats on a dark polished floor. A small, equally plump man stood puffing his pipe by one of the windows. Susan was introduced to Mr. Bailey and talked to him while his wife hustled away to prepare tea for their visitor.

Sitting in a chintz-covered armchair sipping a cup of hot, sweet tea, Susan sighed with delight. Mrs. Bailey beamed and offered her a plate on which lay thick chunks of saffron cake. Susan took a slice but refused the clotted cream offered with it.

"Ah, you'll have to get used to lots of cream if you mean to live here!" Mrs. Bailey chuckled. "We all live on it. Does you the power of good, doesn't it, George?" Her husband smiled, lifting his eyes for a moment from the task of spreading an enormous layer of the cream on top of his wedge of cake.

"Shall miss it while we're away, make no mistake!" he grumbled. Susan liked cream but at the present time she preferred not to risk upsetting her already queasy stomach with too much richness. Later, perhaps, when the first four months had passed and she was feeling better.

The Baileys and Susan discussed the tenancy agreement and rent over the tea-table. Afterwards, Mrs. Bailey showed her over the rest of the cottage. The two bedrooms were small but ideal for Susan's purpose and the bathroom diminutive but adequate. The kitchen, however, was a dream, for, as her hostess explained, she believed in having as many of the latest gadgets as she could fit into the space provided by the recent modernisation of the cottage. The stairs were narrow and steep but Susan knew she would be able to negotiate them with care.

When they were in the lounge again, Susan said:

" Before I accept your very generous offer, I feel I must be fair and ask one question. Have you any objections to a child living here? You see, although I'm separated from my husband, I'm expecting his baby."

" Oh you poor dear!" soothed Mrs. Bailey, putting a motherly arm around Susan's shoulders. " How could any man do such a cruel thing to his wife at such a time!"

" Miriam! I hardly think it's any affair of ours," her husband admonished.

" I'm sorry, my dear. It's just that George and I adore children and never had the good fortune to have any of our own. Now, of course, it's far, far too late to even think of adopting a baby."

Susan sympathised with her hostess and could not help noticing by the way they glanced at each other that the two grey-haired folk obviously adored one another. The lack of a family had not caused any rift, she thought enviously. If only she and Glyn had been as happy as the Baileys!

Their business quickly settled, the Baileys offered to put Susan up for the night, but she regretfully declined, explaining that she already had a room at the inn and hoped to catch the early bus to be at the station in plenty of time for the train the following morning. Her host and hostess insisted that she had supper with them, and this she gladly accepted.

When they parted later that evening, Susan felt strangely at peace. She had not known such happiness. Within two weeks she would be living here!

The following ten days flew by as Susan made her preparations. After a great deal of deliberation, Susan decided to keep the name of " Moore ". Later on, when the baby had been born, she would have to give the name of its father to the registrar of births . . . she could revert to the correct spelling just for that one occasion, perhaps. Anyhow, she'd think of it when the time came.

She gave Elsie and the cleaning woman four weeks pay in lieu of notice, and completely cleared the house of her own personal belongings. They fitted into a large trunk and two small suitcases. She sent the former in advance to Cornwall.

Then there was the question of her car. In the village she would have no use for it. The bus service into the town was regular and she hoped to travel there only once in a while when the need arose. Besides, with a pram, there would be no need to keep on the car, even if she could afford the motor-tax and insurance. The latter was unwarranted, and the money of far more use. She drove the car to a local garage and asked them to make her an offer for it.

What was she to do about her bank accounts? If she transferred them there was always the possibility of one or the other of the Mohrs tracing her through the bank, and this she would not tolerate.

In the manager's office, Susan spoke frankly. She told him she wished to transfer the entire value of Edward Mohr's cheque to the branch in the market town near where she intended to live. She wisely did not give him the name of the village, and informed him that on no account was he to divulge her whereabouts to any member of the Mohr family.

A taxi came to take her to the station. As she locked the front door for the last time, she felt no regrets whatsoever. It had been an unhappy house, and she was thankful to leave it. She put the key in an envelope and asked the taxi driver to take her by a roundabout route to the station so that she could leave the key at Glyn's solicitor's office. This accomplished, she sat back. The house and its contents were no longer her responsibility.

She reached the station in good time and soon was moving westwards, to a completely new life.

Chapter Eleven

FOR the first week, Susan explored the village and surrounding countryside. She familiarised herself with the whereabouts of the shops, and also went into town where she opened a bank account. The bank manager was pleased to accept her transfer and, on request, made several excellent suggestions on how she should best invest the money Glyn's father had given her. He did some quick figuring and Susan was surprised to find out exactly how much these investments would bring in. Naturally, it wouldn't be a fantastic sum, but sufficient for the time. Wisely, she also kept a small amount of capital available should she need some in a hurry. With care and economy, she decided she would be able to live without having to work before the baby's arrival. Afterwards . . . that was a different problem, and one she would tackle the following year.

The village was beautiful. It hugged the steep sides of the valley, with the houses and cottages built almost on top of one another from the water's edge. The harbour was calm and serene, with boats of all kinds bobbing quietly at anchor or tied up to the harbour walls. Some of the cottages clung like limpets to the waterside, so that Susan could well imagine sitting in the window seat of one of their many bay windows and pretending she was on board an old tall master. White-stuccoed, or grey block, timber-faced, and all slate roofed, their windows were small-paned, casement or sash-

cord. There was a unity about the village that impressed
Susan. Everyone seemed to know everyone else.

A family of graceful swans ruled the harbour waters and
the stream tumbling down the hillside towards the sea. They
gathered beneath the overhanging windows in the evenings,
waiting for someone to throw out pieces of bread for them.
They were sleek, healthy birds.

There were also the small boys who, when they were not
attending school during the daytime, spent hours in the
water, shouting and splashing each other. Susan smiled to see
their immense enjoyment. Gulls stood about on the house-
roofs, chimneys, harbour walls and ships' masts; waiting.
They were always waiting. They seemed to sense the arrival
of the fishing boats from a long way off, because they would
fly around the harbour, screeching excitedly before coming
to roost on the housetops nearest the water. When the
catches were being brought ashore, there were gulls everywhere, snatching bits and sometimes whole fish, and quarrelling incessantly.

Susan was surprised to discover how much the village
folk seemed to know about her, although she herself had told
them nothing. They were gentle and kind to her, stopping
to pass the time of day and to ask if she had settled down
in her new home. She began to suspect that her absent landlord and his wife had supplied the villagers with details
about their tenant. However, this did not worry her at all.
In one way it was a blessing in disguise, for she was not sub-
jected to questions on her past home and kind enquiries of
the sort that might embarrass her.

She swiftly discovered a very pleasant walk. Instead of
going down the hill into the village, she turned away from
it and struck out for the open cliffs beyond. About a quarter
of a mile away from her cottage she found a wide cliff path

which led down to a beach. There was also another path which continued westwards, following the configuration of the coastline. The beach was only visible at low tide, she discovered, for when it had turned, the sea soon came right up to the harsh rocks at the foot of the cliff. She liked to sit on the green, springy turf at the cliff edge and watch the foam as it crawled sixty feet below. The spume was like long fingers, seeking and searching, feeling its ways against the rock barrier. She could well imagine how, on rougher days, it would crash up against those same rocks, tilting skywards to a great height before turning slowly and then descending in a tumult of boiling sand-flecked foam.

It was when she was up on the cliff alone, with only the whisper of the sea for company and the cry of a bird above, that Susan found herself thinking again and again of Glyn and the life she had left. Those few months together had been so full of artificiality, with strange, bored faces around her . . . some of whom she could barely remember their names after even this short time . . . soon she would have forgotten them all. They had meant nothing to her, neither she to them. The news of her separation must have ceased to be a seven days' wonder long ago. Even now she could imagine some of those overdressed, artificial women saying in languid voices:

" Susan Mohr? Who on earth is that?"

Yet the memory of Glyn was still very close. She could not prevent herself from wondering how he was. Was he missing her at all? No, that was quite impossible. She missed him terribly, especially now that the baby was growing so fast within her. At home, if she wanted to, she could always take the photo she had of him from the drawer and look at it. Yet she tried to resist such temptation. Better to leave it where it was, face down under a pile of clothes.

If only she had tried to understand him while they had lived together! She realised that they had both been equally to blame for their failure; at the same time, she knew that if she had really made the effort instead of resenting him so bitterly, she might have been able to find some way of beginning to put matters right. She had done nothing constructive whatsoever. She also wondered if she should write and tell her mother what had happened, but decided against it. The time was not yet ripe. She could not have found the words.

It was on one of her walks during the second week that she almost had a very nasty accident. She had reached the cliff top and was standing near the edge, looking out to sea at a lone yacht. The sea breeze gently ruffled her hair and blew her cotton dress against her legs. She lowered her gaze and riveted it on the beach below her. The sand was yellow and wet, unsullied by footprints. The tide was almost out but here and there it curled and sucked around the black rocks. Out of the blue, a fierce wave of faintness assailed her. The world began to sway and mist. She knew she had to come away from the edge before she toppled over, but somehow her feet were too weak to move. The stretch of sand seemed to be coming nearer, stretching up to touch her, to draw her down to itself. She put a hand to her head, panic-stricken.

I mustn't fall! I've got to move back!

Gasping for breath, she heard footsteps running behind her and a strong arm shot out to envelope her. She was jerked roughly to one side whereupon blackness overcame her. When she came to she found herself with her head being forced between her knees and a stern voice commanding her to take great gulps of air. Then the voice went on in a friendlier tone, although it was still scolding:

" That edge is very crumbly, you know. It's very unwise to stand as near as you were."

Susan struggled to sit up properly, her senses fully recovered. Then she turned to look at her rescuer. He was crouching at her side, watching her carefully. She was struck at once by the sincerity in a pair of wide-set green eyes, thick eyebrows and a humorous mouth. His face was almost girlish in shape but there was a determination about the forehead that assured her he was a man not to be trifled with. He looked about thirty, she decided dreamily. His face broke into a smile.

" Better now?" he asked, and his fingers closed over her wrist, feeling for her pulse. She looked down at her hand and then back at him.

There was an unspoken question in her gaze.

" Are you . . .?" she began. He nodded.

" Yes. Doctor Roger Harlow. I know you, naturally. You're our new neighbour, Mrs. Moore. How do you do?" He slipped his hand down from her wrist to shake hers. Susan laughed.

" How do you do?" she replied. " This is a strange place to be introduced!" Roger Harlow changed his crouching position, sitting down to stretch his legs out in front of him. He heaved a sigh of relief.

" That's more like it!" Leaning back on the turf, he rested his chin on his hand and looked at Susan. His eyes were screwed up against the sun's glare. " In future, if you've this tendency to vertigo in high places, you must be careful not to wander too near cliff edges."

" Oh, I don't suffer from that complaint!" she protested, then blushed quickly. His eyes were twinkling and his voice teased. " Now don't tell me that our newest neighbour was actually thinking of *jumping* off that edge?" The ludicrousness of his suggestion made her throw back her head and roar with laughter, as he had intended it should.

"Of course not! Surely it didn't look as if I would? By the way, where *did* you spring from? I thought I was all all alone here today."

"As a matter of fact, it's my free afternoon. For a change, instead of my usual sailing expedition, I decided to amble up here." He yawned. "Sorry, that was rude of me. I was up late last night coping with a particularly cussed delivery, and I felt far too tired to get the dinghy out. Pure laziness, naturally. Still, perhaps it was a good thing I changed my mind. Otherwise there could have been a very unpleasant accident."

"I'm glad you came along, and thank you for what you did just now. I promise not to stand near cliff edges in future."

"Splendid."

"And you're the village doctor?"

"One of them, the junior partner. My boss is a good man, getting on for retirement shortly but still as fit as a fiddle and eager for hard work."

"I've been meaning to come to the surgery because I must register with a doctor fairly soon."

"And we'll be delighted to accept you, Mrs. Moore. I'll care for you myself, if you wish, or my partner will have you as his patient."

"Thank you, but I think I'd like your services, if I may?"
Roger Harlow grinned.

"Before we start, I should warn you that I've the advantage over you, Mrs. Moore. The Baileys and I are very great friends, and it seemed only natural for them to tell me all about their successor. I'm delighted to add that they didn't exaggerate those glowing reports."

Susan blushed.

" Mrs. Bailey was quite right. She said you were very charming and beautiful."

Susan wondered if he realised he had given her an opening.

" Did . . . did she also tell you about my husband?" After all, as her medical adviser, he would have to be told sooner or later.

" Yes. She said you were separated and expecting your first baby. She also told me . . . and this is strictly off the record . . . that I was to take the greatest possible care of you otherwise I'd have her wrath to contend with when she eventually returns to England! "

Susan laughed.

" How kind of her. I'm glad she told you everything because it makes it all so much easier for me." His eyes twinkled mischievously.

" I expect that if we hadn't met today I should have made it my duty to call on you in any case. My partner and I are most particular about our expectant Mums. We don't like them to be left without pre-natal care for any length of time in case anything should be neglected."

Susan's mouth twitched, and she scolded:

" I understand, Doctor. You were going to pay me a visit in order to persuade me to join your panel. In other words, you were cadging for trade. Scandalous, Doctor, absolutely scandalous! I've a good mind to report you to the Medical Council, or whatever is the disciplinary board."

Roger pretended to look hurt.

" Madam, you've misunderstood me completely. I'd never even consider the remotest opportunity of canvassing for ' trade ' as you so delicately put it. No, I was acting as a good neighbour to a stranger in our midst." His voice became serious. "Mrs. Moore, you must book early for a hospital bed, you know. Anyway, I'm off duty now, perhaps you'll call at the surgery soon? You'll find it in the double cottage at the bottom of Macken's lane, that's the turning three doors down from the smithy, so you won't miss it.

"Also, my dear Mrs. Moore, neither I nor my partner can risk losing a patient up here. It would look so terribly bad for business!"

"I'm not on your panel . . . yet," she reminded him gently.

"Just think how appalled the villagers would be to learn of the sudden and unexpected demise of our newest arrival . . . and the most attractive one, too!"

She laughed.

"You flatter me."

"Only on my free afternoons. When I'm on duty, then my behaviour is strictly professional. Of course, the great advantage of a country practice like mine lies in the fact that we can get to know our patients, and they us. Here they're not merely names in a massive filing cabinet as I fear is bound to happen in the large cities. Our patients are people who are born, live, think, breathe, worry, rejoice, make love, age, and eventually die. Each of my patients is unique and I try to learn as much about them as I can so that when they need me, I can be a real help, not just for their physical ills, but also their mental, and occasionally spiritual welfare. There, I've said enough. Now you're looking very much better. May I walk home with you, if you're thinking of returning?"

"Please do," Susan replied, adding shyly: "Perhaps you'd care for a cup of tea?"

"An excellent suggestion."

They walked slowly back to Susan's cottage, during which

time she learned that Roger had qualified four years previously but had not yet yearned to specialise as had so many of his colleagues.

" No. All I cared for was to leave the filth and bustle of the cities and find myself some nice, quiet country practice. It was more by luck than by good management that I came here. Dr. Thomas, he's my partner, needed a younger man because his former partner was retiring early through ill-health. This man was a distant relative of one of the chaps I studied with, and he was asked if he'd care to take over. He loathed the idea, having set his heart on chest surgery, but fortunately he remembered my own yen for the wild, open spaces. I applied, with a helpful letter of introduction from my colleague as well, and Dr. Thomas accepted me at once."

" You like the life here?"

" Love it. My parents were very good. They lent me money with which to purchase the cottage, and I often go up to the old house on the hill to see the man whose place I took. He's bedridden now, of course, but is still very agile mentally. My cottage is built beside the stream, tucked right in behind a row of shops. I expect you've seen it; cream coloured walls and a scarlet front door, with wisteria running riot all over the place and keeping my rooms well supplied with spiders and insects! "

" Do you look after yourself or are you married?"

" No and no. I've a woman who comes in every day. I have two sisters, both of whom I adore, but they don't visit me very often. At the beginning they did. In fact, I could hardly ever get rid of the blighters! " He laughed. " As soon as they learned that I was living by the sea, then they both developed a passion for sailing and fishing. They came to stay for months on end during the summer. That stopped two years ago, and I'm now left in peace."

" Didn't it work out?" Susan enquired gently.

" Oh yes, we all got on like a house on fire, until they suddenly found other interests in the male forms of Hugh and Jack. They're married now. Marian has had two children in quick succession, while Elaine has one daughter and is expecting another child in the late spring. Thanks to Hugh and Jack, I'm now well free of my adorable sisters, although I suspect that when their children are not very much older, I shall be inundated with requests to allow them to stay here for their holidays. It wouldn't surprise me, of course, to learn that my two scheming sisters have already drawn up the rota of who shall descend on me first and who second! " He opened the creaking gate. " Well, that just about finishes my saga."

They went inside the cottage and Susan put the kettle on.

" How do you like living in this cottage?" Roger asked.

" I love it. It's such a happy little house! "

" You're very lucky to get it. I've always looked upon it as being one of the village's nicest. It has such an excellent view and you haven't far to go to the shops and the quay. Also, and it's a great blessing, you're spared the visitors' cars parked right outside. Very few come this way out of the village, the road is too narrow and winding, leading nowhere."

" Since I've been here, I haven't seen very many holidaymakers."

" The bulk of them'll be arriving soon. The worst weeks are the last two in July, right through to the end of August. Then we get hordes of trippers."

Susan's face fell.

" Milk and sugar?" she asked.

" Please."

" I was told we were too far off the beaten track to be inundated with holidaymakers."

He grinned.

" Yes, I suppose we are. I'm sorry. I was pulling your leg.
The lack of holiday facilities here saves us from too many
visitors, although sufficient arrive to satisfy the villagers who
cater for them. People like Amanda Porter and her mother
who run the tea-shop on the quay. There are always folk who
come in cars from the towns and inland places. Some of
them seem to find a tremendous fascination in watching the
fishermen unload their catches, and they'll stand on the
quay for hours on end, just looking. The people who want
sea and sand for their youngsters usually stop at the beach
four miles away. So we're spared most of them, because the
thought of walking four miles in search of a cup of tea on a
boiling hot afternoon doesn't appeal to many folk!"

" Why don't they use the lovely stretch of sand here?"
Susan asked.

" It's only visible at low tide, and no one can swim from
the rocks when the tide's in because the undertow's far too
treacherous."

He declined a further cup of tea.

" I must leave now," he said, standing up reluctantly.
" Thanks very much for the happy hour I've spent in your
company, Mrs. Moore. Now, don't forget to come to the
surgery to see one of us. Nine till ten, or six to seven in the
evenings."

Susan saw him to the door and stood to watch him as he
strode down the lane into the village, covering the distance
in quick, long strides. Then she went inside again.

Suddenly she realised that during the time they had been
together this afternoon, she had not once thought of Glyn.

Chapter Twelve

Two mornings later, Susan visited Roger Harlow professionally. He filled in a card, asking relevant questions; childish ailments, other serious illnesses, vaccinations, etc., name and address of nearest relative, but this she declined to give. He made no comment, merely pausing to peer at her for a moment over the top of the thick-rimmed spectacles he now wore. Then he asked her to prepare herself for examination while he read the letter she had brought him from the private doctor who had confirmed her pregnancy. When it was over, he said:

"Everything's progressing very satisfactorily, Mrs. Moore. Now we must decide what arrangements to make for the actual birth. Where would you like to have the baby? Before you say anything, I must tell you that we've an excellent midwife here, and I also know someone who'd be only too willing to act as home-help during the few weeks after the birth." He smiled gently. "Amanda's an absolute gem! I think I mentioned her the other day. She and her mother run the tea-shop. It's closed from mid-September till Easter every year, and therefore Amanda's free."

Susan frowned.

"I assure you, Mrs. Moore, you'll lack for nothing with Amanda to care for you. I've often used her services during the winter months for my home confinements. A great many

of our patients insist on staying home so that she can be
called in. I suspect many of them of arranging their babies
to fit in with Amanda's free months. She's a hard worker
and a marvel with children. Also, her charges are reasonable.

" If you'd rather have the baby in hospital, I should warn
you that it's over ten miles away, which is really too far in
the case of emergency. Some of my Mums haven't even had
the consideration to wait until they've passed through the
hospital gates, and an ambulance has been known to pull
into the side of the main road to attend to an impatient
baby! I'd like you to think about it for a day or two, and
then let me know, unless of course you've made up your
mind already that you prefer hospital? Or, if you'd like to,
do call on Amanda to discuss my suggestion."

Susan did not need extra time to make up her mind.

" I'd like to see your friend."

" Good. I'll pop in and tell her to expect you, may I?"

" Please."

Susan called at the tea-shop just before eleven the following morning. It was an attractive little place, right on the
harbour. The windows were large, to let in plenty of light,
and the tables of dark mahogany shone with polish, and on
each stood a small bowl of wild flowers. The dark-green door
stood open, although a notice plainly indicated that tea was
not served until three in the afternoon. A yellow board sign,
in the shape of a beehive, proclaimed its name:

" THE HONEYPOT "

Susan stepped over the slate doorstep and knocked on the
door. A small boy carrying an enormous basket over one
arm, came towards her and bid her a cheery " good morn-

ing " before he rushed out into the open, whistling piercingly. He was followed by a tall, red-haired girl whose face broke into a welcoming smile.

" Mrs. Moore! Roger's told me to expect you. Do come in. Mind the boxes," she pointed to a pile of empty cartons lying just inside the tea-room. Then she led the way through a swing door into the kitchen at the back of the building. Mrs. Porter was working at the table, a rolling-pin in her hand. Her face was warm and flushed from the heat of the ovens. Wire trays of biscuits, buns and scones stood in rows to cool.

" Mum, this is Mrs. Moore," Amanda introduced them, and pulled out a chair for Susan.

" I see you're very busy. I shouldn't have come at such an awkward hour," she apologised but her hostess insisted she stay and have a cup of coffee with them. Amanda bustled around.

" We're well up to time today, and we don't open until three. Do you take sugar?"

Mrs. Porter then asked:

" You've come to discuss the new baby, bless its heart. Amanda'll be free in late January, so everything will be all right. Roger told us all about it yesterday and we'll do all we can to help you, dear."

Susan was overwhelmed with their kindness. She had taken an instant liking to Amanda. The younger girl sat on the edge of the table close to her and started to talk animatedly.

" I'll come any time you want me. Roger'll tell me nearer the actual date when I ought to be up at your cottage, so we can arrange all those details later on. You don't know anyone here, do you? We'll soon put that right. Roger's suggested I take you under my wing . . . that's if you've no objection! . . . and I'll be glad to do so. I suppose you started knitting ages ago?"

Susan had to admit that she had not even found any patterns.

" Never mind. Mrs. Arlen has plenty. She's in the haberdashery shop. I'll ask her to pop up to the cottage one evening with the book, shall I, then you'll be able to choose at leisure."

" Oh, I couldn't possibly impose on her! " Susan protested. " I'll go to her shop. Besides, it gives me an excuse to take some exercise."

They all laughed.

Susan's quiet manner and charm endeared her to all the villagers. It was not long before she knew most of them by their first names. Jamie Black, the milkman, a young, studious fellow who sported the most hideous ties Susan had ever seen . . . when he wore one at all . . . and who always picked out the largest eggs for her, and the thickest cream, while Tom Jenkins the butcher cut off the most tender pieces of meat.

" Eating for two now," he'd say. " Only in quality but not in quantity, as Dr. Thomas always tells my missus when she's expecting."

Sometimes Reggie Scobbold, the fifteen-year-old son of one of the fishermen, would arrive on the doorstep and thrust a couple of fine fish into her hands before fleeing, crimson-cheeked. Neither was there ever a dearth of flowers in her vases. Her lawn was cut and the flower beds weeded by members of the local Scouts and Cubs. Often Jean Turner, the schoolgirl daughter of the baker, would bring in wild flowers that she had picked from the hedgerows on her way home from school.

She felt happy and contented, at peace with herself and

the world. Her past unhappiness had faded to the back of her mind, and the trouble with Glyn was being dimmed by the passage of time.

After a great deal of heart-searching, she had eventually decided to write to her mother. In a long letter she told her exactly what had happened and that she had left Glyn. She did not mention the baby at all. She begged her mother to try to see things from her point of view and to understand her motives. She told her how sorry she was but it had seemed the only solution. This letter she enclosed in one to her bank manager in the city, giving no home address, and requesting him to send it on to her mother with the next payment from the account she had left untouched, the one Glyn had opened for her when they first married.

She began to attend church again, and it soon became a regular Sunday habit. It gave her a great feeling of comfort, but also filled her with a sense of guilt for having neglected Sunday worship for so many years. It was Amanda who had persuaded her to go to church again.

When Roger was free, he would also join them as they trudged up the steep hill towards the church perched high above the village and harbour. Susan soon became conscious of the fact that Amanda was in love with Roger and was rather surprised he did not notice. It was in the way she looked at and spoke to him. His eyes, when they looked down at Amanda's eager face, were warm and amused, but Susan could detect no inner sign of love in them.

As for her own feelings towards him, she was not at all uncertain. She liked him tremendously. He was a good doctor and a kind friend. They had quickly forsaken the use of surnames, becoming Roger and Susan to each other. He was always considerate and gentle when they were together, yet at times, Susan was startled to see a quickly veiled expression of something just a little more than pure friendship in his eyes. Could it be that he was in love with her? She sincerely hoped not, for their relationship could never, never pass the bounds of deep friendship. She felt a moment of panic. She did not want Roger to love her! She belonged only to Glyn, regardless of whether he wanted her or not.

If only Roger could be made to love Amanda!

The heat of the summer passed, the last visitor left the village, the " Honeypot " put up its blinds, and cold winds and rain swirled in from the sea, greying everything. People scurried about with their collars turned up and heads covered, while the boats still moored in the harbour no longer rested quietly. Soon the fishermen dragged them onto higher ground, there to stay until the winter tides and storms had passed. The fishing vessels swung out of the agitated harbour waters into the roughness beyond, rearing and plunging as they strove seawards to cast their nets. Smoke belched from the cottage chimneys, to be whipped away by the fretful winds. Inside Susan's home all was snug and warm.

Now that her movements had become slower, Susan settled down to preparing for the baby. She bought wool and material, and spent long happy hours making baby clothes. She wondered what she should do about a cot and pram. Although she had a little extra money to draw upon, she did not want to use too much of it. The prices in the catalogues she had procured from the town seemed very high. It was too much to spend on one child. If she could only find someone with second-hand baby furniture to sell, her needs would be answered!

One afternoon, while Amanda was having tea with Susan, her problem was solved almost accidentally. She had left the catalogues on the table and had to move them before she

could put down the tray. They were amongst a pile of magazines one of the villagers had lent her, and somehow they
slipped from her arms and cascaded all over the floor.
Amanda leapt to her rescue, picking them up for her as Susan
was beginning to find it an effort to bend down these days.

Amanda found one of the catalogues and looked at it
thoughtfully.

"This reminds me," she said. "You haven't ordered one
of these yet, have you?"

"No. Why?"

"Well, don't. I think I know of someone who has some
second-hand stuff she'd like to be rid of, and quite cheaply
too. Mind you," she added somewhat apologetically. "It's
been used for two children, but there's still some life left in
it. Unless, of course, you're wanting to buy new?" She
looked up at Susan whose face shone with relief.

"Oh no, I don't! That is, if I *can* buy second-hand, I'd
far rather."

"Good. I know these people very well. Unfortunately,
you know what most newly-married mums are like . . . nothing but brand new so the bottom's virtually fallen out of
the second-hand market. You ought to be able to purchase
all of their baby stuff for give-away prices."

"Do you really think so?" Susan asked doubtfully.

"Of course. I'll go and see them. What exactly will you
be needing, do you think?"

"Pram. Cot. Ooh, and I'd better have a play-pen and high
chair because I can't allow the baby to mess up the Baileys'
good furniture, can I?"

It was arranged that Amanda should let her know what
she had been able to find out within the next week. What
Susan did not learn, however, was that Roger had been in-
veigled into driving Amanda to the farm-house to inspect

some very battered and badly painted baby furniture.

"What do you think, Roger?"

"She'll never accept it in this condition! But if we take it back to my place, I think we could patch it up between the two of us."

Like conspirators in the night, they squeezed a cot, pram, play-pen and high chair into Roger's shooting brake, and whisked back to the village.

"None of it's very clean," Amanda said. "You give me a few days on this with soap and water and some paint, and we'll have it looking like new."

Three days later, Amanda brought Susan to Roger's cottage and showed her a wooden cot painted pale blue, a polished black pram with new wheels, and a varnished high chair and play-pen. Susan was delighted.

"This is lovely!" she exclaimed. "How much did they want for it?"

"Five pounds the lot," the other girl lied glibly.

"Only five!"

"Yes. I paid for it then and there. You can refund whenever it suits you."

Susan was thrilled with her good fortune. Later, when they were alone, Roger said to Amanda:

"Now then, young lady, how much am I in your debt? We agreed to go fifty-fifty, remember?"

"Let me see, you gave the Walkers the five pounds they asked for, then there was the paint, varnish, new wheels and suspension straps, plus lots of new screws etc., etc. Here," she handed him a piece of paper with some figures scribbled on it. "This is only a very rough calculation."

He leaned over and tweaked her ear affectionately, then took out his wallet.

"Now remember, Amanda," he said as he handed her

some money. " This is a secret just between you and I. Sue's pride would be terribly hurt if she ever found out what we'd been up to! "

Amanda stared up at him, searching his face thoughtfully.

" You like her very much, don't you? "

He smiled.

" Yes. "

She turned away, biting her lip.

" I see. " Roger put his hands on her arms and turned her back to face him.

" Look at me, Amanda. There's one thing you and I must get straight. Sue's my *patient,* and you know darned well that we quacks aren't allowed to mix business with pleasure, therefore I have to be extremely careful in my dealings with her. No matter what private dreams and longings I might have, they must remain for ever unfulfilled, for she already has a husband. "

" I'm so fond of you! " Amanda murmured, burying her face in his jacket while he held her close, looking sadly over the top of her head. Then she jerked back to gaze into his eyes. " Please, please, don't get hurt! "

He touched her nose gently with one finger.

" You're very sweet, my dear, but you needn't worry about me. I can look after myself. As long as you're around to keep on eye on me! " he added, teasingly.

She would not smile.

" Don't go too far away, Roger! " she begged.

" I won't, I promise. "

Amanda wisely let the matter rest there. With an experience beyond her years, she knew that whatever lay in Roger's system, only time would rid him of it and bring him back to her. Any foolish move now on her part might rob her of him for ever. She must wait.

As the weeks passed, Susan found she never had to carry home any of her shopping because wherever she went there was always someone, young or old, ready to take her purchases. Many of the shopkeepers insisted on sending their goods up to the cottage by one of their numerous offspring. Since her arrival in the village she had become very popular and knew that behind her back the villagers referred to her as " Little Mrs. Widow ". This touched her deeply, because she realised most of them had guessed the truth about her marriage.

Christmas approached, but she was not destined to spend it on her own. Mrs. Porter invited her to celebrate the festival with herself and Amanda. Roger came too, when he had finished his rounds. They all went to church in the morning and then sat down to turkey and Christmas pudding topped with brandy butter and thick cream. Roger drove her home early that evening, as she felt very tired these days. He came into the cottage with her, banked up the fire and refilled the coal scuttle, then made her a cup of tea.

When he had gone, she went upstairs. In her room, she opened the bottom drawer and took out Glyn's photo, carrying it to the bed-table so that she could inspect it more closely in the light of the lamp. Mentally she compared the two men in her life.

Roger, so kind, gentle and thoughtful, sincere in everything he said and did. Glyn, selfish to the core and often bitterly unkind. Pampered by his parents, and completely misunderstood by her.

She put down the photo and went over to the mirror to look at herself. Greedy for comfort, selfish and out for herself only. Resentful and not giving way one inch if she could possibly help it. But now, alas, fully aware of all her faults and a sadder but much wiser woman.

Yes, she and Glyn suited each other. Both full of unpleasant traits. If only he too had recognised himself for what he was, they might have had a chance together.

She loved him.

She bent her head and wept quietly.

Chapter Thirteen

THE weeks following Christmas seemed to drag by unendingly. The weather became suddenly very cold, and it was an effort to negotiate the now slippery lanes. Susan longed to lose the burden within her, and wondered if every expectant mother felt as she was feeling towards the end of the ninth month. She was often breathless and her head seemed to ache interminably.

One morning, while she was in the greengrocers, she collapsed and had to be taken home in the delivery van. Roger called almost immediately and ordered her to stay in bed until the baby was born.

" But it's not due for at least another fortnight! " she protested. " And we both know that first babies are notorious for their tardiness."

" Nevertheless, you'll stay where you are, Susan. Of course, if you take it into your head to disobey my orders, then I'll send you to hospital at once." He then dropped his stern tone. " Don't worry. I'll pop in and see Amanda. I'm sure she'll be able to come up here straightaway. She can use your other bedroom. The district nurse will be calling regularly, and I'll drop by whenever I'm passing. So you'll be in excellent hands, with absolutely nothing to do all day but to read or knit. I wish it was me! I could do with a few days of laziness. I'll make out a prescription and Amanda'll bring it with her."

For almost three weeks Susan found herself being treated like a queen. At first she thought she would hate having to keep to her bed, but after two days she began to enjoy herself and to feel thankful there were others to cope with her household chores. She felt much better, but only wanted to go on and on resting. Her blood pressure steadied and the ache left her head.

She told Amanda where to find the baby things, and together they discussed the last-minute arrangements and prepared everything that had to be done prior to the actual birth. It was while Amanda was hunting through the bottom drawer for some flannelette sheets to be put in the airing cupboard, that she accidentally drew out Glyn's photograph. Without really knowing what she was doing, she turned it over and looked at it.

Surprised at the sudden silence, Susan glanced up from the newspaper. Amanda swivelled round to face her, scarlet-cheeked and with the photo in her hands.

" I'm awfully sorry, Sue! I shouldn't have pried."

" May I have it, please?" Susan asked, her voice trembling. Amanda carried it to her.

" He's very good-looking! " she commented.

" Yes. I suppose he is." Susan took it, studying it closely, seeing Glyn's face through the eyes of another. Whereas until just now she had noticed smouldering and scornful eyes, a firm chin and the overall domineering, arrogant expression, today she could see only a pleasant, good-featured, handsome man. She placed the photo face down on the bedspread and stared out at the snow-flecked sky beyond the window. A long, deep sigh escaped her lips. " Put it away again, there's a dear. Underneath all those clothes, at the back of the drawer."

She remained staring blankly into space while Amanda

continued her business at the chest of drawers. Had it only been Christmas when she had last looked at Glyn's photo? When had she *really* thought about him since then? Her mind had been too full of thoughts of the coming baby, yet why was it that today old memories had been vividly revived? They were both bitter and sweet. This unintentional act on Amanda's part had brought Susan face to face once again with the harsh reality that she was missing Glyn intensely. At Christmas, she had known she was going to look at the photo; today it had been thrust upon her when she was totally unprepared.

Where was he now? How had the court case gone? She presumed the authorities must have been satisfied with the eye-witness's account of the accident, as her absence seemed to have been accepted without question. Was he still living with Edward and Beatrice? Did he ever think of her?

Amanda spoke to her, but she did not hear. The younger girl then regarded her thoughtfully for a moment, frowned, and went back to her work. Better to say nothing. It was perfectly plain that Susan had no desire to tell her anything else about her husband.

It was on a cold, sleety day that Susan's labour began. Amanda sent for the midwife and then went upstairs to help Susan. Roger looked in later in the morning, pronounced himself satisfied and then went home to lunch. Dusk came early, and an hour later Amanda came running from the cottage to fetch Roger.

Upstairs, Susan was past caring what happened to her. She was fed up with the whole, horrid business. Why was the baby so long in arriving? All around her was discomfort and utter weariness. She was so very tired!

The midwife bent over her, scolding.

"Mrs. Moore, you're fighting against the pains instead of using them."

"I don't care!" she wailed, full well realising how foolishly she was behaving. She wept with frustration. Roger arrived and joined the midwife but his patient was too full of self-pity to notice anyone but herself and the anguish that was gnawing at her. Suddenly she called out:

"Glyn! I want Glyn! Where is he? Why isn't he here?"

Roger looked across to Amanda who had just come into the room carrying the bowl of instruments he had asked her to sterilise in case they should be needed.

"Glyn, is that you?" Susan called to her and stretched out her arms. "Help me! Hold my hand!"

"Should we send for her husband?" Amanda whispered to Roger.

"How can we? We've no idea where he lives or how to contact him."

"Please!" Amanda pleaded. "It might help her." Roger grinned.

"By the time he gets here, it'll all have been over hours beforehand, by which time she'll have forgotten she even asked for him."

"We could still try!" she insisted. "Besides, it's *his* child and he ought to know about it."

"I wouldn't meddle, if I were you, love. However, if it's what you want, here goes." He bent over the patient. "Sue, tell me, where's Glyn? We'll send for him if you'd like us to."

Susan gripped his hand fiercely.

"No! No, he mustn't come here! He mustn't find me! He doesn't want me, and I haven't told him about the baby. Please, please don't send for him!" she begged, crying. Another spasm seized her.

" Mums!" Roger sighed, and then set to work as the birth appeared to be imminent.

Three-quarters of an hour later, Susan was delivered of a seven-and-a-half pounds boy. She suddenly awoke, coherent again, and her face shone with wonderous delight as the midwife put her son into her arms.

" It's a fine boy!" she told her proudly.

" A son! I have a son!" Susan whispered and pressed her cheek against the new arrival's very soft skin. Then she slept the sleep of exhaustion.

When both mother and son had been made comfortable for the rest of the night, and the midwife had taken herself off home, Amanda sat with Roger in the quiet warmth of the kitchen where they both refreshed themselves with quantities of tea.

They did not talk much, for both were aware of the deep companionship that enveloped them. Eventually, Amanda said:

" Susan's always wanted a boy, Roger. Her dream's come true. She has a son . . . Glyn's son." She was watching Roger's face closely and could not mistake the sudden tightening of his lips. If she had had any doubts before, they were immediately set aside. Roger loved Susan. Her heart felt heavy enough to break, but she said nothing.

" Yes. We've had a successful night," was his comment after a long pause. " I've been thinking over Susan's plea first to send for her husband and then not to. It might have been better had she told us how to contact him. But she's never let drop even a hint about the place she used to live! Still, he has a right to know about his son," he finished thoughtfully.

" He's awfully good-looking, you know."

" Oh? And how do you know?"

Amanda told him about the photo she had found, adding:
" I think the hurt's still very near the surface, although she refuses to talk about him."

" Perhaps it would do her more good to tell someone," Roger suggested. " The hurt must be got out of her system; she can't go through life licking her wounds. Now she has the baby to live for. He'll help, naturally. Life has to go on regardless. Let's hope she'll soon realise it!"

Susan's baby was a very good child and presented her with no problems. He fed and slept well, continuing to grow and flourish. When he was six weeks old, Anthony John was christened in the church on the hilltop, with Roger and Amanda acting as godparents for him. Amanda had offered to travel into town with Susan on the day she wished to register the birth, but the latter declined, asking her to baby-sit for her instead. At the registry, Susan gave the clerk the correct spelling of Glyn's surname. In the years to come, of course, Tony might ask why the spelling had been altered, but that wouldn't be for a very long time . . . not until he would need to present his birth certificate to a future employer . . . years and years hence. She could forget about names for the present.

When the baby went out in his pram, the villagers would stop to coo at him. He adored all the attention, squirming about in the pram and showing toothless gums in a wide, happy smile. Later, Susan discovered he had a very infectious chuckle. She adored her Tony.

Roger also thought the world of him, and made no attempt to hide his affection. Amanda could not help wondering whether he loved the baby for its own sake or because he happened to be Susan's son. She knew she was being unjust and jealous, and she hated herself.

Roger made a point of popping into the cottage regularly

each day to see how his "munchkin" was, as he called Tony. Often, when he had a free afternoon, he would collect Amanda and together they took Susan and the Munchkin for a walk.

Surprisingly, Amanda made no comments about these walks, although her mother shook her head now and again as she watched the quartet walk past the teashop. Little did she realise that beneath her daughter's happy smiling face there lay a heart of lead.

One April afternoon, when Tony was three months old, and Amanda had to stay at home because her mother was not too well, Roger and Susan set out alone. The wind was brisk, but the sun was shining. Roger insisted on pushing the pram on his own towards the cliffs where they had first met. The view was magnificent, and it had become Susan's favourite spot, although she never went near the cliff edge. Later, when Tony was big enough for a pushchair, she hoped to take him down onto the beach and let him play about on the sands.

Roger spread an old mackintosh on the ground, and they sat down to talk while Tony lay sleeping in the pram. He asked Susan what plans she had for the future. She smiled.

"Why should you think I've changed the ones I made almost a year ago? I'll continue to live here, naturally. Perhaps, when Tony's old enough to go to primary school I'll have to think about finding some kind of job. I don't know what I could do, because I only served in a shop before I became a second-rate model." She shrugged. "A very empty life, of course, but I can't do anything else. I wish now I'd had the sense and money to train as a secretary, but training takes time when the money's badly needed at home. Still, I suppose if I'd been really keen, I'd have attended night-school after shop hours. However, I didn't, and that's that. Maybe I could teach myself typing and shorthand, although I doubt it. Also, I'd need a typewriter, and I don't want to spend money rashly. Tony needs my time and money at the moment."

" Can you do dressmaking?" Roger enquired.

" Not on your life!" Susan laughed. " I'm pretty hopeless with a needle. I can make little things, but nothing that has that important professional look you need if you're thinking of taking in work for other people. I couldn't possibly consider dressmaking as a means of making a living."

" Sue, forgive me for asking, but have you heard from your husband at all?"

She shook her head.

" No, Roger, and I don't want to. He doesn't know where I am, and I'm content to leave it that way."

" The night that young man arrived," Roger pointed to the pram, " you called out for Glyn. Do you remember?"

Susan's mouth opened in surprise.

" Did I really? My goodness! I've forgotten such a lot about the night Tony came."

" As I expected you to. At that stage of labour my Mums rarely remember anything at all of what they say or do." He laughed loudly. " Good thing they do, too! I feel sure if I listened to or repeated some of the language they used, I wouldn't have any patients left!" He picked up one of her hands and held it tightly. " I know I shouldn't be speaking like this, but I'm not on duty. Glyn, that's his name, isn't it? Don't you think it's time you made up your mind what to do about him?"

" How do you mean?"

" I know you're not completely happy. Have you considered your joint futures?"

" Surely there's nothing *to* consider? I've done everything I can."

" I know. But is a separation enough in itself? I mean, wouldn't you both be happier if you got a divorce, thus making the break clean?"

" Divorce can never be a ' clean ' break, Roger," Susan said quietly, " as you should very well know. All kinds of unpleasantnesses are brought out into the open for everyone to talk about."

Roger was persistent.

" Yes, I know. Surely divorce would be better than this . . . this emptiness of living apart?"

" I don't know, Roger. I honestly don't! "

"Besides, you're entitled to maintenance money, especially now you have Tony."

Susan jerked her hand away.

" Glyn must never be told about him. He or his parents might try to take him away from me if they knew! "

" They couldn't do that, my dear," he soothed.

" Yes they could! " Susan was quite agitated. " You don't know their type. Glyn's always wanted a son . . . and if he knew about Tony . . ." she left the sentence unfinished. " You needn't worry about me! " she continued bitterly. " I wouldn't come into their plans at all. You see, Glyn's father ' bought me off ' with a very handsome sum. And I accepted it, but only because I knew Tony was on the way. Otherwise I wouldn't have touched a penny of his filthy money." Her voice had risen almost to a shriek. Roger took her hands firmly in his and held them tightly.

" Calm yourself, Sue, there's a good girl, or you'll wake the Munchkin and he'll cry. I realise you've had more than your fair share of trouble, but you must look at the problem from another angle. You're young, you have a bonny child, and you've got to think about him and his future. He needs a fatherly hand to guide him, as well as a mother's love. Don't you see how much better it would be for him to end your unhappy marriage?"

"Glyn can divorce me for desertion after three years are up." Her gaiety was false and bitter, and Roger knew she was close to tears.

"Now, if you were free . . ." he murmured, staring out to sea, "but a man in my position doesn't talk of such things . . ." He cleared his throat and went on in a different tone: "You know, Susan, happiness can be within your grasp, even though you may think it's nowhere near you. Look out there, where the sky meets the sea, in a firm, solid line. That's what happiness is . . . a solid ring surrounding each and every one of us, if we're prepared to notice it."

"Is it?" Susan commented wryly. "How can it be tangible and within our grasp? The sky never actually meets the sea, as we all very well know. No matter where or how far we go in search of it, it's only an illusion. So's happiness . . . a bitter illusion."

"No, darling Sue, it needn't be!" Roger said quickly. "Happiness is where you *want* it to be. If you make up your mind to get fulfilment from life, then happiness comes naturally. On the other hand, if you set out in deliberate pursuit of happiness, then it'll be as you say, just an illusion and forever beyond your grasp." He wrinkled his eyes and stared at her thoughtful face. "Is your future to be over there, where the sky meets the sea, or are you going to pass through life continually searching? Tell me, Sue, I need your answer!"

Bewildered and a little scared at the sudden passion in Roger's voice, Susan murmured:

"You're very sweet, but I'm not the woman for you! Amanda loves you, or didn't you know?"

"Amanda!" His face was stricken and he bit his lip. "What a fool I am not to realise. I should have known she wouldn't joke. The poor, dear child."

"Oh, you exasperate me beyond measure sometimes, Roger! Can't you get it into your head that Amanda isn't a child any longer? She's just as much a woman as I am. Don't hurt her, because of me, I beg you. I'd never forgive you if you did. Give all three of us time. I need it, so do you and Amanda."

"Yes, Susan, you're right. I shouldn't have said what I did."

"Please, please don't tell Amanda that I've told you her secret!" Susan pleaded.

"I won't, I promise. Only I wish in a way I hadn't been made to see the truth . . . fool that I am."

"Be gentle with her, Roger. Very gentle. She's a good girl and lucky will be the man who eventually wins her."

He held her hand very tightly.

"Because I love you, I'll keep my promises."

Susan rose.

"Come on. I think it's high time we went home."

They stared at each other and then broke into spontaneous laughter. With it, and the breeze from the sea, the embarrassment at the revelation of secrets vanished completely.

Chapter Fourteen

FROM that day on, Roger was very careful not to go out alone with Susan, or to call too often at the cottage. She understood his motives and praised him secretly for his determination, yet she missed his gay company. He seemed to sense when Amanda was with Susan, for it was on these occasions that he would visit her and Tony.

The summer came in with a blast of heat which lasted for three whole weeks. The turf on the cliffs grew brown and crackled as the sun baked it. The sea was calm and sparkled with a cobalt blue; a brilliant, peaceful and bottomless expanse of water. The village was inundated with visitors as the holiday season started up again with a swing. The villagers were both flabbergasted and pleased with the number of their visitors.

"There seem to be more this year than ever before!" Amanda's mother declared as she toiled in the kitchen. Both she and Amanda were being overworked, and because Mrs. Porter had had a bad attack of bronchitis during the winter, Roger insisted that she should on no account overtax herself. Susan suggested she should help out instead.

"Oh Sue, would you really?" Amanda cried delightedly. "Do you think you can manage?"

"Of course."

"What about Tony?"

" He'll be all right in his pram in the back garden during the mornings while we're cooking. If I can find someone to mind him after lunch until we close at six, it'd be a great help. He can't be expected to lie in his pram alone all day long. He must have someone to take him out and play with."

In the middle of June, when trade was beginning to get hectic, Susan joined the staff of the " Honeypot ". By this time Tony had become a very active young man, and was taking a great deal of notice of what went on round him. Mrs. Martin, who owned the grocer's shop at the end of the main street, was willing to care for him each afternoon until her daughter, Fiona, came home from school at five, when she took over the task of baby-minding. Mrs. Martin assured Susan that Fiona would be only too delighted to take full charge once the summer holidays started in late July.

Susan enjoyed her new life. She rose very early in the mornings in order to get all her own chores done before wheeling Tony down to the teashop at nine o'clock. The baby had his morning nap in the small garden while Susan and Amanda prepared the dining-room and did the baking for the day's customers. Mrs. Porter did very little in the kitchen, although she was kept busy in the tea-room. When they were open, she sat in a corner at the till while Susan waited at table.

June and July came and went, and August was upon them. Business had never been busier, the two girls being almost rushed off their feet. Teas were served between three and six, but even these hours were filled to capacity, to say nothing of the hours of preparation that went on beforehand. The shop was rarely empty of customers. Susan quickly realised why Amanda had decided not to serve lunches. There would never have been any free time at all for either girl, with the teashop filled for many long hours daily. The dining-room itself was as full as they could allow. Fourteen tables, with four chairs at each, had been packed into the room, leaving just sufficient space for Mrs. Porter's cash desk and room for the girls to pass the customers as they ate.

Amanda's specialities were lobster—and cream teas. The lobsters were purchased from the fishermen on the quay, and all the fancy cakes and dainties were home-made.

The weather continued fine until the end of the second week in August when it broke suddenly in a tremendous thunderstorm. Afterwards, the heat lessened and dull, drizzling days took over from fine, sun-filled ones. The drizzle fell day after day, which gave the two girls a well-earned breathing space because the number of holiday-makers slackened off considerably. It was only the spartan few who braved the weather in mackintoshes and armed with umbrellas to trudge through the rain-soaked village.

It was on one of these afternoons late in August . One couple remained sipping tea and smoking cigarettes as the clock hands crept towards six . . . Mrs. Porter had joined her daughter and Susan in the kitchen where they were also drinking tea and finishing some of the many cakes that were left over. Suddenly the bell on the front door tinkled. Amanda fastened her eyes on the hatch.

" Coming in or going?" Susan asked.

" They'd better not be leaving because they haven't paid yet! " Mrs. Porter murmured.

Susan stood up, and smoothed down her pale green nylon apron.

" I'll see to it."

" It's a man, and he's alone," Amanda told her. " He's gone to the window table."

Susan picked up her note-pad and pushed the swing-door leading into the dining-room. She saw that the newcomer had taken the nearer of the two window tables and was sitting with his back to her, looking out onto the rain-soaked quay beyond. She went up to him, pencil poised.

" Will you order, sir?" she asked.

The man turned and Susan thought she would faint. She went sheet-white and trembled violently.

It was Glyn.

For a moment the world rocked dizzily before it steadied again. Grey eyes held blue, with a depth of unspoken misery and meaning. She could see that he was just as shocked as she was. Masculine mouth quivered as he struggled to find words which refused to come, and the muscles of his left cheek worked frantically.

Very slowly he rose, until he stood looking down at her.

Susan gulped, longing to flee but somehow her feet were stuck to the ground almost as if this was nothing more than a very bad dream.

" Sue! Oh, Sue!" he whispered, his voice thick with emotion.

The spell broken at last, Susan fled, fear lending her wings.

" I'm sorry," she gasped. " Someone else'll come." Then she stumbled into the kitchen, knocking over a chair as she went and oblivious of two pairs of interested eyes that watched her progress from the other table. Amanda jumped as Susan fell against the table, panting hard.

" Whatever's wrong?" she demanded, hurrying to her side.

" I can't tell you now, but I must go home . . . please! At once!" Susan cried, distraught. Amanda made no move to stop her. Susan's eyes were blinded by tears as she ripped off her apron and reached for her mack. Without another word, she opened the door and ran away.

"Well!" Mrs. Porter declared. "Whatever's come over our Sue?"

"Leave this to me, Mother," Amanda advised as her mother started to move towards the tea-room. When she entered it, Glyn walked quickly towards her. She recognised his face but for the moment was unable to place it.

"My wife, where is she?" he demanded anxiously. "I must talk to her."

Of course! Glyn Moore. No wonder Susan had fled in such terror.

"May I come into your kitchen?" he persisted, shepherding her expertly back to the door.

"This way," Amanda said. When the door had swung to behind them both, she went on, "Your wife's gone, Mr. Moore."

"Where? Tell me, where can I find her? Which way did she go?" Glyn was desperate and Amanda's heart went out to him. In the fleeting moment she had come face to face with this man, she had learned one important fact. He was as desperate for his wife as she was for him, although wild horses wouldn't permit her to admit it.

Amanda made up her mind. Susan and Glyn needed each other and must be forced to sort out their differences somehow, and she would help them as much as possible. She told him how to find Susan's cottage. He thanked her, went back into the tea-room for his coat, and then left. Amanda watched him from the swing-door, thinking grimly to herself.

Now try and get yourself out of this little muddle, Susan, my poor misguided friend!

Chapter Fifteen

How Susan reached home, she never knew. She stumbled through the puddles in the narrow, twisting streets, her head lowered to keep the incessant drizzle out of her eyes, and blundered into people. Acquaintances turned to stare after her in amazement when she ignored their greetings. Thrusting the cottage key into the lock, she went inside and slammed the door. She then ran into the kitchen and sank down onto a chair, with her head on the table.

Why had Glyn come here today? What stroke of bad luck had directed his feet to this particular village, or had he known beforehand where to find her? She wanted to cry but shock had dried up all her tears, leaving her throat stiff and sore.

Would he follow her from the 'Honeypot'? If so, what should she say to him? On the other hand, there was no reason for him to come up here to the cottage for he had made it perfectly clear he wanted nothing further to do with her.

The old ship's bell rang.

She stood up slowly, her hands cold and trembling. She must answer the door; it need not necessarily be Glyn outside. As she walked through the small hallway she knew without doubt whom she would find standing on the doorstep. Her hand hovered on the latch, and she wondered if she could thrust the bolt noiselessly, and pretend she was not in. He was a persistent person, and would only return later, so what was the point in postponing their meeting? Better to get it over and done with.

She lifted the latch and drew the door back carefully.

They stared at each other. Glyn's face was inscrutable, although guarded. Her own lips were firm, will-power forcing her to stop their trembling.

" You'd better come in," she said at last.

" Thanks."

She led the way into the sitting-room and stood by the fireplace while Glyn went over to the large window, to look out.

" I should imagine that without this hovering sea mist, you get a magnificent view from here," he began conversationally, trying to break the ice.

" Yes. It is beautiful on a fine day."

There was a silence, then Glyn cleared his throat and turned to face her.

" It was pure chance that brought me to this village to-day."

" Oh?" She tried to sound disinterested.

" Yes. I've been spending a fortnight or so at St. Ives and decided to spend the last few days travelling home slowly to see the countryside as I went. Today I had the impulse to explore the coves and inlets along this part of the south coast. This place was to be my last port of call because I'm due back at work the day after tomorrow."

" So you work now, do you?" Susan's voice was scornful as she remembered past occasions when it had not mattered one iota to him whether he turned up at the office punctually or not. Glyn allowed the remark to pass. He went on:

" The weather's been so poor recently that I felt it was

an excellent opportunity of seeing a few of the places one hasn't time for when the roads are crowded with holiday-makers. Most of the cars I passed were *en route* for the towns and not the coast because of this drizzle."

"You came by car?"

"Yes. I'm permitted to drive again. My licence was suspended for a short time after . . . after the accident. When I'd parked my car farther up the lane leading from the village, I walked around a bit and then saw the 'Honeypot' sign, which reminded me that I was very hungry."

"Another half an hour and you'd have been too late!" she declared fiercely. "We close at six."

"Then it was even more fortuitous I found the tea-shop in time. I think Fate must have brought me here and guided my steps towards you again." He moved to her but she turned away quickly. His voice was vibrant with a great sadness.

"I've had many months in which to think over what I quickly came to realise was over-hasty action. I've missed you, Sue."

"Have you?" She tried to make her tone disinterested. She did not trust Glyn, and was wondering exactly what game he was playing. Watch out for the Mohr cunning! a small voice urged although she longed to throw herself at him and tell him how much she had missed him too. Things were different now. She had pushed him out of her life, it must stay that way.

"Yes," he went on. "After you'd left, and I felt better, I sold that terrible house. Suddenly I began to see it as you had . . . a monstrosity of bricks and mortar, not a home. I also sold all the furniture you'd hated so much. Then I bought a modern house. It's very much smaller, of course, but far easier to run. The tragedy is that it's exactly the kind of place you'd asked me to buy in the very beginning! I think it must have been the passage of time and living away from it that made me realise how appalling the other place was!" He smiled ruefully. " If only I'd done so before we were married then perhaps . . .? But no," he added quickly, his voice firm and brisk. " It wouldn't have made any difference to us."

" So you're not living with your parents after all?" Susan's tone was bitterly sarcastic.

" No. I was mad even to have considered it. Believe me, Sue, it must have been that bang on the head. For months I couldn't bring myself to think coherently. I realise I must have been an extremely difficult person to deal with."

" No more so than before," Susan interrupted spitefully, then bit her lip. " I shouldn't have said that."

However, Glyn appeared completely unruffled.

" As soon as I'd recovered full use of this leg . . . and I don't even limp now . . . I decided to leave my parents. Naturally, there was an awful fuss, but you know, Susan, when you've lived with someone else away from your parents for even a short time, it's very, very difficult to go back to the mode of life you'd had previously. I didn't like being alone."

Susan made no reply. She too knew the meaning of loneliness! How dared he complain that *he* was lonely, almost as if he was blaming her for being responsible!

" How've you been keeping?" he asked, after an awkward pause.

" Quite well, thanks."

Glyn wandered about the room, inspecting the furnishings and knick-knacks. He looked at her, his mouth twisted in a sneer.

"I see you made excellent use of the money you took from Father."

"Please! You're being unfair."

"Am I? It was true, wasn't it? All along you'd deceived me. You hadn't wanted me, while I, like a fool, had flattered myself into thinking I could make you want me. And all the time it was money you were after!" he added bitterly. "I'll tell you something, Susan. There isn't a man on this earth who can stomach the knowledge that he's a failure with the woman he loves. Of course, most of it was my own stupid fault. I realise now how wrong and selfish I'd been. I blamed you for my failure, with the unhappy result that I tried to hurt and bully you into loving me, thereby raising my own ego.

"You were right, of course. From the very beginning you were right! We were totally unsuited and should not have risked marriage. Now do you understand why I'm glad to have met you today? We can sit down and have a sane, unemotional discussion on where we go from here. A separation is neither one thing nor the other, and is consequently useless to us both. I suggest we make a final, clean break."

"Divorce?"

"Naturally. What other course lies open?"

"I see." Susan paused, then asked: "Do you wish to remarry, is that it?"

"I've no one in mind at the moment, but it's quite possible both of us may want to marry someone else in the near future."

Susan looked down at her hands.

"I suppose it might happen . . . one day," she said in a small voice, although she knew she would never want to.

"Can I rent a room in the village?" Glyn asked.

"There's an inn. I expect they'll have a free room."

" Good. Then I suggest I stay there tonight and we'll meet in the morning to discuss the matter of a divorce."

" It'll have to be very early. I start work at nine. I'm sure Amanda won't mind if I spare you an hour from nine till ten."

" You needn't worry about evidence, Susan. I'll provide it if you wish. Save you the embarrassment."

" Indeed? Surely such action on your part won't exactly meet with your parents' approval?" she enquired, her voice heavy with sarcasm. Glyn was about to protest when they both heard the front door open and Fiona's cheerful voice.

Tony!

Susan knew panic. She had forgotten time was passing so swiftly. What a fool she'd been to let Glyn into the cottage in the first place! If he should see Tony, or even find out about him, he'd know at once whose child he was because the baby was growing more and more like his father every day. What could she do?

Nothing. It was far, far too late.

Perhaps Fiona would take Tony straight upstairs, then Glyn could be whisked out of the house before he found out.

In the hallway Fiona chattered to Tony, and the child laughed gaily. Glyn frowned suddenly, and looked searchingly at Susan who was standing in the middle of the room, her hand at her throat, and a terrified expression on her face.

Then the worst happened. Fiona opened the door and came in, carrying Tony. She caught sight of Glyn, and stopped, confused.

" I'm sorry, Mrs. Moore. I didn't realise you had a guest. I'll take Tony straight upstairs, shall I? I can stay to put him to bed, if you'd like me to."

" Yes. Yes, please, Fiona," Susan replied wildly. The girl turned to leave the room but it was now that Tony asserted his own authority. He suddenly decided he wanted his mother. His face wrinkled with disgust and he thrust out both arms, crying:

" Mmmmmmumumum! "

Fiona smiled and patted his back gently. She carried him over to Susan.

" I'm sorry, Mrs. Moore, it seems he wants you for a moment before I take him up to bed. There you are, my poppet, Mummy'll have you."

Tony burbled and bounced delightedly, clinging onto Susan's neck and dribbling down her cheek. Then he turned to beam at Glyn.

Susan was watching her husband's reaction, and she saw the unmistakable signs of strain and shock. He gripped the back of the armchair until his knuckles stood out very white. His eyes were bleak and his mouth quivered. Then he blinked rapidly four or five times . . .

" Thank you for bringing him home, Fiona. You needn't stay now. I'll put him to bed."

" That's all right, Mrs. Moore. You know I love doing anything for this gorgeous little man! " Fiona came over to Susan and kissed Tony's chubby cheek. She turned to Glyn and smiled; " He's a beautiful baby, isn't he, sir?"

Glyn's mouth had steadied into a hard, white line, but he managed to nod to Fiona before she left.

Susan decided to forestall his comments.

" Glyn, Tony's *our* son," she said shakily. Glyn flinched and came over to her, put his hand under the baby's chin and turned his head fully towards him. Naturally, Tony resented this high-handed treatment. He pursed up his mouth and began to cry before cringing back to the safety of Susan's neck. From then on, he kept casting suspicious glances at his father.

"Now you've frightened him!" Susan scolded Glyn.

"If I'd had any doubts when the girl brought the baby in just now, they've been dispelled. I've only had to look at him closely to see he's indeed my own son. He even has my colouring!" he declared angrily as if it was a personal affront. Susan could not help a smile.

"Children have a habit of taking after their parents, you know. Tony's always been more like you than me, ever since he was born."

"And when was that?" Glyn demanded.

"I . . . oh, I see what you mean. Tony arrived on January 22nd."

Glyn looked at her quickly and she could see him doing some rapid mental calculations.

"Then . . . and you say he's my child . . . yet how can he be?" he murmured. "Unless . . . unless," he paced the room, frowning so hard that the devil's eyebrows met and blended. Suddenly he looked at her. "It must have been sometime near the accident. It could only be then . . . it must have been! It's impossible, because we hadn't been sharing beds for months before the car smash." He resumed his pacing, while Susan watched him.

"Sue, I don't quite know how to say this, but has Tony anything to do with our quarrel? I realise I ought to know but I don't! Confound it, Susan, those lost hours are still quite blank. You must tell me! Did I force you to make love to me a short time before the accident? Did I? Tell me, *did* I?" He had raised his voice and Tony started whimpering again.

"Yes, yes, yes!" Susan yelled back at him. "But it's of no importance now. I have Tony, and until you came here today we were both happy. Now please go, Glyn. I want to put him to bed. I can't speak to you tonight. Oh, please, please . . . *go!*" Her own eyes were full of tears, and the baby was clinging so tightly around her neck that she was almost choking.

Glyn swallowed hard.

"Very well, Susan, I'll leave. I hope you realise what a tremendous shock this has been to me, but we'll talk about it in the morning . . . early."

"Yes, yes. In the morning. We'll thrash it out tomorrow."

Chapter Sixteen

Susan hardly slept at all that night. Her encounter with Glyn had been so completely unexpected; she felt as though she had stepped heedlessly into a quagmire and was now sinking slowly. Glyn had made it abundantly clear that he wanted a divorce. Almost from the moment he had stepped inside the cottage she had known he had not come to ask her to return to him, but now there was another, far more terrible dread in her mind. Until today he had been in ignorance about the baby. Unfortunately, since he now knew Tony existed, and was his own son, it was impossible not to believe he would try to take him away from her.

She spent hours tossing and turning on her bed, wondering. Then common sense reasserted itself to remind her that a very young baby's place was with its mother.

What about the proposed divorce? Would Glyn now try to win custody of Tony so that his son would be brought up in the way he stipulated? If this was the plan, then she was prepared to fight him tooth and nail to keep her child.

Just before dark that evening, Amanda had called at the cottage.

"I know Mr. Moore has gone," she began. "I saw him go into the inn. May I come in?"

"Of course." Wearily Susan held the door for her friend.

"Please don't think I'm being nosy, but I felt you might

like someone to talk to after the sudden encounter with your husband."

"Yes. Yes, I must talk to you," Susan had agreed and together the two girls had sat long into the night talking. Amanda commented little, until she had asked:

"What are you going to do?"

"I just don't know! I suppose I'd better wait until the morning to hear what Glyn's proposing. Oh, how I *wish* he hadn't seen Tony!"

"He'd have found out sometime, you know, Sue," Amanda told her tactfully. "I know everything looks very bad at the moment, but something's bound to turn up."

"You don't know Glyn!" Susan had wailed miserably.

"No, I don't. From the little I've seen of him, I didn't get the impression he was planning to hurt you. Far from it."

"Really? Which all goes to show how little you *do* know about him! I've been tricked in the past, and I'm not going to allow him to get his own way ever again. Especially where Tony's concerned."

"Go to bed, Sue, you look absolutely worn out. Shall I get you anything before I leave?"

Susan had declined.

"Then I'll leave you to your thoughts."

"I might be a little late at the shop in the morning, if that's all right with you?"

"You come along whenever you and Glyn have finished your discussion. Mother and I can cope for a few hours." Amanda had gone to the door to let herself out, then she turned to say: "Oh, Sue, I've a suggestion. Wouldn't it be easier if I came up here about half past eight and took Tony off your hands? Then his presence won't be an added distraction while you're with your husband."

"Would you? That *is* a load off my mind."

Early the following morning Susan began to tidy away as much evidence of Tony's occupation as she could find. His bricks and toys she put out of sight in a cupboard, the mending was pushed into a corner of the bedroom instead of being left in its usual pile on the table beside her armchair. The only items she was obliged to leave was a clothes-line of nappies fluttering in the breeze outside the back door, but men never noticed that kind of thing.

Amanda arrived to collect Tony in his pram at twenty-five past eight, after which Susan sat down to wait for Glyn. She picked up a book to pass the time but her eyes were for ever straying towards the clock.

Why, oh why did time drag so?

After what seemed hours of impatient waiting, Glyn eventually arrived a few minutes past nine o'clock. Once inside the cottage he looked round hopefully, then scowled.

"Where's my son?" he demanded, his voice arrogant.

"With friends. I thought it better we should be alone while discussing our matrimonial problem. Glyn, I haven't much time, so I'd be grateful if we got straight down to business. I ought really to be at work by now."

"I see. By the way, one small but very important point. What happens to our child while you work?"

Susan explained the arrangements she had made.

"Do you honestly think it's a good idea?" he asked.

"Yes. I'm helping Amanda and her mother who have been very good to me ever since I arrived here last year. At the same time I'm earning a small wage. Tony's also well cared for. He sleeps in his pram most of the morning, a thing he'd do in any case, whether I went to work or not, and then he has the company of other young children after I've given him his dinner. Fiona's brother and sisters love Tony and are very good for him, I'm certain."

"What of the future? Do you intend to continue living in this way?"

"For a while, yes. The summer season ends soon, then I'll be free to be with Tony all the time. Next summer, of course, he'll be very much more active and walking. He'll be able to play with the other village children by then. As soon as he's old enough to go to the local primary school, I'll be able to think about getting some other kind of job."

"I understand." Suddenly he swung round on her and snapped, "Why the hell didn't you tell me you were pregnant?" Susan jumped, then reminded him:

"I tried to, Glyn. I wanted to come and tell you in person if you think back, only your father refused to allow me near his house. He told me that *you* couldn't be bothered with me any more," she added, the scorn in her voice cutting him like a knife. "After that I knew how useless it was to go on trying to tell you. I thought I'd probably be able to struggle along on my own somehow or other, then your father offered me a large sum of money."

"Which you accepted without any hesitation whatsoever, so he informed me!" Glyn's voice was hard and bitter. Susan's eyes widened.

"But of course! It was the most natural thing to do, to take that money. Don't you understand? It came as the answer to all my worries, therefore I was able to take it without any qualms of conscience because I meant to use it solely for the baby. I invested most of it and have managed to live reasonably well, as long as I go carefully, on the small income it's brought me."

"You had money in your own banking account! The account I opened for you when we married. Why didn't you use that as well?"

"I did."

"Only to send regular monthly gifts to your mother." Susan turned from him. "Oh yes, Sue, I know all about it. I had a heated argument with the bank manager and, in the end, he grudgingly told me what I needed to know about your money. I wanted to give you more, and I even tried to reach you through him, but he refused to tell me where he thought you must have gone."

"Under my instructions, naturally, although I was careful not to tell him exactly where I was going to live. Still, he might have guessed to within a radius of ten miles or so."

"Why didn't you use the money I gave you?" Glyn demanded angrily. "Why continue to give it to your mother when your own need was greater? Damn it all, you're my wife and have the right to sufficient money for our child!"

"I didn't think so. I didn't want to touch any money that came from you."

"I was bitterly shocked on learning you hadn't touched a penny for yourself," he stated unhappily.

Susan swung away from the mantelpiece and crossed to the chair nearest him where she stood looking down at him as he sat on the settee.

"Of course you were shocked . . . but only because on discovering that I *wasn't* using it, you had the uneasy feeling that perhaps I hadn't married you for your money after all! I had my pride, Glyn. I wasn't going to be dependent on you any longer."

"A damned silly kind of pride, I must say!" he snapped angrily. "I'm your husband and you'd a right to that money."

"As I'd a right to everything else of yours, including your companionship and a share of your household, perhaps?" Susan jeered.

Glyn lowered his gaze, ashamed.

" I'm sorry, Sue. I did wrong. I acted too hastily in accepting my parents' offer of care. I ought to have thought more of you and less of myself."

" You may be apologetic now, but you were perfectly clear-headed and adamant when you made your original decision not to come home to me. Anyway, where the money was concerned, I felt your father owed me every penny he offered . . . and more . . . He had set out to drive a wedge between us, and he'd succeeded very well indeed. Beyond his wildest hopes and dreams, in fact." Susan raised her chin determinedly.

" Oh yes, Glyn Mohr, I'd have taken all of your father's fortune, had he offered it, yet your own money I wouldn't have touched. Wild horses couldn't have made me! I had to keep up my small contribution to my mother, though."

" What a strange girl you are! "

" No, I'm not. It's quite possible I prefer to stretch the pennies rather than be censured by Mother."

" Sue, I saw her a few months ago," Glyn said slowly.

" Oh? How . . . how was she?"

" Quite well, and very sorry to have received your letter."

" Did . . . did she say anything to you about it?" Susan asked with reluctance. Glyn looked at her thoughtfully.

" As a matter of fact, she did. She said that when I found you I was to tell you that until you could learn to love your husband as you should . . . as she had told you . . . then she'd rather you didn't come to see her again." Susan turned away, biting her lip. " I'm sorry, my dear, but she wasn't too pleased with *either* of us! As a matter of fact, I rather threw myself at her mercy, begging her to tell me where I could find you. But she didn't know."

Susan's hands began to shake and she had to clasp them firmly together. " Yes, my dear, hasn't it occurred to you that I might have wanted to find you in order to sort out our affairs?"

"No. I'm afraid I never thought of it like that."

Glyn continued more cheerfully.

"Yet your poor mother knew as little as I did."

Susan suddenly laughed.

"After all the elaborate precautions I took to keep our paths separate! I needn't have bothered, need I? Fate steps in and plays her dirty trick by showing you exactly where to find me. Bang! Just like that. Oh, cruel, cruel Destiny. Why, oh why did you have to come here?" she cried, her voice harsh and bitter.

There was a long pause before Glyn said:

"Yesterday, when we met, I told you I wanted to discuss divorce. At the time I was unaware I had a son."

"What difference does it make to the divorce?" Susan demanded hastily, fear pounding in her chest. "You can't take him away from me, because I won't let you! Anyway, the Court would never allow such a thing."

"Susan! Will you *please* let me finish what I'd started to say? Yesterday I didn't know about Tony, but today I see that divorce is completely out of the question."

Susan's heart leapt uncontrollably. What was he getting at now? "Why?" she asked, guardedly.

Glyn looked at her, his expression unfathomable.

"It's out of the question because I want my son. I'm not going to allow you to have sole charge of him," he added firmly.

Susan gasped with horror.

"I . . . I," she began, then stopped, at a loss for words.

"All night I've lain awake thinking about you and the baby. Fortunately I came to this conclusion. For all our sakes, but mainly for the child's, I want you to leave here and come home with me. Back to my new house where Tony can be raised by both his parents guiding and caring for him."

"How strange you should say such a thing!" she mused almost to herself. "Someone else used almost the same argument to me not so very long ago. I mean, where Tony and I are concerned . . . Tony needing a father as well as a mother."

"Who said it?" Glyn demanded, suspicion on his face.

"A friend . . . a very dear friend," Susan replied haughtily.

"Male?"

Susan did not reply.

"I see." Glyn cleared his throat. "I've made my proposition. I'm asking you to come back with me so we may live together again and have the enjoyment of bringing up our own child."

Susan threw back her head and laughed gaily. Glyn lurched towards her, grabbed her arms and shook her hard.

"Stop it! Stop it at once! You're hysterical."

"I'm not. I'm just highly amused." Carefully she removed his restraining hands and moved away from him, all laughter gone. "You're so two-faced! Less than eighteen hours ago, you stood in this very room telling me in detail why you thought we should get divorced. This morning, however, we've a complete change of tune, and all because you've discovered you'd been a father for seven months. Today you're asking me to come and live with you again." She went over to him, demanding angrily:

"What do you think I am? I'm not prepared to make the same mistake twice, even if you are. As you so very, very kindly explained yesterday, we just don't belong together, and I'm really interested in your wealth. Face the truth, Glyn. You don't want *me*! You feel you have to ask me because I'm the commodity which comes with the baby, but he's the only one you really want, isn't he? Let me say one thing, Glyn Mohr, for seven months Tony and I've got on extremely well, each needing the other, and no one else. We've sufficient money to keep us, as long as I'm careful. We've made our lives in this village, and are happy in them. Why, I've even altered the spelling of our surname to get away from my memories! M-O-O-R-E. Don't disrupt everything now, please! For many reasons, most of them too complicated and personal to explain at the moment, I just don't want to go back with you. I'm used to living here and I'm set in my ways because I like living here. So please go away and leave us alone, will you? Tony's still a baby. We shall not run away, I promise, but let's go ahead with the divorce as you suggested yesterday. You wanted it, you said so. I expect the Court will allow you reasonable access to Tony."

" I want my child all the time! " Glyn stated harshly.

" Oh no, that I can't permit. You'd have to fight me in court before I allowed you to take him away from me." She touched his arm, her voice now gentle. " Be reasonable, Glyn. There's still over a year to run before you can sue me for desertion. Get your divorce then, I won't try to stop you, although I'll fight to keep Tony." Her eyes were alight with the fire of battle. " He's my baby and no one, not even you, shall take him from me! I certainly don't want to live with you again, so you can forget that idea. It'd be inflicting utter misery on both of us because you told me *it wouldn't work*."

" Yesterday I thought differently," he mumbled.

" Nothing important's changed. How could it?" Susan gripped Glyn's arm fiercely. She felt tongues of fire sweep upward as she touched his firm muscles beneath the coat sleeve. If she gave in now all would be lost.

"Glyn, please, please leave us alone!" she implored.

"Very well, Susan, I know when I'm beaten. I'll do as you wish. I'll not force you to come with me."

Suddenly he smiled.

"Don't look so scared, Sue. I'll not hurt you or him, but I want you to promise not to refuse me permission to see Tony should I come back to the village any time. Just before I go, may I see Tony?" he asked gently.

"Yes, Glyn. I can't prevent you seeing Tony if you're here. But how often will that be? You have your work in Town. Or are you..." she stopped.

"I knew you probably wouldn't believe me if I told you but I now work regular hours each week, Monday to Saturday. Quite a surprise, isn't it?"

"After the accident I learned many home truths, one of them resulting in my decision to earn a salary by honest, hard work. Secondly, I've forsaken all forms of alcohol..."

"But you weren't drunk that night! I don't care what they said, you were *not* drunk..."

"Whether I was or not, I've taken a distinct disliking for the stuff. Many's the occasion in the past when I *have* come very near to one too many, whatever you say. In the meantime, you'll oblige me by accepting a cheque."

"I... I," she began, then shut her mouth. Glyn unscrewed his gold fountain-pen, looking at her wistfully.

"I'll not insult you by giving you money, but please take this, as a gift for Tony."

"Not... not too much," she begged.

"Here are my home and office telephone numbers, in case you need them."

"I doubt it."

"Sue! I know you distrust me, and I can't say I blame you. However, I want you to have this. Of course, you may never need to ring me, but if Tony should be ill, or you yourself need something urgently, then you can call on me at once."

Susan pouted.

"As Tony's father I have a right to be told immediately if anything's wrong," Glyn declared angrily. They walked down the hill into the village in silence. Neighbours nodded greetings and stared with interest at Glyn.

"Do you know everyone?" he asked, smiling.

"Most of them. Here we are." Susan opened the gate into the garden behind the 'Honeypot'. Tony lay in his pram, fast asleep. Glyn bent over him, the eagerness leaving his face and keen disappointment taking its place.

"I won't stay, Sue. I mustn't wake him now, must I?" He stared down at the angelic sleeping face with its golden wisps of hairs, and a slow delighted smile lightened his expression. Susan saw the gentle wistfulness and her heart quivered.

Glyn broke the silence.

"Goodbye, Susan." he said and turned away from the pram. "I'll let you know in good time when I'll next be in the village. I don't expect I can make it before three weeks."

He hurried away. Susan stayed to watch him, hoping he would turn back to wave, but he did not do so. Then she went into the kitchen where Amanda and her mother were waiting, their faces eager.

"Well?" said Amanda. "We saw you through the window, deep in conversation. What's been decided?"

"Amanda!" her mother remonstrated.

Susan smiled, knowing neither would be satisfied until they had been told what she and Glyn had decided.

"He doesn't want a divorce, not now he knows about Tony," she explained. 'He asked me to go back to him, but only for Tony's sake."

"You agreed, naturally," Amanda commented.

"Goodness, no! Why should I?"

"Because you love him, of course."

Susan blushed furiously.

"That has nothing to do with it. I admit I do love him, but he mustn't ever know because he plainly doesn't want me. He told me so yesterday when we talked of divorce."

"What other plans has he?"

"Nothing at the moment, or so he said. He wants to see the baby again and I've agreed."

Amanda regarded her friend with one eyebrow raised.

"All right, then, you tell me, Amanda! How can I stop Glyn seeing Tony?" Susan demanded.

The other girl wagged a floury finger at her.

"Surely this is the point, do you really want to stop him?"

Susan shuffled her feet.

"No. No, of course not. All I want is for Glyn to find out that he wants me just as much, if not more, than he wants Tony. But at the moment," she finished sadly, "I figure very little in his thoughts."

"Huh!" Amanda scoffed.

"What do you mean . . . 'huh!'?"

"Nothing. Just huh!"

Chapter Seventeen

SUSAN did not return to the 'Honeypot' for four days. Tony was by no means his usual smiling self. He was teasy and fretful, and dribbled a great deal.

Susan suggested to Fiona that she go up to the cottage to look after Tony for a couple of days rather than allow the child to spread his cold germs around the rest of her family. Fiona agreed and called at the tea-shop to collect the pram after lunch. Before she left, Susan promised to be home as early as she could that evening.

Unfortunately, luck was against her that Wednesday. At five o'clock a coachload of trippers arrived on their doorstep, demanding tea.

Susan was kept busy hurrying in and out of the kitchen with dirty crockery and fresh plates piled high with cakes and buns and teapots that always seemed to need replenishing. It was with considerable surprise, therefore, that she saw the back door open and Fiona rush into the kitchen, panting hard. Alarm filled her.

"Mrs. Moore...come quickly! Oh, please come quickly!" she cried, tugging at Susan's arm. Two cups fell off the tray to shatter on the floor as Susan slammed it down on the table. Amanda's mother turned from the sink where she was washing dishes and stared at the distraught young girl.

"What's happened?" Susan gasped. "Tony! Where is he?"

"They're taking him away. Oh, please let's be quick before it's too late."

"I tried to stop them. I said he'd just had a bad cold and was going to bed, but they wouldn't listen. The woman dressed him again after I'd finished the bath. They said they were his grandparents, and that they'd come to take him back to his rightful home."

Susan stopped dead.

"Fiona! The cottage!" she called. When she reached the garden she saw the front door standing open. She dashed inside shouting Tony's name. The pram in the hall stood empty. Even the rugs and blankets were missing. She went into the lounge and stared down at the floor. The playpen stood as Fiona had left it when she had taken Tony up for his bath. Bricks lay higgledy-piggledy on the carpet while Tony's teddy bear rested face down under the table. She ran upstairs to look into the bathroom and Tony's bedroom, both of which were empty. She came down again and went into the lounge. Then she dropped onto the settee.

Fiona joined her. She was crying bitterly.

"I'd just brought him down from the bathroom in his dressing-gown and sleeping suit. We were playing together on the floor when ... they came. I opened the front door, then that ... that awful woman marched right in and demanded to know where the baby was." She gripped Susan's arm.

"Oh, I tried to stop them, really I did, but I didn't know whether I ought to stay with Tony or come straight for you."

Susan drew the girl close and folded her arms around

her, holding her tightly.

"There, there, my dear, you did all you could. You were very brave and sensible. It wasn't your fault at all. I ought to have guessed something like this would happen."

"You'll never forgive me!" Fiona wailed.

"There's nothing to forgive. I know you did everything in your power to protect Tony. I know both the persons concerned, and I think you stood up to them marvellously."

Fiona caught sight of the teddy bear under the table. She bent down to pick it up. Then she gave it to Susan.

"Look, they've left his little teddy! He'll be miserable without it."

Susan held the toy to her cheek. At that moment there was a screeching of brakes outside the cottage. Susan's heart leapt. Was it possible her in-laws had had a change of heart and were now returning?

Together they dashed out into the hall and Fiona pulled open the front door. It was Roger. Fiona hung onto his arm and poured out an incoherent tale. His face was grim. He went at once to Susan and put his arm round her, leading her back to the settee. She leaned against him, weeping.

"Amanda phoned me and told me to get up here at once. What's all this Fiona's been saying about young Tony?"

Through her sobs Susan began the story. Throughout it all, Roger smoothed her hair gently.

"There, darling!" he murmured.

"Oh, Roger, I trusted Glyn!" she wailed reproachfully. "Fool that I was, I should have known better. He never did allow anything to stand in the way of what he wanted."

"Calm yourself, Sue. We'll get Tony back. His place is with you, his mother. Now, tell me, is there any way in which you can contact Glyn?"

"Yes! He made me take his phone numbers."

"Splendid." Roger stood up and helped her to her feet. Then he put his other arm round Fiona and gave her a comforting hug. "I'll drive you straight down to my place where you shall ring him. The sooner you two talk the better."

In Roger's cottage, Roger dialled the exchange and asked for the number of Glyn's office.

"I hope he hasn't gone home yet!" Susan murmured, wringing her hands anxiously.

"Mr. Moore please!" Roger snapped. "Mrs. Moore . . . it's urgent . . . Well, find him girl!"

Almost immediately Glyn was on the line. Silently Susan took the receiver from Roger.

"Susan, is something wrong?"

"You know there is. Glyn, I want Tony back . . . tonight," she demanded fiercely.

"I'm sorry. I'm not with you. What do you mean?"

Her voice rose hysterically.

"You know right well what I mean. You're to bring Tony home at once."

"I'm awfully sorry, Sue, dear, but I honestly don't get it. Want Tony back . . . why? Is he ill, or something?"

She stamped her foot impatiently.

"Stop fooling, Glyn," she hissed. "You needn't pretend with me. I know quite well you used your parents to come and take Tony away from me."

There was a sudden, shocked pause. She heard Glyn gasp. Then he said in a voice of ice:

"Tell my parents to take Tony away from you? O
course not, stupid!" He was now furiously, blindly, an
gry, and Susan quivered as he spat the words at her
"Haven't I given you my promise that I wouldn't ask fo
Tony just yet? I think you'd better be more explicit."

She began to cry bitterly.

"Then ... then it's nothing to do with you at all?" He
voice faltered. Roger took the receiver from her and said

"Mr. Moore. This is Dr. Harlow, Susan's practitioner
Less than half an hour ago, a man and a woman, whom
Susan assured me are your own parents, forced their way
into Susan's home, terrified the young girl whom Susan
had left in charge of her baby, and took the child away
with them. The baby-sitter did her very best to dissuade
you parents but they over-ruled her ... rudely, too, i
would appear. She rushed to fetch your wife, but by the
time they got back to the cottage, your parents had
left ... with the baby."

Susan could hear the angry exclamation and torrent o
words on the other end of the line.

"I might also add, Mr. Moore, that the child has beer
under my care recently, and I consider it extremely inad
visable to have taken him out in a car at the present time
I cannot stress strongly enough how vital it is for Tony te
be returned with all speed to his mother."

Glyn now spoke at length.

"Yes ... yes, Mr. Moore ... I'll do that ... very
well ... then we'll leave it entirely in your
hands ... Thank you." Roger put the receiver back into
Susan's hands, and she listened eagerly.

"Sue, you're not to worry, understand?" Glyn said
"Your doctor will look after you until I arrive later to
night. You're not to do anything until I'm with you."

Chapter Eighteen

ROGER took Susan back to the cottage where he made her a cup of tea and gave her a sedative. Outside the gate, the police constable waited, while eager faces in the neighbouring cottages watched the comings and goings.

"Good evenin', sir. Anything I can do for the lady?"

"No thank you, Frank. Everything's well under control."

"Ay. So the County Office told me. Seems the gentleman's called on us to stop the car. I expect they'll catch it at the Tamar Bridge."

The hours passed slowly. Amanda did her knitting while Susan lay staring up at the ceiling, saying nothing. The sun set and it became dark. Shortly after twelve, they heard a car coming up the road.

"Is it . . .?" she faltered, her hand at her throat. Her knees were shaking. She felt too weak to move.

"I can't quite make it out," said Amanda peering out into the darkness, "but I think it's your husband." She saw him open the rear door, lean inside and pick up a large bundle, wrapped in rugs. She turned a radiant face to Susan.

"Sue! He's got Tony!"

With wings on her feet, Susan rushed out into the hall and threw open the front door. Then she dashed down the garden path to meet Glyn.

"Tony! Tony!" she cried joyfully. They met, but Susan had eyes only for her child.

"Careful, he's fast asleep," Glyn warned. "Completely worn out, the poor little fellow." Then he placed the sleeping baby into his wife's open arms.

"He's safe, oh, he's safe! My darling baby." She pressed her cheek softly against the sleeping child.

Amanda came out, put her arm round Susan's waist and led her back to the cottage, followed by Glyn.

"Sue, darling, hadn't you better put him straight to bed?" she advised.

Tony stirred, opened his eyes and began to wail. He blinked up at Susan then recognised her. This seemed to reassure him completely, for he turned away at once and promptly went to sleep again.

Glyn touched her shoulder.

"Your friend's right, dear. Tony ought to be in bed."

Susan looked at him for the first time since he had given her back her child. Until that moment it had been as if he hadn't existed. Now she was filled with a surge of compassion for her neglect.

"Oh, Glyn, how can I ever thank you?" she murmured.

"We'll discuss that later," he said, and put his hand under her arm to guide her to the narrow staircase.

Amanda disappeared into the kitchen. A minute later there was a knock at the front door. She hurried to open it, admitting Roger.

"The child's home?"

"Yes. Upstairs with Sue."

"In that case I'd rather make sure he's all right before she tucks him in."

He took the stairs two at a time and went into Tony's room. She smiled gaily at him.

"Just a quick check before you finish," he said, pulling out his stethoscope. He made a rapid examination, then nodded. "No harm's been done, as far as I can tell. However, I'll pop in and see him first thing in the morning."

Roger joined the other two in the lounge. Glyn looked up hopefully as he entered the room.

"Your son's none the worse for his adventure," Roger told him.

"Thank heaven!"

"Mr. Mohr, naturally you won't be driving back to town at once will you? May my mother and I offer you a bed for the rest of the night? The inn's closed at this hour. They'll all have gone to bed ages ago."

"That's very kind of you, Miss Porter."

"Amanda, please."

"Amanda. I'll gladly accept your offer. I was a little worried because naturally Sue doesn't want me here. Are you quite sure I won't be causing you any inconvenience?"

Amanda reassured him and Susan entered the room, her face radiating her joy. She was handed a cup of tea which Roger had liberally sugared beforehand.

"Ugh!' she said, grimacing. "Far too sweet."

"Drink it up," Roger ordered. Glyn looked at him and caught the gentle expression of love. So that was it! The doctor was the man Susan loved.

"Now please tell us, how did you find Tony?" Susan asked Glyn.

"As soon as you'd rung off, I rang the police. I realised they'd be the only ones with authority to halt my parent's car. I soon learned that the car had been stopped on the

Tamar Bridge. Arriving there, I found Father ranting
and raging and Mother hysterical." He scowled. "By the
time I'd finished what I had to say to them, they were
even more displeased. I want you to understand, Sue, before we go any further, that I'd no idea whatsoever of
their plans. When I arrived home after seeing you recently, I was too pleased with the knowledge that I was a
father to worry over their reactions. Both of them did
their utmost to persuade me to come back here and remove Tony from your care. I refused, explaining that
what you and I did was entirely up to us and no one else.
I've very little doubt that my father's fertile brain
hatched today's plot. And Mother simply cannot see that
they'd done wrong! She only wanted to surprise me, by
giving me back my son. Even though I argued and
argued, she refuses to see it from your point of view. Tony
is my child and, according to her, he should be living
either in my house or in hers, with a nanny to care for
him."

"They've now driven off home in a fearful huff. I simply cannot understand my mother! How on earth she
thought I'd care for a child while I'm at work all day, I
don't know! Anyway, it's over now. I'm master in my own
home, and intend it to stay that way. What I decide to do
with my own son is my business . . . and yours too, my
dear." He smiled at Susan and squeezed her hand
quickly. She looked at him searchingly while Amanda
glanced at Roger who was showing signs of jealousy. She
stepped in at once.

"Sue, I've already told Glyn he can have a bed at the
'Honeypot'."

"Thanks, Amanda."

"I'll drive you home," Roger murmured while Amanda

turned to Glyn.

"I'll leave with you, I expect poor Sue's dead tired and wants to go to bed after such a worrying evening." He went over to Susan who was now standing at the table, collecting cups and putting them on the tea-tray. "Sleep well, my dear. I'm quite sure Tony'll be none the worse for his outing."

"What can I say, Glyn, except... thank you, from the bottom of my heart." He took her hands and held them very tightly. His voice was slightly husky.

"Nonsense! I'll call early in the morning. It'll have to be before nine, I'm afraid."

"Do you... do you have to return so soon?" Susan asked, with a twinge of disappointment.

"Yes. I'm sorry, but there's nothing I can do about it... much as I'd like to," he added softly.

Glyn's car arrived outside the cottage just after eight. He followed Susan into the kitchen where she was in the middle of giving Tony his breakfast.

"Do you mind helping Tony while I work around? Take care, though, he has a horrid habit of upending the cup when my back's turned. I'll make the tea."

Glyn sat down beside Tony who watched him thoughtfully. Suddenly he gurgled and smiled sunnily. Then he thrust a sodden rusk straight into his father's eye. Susan laughed.

"You're now his friend for life!"

"I'm glad. What about you?" he went on, looking at her. She turned away, confused, and fussed with the kettle.

"Sue, I want to talk to you. The milk's gone and he seems to have finished eating. Shall I put him in his play-pen for a few minutes?"

"Please."

She sat at the table and poured out a second cup of coffee.

"You might as well drink it while we talk," she said, replenishing her own.

"Sue, first of all, I promise that there'll never, never be a recurrence of yesterday's pantomime. We needn't worry about my parents. I'm certain they won't dare interfere again. As I told you when we met, I am prepared to wait, but since yesterday my opinions have changed. We'll have to make up our minds one way or the other sooner than agreed. This is my plan. I'll take leave of absence for about ten days, depending on how work goes. I intend staying here in the village ... at the inn." he added pointedly as her eyes widened apprehensively.

"During this time I suggest we see as much of each other as we can, so that we may decide for certain whether there's any possibility of our living together again.

"We must try to see the problem from the other's angle. At the end of my visit, I'm confident we'll have had sufficient time to make up our minds."

"And I give you my word of honour now, Sue, that if you still find you can't bear the thought of coming back to live with me again, then I'll go away ... for good. I'll make no more claims on Tony ... and I'll also provide the necessary evidence so that you may divorce me. That's a fair bargain, isn't it?"

"Oh, Glyn!" her voice was sorrowful.

"Yes, it'll be a wrench for me but I'll weather it if you give me your word now that you'll make an honest effort to see this from my angle. Will you Sue?" "Yes, Glyn. Of course I will."

"And, as I've said, at the end, if you still want to live

alone, then I won't prevent you. On the other hand, if you decide you'd like to come back to me, I promise I'll make no unnecessary demands on you. We have one child, and I'll be content to leave it so."

"Glyn ... if, if I can't bring myself to return to you, you'll understand and forgive me, won't you?"

"Naturally." His voice had become hard.

"That doesn't sound over-convincing!" she chided him gently, then added: "Promise me that you'll try to see how I feel about all this?"

"Yes."

"Good."

"Then it's all settled?"

She nodded.

"I'll write and let you know which day to expect me. And, remember, Sue, they'll be the most important days of our lives." He stood up. "Thermos ready? I must go now."

He kissed the baby's chubby hand and gave Susan's arm a gentle squeeze.

"Goodbye, Sue."

She swallowed.

"'Bye, Glyn."

He started the engine, then leaned towards her again, his face tense and anxious.

"Oh, and Sue, you'll give me a fair chance?" She nodded.

"I will."

"Splendid. 'Bye!"

Glyn smiled and drove away. Susan saw him look in the mirror and this time he raised a hand to her before the car rounded the corner.

Chapter Nineteen

SUSAN began to feel like a girl again. Each morning
before she took Tony down to the tea-shop, she would
watch for the postman. Then at last, the longed-for letter
arrived. She ripped open the envelope impatiently and
quickly read Glyn's untidy handwriting.

He was taking fourteen days' leave, not ten, and expected to reach the village some time in the early evening
on Saturday ... in four days! He told her he had wanted
to make it a late Friday arrival but pressure of work obliged him to spend a few hours in the office on Saturday.

As Saturday approached, Susan decided to keep Tony
up until after Glyn's arrival, as long as it was no later than
seven o'clock. After all, wasn't the child the reason for her
husband's visit?

On Saturday, Susan left the 'Honeypot' at half-past
four and collected Tony from Fiona. She took him home
and gave him his tea. It was therefore a complete surprise
to find Glyn on her doorstep shortly before five.

"Come in," she told him. "I didn't expect you so soon.
We were coming down to the quay to surprise you. It was
a special treat for Tony. I'll get you some tea."

After he had finished tea, they played with Tony until
it ws time for Susan to take him upstairs for a bath. Glyn
remained in the lounge. Later, Susan reappeared in the

doorway, her towelling apron soaked.

"Glyn," she began awkwardly, "I've tucked him in. Would you like to go up and say good night?"

"Please don't tickle or over-excite him in any way, will you, because the little rascal'll play up all evening. He's just like other children . . . loves a lot of attention."

Glyn stood up.

"Takes after me, I suppose," he said and grinned wickedly. "I was a poisonous brat, you know, and you needn't start to agree with me. Oh, while I'm away, you might care to read this. Mother asked me to give it to you." He handed her a sealed envelope which Susan took, puzzled.

She could hardly believe her eyes on reading the letter's contents. In it, Beatrice and Edward begged her to forgive them for their appalling treatment of her over Tony and the cruel, unkind things they had said to her in the past.

She sat in a chair listening to Glyn talking upstairs with Tony. It must have taken Beatrice a tremendous amount of courage to write as she had done, and her heart thawed a little. If she went back to Glyn, then she too would try to help the elder Mohrs forget the past, but it was far too early to say what she was planning to do.

Five minutes later, Glyn returned, looking pleased. She put the letter back into its envelope and left it on the table. He did not ask her what it had been about.

"He's a wonderful child, Sue. You've done well." Then he sat in a chair and glanced up at her.

"Glyn, have you planned to have supper at the inn, or would you like to eat here with me?"

"With you, please. There are lots and lots of questions I want to ask about Tony, and the sort of things he does."

"Glyn, before we go any further, I want to know one

thing. That awful business the other day, was it honestly nothing to do with you?"

He stared at her, his face suddenly bleak.

"Go on," he ordered harshly. "You've said so much you might as well finish."

"Well, it had crossed my mind that perhaps you had all planned it between you," she explained, unhappily.

"You accuse me of duplicity. You think the abduction was a put-up job?"

"Oh no Glyn, I'm sorry! I see I was quite wrong . . . it's just that I . . ." she faltered as she went quickly to join him.

"I know exactly what you meant, my dear. You distrust everything I do. I suppose you even have suspicions concerning my visit now?"

"Look at me, Sue, look hard at me! Oh, I can read your mind, my dear. You suspect me of coming here solely to get to know Tony so well that it'll make it far too difficult for you to decide once you've seen how closely Tony and I become. Am I right?" He paused, and she nodded her head almost imperceptibly.

"I swear to you, Sue, that I don't want it to happen like that! Even if I never see my son again after this fortnight, I don't want you to come back to me because you ought to for Tony's sake. I want you to come because you want to . . ."

She felt a surge of excitement. Was it possible . . . ?

Eagerly she searched his face but he had his emotions well under control and she could read nothing at all behind that carefully veiled and inscrutable facade. She sighed.

On Monday morning, Glyn arrived with a pile of newspapers and a bulging brief-case. He grimaced.

"I hope you don't mind, Sue, but I couldn't get all my work finished before I left. If you're busy with the chores, perhaps I could sort out some of this mess in the privacy of the lounge? When you've finished, I'll take you and Tony into town for lunch."

"If you don't mind, it'd be easier to give him his lunch here. Perhaps we could go out in the car afterwards?" Susan suggested.

She experienced a strange feeling of satisfaction to work in the kitchen, knowing that Glyn was busy in the next room. It was homely and warming. Halfway through the morning she took him a cup of coffee. He was sitting in front of the table, with papers strewn all over the place and the dailies open at the commercial pages. He was completely absorbed in his work, so she put the cup at his side and turned to go. Then he looked up, peering at her through heavy-rimmed spectacles.

"How about packing a picnic tea for later?" he suggested. "I found some attractive and secluded coves on my meanderings a few weeks ago."

They drove into a small cove where they found two other cars parked. The beach was wide and with plenty of clean, yellow sand. Glyn spread the car rug for Susan and Tony, and they all sat down. It was a happy afternoon, sitting there and gazing out to sea. The breeze was still warm, although it was late in the season, and the sky was almost cloudless. Tony shuffled about on his rear, playing with handfuls of sand and a small wooden spade they had bought him.

Each morning she found herself eagerly awaiting his arrival. She became anxious if he was a few minutes late, although she took care he did not notice her concern. When he left the cottage every evening, it was at a reasonably early hour.

"Mustn't give your neighbours anything to gossip about!" he said jokingly when she tried to persuade him to stay longer. Her eyes widened in astonishment.

"Why not? You're still my husband, aren't you?"

"Am I?" he asked searchingly. "I think if I stayed too long, I might be tempted not to leave at all." He moved closer to her. "Sue . . ."

She pushed him away.

"Please, Glyn, this wasn't part of the agreement."

"Now you understand why I go back to the inn early," he said grinning. He opened the front door. "'Night, Sue."

"Good night, Glyn." She closed the door after him, and walked slowly back into the lounge where the smell of his pipe lingered.

The days passed quickly. Glyn and Susan went for walks and outings in his car, lazed on the beach or in the garden, and on one or two occasions they braved the cold sea for a bathe.

On another occasion, Glyn absented himself to take Roger out. They drove to a hotel in town where they dined. Susan suspected that Glyn wanted to discuss her with Roger, and she was right.

Glyn came straight to the point.

"This won't take long," he began, "but I'm going to put my cards on the table. I want Sue back, although I know you love her. So, the best man wins. If she won't return to me, then I promise to provide the necessary evidence for her to divorce me, after which she'll marry you."

"You have the advantage over me, Glyn. You're already married to Sue."

Glyn shrugged.

"But she loves you, or so I have strong reason to believe . . . unfortunately for me."

"I wish I had your confidence," Roger mused.

They went sailing the following week. Roger and Amanda returned to the cottage to partake of a cold supper Sue and Glyn had prepared beforehand.

"Would you like a hot drink?" Susan asked Glyn, as she shut the door behind her two friends. "I can warm the coffee again, there's still a little left."

"No thanks. I'm not staying long. I just wanted to tell you something . . . for your ears alone, you might say."

"Oh?"

"Yes. I've enjoyed every moment of today, and I wanted to say a special thank you." He picked up his thick sweater from the back of the armchair, then went out into the hall.

Suddenly his arms were round her like a tight band and he was pulling her against his chest. Then he kissed her.

"Good-night, Sue," he said as she jerked away.

"Glyn! I don't know yet. That ws unfair."

"Course it was! he grinned good-naturedly back at her. "That was just to give you something to think about until we meet in the morning."

As she went to bed, she was very thoughtful. Glyn's kiss had been almost flippant. She knew what she had to do the day after tomorrow, but did he? Was he prepared to face the truth which she believed to lie within him? Even though she loved him she couldn't possibly go back to him unless he told her he also loved her.

Chapter Twenty

THERE were only twenty-four hours left. Thinking back over the past thirteen days, Susan knew they had been a success after all. Glyn had been generous and kind to both her and Tony. It had been a pleasant change to be able to afford the more expensive foodstuffs and vary her diet. She had accepted Glyn's financial help as a matter of course and now that it was over she would have to return to careful household management.

Unless he told her he loved her . . .

Roger came to the cottage that morning, while Glyn was down in the village.

" I know Glyn isn't here," he said, coming straight to the point. " But I had to see you alone. Sue, I can't bear this suspense any more. I had to come this way to see old Mrs. Hawker, and decided to have your answer one way or the other. Please, what are you going to do?"

He looked like a small boy, standing there by the lounge door, a hurt expression on his usually cheerful face.

Susan had to smile.

" Oh, Roger! You and Glyn are so amusing. As if having a time limit set to a problem could ever hope to bring it to a satisfactory solution! Especially where love's concerned. No, Roger, a fortnight isn't enough."

" Then . . . ?"

"I knew long, long ago what I wanted to do!" she declared. "The question is, does Glyn? Yes, Roger, my place is with him. How could it possibly be otherwise? It's always been Glyn," she added gently.

"I see. I'm sorry, Sue, but I'd hoped you might find it in your heart to love me instead."

She touched his arm.

"Dear Roger! I'm afraid I haven't been very fair. You see, I love my husband, and I hope and pray he still loves me. I *think* he does, but I want him to tell me so."

Outside the cottage, Glyn walked up the garden path.

"In the past week," Susan went on, "his interest in Tony has taken second place in my favour and I *know* he needs me. If only he'd find the courage to tell me in so many words!" She sighed.

Glyn quietly opened the front door and came into the hall.

"I'm glad, Sue, I hope you'll be happy," Roger replied softly.

Glyn walked towards the open lounge and paused, un-noticed, as he heard Roger say:

"You know I love you, Sue, and your happiness comes first. Are you sure you know what you're doing?"

"Yes, Roger, I'm quite sure."

He smiled ruefully and took her hands in his, unaware of the silent onlooker standing in the shadowed hall.

"Kiss me, Sue!" he urged. Obediently she raised her face to his. At once the watcher turned and walked quickly out of the cottage, as silently as he had arrived. He went down the path and swung his step towards the village. His face was set. It was as if the bottom had fallen out of his world. Yet who was to blame? Himself, naturally, for he had known Susan had not loved him. He realised he ought to have been prepared for this to happen, but somehow he had put off thinking about it, and had just hoped . . . and hoped. It was time he moved off homeward. No Susan, no Tony . . . nothing but a life of agonising loneliness ahead.

He went into the inn and asked for his bill. Then he went upstairs to pack.

Less than five minutes after Glyn had left the cottage, Roger also came out. Susan waved cheerfully to him, and then returned to wait for Glyn. He had promised to be there by ten, and he was never late.

The minutes ticked by and still he did not arrive.

What had happened? Susan wondered as the minute hand crept on and on. It was nearly a quarter to eleven.

By this time she was considerably alarmed. She decided to go down to the village and find out where he was. Tony was asleep in the pram, so she wheeled him out of the garden and along the street. She enquired for Glyn at the inn.

" Is Mr. Mohr here?" she asked anxiously.

" No, ma'am. He vacated his room less than half an hour ago."

"You mean . . . he's gone?" She could not believe it. " Are you sure? Perhaps his car's still in the car park?"

The innkeeper went out to the back, and then returned almost at once, shaking his head.

" I'm sorry, Mrs. Mohr. The car isn't there either."

" Oh no!" Susan wailed. " Thank you." She ran out of the inn, looking to left and right.

Why had Glyn gone so suddenly? Where was he? Surely he couldn't have started on his journey home without coming to see her, to explain?

She wheeled the pram into the back garden of the ' Honeypot '.

"Look after Tony, will you, please?" she begged Amanda who came out to greet her. "I can't explain now, but I won't be very long. Glyn's taken it into his head to go off somewhere, and I must find him before he returns to town . . . if he hasn't gone already."

She rushed away, heading for the cliffs. Instinct guided her feet towards that particular cliff path. It was possible she might find Glyn on the beach. He had told her how beautiful it was, and the peace it gave him. The skirt of her white jersey dress was tight, impeding her progress.

She heaved a sigh of relief when she caught sight of his car parked at the side of the lane fifty yards from the cliff edge. She ran across the turf and stood on the edge panting. Shielding her eyes against the sun she searched the long stretch of grey-gold sand beneath.

A lone figure, with head bent, was ambling along the water's edge.

"Glyn! Glyn!" she called, but the wind whipped away her voice. He did not turn.

Scrambling down the cliff path, she hurried towards him, calling out as she went. The sea murmured, growing louder as she ran nearer. The sand was wet and clinging, hampering her impatient progress. She stopped, tugged off her sandals and carried them. The wet sand tickled her bare toes, but she did not care.

"Glyn, wait!" she shouted. This time he heard her. He stopped and looked around. Gasping for breath she rushed up to him and stood before him, her chest heaving.

"Oh, Glyn, why did you give me such a beastly fright? I thought you'd gone without saying good-bye."

"No, Sue. I was coming to see you, but I hadn't been able to find the courage. I needed time to think, so I came down here to work out what I had to say to you before we parted."

" Then you're really going home to the city?"

" Yes."

" Why?"

" Sue, let me explain. I badly want my son, but I'm not selfish enough to take him away from you. It'd be a wicked, cruel deed. You want Roger . . ."

" What makes you think that?" she interrupted.

" I saw you both earlier on."

Susan frowned.

" Saw us? What are you talking about? And what makes you think it's Roger I want? Have you gone out of your mind?"

" There's no need to lie, just to be kind," he said gently. " I saw you both, through the open lounge door. I came into the cottage . . . perhaps you didn't hear me . . . and you were talking. I shouldn't have listened, but somehow I couldn't help overhearing. Then I saw you kissing."

Realisation dawned.

" Oh!" she sighed, relieved. " Is that all? Now I understand." She caught hold of his elbows and shook him, her smile impish. " You didn't stay very long, did you?"

" Of course not! One quick glance told me all I needed to know."

" Did it, indeed! Then perhaps I'd better refresh your memory. This is how I was kissing Roger." She pulled his head down to hers and gave him a demure kiss on the mouth. Then she released him, and her eyes sparkled. " Yet this is different," she went on, her face suddenly solemn. " *This* is the way I might have kissed him had he been the man I loved." She flung her arms tightly around his neck, pressed one hand hard against the back of his head and strained upwards. Her parted lips then met his with an ardency that amazed and thrilled him. She arched her body against his and began to tremble.

" Oh, you fool, you fool! " she moaned. " Can't you understand?" He tasted the salt tears welling out from under her closed eyelids. Then she flung herself away from him.

" Show me, Glyn, show me you love me! Kiss me, oh kiss me! " she begged.

With an inarticulate cry, he pulled her back into his arms and brought his mouth down on hers so roughly that she felt bruised and hurt, but did not mind. He pressed himself against her, then buried his face in her neck while she clung wildly to him, weeping with joy.

" Sue, my darling Sue! I've been so very, very stupid! "

" I know, my love, but I haven't helped you, have I?"

" I wanted to throw myself at your feet, begging you to love me, but I was afraid. Afraid of being hurt and spurned as you so often did in the past."

" Sh! That was over long ago," she whispered against his searching mouth.

Time seemed endless as they stood in each other's arms, with the sea murmuring and fussing about their feet, soaking Glyn's town shoes. At long last they released each other, smiling tremulously. Then he took out a handkerchief and wiped the tears from Susan's cheeks.

" Don't cry, darling. The time for sorrow's past now."

She clung to his waist and they stood looking out to sea, where the mid-day sun sparkled on the wide waters. His lips caressed her neck as he murmured:

" I must know one thing! Tell me now, and I'll never again refer to it. Tony . . . how and when did it happen?"

Without embarrassment Susan answered, while he

watched her thoughtfully. When she had finished he smiled and looked relieved.

" Now I'm content. I know the whole truth. It's been worrying me for so long . . . even before I knew about Tony. Until I saw him I couldn't believe it had been true. You see, Sue, once I began to get better, I kept remembering little things here and there. That fateful evening was like a jig-saw with many missing pieces. I knew we'd quarrelled, that was confirmed by my friends. Yet I had strange memories . . . fantasies, if you like . . . of the events in the garden. At first I dismissed it as part of the nightmare caused by a cracked skull. Then I met you again . . . with Tony . . . and knew it must have been true after all. Then the jigsaw began to fit together perfectly, except for one small piece. My first recollection after the accident was a feeling of tremendous exultation . . . I was glad about something, but didn't know what. Later, I decided it must be because I was glad our marriage was over. Then . . . I saw you, and Tony . . .

" You see, I couldn't believe you'd welcomed me that night. I thought it must have been a figment of my imagina-tion, wishful thinking, if you like. Now that you've told me yourself, I know I wasn't mistaken. Seeing you with Roger I was hurt, yet I wanted you to be happy even if it meant the end of all my dreams."

Susan kissed him again.

" I'm very fond of him, but he knew long ago that I wasn't the woman for him. I told him he ought to love Amanda. Glyn, you're the man I need and love."

" And it's taken us almost two years to find out!"

" Glyn, you don't have to go back today, do you?"

He smiled at her.

" Nothing could drag me away from you now, my darling.

To hell with the work for another week. I'll ring them and say I'm ill, or something equally untrue. Terrible disease is love; all the worse when it comes late in life, as someone once said."

"Glyn, what are we going to do about the future? I love it here, but I want to be with you."

"You've still part of your lease to run, haven't you? Good. Then we'll live in my . . . I mean, our . . . new house during the week and drive down here every week-end. Then we'll think about some different job."

"Oh no!" she began to protest.

"Don't worry, it's a question that's been given a great deal of thought for quite some time. I'm not particularly happy working for my father. I've always wanted to try my hand at something else. I'd like to live away from the big cities . . . in a place like this, perhaps, and travel a few miles to my job every day."

"Oh, darling, if only you could!" Susan sighed and snuggled into Glyn's side. "We'd be so happy here." He grinned down at her.

"We can discuss all this later. In the meantime, and especially for the benefit of anyone up there on the cliff top, I'm going to kiss you again. I've got a lot of time to make up, and don't think you're going to find it easy to wriggle out of it!"

"Who said I'd want to!" she murmured, screwing her head around to look back at the land, but there was not a soul in sight. They were quite alone, with only the sea and the sky for company. She turned towards Glyn. He cupped her face in one hand and his smile was gentle. She touched his greying hair and murmured:

"To think you once terrified me!"

"I was selfish and thoughtless. You were right to spurn

me. I promise you, darling, that from now on you'll find me the most loving and gentle of husbands."

"But still the master of the house!" she urged anxiously.

"Very much the master! That's one post I refuse to relinquish to you, my girl." He pulled her to him, his mouth touching her cheek and his hand caressing her neck.

"I love you, Sue," he whispered.

"I love you, Glyn," she managed to reply before their mouths met.